READ SEC

W

2

WITHDRAWN FROM STOCK

C000145464

Recent Titles by James Follett from Severn House

WICCA

James Follett

This first world edition published in Great Britain 2000 by
SEVERN HOUSE PUBLISHERS LTD of
9–15 High Street, Sutton, Surrey SM1 1DF.
This first world edition published in the USA 2001 by
SEVERN HOUSE PUBLISHERS INC of
595 Madison Avenue, New York, N.Y. 10022.

Copyright © 2000 by James Follett.

All rights reserved.
The moral right of the author has been asserted.

British Library Cataloguing in Publication Data

Follett, James, 1939-
    Wicca
    1.   Science fiction
    I.   Title
    823.9'14 [F]

    ISBN 0-7278-5626-X

NORTH LANCS
DIVISION

NFR 7|01   NBO 9|12
NKN   1|02   08230875
NPO |04

All situations in this publication are fictitious and
any resemblance to living persons is purely coincidental.

Typeset by Palimpsest Book Production Ltd.,
Polmont, Stirlingshire, Scotland.
Printed and bound in Great Britain by
MPG Books Ltd., Bodmin, Cornwall.

Acknowledgements

My thanks to Ivan Bunn for providing much valuable information on that shadowy figure, Matthew Hopkins – the so-called Witchfinder General; and to Deborah Smith for her helpful comments in the early days.

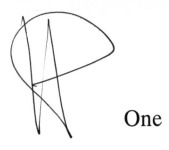

One

Vikki pressed the back of her hands to her eyes and started wailing.

The four-year-old was tired and hungry. The Gatwick–Alicante holiday flight had been delayed eight hours. She wanted the familiar surroundings of her bedroom, the reassurance of her cuddly toys.

Anne Taylor scooped up her daughter and carried the lightest case into the holiday apartment block's deserted lobby while her husband struggled with the larger cases. The lift was typical of Spain's 1960s-built apartment blocks: a tiny car barely large enough for four adults, with a hinged outer door that had to be propped open with a bag while it was loaded. Anne entered the lift first and put Vikki down so she could help Jack stack the cases.

"Bloody courier and coach scooting off like that," he grumbled. "Not showing us what's where or anything."

"It's gone one o'clock, Jack."

Once all three and their belongings were crowded into the lift and the outer door closed, Jack checked the tag on the keys the courier had virtually thrown at them as the airport coach pulled away. He pushed the button for the fourth floor.

Time would never blot out the memory of Vikki's terrible scream of agony when the lift started moving. The couple had never encountered a lift without an inner door. Anne's cry of terror when she saw her daughter's hand being dragged into the gap between the lift's floor and the side of the lift shaft as the car started rising was lost in the sheer volume of Vikki's scream. Jack's horrified glance took in everything as Anne fell to her knees beside her stricken daughter. Priceless seconds were lost as he struggled with the unfamiliar control panel to stop the lift. It jerked to a halt and he threw himself dementedly against the door in a futile attempt to spring it open, but the lift had risen two metres; the safety interlocks and the floor above held the outer door closed.

The next two hours passed in a nightmare montage of sounds and images. English voices in the lobby; Jack pleading with them not

1

to try to move the lift, shouting above Vikki's terrible screams; the blood pooling across the floor; the sudden silence when Vikki mercifully fainted; the blood; Anne's handkerchief as a makeshift tourniquet; Spanish voices; arguments; a crash overhead as the roof panel was ripped off and an engineer adding to the crush in the lift; the blood; the luggage being passed up to make room for a doctor and a nurse; the blood; Anne refusing to leave Vikki; the blue flare and crackle of cutting equipment slicing into the door; Vikki being carried unconscious to an ambulance that disappeared into the night, sirens howling despite the hour, with Jack and Anne following in a Guardia Civil car.

Four hours after the terrible accident, a surgeon in the general hospital at Denia told Anne and Jack that Vikki was out of danger. He normally spoke good English but exhaustion had him reverting to Spanish as he tried to explain that the damage was too severe and that it had been too late to save their daughter's left hand. Amputation of the hand's shredded remains had been essential.

Anne's sobs of despair were swamped by Vikki's anguished scream. *"Please!"* she begged. *"Please don't take my hand away! Please!"*

A voice invaded Vikki's nightmare.

"Viks – it's all right. Everything's all right. You've got a fabulous new hand."

"No! No! They're going to take it away!"

Two

A stinging slap across the cheek brought Vikki weaving erratically to full wakefulness. She opened her eyes and stared uncomprehendingly up at the thin-faced girl with the straggling blonde hair. It was some seconds before she recognised the face as belonging to Sarah Gale – her classmate and best friend.

"Bloody hell," said Sarah worriedly, shaking the pain out of her fingers. "I thought that belting someone having a nightmare only worked in the movies."

"What's going on up there?" Anne Taylor's voice called from the foot of the narrow flight of stairs that led to the girls' bedroom.

"It's all right, Mrs Taylor," Sarah answered. "Vikki had a bad dream."

"Vikki! Are you OK?"

Vikki propped herself on her elbows. "I'm fine, Mum!"

"Breakfast in ten minutes," Anne replied. "And go easy on the hot water, ladies – it's got to last. The radio said it might be another cloudy day today."

Sarah slid her gawky frame on to the bed beside Vikki and put her skinny arms around her friend. The two sixteen-year-olds clung to each other – a tangle of Vikki's natural blonde hair and Sarah's not so natural blonde hair. "What happened, Viks?"

Vikki stared at Dario – her full-length, life-size wall poster of a magnificent Zulu warrior. He was holding a leopard-skin-covered shield in one hand and a short, stabbing assegai in the other. His crane-feather headdress erect, his skin a fine honey-coloured sheen from its treatment with ox tallow. Vikki had named him Dario because it seemed to suit his majestic bearing.

"It's not going away," said Vikki unsteadily. "I mean – dreams when you wake up start going away. But it's still clear, sort of. They made my hand, Sarah. Made it whole."

The girls separated. Sarah took Vikki's left hand and stroked it. It was a perfect hand. As always when she wasn't using it, Vikki

3

had closed the fingers in a slight clench – the default position of the artificial hand she used to wear. "Who did, Viks?"

"The visitors in Pentworth Lake."

Sarah stared quizzically at her friend. Pentworth Lake was at the precise centre of an invisible force wall that completely enclosed Pentworth and the surrounding West Sussex countryside. The Wall had appeared three months previously at the end of March. It was thought that the visitors' UFO – dubbed "The Silent Vulcan" – or whatever it was they had arrived in, was buried deep in the silt that filled the bottom of the seemingly bottomless lake.

"Well," said Sarah. "I always thought it had to be them. And I bet they had something to do with Cathy Price being able to walk again. But how do you know for sure?"

"I dreamed that they called me to the lake," Vikki replied, washing at the bedroom hand basin.

"And you went?"

"Yes."

Sarah grimaced. "Had to be a dream then. The morris police are taking this stupid curfew seriously. Nothing under eighteen moves at night without an adult."

Vikki had a vague recollection of being caught by a morris police patrol and being dropped at the end of the lane in their Range Rover but daylight was making the edges of her memory fuzzy.

"So the visitors told you that they gave you your new hand?"

A hook came away from Vikki's bra. She placed it carefully in a pot on her dressingtable. Hooks and eyes were precious now. "Yes."

"Anything else?"

"They said that they came from a place called . . ." Vikki frowned as she tried to recall details. "Sirius."

"I am being serious," Sarah replied.

"No – what we call Sirius. It's a star or planet or something."

"Did they speak English in this dream?"

"Now you're laughing at me."

"No," said Sarah earnestly as she started dressing. "If they spoke to you they must've used some sort of language."

Vikki sat on her bed and wriggled her jeans over her hips. "These feel damp."

"Heavy dew last night and the window was open."

"They spoke in pictures," said Vikki, tugging carefully on the zip fly. A broken zip was a disaster. She stared at Sarah, her large

4

green eyes clouded with worry. "They said that they wanted me to do something but not yet."

"What?"

"I can't remember."

"You said everything was clear."

Vikki struggled manfully not to cry. "Supposing I can't do it? They'll take my hand away."

"I wish they'd take their bloody force wall away."

"I wish you'd take me seriously."

"I wish you'd take yourself seriously," Sarah snapped back. "Look at you – putting that stupid glove on. You're going to have to 'out' your hand sooner or later, Vikki."

"I'd rather it were later."

"But you've had it three months now! Ever since the Wall appeared. You can't go on hiding it inside a glove just because of this stupid idea that you're going to lose it again. It's a *real* hand, Vikki. It's yours for keeps."

Vikki stared down at her gloved left hand, resting on her lap, the fingers looking unnatural in their usual half-clenched position of her old artificial hand. "The dream was so real, Sarah," she said in a low voice.

"It was just a dream, stupid!"

"Vikki! Sarah!" Anne Taylor's voice called from the foot of the stairs. "Breakfast is nearly ready. Now come on!"

Vikki reached down for her trainers. She picked one up. Both girls stared at it in astonishment. Vikki found the other and held both up, her eyes widening in fear.

The trainers were caked with fresh mud.

Three

D etective Sergeant Mike Malone's regular jogs rarely took him this close to the Wall but today was an exception.

He swung his rangy, muscular frame over the farm gate in an easy vault and paused to wring out his sodden sweatband, and tighten the drawstring on his white tracksuit. He seemed engrossed but his eyes missed nothing. The morning sun was evaporating the dew quite rapidly but he had no difficulty picking out the two recent trails that crossed the field from the gate where he was standing.

He resumed jogging – long, easy strides across the close-cropped grass – following the pony and trap tracks in the disturbed dew. The second set of tracks were made by someone on foot. In places where the over-grazed field was bare of grass he noted that the footprints partially obliterated the wheel ruts. Cuban heel boots. He knew of one person in Pentworth who wore such boots and who had reason to follow the trap – a suspicion that was confirmed a few minutes later as he breasted a rise and saw the footprints veer into a small, bramble-protected stand of chestnut and larch saplings – a future crop of fencing posts and an ideal hiding place to observe the valley and the tall, stooping figure of Bob Harding.

Malone slowed his pace as he took in the strange splendour of the alien landscape that lay beyond the valley. It was the icy, frost-crisped wilderness of Farside – the unattainable land beyond the Wall.

What should have been the rolling hills of West Sussex were the bleak steppes of Northern Europe of 40,000 years ago – an endless vista of sturdy sedge grasses swept by ceaseless, loess-laden winds that bore no moisture for they were chilled and desiccated by the mighty glaciers to the north. Only when the glaciers had receded would the winds become warmer and bring moisture instead of dust, thus enabling forests of the pre-Ice Age to re-establish. But, for the time being, the steady rain of loess was building the rich top soil of what would become the fertile pastures and downs of southern England 400 centuries in the future.

The picture was very different within the invisible ten-kilometre diameter dome that had isolated Pentworth for thirteen weeks from the rest of the world. Trees were making vigorous growth in the longer hours of daylight compared with the barren wilderness of Farside.

The early summer sun was already uncomfortably hot, and the relative humidity rising to its now customary and uncomfortable eighty per cent. Bob Harding's prediction in the spring that the greenhouse effect of the dome would create a Mediterranean climate was turning out to be correct. The benefits were doubtful, as people were now discovering. Traditional crops such as brassicas were not faring so well, whereas less nourishing fruit and salad crops were flourishing. There was a prospect of more food rationing ahead.

Bob Harding was near some old tree stumps on the far side of a small field of sugar beet. Tethered nearby was his government-issue pony and trap. The retired scientist was right at the periphery of the invisible Wall – indicated by black and white striped survey poles that had been driven into the ground at hundred-metre intervals around the dome's thirty-kilometre circumference. They had been put in place, not as a warning – no one had ever been harmed by coming into contact with the Wall – but to aid the careful mapping of the dome the previous March when it had appeared.

There was no way across the field because salad catch crops had been sown between the slower growing rows of beet. Intensive cultivation was essential to provide food stocks for Pentworth's 6000 inhabitants – particularly during the coming winter. The former Pentworth Town Council, now the government, had given itself emergency powers to ensure that every hectare was put to good use.

Malone jogged around the perimeter of the field and pounded up to Bob Harding. There were few men in Pentworth that commanded the police officer's respect but the retired government scientific adviser was one of them. Tired of London and its fumes that played hell with his asthma, and made the pursuit of amateur astronomy impossible, Bob Harding had taken early retirement and moved to Pentworth where he had supplemented his pension by running an electrical repair shop – now an important part of Pentworth's social structure. He had also married a former student nearly forty years his junior and had been voted on to the town council. Shortly after the Wall's appearance, it was Bob Harding who had calculated that Pentworth's night sky was 40,000 years in the past following his discovery that the Pole Star was no longer in its proper place.

7

"Good morning, counsellor," said Malone.

A flash of blinding light from the clump of saplings and brambles. The unseen watcher was being careless with a camera or binoculars.

The scientist ignored Malone. Harding was standing on one of the stumps, staring intently southward across the frost-scorched sedge grasses of Farside. Malone's eyes were sharp. Despite the slight distortion caused by the Wall, he spotted the distant family group of slow-moving reddish-brown creatures immediately. They were about three kilometres away – their breath leaving clouds of swirling vapour in the freezing air beyond the Wall.

"Woolly mammoths!" Malone breathed in wonder, his usual phlegmatic nature forgotten.

"Goddamn it – I should've brought my camcorder," Harding grumbled.

"It would be a recording of a recording," Malone observed.

Harding chuckled. "Good morning, Mr Malone. You still really believe that Farside has been created artificially by the visitors? After all these weeks?"

Malone shrugged. "I recall telling you the day the Wall first appeared that I'd seen a similar trick at the London Planetarium."

"A dome some five kilometres high at the centre and covering thirty square miles is some planetarium," said Harding quietly. "Besides, it's not a dome – it's a completely enclosing sphere."

"How's Suzi?" Malone enquired.

"Looking after the shop. Slave-driving my assistants, I hope."

The two men watched the mammoths disappear into a valley.

"I suppose our erstwhile Chairman has sent you to spy on me?" Harding enquired.

"Mr Prescott has his own informants he can call on," Malone replied evenly, his expression giving nothing away. "I'm spying on my own account."

The older man grinned and met the police officer's wide-set brown eyes. "My apologies. Mike Malone owes no allegiance to anyone."

"Any spying on you is too late," said Malone ruefully. "That museum-piece manual telephone exchange you've got up and running was a mistake."

"You don't approve?"

"I suppose it's OK, being limited to essential services and a few kiosks. But I'd hate to think of the telephone returning as an instrument to rule our lives and drain our bank accounts."

"This Ludditism is a bit rich coming from someone whose idea it was that I set up Radio Pentworth using one of my old Spectrum transmitters," Harding observed.

"I worry about this talk of moving the station to Government House," said Malone. "It will lose its independence."

"I need the room. You've seen how crowded my workshop is these days. Turning the old courthouse into centralised government offices was a sensible move. It's a big building which gives them plenty of room for a proper studio."

"I'm not a Luddite, Councillor Harding," said Malone seriously. "My two kids are Farside."

"I'd forgotten . . . I'm sorry."

The scientist recalled how Malone's eyes had been fixed on him at the first meeting of the town council the day after the Wall's awesome appearance. At that meeting Harding had surmised that the visitors' Silent Vulcan UFO was deep in the mud and silt of Pentworth Lake because that was the precise centre of the Wall's circumference. Also his gravimeter had detected an anomaly in the lake. He had speculated that perhaps the UFO had been damaged and that the Wall was the visitors' means of defending themselves until help arrived, called by their powerful radio emissions from the lake. Assuming that they were from the nearest star, Proxima Centauri, this could take as long as twenty-seven years, or many thousands of years if the visitors were from the centre of the galaxy.

Malone stretched his hand tentatively towards the force wall. The tingling sensation in his fingertips was not unpleasant. He pushed harder and watched the strange blackening effect around his hand as the Wall became visible. "I want to see this . . . obscenity destroyed, Mr Harding. If that makes me a Luddite, then so be it."

"And that's what I'm working on," said Harding.

Malone pushed harder and felt the Wall pushing back – matching his efforts with an exact counter force needed to repel him. No more and no less. He took his hand away and the Wall became transparent again.

"Most of us have got bored with playing with it, Mr Malone."

Malone shrugged and peeled off his tracksuit top. "Radio Pentworth got the weather forecast wrong," he observed, glancing up at the strengthening sun. "Why don't they just play a tape? 'Today will be hot and humid just like yesterday, and the day before, and the day before that'."

"'And more rain is forecast for tonight and every night'," Bob

Harding added. "It keeps the pollen down – otherwise it'd play hell with my asthma."

"Life in a greenhouse."

"A productive greenhouse," said the scientist, nodding to the crops. "I'm sure those lettuces have grown since I arrived. Right – the best way to spy on me is to give me a hand."

The heaviest item Harding had brought in the trap was a Dowty hydraulic mining jack, borrowed from the fire station – a massive device, resembling a village pump. It was used as an emergency prop to support buildings made unsafe by trucks or tourist coaches attempting to park in them. Such accidents had been not uncommon before the Wall in homes and shops fronting Pentworth's narrow, winding streets.

The two men positioned the jack flat on the grass so that its base was touching the sturdiest of the tree stumps. Harding cranked the handle vigorously, causing a gleaming ram shaft to appear. The lifting shoe made contact with the Wall and immediately a blackened, opaque area seemed to spread from the point of contact – rising up like a surreal, two-dimensional bush.

The scientist stopped cranking and recorded the jack's load gauge reading in a notebook. He measured the diameter of the blackened patch of force wall, calculated the area and noted the information.

"You're not expecting to break through with this thing, are you?" Malone asked.

Harding shook his head and resumed pumping while watching the load gauge. "I don't think that's likely."

The jack's shoe disappeared into the blackness which spread outwards and upwards for two metres from the point of contact. Harding entered the new figures in his notebook. After more cranking and two further readings, the strange blackness of the Wall made visible was the size of a double-track railway tunnel. Harding's mounting excitement was evident.

"Just as I hoped," he exclaimed in answer to Malone's query. "The counter force has a linear progression. Double the load and it doubles the area of blackness."

"Meaning?"

"Meaning that I'm sure we can defeat this thing with a massive overload," the scientist replied. "Damn – the gauge is nearly on maximum reading."

Harding resumed working the crank handle, more slowly because it required considerable effort. A few more centimetres of ram appeared and a little oil seeped around its O-ring gland under the enormous pressure. He stopped and wiped his forehead with his sleeve. "That's it – needle's on the stop." He stared into the featureless blackness. "Amazing engineering," he breathed. "Truly amazing. A hundred tonne load bearing on a few square centimetres and look at it. Let's leave it under load and see what happens."

"Cathy Price reckons she hit the Wall at about a hundred miles per hour in her E-Type," said Malone conversationally. "That was the night that the Wall first materialised."

"Yes – she told me. She said it was like running into a pile of mattresses." Harding returned his attention to the jack's load gauge. He thought he had seen the needle quiver. "What are you trying to tell me, Mr Malone?"

"That I don't think we'd ever be able to beat such technology but I accept that we won't know until we try."

"If we fail," said Harding, "I shall attempt to communicate with the so-called Silent Vulcan UFO in Pentworth Lake."

"Their spyder made no attempt to communicate with me," Malone observed.

The detective sergeant was referring to the time when a machine that could have only belonged to the visitors had followed him home one night. It had resembled a mechanical crab, moving purposefully on curiously articulated legs. When he had tried to catch it, it had sprouted helicopter rotors and taken off into the night sky. Several other people had seen the strange device. Cathy Price had nicknamed it a "spyder" – and the name had stuck. It had not been seen again since the day after its close encounter with Malone.

Both men saw the needle drop back.

"By God!" Harding yelled as the needle fell to fifty tonnes. "The pressure's dropping! The jack's breaking through!"

"I don't think so," said Malone.

The scientist heard the soft snapping sound of buried roots being wrenched apart and felt the tremors underfoot. Both men stared at the massive tree stump as it keeled slowly away from the Wall. A hard-packed pan of leaf mould near the base of the stump yawned like a mouth. Freed of its mighty load, the jack rolled on to its side and the huge black patch of nothingness in the Wall disappeared.

"Bugger," said Harding succinctly.

Four

"**R**ight," said Anne Taylor firmly when breakfast in the garden was over. "Vikki – your turn to wash up. Sarah – help me position the cooker for dinner."

As always, it irritated Anne to see her daughter clear the garden table by expertly balancing the plates on her forearm instead of making proper use of her left hand. Before leaving, Vikki gave Sarah a warning glance to say nothing about her strange dream, although she knew it was unnecessary. Sarah would never betray a confidence.

Anne treated Sarah to a frosty look but said nothing as she and the girl swung the four-metre-diameter solar dish into the optimum position for cooking the evening meal. The silver-painted, papier-mâché parabolic reflector, mounted on a stout, cross-braced framework of hazel and ash, was one of several hundred manufactured by Selby Engineering. It was a bulky yet simple device: the cooking area was little more than a shelf at the dish's focal point – concentrating the sun's energy on to saucepans and pressure cookers. The people of Pentworth had become expert at cooking casseroles and stews while standing on stepladders.

The Taylor household was luckier than many. They had water from a borehole, and Anne had converted a large, old-fashioned cast-iron radiator into a solar heat exchanger that kept the well-insulated hot water tank primed. The radiator was in position on the lawn, painted black, and propped against a post.

With her husband, Jack, Farside, the entire burden of running the two farm cottages knocked into one dwelling had fallen on Anne's capable shoulders. She coped admirably with all the problems of the "new life" as it was now called, the most significant being no electricity, but she was now used even to that. Her hand no longer went automatically to the light switch when entering a room. There was no television, no piped gas, no petrol for her ancient Mini. Life for everyone in Pentworth was akin to life in the early nineteenth century, but with the knowledge of the twenty-first century.

Anne was proud of the way she had come to terms with the "new life". She rose at dawn and went to bed at nightfall after listening to the daily radio play or the reading on Radio Pentworth. The Wall had pushed her into finally giving up smoking and she felt better for it. And the air was so much cleaner without diesel and petrol pollution. But what she really appreciated was the new community spirit that the Wall had brought to Pentworth.

It was now the end of June. Asquith Prescott and the council had achieved much in thirteen weeks. The campaign to revive ancient but vital skills that were essential for Pentworth's survival was proving a success. A cooper, who had made his last barrel twenty years before, had been winkled out of retirement, given a workshop and two willing lads, and asked to make barrels.

A shoe repairer had, to his joy, been supplied with four youngsters who were already keen on leather work, and tasked with teaching them to make good-quality working boots – the supply of rawhide and leather was assured by the revival of the tanning workshops, where young and old trainees scraped and worked hides on stretcher frames and used cows' brains for the tanning process.

Pentworth was reverting to what English towns had always been before industry had been driven out by planning regulations and rocketing rents and rates. The antique shops were fast disappearing to be replaced by shirtmakers, farriers, blacksmiths, seamstresses, spinners, candle makers, tanners, saddlers, and all the socially useful trades that contributed to the wealth and well-being of a thriving community.

It was a similar story on the farms where old skills were being relearned. David Weir's Temple Farm was among the busiest, running training courses in which Charlie Crittenden and his family of travellers introduced classes of the young and old to the crafts of hurdle-making, hedge-layering, coppicing, pollarding, ploughing and harrowing, and care of horses and farm implements. The once-despised Crittendens, that David Weir had welcomed to Temple Farm before the appearance of the Wall, were now held in high esteem for the skills that had been in their blood for generations.

Under the direction of Charlie Crittenden's sons, parties of apprentices were hard at work clearing long-neglected and overgrown woodland. The piles of brushwood of their labours were collected and taken to Pentworth Paper Mills for pulping and shredding to make a wide variety of paper goods that included huge sheets of low-grade but adequate tissue paper that were dried in the sun and rolled and sliced to make toilet paper and even sanitary towels. Nothing was burned.

Anne Taylor's main regret was not separation from her husband – their marriage was on the point of break-up anyway – but her failure to persuade Vikki to accept her miraculous new hand – a wonderful gift from God that had grown on that unforgettable weekend in March when the Wall had appeared and Pentworth's isolation had begun. Vikki's wish to say nothing to anyone about the hand had been respected.

Once the solar dish was in position, Sarah tried to flee to the kitchen to help Vikki but Anne commanded the girl to sit at the table. Woman and schoolgirl faced each other.

"Well?" Anne demanded.

"Well what, Mrs Taylor?"

"Vikki's hand. You promised to get her to end this secrecy nonsense. It's gone on too long."

"I promised to do my best," said Sarah, with a hint of defiance. "You know how stubborn Viks can be. She says she's not ready."

"I was counting on you, Sarah. It's bound to come out sooner or later. Too many people know."

Sarah looked puzzled. "Who else knows? Vikki. You. Me. And Dr Vaughan. She's your doctor, so she won't say nothing."

"Say anything," said Anne absently, brushing her long, blonde hair away from her face. At thirty-six, she looked more like Vikki's older sister than her mother. "I'm sure Mike Malone suspects something. Vikki was using both hands that time we were fixing up that radiator and he turned up."

Sarah looked contemptuous. "He's a thick plod." She gave an impish grin and looked speculatively at Anne. "Wouldn't mind finding out just how thick. I bet you've found out."

"Don't you think about anything but sex?"

"No. But who mentioned sex?"

Anne smiled. Sarah was a likeable little trollop. "You seriously underestimate Mike . . . *Mr* Malone. He's the shrewdest man I've ever met. The scrapping of bars and having waiter-only service at tables for drinks in pubs and clubs was his idea. And it's worked. It means that juveniles like you and Vikki can go into pubs for soft drinks. So don't go knocking Mr Malone."

"Well – he would've said something by now if he'd seen anything."

Anne's green eyes regarded the girl steadily. "One of the

14

Pentworth House girls delivering milk saw Vikki climbing out of the swimming pool using both her hands."

"Must've been before the water turned green."

"It was a couple of days after the Wall appeared. The girl returned Vikki's artificial hand which she lost at the Pentworth House party."

"No one takes any notice of those Bodian Brethren loonies at Pentworth House," said Sarah pointedly. "They're all nutters."

"Obviously you've never heard Father Roscoe preaching from the back of a dogcart," Anne replied. "A lot of people are beginning to take him very seriously. That the Wall is a punishment for our sins. Although I'd be sorry now to see it go." Anne experienced a twist of guilt, knowing how much Vikki missed her father.

Sarah remained silent, wondering what was coming next.

"You're good for Vikki, Sarah," said Anne slowly. "If your mother doesn't mind, you're welcome to stay on here as long as you like."

"I'd like that, Mrs Taylor. Thanks. I like having a sister. Vikki thinks she can get me a holiday and weekend job with her in Ellen Duncan's herb shop. Or in her fields. I could give you some housekeeping."

"I'll have to check with your mother first."

"Mum won't care. She's got a new boyfriend."

"Another one? Your mother is going to run out of Pentworth men at this rate."

"Oh – she only has 'em one at a time, Mrs Taylor. They come and go with monogamous regularity."

"Her daughter's also heading for a reputation as a man-eater, the way she carries on," said Anne drily.

"But a lot of men like being eaten," said Sarah innocently.

Vikki emerged from the kitchen and wondered what her mother and Sarah were laughing about.

Five

The visitors chose a night when there was no moon; therefore the only witness of the sudden disturbance in the centre of Pentworth Lake was a marauding barn owl. It circled, scrutinising the erupting bubbles before deciding that they were inedible and continuing its flight.

The spyder surfaced, the many metres of bottom silt it had had to push through still streaming from its strange, crab-like body. It crawled clear of the water and tested each of its articulated legs and manipulators in turn while its sensors listened and watched, monitoring the entire spectrum of human perception and beyond. The nearby cry of a nightjar had to be pinpointed and accounted for before its casing opened and contra-rotating helicopter rotors appeared.

Motors hummed faintly, the rotors spun, and the spyder lifted vertically, high into the humid night sky before swinging towards Pentworth.

During the early days of their arrival the visitors' spyder had come close to being captured, and on another it had been forced to use a spray of non-lethal nerve gas. They didn't want to use the spyder again to venture into a house – their summonsing of Vikki to the lake had satisfied them that their triggering of the correct stem cells to regrow her hand had been a success, but they needed information on the repair of neural networks in the human brain. They had already carried out some simple repairs on a person, so they decided that it would be sensible to visit that person again to obtain the additional information and confirm that the repairs had worked.

They didn't know her name – Vikki was the only person with whom they had established contact – but they knew where Cathy Price lived. A house with an octagonal tower on a hill on the outskirts of Pentworth.

The spyder found Hill House, stopped, and descended rapidly, arresting its fall with a surge of power in the final seconds so that it settled silently on the roof of the octagonal tower. Two manipulators were extended quickly to secure a purchase.

It waited for over an hour, not moving, listening for the characteristic pattern of cerebral rhythms that told it that its quarry was in deep sleep. This time the warmth and humidity made its task of entering the house easy because all the windows were open to catch the light breeze of the night convection currents. Extending its manipulators allowed it to lower itself level with an open window. Dropping silently from the sill to the bedroom floor was achieved by the same means.

Through the eyes of their spyder, the visitors studied the spacious bedroom. Their machine had been in the room before but had had to leave in a hurry when Cathy had woken.

Despite being able to walk again, the woman still had a combined studio and bedroom. The visitors surveyed the professional workstation and had no difficulty divining the purpose of the Macintosh computer, a large A3 laser printer and an equally large flatbed scanner, but the purpose of a bicycle exercise machine took them several milliseconds to comprehend. There had been another device in the bedroom that had been noted on its first visit but there was no sign of it now: a wheelchair.

The spyder moved towards the dark-haired young woman, sprawled naked on her stomach on the bed, her fingers touching the floor. A small manipulator took a tiny tissue sample from the woman's wrist. She didn't stir. The biological identification corroborated the visual identification that they had the right person. A neural scan of Cathy's brain was performed in less than a minute. The findings confirmed what the visitors had hoped: that the repairs to the young woman's brain carried out by their spyder during its first visit had been a success. Even without the positive information of the scan, the worn state of the young woman's shoes and the absence of the wheelchair suggested that she could now walk.

The spyder returned to Pentworth Lake and disappeared into its depths. Its makers were satisfied with the results of the sortie. Work could resume on the human being they were rebuilding.

Six

Ellen Duncan was in a reasonably good mood, so she tore into David Weir for only a minute on her visit to Temple Farm.

"I'm slaving my guts out to increase herb production to make remedies for the hospital!" she railed. "I'm having to work all hours God made in the shop. Cope with a bunch of cretins I've been lumbered with, and I find you and Charlie Crittenden and his boys messing about with this useless rust box on wheels! You promised to plough and harrow my lower field by the weekend!"

The target for Ellen's ire was David Weir, owner of Temple Farm. Good-natured, blond, forty, with an unlikely aristocratic demeanour for a farmer. Five years ago he had sold his share in a London art gallery, bought the rundown Temple Farm, and turned it into an agricultural museum – a working theme farm with horse-drawn and steam-powered farming implements. The useless rust box on wheels that Ellen had referred to was "Brenda" – a partly restored showman's engine. It was a Charles Burrell and Sons steam-driven traction engine that had been abandoned in a field for half a century. In its day the formidable machine had generated the electricity for travelling fairs. David was standing on the driver's platform beside Charlie Crittenden – head of a family of travellers whose caravans were now a permanent feature of Temple Farm. Charlie's eldest sons, Gus and Carl, were sitting astride "Brenda"'s boiler, regarding Ellen in some awe. Tight shorts that had been jeans in another life, a loose halter top, the breeze tangling her rich, black tresses around her face, the voluptuous herbalist was a stirring sight for two young men, or any number of men of any age.

David eventually managed to interrupt her tirade by pointing out that he was doing his best and that—

"Down!" yelled Ellen.

"I feel safe up here, m'dear."

"You won't be if I come up there and throw you off!" Ellen retorted and took a threatening step forward.

David knew Ellen well enough to know that it was no idle

18

threat. Their affair, which varied between the tempestuous and desultory depending on Ellen's uncertain mood swings, had started the previous year when Ellen had discovered a palaeolithic flint mine on land adjoining a field that David rented from her. Since then their interest in palaeontology, each other, and arguments had developed.

But their biggest find had been the day before the Wall appeared when Ellen had urged David to use his Kubuta miniature digger to burrow into the side of hill on her land near the Temple of the Winds. They had broken through into a cave whose walls were decorated with vivid hunting scenes from, as near as they could date from the techniques used, 40,000 years ago. Without the resources to maintain a twenty-four-hour guard over the priceless find, they had filled in the cave's tiny entrance and decided to keep it a secret until the Wall was no more.

David jumped down hurriedly when Ellen made a move to climb on to the traction engine. "Let's discuss it in the office," he suggested.

Ellen pushed him away when he tried to put his arm around her waist. "Good idea," she said tartly, moving off. "There won't be anyone to witness the unspeakable things I shall do to you."

In the farm office she resumed her forcible opinions of David and his parentage while the object of her affections poured nettle tea from a thermos flask. One sip stopped her in mid-insult. "This is disgusting, David."

"I bought it in your shop, m'dear. You think I ought to sue?"

"I'm the one who should be suing you for breach of promise."

"But I've never proposed to you," David protested, although he had often entertained the idea, hazardous though it was.

"For failing to plough my field! If the inspectors jump on me there'll be hell to pay. I can just see Asquith bloody Prescott gloating at the next council meeting – telling us that, as councillors, we should be setting an example."

"It'll be done tomorrow afternoon."

"Is that a farmer's promise or a David Weir promise?"

"A David Weir promise. It'll be done, Ellen."

Ellen calmed down. "You're seriously dead if it isn't."

"I believe you, m'dear."

She regarded David thoughtfully. "There's something else on my mind. We ought to take a look at the cave. I worry about those paintings – wondering if we've changed the humidity or something when we broke through."

It was a lame excuse. David knew that Ellen was aching to see those wonderful hunting scenes again. "It's risky in the daytime. It's not too good at night, either. Morris patrols everywhere."

"If you refuse, I shall do something of a gruesomely violent nature to you. If you agree, it'll be something of a sexually depraved nature."

"Looks like I'd better check the torches."

Ellen kissed him. "Thanks, David. You're wonderful. Sometimes."

"Weak is the word, m'dear. But on one condition."

"Which is?"

"That you tell me how you knew the cave was there."

"I didn't know for sure."

"You knew exactly where I was to dig into the side of the hill with the Kubuta."

"I told you – soil discolouration in those aerial photographs that Harvey Evans took last year."

David tilted her chin towards him. "I'm going to take a tape measure to your nose."

Ellen stared at him and gave a sudden smile. "If I told you, you wouldn't believe me."

"In our present crazy situation, I'm prepared to believe anything but not, to put it crudely, a load of bollocks about aerial photographs. So tell me."

Ellen sat at David's desk and fiddled with a pen. "If you remember, that day I'd been down to the lake to see Inspector Harvey Evans about those two radio interference blokes who'd been drowned the day before."

"Their bodies never have come to light," David observed. "And?"

"I'd climbed about halfway up the hill and sat down to rest. I'd hardly slept that night. I must've dozed off for a few minutes." Ellen paused and looked up at David. "This is where it gets weird. I woke up suddenly and everything had changed. The countryside was like Farside. Bleak. Terribly cold. No trees. There was a huge waterfall cascading into the lake – but it was more like a crater, tremendously deep . . ." Her voice trailed into silence as she recalled her confusion during those strange moments. David waited, not prompting. "And there was smoke coming from nearby."

"From where the cave is?" David guessed.

Ellen nodded. "David – I swear I'm not making this up but the entrance was much bigger than the little hole we made, and there was a man standing there, nearly naked, covered in red ochre – all over his hands and arms. He was engulfed in the smoke. It was pouring out of the cave."

"What sort of build was he?"

She looked carefully to see if he was mocking her but his expression was impassive. "A bit shorter than you. Thin. Long, straggly hair and beard. But his face . . . His eyes, large, intelligent. He was like us and yet not like us . . ." Then a hint of pleading in her voice. "David . . . I *know* he was a Cro-Magnon man and that he was one of the artists that painted those hunting scenes. *He* had hunted mammoth and therefore what I was seeing was someone who had lived at least forty thousand years ago."

"Then what?"

Ellen managed a crooked smile. "I think I scared him. I said something stupid – hallo or something – and he took off into the cave. I tried to go after him but was choked by the smoke. When I managed to stop coughing and could open my eyes, everything had gone. I was back in the present. Where the cave had been was just a grassy slope."

They looked at each other in silence. For several moments the only sound in the office was the harsh crackle of an oxyacetylene torch as Charlie Crittenden used some of his precious gas on repairs to the showman's engine.

"If I recall, you saw the spyder that day."

"A glimpse," said Ellen. Intrigued by his thoughtful frown, she added, "Why?"

"Cathy Price also saw it. Your burning ambition has always been to discover palaeolithic cave paintings to equal the finds in France. And you did so. Cathy Price's dream has been to walk again – and now she can. And you both saw the visitors' spyder thing."

"One crackpot make-a-wish theory from Professor David Weir coming up."

"Why so crackpot? Perhaps the visitors are trying to compensate us for the misery they've inflicted?"

Ellen sighed. "Mike Malone also saw it, and so did Vikki Taylor. Mike Malone's wish would be to see his children. No prizes for guessing what Vikki's wish would be."

David nodded. "You have a point," he conceded.

From outside came a yell of pain caused by something soft and animate being hit with something hard and inanimate. A string of curses followed.

"So why are you messing about with "Brenda"?" Ellen demanded. "The resources committee have given it a low priority because you said yourself that the dynamo will have to be completely rewound."

"We're concentrating on getting it mobile," said David. "We're only putting in an hour or so a day." His move to the door was thwarted by Ellen putting her arms around his neck.

"That doesn't answer my question."

David smiled and kissed her on the cheek – an adventurous foreplay move for him. "A favour for Bob Harding."

"I've told you the truth about the cave, David. Only a low-life swede-basher would make me have to resort to sexually depraved ploys now."

David grinned. "Ah, but I'm a particularly disgusting form of low life swede-basher, m'dear. Ploy away."

Seven

Asquith Prescott, Chairman of Pentworth Council, switched off the camcorder and placed it on his desk. The camera had an effective zoom lens; the scene with Harding and Malone struggling with the hydraulic jack had been captured in detail. The seeming invincibility of the Wall pleased him. Without it he was Chairman, just by virtue of it being his turn by rotation, of the council of a small town with hardly any powers. With the Wall he had almost total control over an area of thirty square miles and over 6000 inhabitants, and a satisfyingly large office on the top floor of the recently requisitioned old courthouse, now renamed Government House. Thirty square miles didn't add up to much but there had been smaller city-states in history. The Wall was his source of power. Long may it remain so.

His smile saturated his visitor with bonhomie radiation. He picked a fleck of dust from his immaculate white safari suit. The government-run laundry took particular care of his safari suits. The gesture enabled him to avoid his visitor's disturbing blue eyes.

"A most interesting, tape, Adrian. It would seem that Councillor Harding is wasting his time."

"He is raising his hand against God," Roscoe answered. His gaunt appearance, compelling blue eyes that rarely blinked, and a rich, resonant voice, made him an accomplished orator and a formidable enemy. No one crossed Adrian Roscoe.

"Oh – I hardly think so," said Prescott, who had heard all this before. He had to tread carefully with the self-styled Father Adrian Roscoe, leader of the Bodian Brethren. The cult leader had a long lease on Pentworth House and the estate's farmland. His band of followers plus a number of party guests and security men hired for the party who had been trapped within the Wall meant that he had a useful labour force at his command. Although Prescott had recently done a deal with Roscoe that placed the security men under his control, guarding Government House. Roscoe's ace was that he controlled Pentworth House's methane-fired bakery ovens – now a vital part of the community's economy. Pentworth had large stocks of European Union grain that had to be used before it was spoiled by the high humidity.

Roscoe's gown fell away from his bony arms as he leaned forward, resting his elbows on Prescott's desk. "The Wall was put in place by God as a punishment for our sins! To isolate the evil we're harbouring in our midst from the rest of the world. It was either that or the total destruction of this planet, just as He destroyed the fourth planet, and just as He will destroy the earth if we don't heed His warning!"

The belief was the foundation of the Bodian Brethren's philosophy – that the asteroid belt beyond Mars was the remains of a planet that had defied God, and that continual prayer was the only way to prevent similar punishment being meted out to earth.

It took courage to meet Roscoe's cobalt-blue stare. Prescott was vain and self-opinionated, but he didn't lack courage. He met the stare head on. "As you know, Councillor Harding thinks the Wall is the work of an advanced intelligence. He's theorised that the visitors and their damaged UFO or Silent Vulcan, or whatever, is in Pentworth Lake. That the dome is a defence mechanism while they're awaiting help from some sort of interstellar AA service."

"Councillor Harding is a fool, as you saw from that video tape!" Roscoe snapped.

Prescott shrugged and said nothing. For a few moments the only sound in the fourth floor office was the clatter of cartwheels and horses hooves from Market Square.

"Also he's a friend of that infernal wicca woman!"

Here we go, thought Prescott. "You mean Ellen Duncan, Adrian?"

"She is an acolyte of Satan! And that Taylor girl is her apprentice!"

"There is no proof—" Prescott began.

"The proof's in that camcorder! Rewind the tape to the start! It's the shots showing the Taylor girl playing table tennis in her garden using a perfectly normal left hand! What more proof do you want?"

Roscoe had shown Prescott the secretly taped video recording of Vikki Taylor on an earlier occasion – after a private dinner at Pentworth House when the real reason for Roscoe's hatred of Ellen Duncan had emerged.

"Then there's the Catherine Price woman," said Roscoe, calming down. "She was unable to walk since a riding accident as a child, and now she can walk. A friend of the Duncan woman. Ellen Duncan is wicca through and through, Asquith – an affront to God, and someone who opposes you in council at every turn." He rose and picked up the camcorder. "We must apply ourselves to getting rid of her so that God will remove His Wall. That's what we agreed, isn't it?"

Prescott beamed. He certainly wanted Ellen Duncan off the council and saw no harm in shaking hands with Roscoe before the cult leader swept out of his office. He was lost in thought for several minutes when there was a tap on his door and Diana Sheldon entered from her outer office.

The Town Clerk was a greying, self-effacing woman of fifty-five who had never had a lover in her life before Prescott, seeing many advantages in her subservience, had made her his mistress. She had been flattered by his attentions at first and had proved an easy victim, even dressing to please him, and had been eager to use her legal training to find ways of helping Prescott tighten his grip on power, but now her innate good sense was making room for doubts.

"How was he?" she asked.

"Difficult, as usual. Will no one rid me of this tiresome priest? Has Nelson Faraday arrived?"

"He's outside. Chatting up Vanessa Grossman. I doubt if he'll get very far with her."

"Vanessa Grossman? Rings a bell."

"My new assistant."

"Ah, yes. The tall brunette. Any good?"

"A brilliant organiser," said Diana warmly, moving to the door. "She's got all the filing straightened out. A proper registry set up. I don't know how I managed without her."

"Good. Good. Send Faraday in please, Diana."

Vanessa Grossman showed Faraday in a few moments later. Without waiting for an invitation, he sat before the huge desk, while Prescott stood at the window overlooking Market Square, waving to the knot of his supporters who always gathered outside when the presence of the Pentworth coat of arms flag on the rooftop flagstaff indicated that he was "at home".

Nelson Faraday would have been an imposing figure in any colour but he was particularly so in black leather. Everything about him was black, from his turntop cavalier boots to his lantern-jawed, sullen expression. The only relief was the crimson lining of his leather cloak. Nelson Faraday would have made an excellent Count Dracula. The difference being that Dracula had a certain charm; Faraday had none.

Prescott dropped his large frame into his swivel chair and smiled benignly at his visitor. "Government House is a large building, Nelson. When we took it over, its size worried me, but you and your men are doing an excellent job looking after its security."

"Thank you, sir."

"What disappoints me is that you seem to be under the impression that you're still working for Father Roscoe." Prescott cut off the beginning of Faraday's protest by raising a hand. He continued in a mild tone. "I asked you to keep tabs on Councillor Harding. Perhaps I didn't make it clear that eyewitness reports would've been adequate. I certainly didn't want you borrowing Father Roscoe's camcorder for the purpose. No doubt he asked you why you wanted it, and no doubt, as a former employee of his, you told him."

Faraday was astute enough to know that there was little point in lying; Adrian Roscoe's brief visit to Government House had been reported to him by his duty guard at the front desk. "I'm sorry, sir."

Prescott gave a dismissive wave. "Oh, I'm not being critical, you understand. Divided loyalty and all that."

"It won't happen again, sir."

"I'm glad to hear it, Nelson. Glad to hear it. But, of course, you should still be of help to Father Roscoe in any way if he asks, within reason, of course. But do remember who is now paying you a proper salary with decent bonuses."

"Understood, sir."

"Excellent, Nelson. I look forward to our long and successful partnership. Well . . . I'm sure you have much to do. Don't let me keep you." He added a rider when Faraday reached the door. "I see that Detective Sergeant Malone was with Councillor Harding during that nonsense with the hydraulic jack."

Faraday was uncertain what was coming next. "He was, sir."

"Malone is a shrewd operator, Nelson. I hope he didn't see you?"

"He didn't, sir." This time Faraday was lying. When Malone had left Harding and jogged past his hiding place, the police officer had called out: "Mind you don't tear that fine cloak on those brambles, Nelson."

Eight

Harvey Evans levelled his Durand microlight biplane at 1000
feet above Pentworth Lake and flew in a slow circle, gripping
the simple yoke between his knees while sweeping the entire area
enclosed by the dome with his binoculars. The moisture-laden
thermals rising from the lake were meeting colder air at 3000
feet and condensing as clouds that would fall as rain at night
when the temperature fell. The air currents caused the tiny aircraft
to buck slightly but he was a skilled pilot and had no difficulty
retaining control. Unlike most microlights, in which the pilot was
suspended precariously beneath the wing, the French-built Durand
was a miniature aircraft with a partially enclosing cockpit in a
fuselage.

He scoured the lake with his binoculars, paying particular attention
to the sandy bathing area that was now Pentworth's favourite
picnic spot. It was several months since the two radio interference
investigators had drowned when the lake was in flood following a
storm and had become a swamp. It had been two days before the
Wall had appeared. They had been weighed down with equipment
used to trace the source of powerful radio emissions from the lake.
It was unlikely that their bodies would appear now, and the banks
were always checked at first light each day by a morris police patrol,
but there was no harm in a double check.

He spotted a wisp of smoke above the town and altered course
to investigate.

Harvey Evans was sixty. A powerfully built, thickset dependable
man. Until recently he had been Sussex Police's sector inspector
for Pentworth but had resigned rather than accept Asquith Prescott's
restructuring of the police force. Evans had conceded that recruiting
morris men for a rapid build-up of police strength to fifty men hadn't
been such a bad idea – the core of the new police force was the
Pentworth Morris Men side. Evans had been their "squire" and had
nurtured them through many changes. The side now had a reputation
for toughness since he had introduced sword dances and scrapped the

fluttering handkerchiefs. The men were all well-known – unarmed apart from their staffs, and the public had been surprisingly quick to accept them and their now familiar uniforms of straw hats, white blouses, and buckle shoes.

What Evans had vehemently objected to was Prescott's proposal to recruit the security men, that Adrian Roscoe had been stuck with, as a private army under the command of Nelson Faraday to guard Government House and its immediate surroundings. That meant a gang of untrained black-shirted heavies keeping their idea of law and order in Pentworth's town centre. Nelson Faraday was a sadistic thug. His PNC printout made for chilling reading: the thirty-five-year-old Londoner had a long string of previous convictions ranging from pimping to serious assault. His victims were usually women.

Evans had resigned knowing full well that he was being pushed into doing so. The result was that Prescott got what he wanted and was now commander of the morris police and the blackshirts. Evans had hoped that the council would refuse to ratify the situation, but it had proved a slender hope because the perception of Prescott's stealthy tightening of his grip on power was eclipsed by the many sensible but tough measures he was pushing through council that were necessary to ensure Pentworth's survival – and they were sufficient to override opposition.

Out of loyalty, Malone had offered to resign from the police too, but Evans had wanted him to stay on, saying he'd be happier if there was at least one sane officer on the force come the day when they'd have to pick up the pieces.

On balance, retirement wasn't so bad. Prescott had honoured Evans' pension. The former police officer had his hives to look after and, above all, he could continue to indulge his passion for flying because the council had voted him a fuel allowance for weekly aerial inspections.

As the tiny biplane neared the town, Evans identified the strands of smoke as coming from North Street – near Ellen Duncan's "Earthforce" herbal shop. Someone had lit an unauthorised fire that night and put it out before daybreak, not realising that their chimney was still emitting tell-tale traces of smoke. Pentworth was built on a buff therefore maintaining level flight resulted in him flying above the rooftops at less than 500 feet.

The streets were busy with hand carts and a few horse-drawn vehicles. There was a crowd gathering in Market Square near the town stocks. Probably someone who was having a clear-out and had set up a stall. All junk had value these days. A queue had formed outside the battery-charging centre. He altered course and flew parallel to North Street, enabling him to pinpoint the exact property emitting smoke. He keyed his PMR radio.

"Alpha Zero One – Oscar Papa."

"Go ahead, Alpha Zero One," the Pentworth operations duty officer at the police station acknowledged.

Evans had to press the handset's speaker-microphone to his ear to hear above the harsh buzz of the microlight's air-cooled engine. "A possible recently extinguished fire," he reported. "Warren's butcher's shop, North Street."

"Thank you, Alpha Zero One. We'll send a unit to take a look."

A fire warranted a prompt response. The morris police would check fireplaces and test the temperature of chimney masonry. If Tony Warren had lit an illegal fire, he faced an automatic fine of 500 euros. Among the first measures taken by the council the previous March when the Wall appeared were strict controls on carbon dioxide emissions. Fire licences were issued by Government House for public barbecues, charcoal production, and essential engineering work, and that was all.

Evans banked and flew south-east, passing directly over Ellen Duncan's property. Her wedge-shaped plot started at the narrow frontage of her shop and widened rapidly in a series of terraced fields as it dropped down the slope. Ellen also owned the adjoining farmland and Pentworth Lake itself. One of her small fields was on a checklist provided by Government House, but it had been ploughed and harrowed since his last inspection flight, so his digital camera remained in its case.

He spotted Ellen near the back door of her house, shading her eyes as she stared up at him. He waggled his wings. There was a pause before she waved in acknowledgement. He chuckled to himself when he recalled a flight two years previously when he had caught her unawares.

He glanced at his watch. The time allowed for his inspection flight was nearly over. Just a quick check of Temple Farm to the east and then home to a landing in his paddock where his son would be waiting for him.

Before him lay the Temple of the Winds with its massive sandstone outcrop projecting from the hill's wooded slopes near its brow. The winds of a hundred centuries had carved the edge of the great slab into a strange, gargoyle-like face that scowled southward across the valley to the alien crags and tors of the Farside steppes.

The high outcrop was steeped in legend, the most ancient being that the Beaker people had thrown virgins off the precipice to appease their gods.

If the couple that Evans spotted on the slab near the lookout obelisk were virgins before they climbed the hill, they were now doing their damnedest with horizontal aerobics on a blanket to remedy the situation.

What Harvey Evans did next was more than merely cruel and immature – it was downright malicious, but he was downwind, was weak, and had a sense of humour.

He throttled back and lost height so that he was below the level of the slab, thus the engrossed couple would be unlikely to hear his approach.

They didn't.

The realisation that their party for two had become a *ménage à trois* came when the Durand microlight appeared from nowhere and roared over them at a height of ten metres. Evans could not have joined in at a worse moment: coitus interruptus with wings. His startled male victim suddenly reared up from between his partner's spread thighs and splattered her. Evans looked back and caught a glimpse of the man bundling his girlfriend towards the sanctuary of nearby trees, trying frantically to yank his zip over a diminishing erection, while the girl played hopscotch with a pair of panties. They became entangled and fell over. The man jumped up and shook an enraged fist at the biplane. Evans recognised them: Josie Smith and her husband. He held his course away from them to spare them further embarrassment.

A married couple having it off in the outdoors? Well – it wasn't that unusual. There was a local belief that children conceived at the Temple of Winds were destined for good health and prosperity.

Strange how 2000-year-old pagan beliefs still exerted such a hold over supposedly rational people in the twenty-first century.

Nine

Ellen glowered up at the microlight biplane as it flew over her house. A mixture of embarrassment and anger pricked her cheeks whenever she saw the diminutive aircraft. Before the discovery of the flint mine the previous year, when she had had more time on her hands, she had often taken the steep path up to the Temple of Winds on fine days to sunbathe, read, and listen to music. On one occasion she had been reading a book about Isadora Duncan and, feeling exuberant, had emulated her namesake by performing a little dance to Stravinski's *Rite of Spring*, naked. Harvey Evans had chanced on her so suddenly in his damned flying flea of an aeroplane that she had had no time to grab her towel. According to David Weir, Evans had talked in the Crown about the incident but, thankfully, had never mentioned her name.

Now the nosy old sod was making life a misery with his damned Prescott-inspired inspection flights. David's fellow farmers were complaining about the fines they were having to pay for minor infractions of a whole raft of new anti-pollution rules and regulations.

The Durand waggled its wings. Ellen returned the salute with a wave but two upturned fingers tended to undermine the friendliness of the gesture. A large black cat, Thomas, rubbed around her ankles and looked up at his mistress with the woebegone expression of a cat forced to accept the ugly truth that the last tin of Felix had been opened several weeks ago. Ellen pushed him away with her foot and turned to berate a herb or a helper.

"Where's that Sarah Gale and Robbie Hammond?" she demanded.

Tracy stopped hoeing between the rows of chicory and pointed down the terraced slopes. "They went that way, Mrs Duncan. They said—"

"*Miss* Duncan!"

"Sorry, Miss Duncan. They were carrying boxes of digital seedlings to plant in that new bottom field."

"I'll give 'em hell if they're not," said Ellen grimly. "It's digitalis – good for heart remedies. And careful with that hoe! Can you call

31

upon a working corner of your addled brain to recall why I've marked some plants with coloured raffia?"

The girl regarded her, doe-eyed. "Because they're the best and therefore they're going to be allowed to go to seed for next year's crop?"

"Excellent, Tracy. Perhaps your cerebrally challenged condition was over-estimated by the Apprentice Assignment Committee."

Ellen turned her back and set off in search of her missing helpers, leaving the doe-eyed girl wondering if she'd been complimented or insulted. Thomas followed, pausing to outwit and kill the occasional dead leaf.

Apprentices! thought Ellen, tramping downhill. The delinquents she'd been saddled with by the assignment committee were real dumbos. All they would ever grow was bored, and they were already experts at that.

Ellen was not wholly in favour of Prescott's apprenticeship scheme. Having less bright kids completing their education in apprenticeships to wheelwrights, cartwrights, wainwrights, bakers, candlestick makers and all the other many vital trades that had been on the point of extinction might be a practical idea, but to Ellen it smacked of selection.

But, whatever the rights and wrongs of the scheme, she grudgingly had to admit that it seemed to be working. They were nearly into July – thirteen weeks of the Wall and the whole community was abuzz with activity, taking advantage of the long, hot hours of daylight.

Some kids were taking the wrong sort of advantage; shrieks of laughter enabled Ellen to locate her missing helpers. Sarah Gale and Robbie Hammond were naked, splashing each other in the depleted stream, the boy doing his best to kiss Sarah's breasts but she kept pushing him away with playful flicks at his hopeful coat-peg erection.

"When you two have finished," Ellen bellowed, her hands cupped to her mouth, "there's digitalis to be planted!"

The couple stopped their horseplay. The boy clapped his hands in front of himself and hid behind Sarah who was quite unabashed by her nakedness.

"We're taking a break from the stink of that tree down there!" said Sarah defiantly. She was referring to Ellen's ginkgo tree, whose terrible smell kept deer away from her herb crops. It had also deterred weekend ramblers in the days when they had been a problem. In fact the tree deterred anything that could walk, crawl, swim or fly. It was a biological stink bomb of awesome potency.

"You'll get used to it!"

"No way!" Sarah declared.

"Sorry, Miss Duncan!" the lad called out over Sarah's shoulder. He was fearful of Ellen's temper. "We'll get back now."

"Not without gas masks!" Sarah yelled.

Ellen's explosion of anger was checked by someone calling her. She wheeled around. It was Tracy, the doe with the hoe, out of breath. "Message from Vikki, Mrs . . . Miss Duncan. There's a Mr Hardy to see you urgent in the shop!"

"Urgent*ly*! It should be an adverb!"

"I don't think so. Vikki didn't say he was selling anything."

Ellen didn't bother trying to work that one out. She hurried back to her little herbal shop to discover that Tracy's Mr Hardy was Bob Harding.

The scientist's expression was grim. He came straight to the point. "I owe you an apology, Ellen, for the number of times I've not voted with you. Until now, I've usually gone along with Prescott because I think he's been doing a good job and always has the best interests of the community at heart. But this time he's gone too far. You'd better come and see what's happening in Market Square."

Ellen asked him to wait while she changed quickly into clean shorts and a T-shirt. She left Vikki and Thomas in charge of the shop and had to trot to keep up with the scientist as he strode towards Market Square. In answer to her questions he said, "You'll see," and kept walking.

They were nearly at the square when Harding asked: "By the way, Ellen, how's the work going on David's traction engine?"

"Charlie Crittenden is testing the boiler tomorrow."

"Excellent. We can set a date for the operation for next week if our wonderful Chairman agrees."

Ellen's scathing response that the decision to carry out the scientist's crazy plan for an assault on the Wall would be taken in full council never materialised. She followed Harding through the small crowd and stared in a mixture of astonishment and horror at the scene before her, not hearing Harding's excuses that there were problems at the new ice-making plant that he had to attend to.

Brad Jackson, the scourge of Pentworth, was in the town stocks. The delinquent was naked and sobbing in terror, writhing and twisting – his wrists and neck bleeding from abrasion against the rough timbers in his desperate but futile efforts to avoid jets of urine being fired at him by a big woman wielding a formidable plastic water rifle with a large reservoir. A jeering crowd had gathered, some trying to get near enough to spit but prevented by three white-bloused morris men. A fourth morris man was moving through the throng, warning people not to throw anything. Nelson Faraday, dressed in his customary black leather, was standing nearby, idly twirling some keys on a chain and scowling at everyone.

A group of teenage girls were pointing and laughing at the youth's genitals while chanting, "Brad's got a little one! . . . Brad's got a little one! . . ."

Ellen didn't know any of the morris policemen because there had been many new recruits recently. Faraday seemed to be in charge, so she rounded on him. "This is inhuman! Release him immediately!"

Faraday took a step back, folded his arms, and studied Ellen quizzically, looking her up and down like a Roman senator contemplating the purchase of a slave. His gaze lingered approvingly on her breasts before he gave her a sardonic smile.

"I will in forty-five minutes," he said. "Then it'll be the turn of his mates. An hour each. Chairman's orders." He jerked his thumb at a dogcart where two members of Brad Jackson's gang were manacled to a cross-bar, their eyes wide with terror.

The women with the water rifle ran out of ammunition. She started forward with the intention of kicking the youth but was restrained by a morris man. Nevertheless she managed a well-aimed glob of saliva that trickled down her target's tear-stained face.

Ellen stared around at the crowd and saw the same faces and the same twisted expressions of hate that she saw in her recurring nightmare of a terrified young woman being driven around the town. It was a bright, sunny day, yet the vision sprang at Ellen, swamping her senses. The young woman had luxuriate black hair like Ellen. She was chained naked to the cross-bar of a dogcart, her legs streaked with mucus and semen from the mass rape she had suffered at the Temple of the Winds. She gave a scream at something she had seen in the middle of the square. But it was a silent scream. It was Brad Jackson's real scream of pain from a well-aimed stone that banished the stark images, bringing Ellen to her senses.

For some moments she was disorientated, her brain a madly spinning kaleidoscope, but she managed to marshal her thoughts and square up to Faraday. "Listen, you scumbag – what you're doing here is illegal and a flagrant violation of human rights!" she snapped, her face white with fury.

Faraday's smile faded. His expression hardened to a scowl. "No one calls me a scumbag."

"I call you what I damn well like. This is illegal."

Faraday's eyes glittered hatred. "Best you argue with this little delinquent about what's legal and what's illegal. He and his mates were caught trashing this lady's home this morning. He stays in the stocks another forty-five minutes. Chairman's orders."

Ellen controlled her temper. "So you're saying that it's not much use my talking to the monkey when my argument's with the organ-grinder?"

Without waiting for an answer, Ellen glanced up at Pentworth's coat of arms fluttering from the flagstaff on top of Government House, indicating that Prescott was in, and walked slowly away. Faraday and the hostile crowd watched her crossing the square. Ellen was too intent on her next course of action to notice Detective Sergeant Mike Malone also watching the proceedings with interest from his favourite table outside the Crown public house. He was off duty, enjoying the sun and a tankard of Pentworth Breweries latest special malt beer. Much as he admired Ellen, the detective's attention remained on the small crowd, particularly the nucleus – the twenty or so who had gathered even before Brad Jackson had been locked in the stocks.

Suddenly Ellen broke into a run and veered towards Government House.

"Stop her!" Faraday yelled.

The two black-shirted men standing each side of the entrance were members of the security team donated by Adrian Roscoe. They knew Ellen was a councillor and hesitated. Their momentary indecision was enough for her to thrust them aside and storm into the lobby.

Jesus Christ! she thought, racing up the stairs. Blackshirt palace guards now!

On the fourth floor Diana Sheldon and Vanessa Grossman tried to stop Ellen but weren't quick enough. The infuriated woman burst into Prescott's office. The Chairman was sitting behind his expanse of desk and had a warm smile of welcome in place that masked his concern. He had seen Ellen break into a run and head for Government House and was alarmed at the ease with which she had entered the building and his office. Security would have to be stepped up. He rose, hand outstretched in welcome. As usual, he was wearing a spotless white safari suit, open-necked, his ruddy cheeks a little less rounded now because he was losing weight and looking better for it. He motioned Diana and Vanessa to withdraw.

"Ah. Councillor Duncan. An unexpected pleas—"

Faraday and the blackshirts hurled themselves into the office and pulled up when they saw Prescott's upraised hand.

"It's all right everyone. Councillor Duncan and I are old friends. Leave us please, and close the door."

"Release him!" Ellen snapped when they were alone. "Release him and the other two this instant!"

Prescott regarded Ellen with unconcealed admiration. Her long, dark hair was entangled around her face, her eyes blazing with a savage beauty. The fine sheen of perspiration caused by her racing up four flights of stairs gave her an animal quality that he found decidedly exciting, particularly the way her T-shirt clung to her full breasts. A real woman – a woman with spirit and passion – unlike the fawning Diana Sheldon who now bored him. He had never forgotten the time at a ball when Ellen had underlined her rejection of his advances with a knee in the groin. It was only a matter of time before this magnificent creature was before him, helpless and terrified – promising him anything to secure his mercy.

That day would come . . . It would surely come . . .

"I'm surprised, Ellen," said Prescott comfortably. "You've been the victim of Brad Jackson's shoplifting activities on several occasions. Now he and his cronies are being punished – properly punished – and you're angry."

"That's not punishment!" Ellen snapped. "That's—"

"Nor was what they've received in the past," Prescott interrupted. "Endless probation orders which they've broken; supervision orders, bail conditions, court orders which they've repeatedly ignored. Those little street rats have been house-breaking and shoplifting and vandalising property since they could walk. They've caused untold misery in this community over the years, and now the community is fighting back."

"You're punishing children because of their backgrounds—"

"They're not children any more. All three have turned eighteen. They're being punished to show them that the people of Pentworth won't stand for their behaviour any longer. The days when they could cock a snoot at the law are over—"

"You're the one cocking a snoot at the law!" Ellen fired back. "What's being done out there is illegal!"

"I am acting one hundred per cent within the laws of England and Wales," Prescott stated flatly.

Ellen stared at him. "How can you be? This situation is unprecedented!"

"Perhaps. Yet it is covered by existing law." Prescott opened a drawer and slid a document across his desk that bore the seal of the local notary. "That's a ruling from His Honour Judge John Harleston-Hooper. He spent many years of his working life in Hong Kong, so he's more familiar with colonial law than most. A somewhat lengthy ruling, so I suggest you read the marked paragraphs in his summing-up on the last page."

Ellen leafed through the typescript. Every alteration had been signed in full by the judge and each page had been separately notarised. She came to two paragraphs marked with a yellow highlighter pen.

> It will be seen from the foregoing that the extraordinary situation that has arisen in Pentworth, with its mysteriously imposed isolation from the rest of the world, has precise parallels with the situation confronting the governor of a remote crown colony where communications between the colony and the Crown and parliament are difficult or impossible. In my opinion, in such circumstances, the governor of a crown colony has statutory powers equal to that of the Crown and parliament combined in the keeping of the sovereign's peace and preservation of religious harmony, and discretionary powers which are also equal to the powers of the Crown and parliament combined in the enforcing of such peace.
>
> In my opinion, a governor (or acting governor, as we have in Pentworth) can promulgate emergency legislation in the interests of the colony, raise militias, and even declare and wage war if necessary to defend the colony when all diplomatic methods have failed. In previous such extreme cases, it is has been usual for the then Colonial Office to retrospectively endorse the actions of the governor or acting governor. I know of no cases that can be considered closely pertinent to this situation where such endorsement has been denied.

"A remarkably concise document for a lawyer, wouldn't you say, Ellen?" said Prescott when she had finished reading. He took the papers from her and smiled complacently at her shaken expression for a moment before producing another document, a single sheet of paper this time, and pushing it across the desk. "Now take a look at that please."

He sighed when his visitor didn't even glance at the paper. "Since the beginning of the crisis," he continued, "four custodial sentences have been passed down by the bench. As you know, the basement of the Old Malt House has been converted into a custody unit. What you don't know, and what I didn't know until yesterday, was the extent of the burden on the community that running the custody unit has become."

"The morris police officers are OK," said Ellen. "That was a good idea – we needed them. But the team of Roscoe's blackshirts you've got guarding this pile and the custody unit are nothing but thugs."

Prescott shrugged. "But they *are* legally recruited, whatever you may think of them, Ellen. Manning the custody unit is tying up several black— Government House security officers full time. In addition there is a support staff of two cooks and a clerk. At the moment we have eleven full-time employees to look after four prisoners. Next week two women come up for sentencing. The nature of their crimes is such that they're certain to receive custodial sentences – and that means recruiting more staff and building more permanent cells. Unless we do something now, before we know what's happening, we'll have a prison, prison warders, an army of probation officers, clerks of court, ushers, and God knows what else to support. Pentworth cannot afford that sort of judicial infrastructure. The people are working hard and it would be grossly unfair to impose even more taxes on them. Therefore I've decided on a fast-track system of justice. Offenders are to be brought straight here following their arrest. I've appointed the food control officer as a lay magistrate. She will break off her work, hear the evidence and pass sentence on the spot. No masses of forms – paperwork and records will be kept to the absolute minimum. No adjournments; no probation officer reports or any of that nonsense. Just fast, effective justice."

"Putting offenders in the stocks," said Ellen contemptuously. "That's your idea of justice, is it? Turn back the clock five hundred years. What's it to be next? Torture chambers? Breaking people on the rack?"

"Now you're just being silly and over-dramatic."

"The majority of the people of Pentworth are decent, honest, hard-working," Ellen retorted angrily. "Do you really think they will tolerate a barbarity such as the *stocks* in the twenty-first century?"

"I agree with you about the people, Ellen. Decent and hard-working. They've had it up to here with petty crime and vandalism. And some of it not so petty. Time and time again politicians have promised action and nothing's been done other than to cut back on the police. Well, the time has come for the people to have their say.

"The stocks will be used as a last resort for habitual criminals instead of custodial sentences. On the spot fines and the seizure of chattels has proved most effective so far, so I doubt if they'll need to be used that often." Prescott swung his chair around and gazed down at the square. Word had spread fast – there was now a large crowd gathered around the stocks. The woman with the water rifle had refilled her weapon and was using it on the manacled prisoners, cringing helplessly on the dogcart. "But those little skunks down there need a lesson that they'll never forget. Humiliation is a powerful deterrent."

"It's not the behaviour of the skunks down there that worries me," Ellen retorted.

Prescott's scalp went back but he remained calm. He rose. "Very well, Ellen. If you feel so strongly, you can be responsible for their release. Come."

Despite her natural inclination not to obey any order given by Prescott, Ellen followed him down the stairs and out of the building. The crowd around the stocks fell silent and made a passage. Some tried to shake Prescott's hand but he brushed them politely aside. Faraday's eyes bored into Ellen.

"Mrs Edmunds," said Prescott to the woman with the water rifle. "Perhaps you would be good enough to tell Councillor Duncan what these vandals did to your home, please."

Mrs Edmunds was about sixty. Fat and friendly was the way she liked to describe herself but now her normally cheery, round face was sagging with sorrow. She had been crying recently. "I was going to see my daughter at Tillington," she began. "But the bus couldn't leave because one of the horses went lame, so I went home. I knew something was wrong the minute I opened my front door." Her accusing eyes went to the sobbing youth in the stocks and his two mates on the dogcart awaiting their punishment. "They was in my back room – playing an old wind-up gramophone which is why they didn't hear me . . . They'd smashed everything . . . Pictures of my late husband . . . All my china . . . Royal Doulton . . . Everything . . . Killed my budgie." Her eyes filled with tears and she was unable to continue.

Ellen put an arm around her to comfort her but couldn't think of anything helpful to say.

"There's more," said Prescott grimly. "Tell her, Mrs Edmunds."

The woman wiped her eyes on her sleeve. "They pushed past

me and ran off. Hands over their faces. Laughing. But I knew who they was all right. There was a terrible smell . . . Really bad – I wanted to be sick. They'd smeared . . ." She was unable to continue until she had taken a deep breath, and then the words came out in a rush. "They'd smeared it everywhere . . . Walls, carpet . . . Everywhere . . . Why'd they want to do that? Why? I'd never done them no harm." She dissolved into tears.

"Mrs Edmunds," said Ellen, feeling foolish and ineffectual. "What they did was wicked and they must be punished. But this sort of punishment is wrong. If we treat them like this, like animals, then we're letting them drag us down to their level."

"That's what they are!" the woman spat. "Animals! They get an hour each in this thing. That's all! An hour for wrecking a lifetime!"

The crowd murmured in sympathy. Prescott took the keys from Faraday and held them out to Ellen. "If you want to let them go, Councillor Duncan, then so be it. I daresay they've received a sufficiently salutary lesson."

"Let the little bastards trash her shop!" someone shouted. "See how she likes it!"

Prescott was trying to call Ellen's bluff, but it was not in her nature to allow intimidation to undermine her principles or weaken her courage. Nevertheless her heartbeat quickened as she calmly took the keys from Prescott and unlocked the padlock on the stocks. She lifted the hinged yoke so that Brad Jackson was free to stagger clear, rubbing his neck and wrists, his eyes blazing raw hatred at Prescott. A morris man tossed him his pants.

To release the other two meant climbing on to the dogcart. By the time she had unlocked the manacles, the crowd had gathered around – a silent sea of hard, unfriendly, unforgiving faces. The youths scrambled down, white with fear at what the mob might do but a passage opened up for them to make their escape. It was Ellen that the silent faces were watching. Someone took hold of the dogcart's hafts. It moved suddenly, causing her to grab the crossbar to keep her balance.

"Mekhashshepheh!"

The ancient curse that predated Christianity sent a flood of cold terror surging through Ellen, and the hate in the gathering crowd rose around her like a black, suffocating night that produced eerie patterns of light and swirling smoke from blazing torches held by the mob. The nightmare would not leave her alone. Shadows danced on the façades of buildings that did not belong in the Market Square

Ellen knew. She heard the girl on the dogcart scream again but this time Ellen saw the cause of her terror. The Crown tavern looked very much as it always had but it was partially obscured by piles of faggots and bundled brushwood surrounding a stout wooden stake driven through the surface mud and into the hard-packed ground.

"OK. The show's over. That's enough, everyone. Let's all get back to work."

The friendly yet assertive voice banished the terrifying vision. Daylight returned and Ellen saw Malone holding out his hand to her. She took it gratefully and allowed him to help her down from the dogcart.

Malone would have made an excellent schoolteacher; his cold, disapproving eye seemed to take in everyone in the crowd in turn, stirring gremlins of personal guilt. They quickly dispersed so that only Prescott and a few of his acolytes remained. Their beloved leader treated Malone and Ellen to a sneering smile of triumph and beckoned to Faraday before marching into Government House, pausing on the steps to shake hands with his supporters and accept their congratulations.

"*That*," said Malone with heavy emphasis, "took real balls, Miss Duncan."

"Mixed with three parts stupidity," Ellen added bitterly.

Malone smiled enigmatically. He had always harboured a secret admiration of Ellen Duncan. He correctly guessed that the last thing she wanted was to be hustled away from the scene. He took her arm and sat her at his table. He ordered two Pentworth beers from the waiter and regarded his guest thoughtfully. "I wouldn't say that what you did was stupid, Miss Duncan. Impetuous – yes. But not stupid."

"When I decide to act, it has to be immediate."

"Like the time you rushed into the street in your nightie when those yobs from Pentworth House sprayed graffiti on your shop windows?" Malone queried.

It had been a Friday night – the day before the Wall had appeared. Malone had nearly caught the two aerosol artists who had written "EX2218" in large letters on Ellen's shop windows. Whatever it meant had been enough to cause Ellen to faint. Malone had scooped her up and carried her into her shop. She had later denied knowing what the strange inscription meant but Malone had been certain she was lying.

Ellen refused to acknowledge the police officer's query or meet his eye. Instead she returned the stares of a couple sitting at a nearby table. She recognised them as her customers and was about to make a cutting remark, but they looked sheepishly away and left. The group of Prescott's admirers were not so easily intimidated by Ellen's glares and remained at their post on the steps of Government House.

"I don't understand it," she muttered. "I just don't understand it. How could so many people support such inhuman treatment?"

The waiter bought their drinks, which Malone paid for. "They won't reoffend," he said, sipping his beer appreciatively. It was a strong, malty brew.

Ellen glared at him, making no attempt to pick up her glass. "Are you saying that you support Prescott?"

"I am pointing out that those three little street rats won't commit that sort of offence again. Public humiliation as a punishment is the most powerful deterrent of all, not only to wrongdoers, but would-be wrongdoers: the dunce's cap, the van bearing a debt-collecting sign, local shops and businesses publishing debtors' blacklists – all effective methods, which is why only wealthy societies can afford to ban them."

"So Pentworth is a poor society?"

"In many respects – yes. Poor in the most precious commodity of all – people."

"I'll ask you again: do you support Prescott?"

Malone's hesitation was all the excuse Ellen needed to go on to the offensive. "Obviously, you do. He's sacked your sector inspector. You told me yourself that Harvey Evans was a decent man, and yet you're staying on."

"Inspector Evans resigned," said Malone.

"Mr Evans was pushed into an intolerable situation!" Ellen snapped. "Oh, you don't have to be ashamed, Mr Malone – Prescott's got the entire community behind him – but forgive me if I don't drink with you." She stood.

"Please don't go, Miss Duncan. I'd like you to hear what I have to say."

The uncharacteristic, almost pleading note in Malone's voice caused Ellen's curiosity to triumph over her anger. She sat and stared fixedly at the police officer but made no attempt to touch her drink.

"Firstly," said Malone evenly. "Despite appearances, Prescott does not have wide support. And certainly not from me."

Ellen's reply was scathing. "You've not been very observant. Every time Prescott appears he attracts dozens of supporters."

"He attracts supporters – but not dozens of them. It only seems like that because they always make such a fuss of him." Malone produced a sheaf of papers and placed it before Ellen. It was a handwritten list of names and addresses. "Those are his supporters," he continued. "Pentworth's voting population is about five thousand seven hundred. Of that about two per cent – exactly one hundred and ten people – are dependent on him either directly or indirectly: his tenants and their families, and his employees and their families. Those are the ones who are always hanging around here, waiting for him to appear. Cheering him when he does show up and telling him what a splendid fellow he is. They've even got a rota system worked out so that there are always at least six of them on 'duty' – just as we have now."

Ellen glanced at the small knot of people outside Government House and looked questioningly at Malone. He studied the head on his beer. "The elderly woman is the sister-in-law of his estate manager. The two young men are sons of his tenants. The other three are friends. When St Mary's chimes noon in a few minutes, two of them will be relieved by two more. Prescott's rota is better organised than our police response cover."

"Did you compile this, Mr Malone?"

"I did indeed. Also, as I'm sure David Weir will confirm, Prescott does not enjoy widespread support among the farming community. In many ways they've borne the brunt of his stream of decrees and been unfairly blamed for some food shortages. This increasing dichotomy between town and country is the real danger and one that Prescott has failed to address."

Ellen grimaced. "The council hardly gets a chance to discuss anything now. Meetings cancelled. Items scrubbed from the agenda."

Malone held up his glass to the light. It took his mind and eyes off Ellen's legs. "Elective dictators need a high level of control of the political arm by intimidation," he observed. "It doesn't have to be overt intimidation. A couple of dozen supporters outside waving placards and chanting their leader's praises can do the trick."

"Such as we get at council meetings?"

"And which you're certain to have with a vengeance on Monday evening when you vote on Bob Harding's plan to breach the Wall," said Malone. "Prescott has made no secret of his opposition to any scheme. If the Wall is destroyed, bang goes his power and prestige. So he'll ensure that there'll be a good turn out of his supporters here in the square. Their yelling and chanting will be heard in the council chamber. You may not think it will affect your voting, but it will."

"He showed me a ruling by Judge Hooper just now that gives him total power anyway," said Ellen sourly. "If the council votes against him, he could legally wind up the council."

"Judge Hooper's analysis of the situation," said Malone off-handedly.

Ellen was surprised. "You've seen it?"

"Not officially. I don't think it could be considered a ruling without the weight of the Crown and the Lord Chancellor behind it. Hooper's a circuit judge, not High Court – and he's not the sort of man to drop into Prescott's pocket that easily. What he's given Prescott is more like a counsel's opinion, but that's something lawyers could argue over for years. Getting Judge Hooper to draft something was a shrewd move by Prescott. A bit of legal armour to cover his arse." He leaned forward, fixing his wide-set eyes intently on his guest. "It's too soon for him to grab total power. Right now he's doing very nicely with a stream of decrees – sorry, guidelines – that are slowly eroding Pentworth's democracy." Malone paused and glanced around the square before returning his gaze to Ellen. "What worries me, Miss Duncan, is that when food shortages start to bite in the autumn it will be the time when the people will want a democratic voice. That's when they'll find that they no longer have it and that's when the right conditions will be in place for civil unrest – possibly leading to serious trouble."

Ellen looked sharply at the police officer. "Meaning bloodshed?"

"Or worse – civil war. We have the ancient protagonists of town versus country in place. In many ways Prescott is doing a good job, but he does need a sharp, salutary lesson in democracy that will stop him in his tracks and prevent him increasing his power."

"That's what I've been saying all along, but no one will listen," said Ellen bitterly.

"So now's the time for action," said Malone. "A small step but an effective one. What you have to do at Monday's council meeting is expose any demonstration that takes place outside the chamber as the rent-a-mob sham that it is."

"How?"

Malone smiled enigmatically. "You have lovely, long hair, Miss Duncan."

Before Ellen had a chance to unleash a broadside, Malone quickly outlined a simple plan that had Ellen smiling by the time he had finished.

St Mary's clock tower started chiming twelve. The number of

people hanging around outside Government House swelled to eight. By the time the clock had finished striking, two of Prescott's original supporters had drifted casually away.

Ellen studied the list closely. The neat listings, with carefully recorded times of comings and goings, said as much about Malone as it did about Prescott's deviousness. She picked up her glass and raised it to Malone. "Your health, Mike. Do you mind if I call you Mike?"

Malone was delighted.

"In which case I insist that you call me Ellen." She finished her drink and stood. "I need to pick up some recharged radio batteries, and then I'd better get back to the shop. So when do I get the gizmo?" "I'll drop it in tomorrow morning . . . Ellen. And I'll show you how to use it."

Ellen flashed the policeman a warm smile. She would have been surprised had she known the effect it had on the otherwise enigmatic Malone. "See you then . . . Mike."

Malone thought thoughts of the impossible that might just be possible as he watched Ellen walking across the square.

She paused near the centre of the square and studied the worn inscription cut into the flagstones. It was something she had seen hundreds of times without noticing. This had to be what had triggered those terrible visions. The explanation, weak as it was, restored her confidence. Her step was a little lighter as she left the square.

Two gossiping women broke off to stare after Ellen. One gave a shrug of indifference. An insignificant gesture but Malone had seen enough such gestures to be deeply concerned for Ellen's safety. He pulled out his notebook and wrote down a phonetic approximation of the curse "*Mekhashshepheh!*" that he had heard spat at Ellen on two occasions now. At least, he presumed that Pentworth's ritual May Day shout was a curse. The problem was that he was grappling with a subject that he knew little about.

Malone was a man of considerable learning, particularly philosophy – the analysis and codification of the rational. He had little interest in religion or witchcraft, believing that all they provided was a measure of Man's gullibility and his ability to rationalise the irrational, and that one didn't need to study religion and witchcraft to know that.

He drained his glass and crossed to the inscription. Like Ellen, he knew what it said but had never taken much notice of it. The words were worn but readable:

On this spot, Eleanor of Fittleworth, convicted of witchcraft,
was burned at the stake, 12th April 1646.

Why was she burned when hanging was the traditional method
of execution in England that predated the seventeenth century? He
stared down and cursed his lack of knowledge. Bundles of books
being unloaded from a cart and carried into Government House under
the supervision of Dennis Davies, the librarian, gave him an idea.

Ten

Cathy Price heard a motor vehicle turn into her drive. Good – more government printing work just when money was getting low.

Even after fourteen weeks of being able to walk, she still experienced a thrill at being able to rise from a chair and cross to a window.

Her pony had thrown her at the age of ten. The neural damage controlling balance had confined her to a wheelchair for twenty-two years until after a particularly vivid dream in which the visitors' spyder had entered her bedroom while she was asleep. The following morning she discovered that her sense of balance was returning. A week later, to the astonishment of Dr Millicent Vaughan, she could walk normally.

In a way Cathy had always been 100 per cent fit although disabled. She had lived life to the full, had kept her body in good shape with exercise machines, run a successful graphic design studio from her home, and conducted a passionate affair with Josh, a weekend lover, now Farside and lost to her. Josh had exploited Cathy's magnificent body and wild, exhibitionist nature by setting her up with a web camera in her studio-bedroom that fed a stream of pictures of an anonymous "Cathy" at work and play to paying subscribers via an Internet website in France. Some even liked to watch her asleep.

The Wall had ended all that, particularly her passion for thrashing her restored E-Type Jaguar along motorways. But the return of her sense of balance had been a million compensations.

From the window she saw that the government's usual, unmarked van had turned into her drive and was parked in front of her E-type. Odd that this time the van didn't have its mobile generator in tow.

Three times since the Wall had appeared Diana Sheldon and Vernon Kelly, a banker and Pentworth's financial advisor, had descended on Cathy unannounced with a supply of special paper and required her to print banknotes that she had designed for them on her Mac.

Following the appearance of the Wall, Pentworth's surviving branch banks and building society offices had stopped the banking clock by freezing accounts. They were cut off from their computers therefore they had little choice. They had appointed the humourless Vernon Kelly as the chairman of their working group which had advised Pentworth's government to issue its own promissory notes in the form of euro denomination vouchers printed on Cathy's professional colour laser printer – the only one of its type in Pentworth. The vouchers were now accepted in the community as banknotes.

Two million euros worth churned out only last week, thought Cathy as she went to answer the door. Surely they didn't want more already?

During the last print-run she had jokingly said to Vernon Kelly that the government merely had to print money when they needed it. The banker had looked at her in horror.

"The money is only a measure of labour available, Miss Price," he had said stiffly. "Pentworth is short of labour. Too much money chasing after too little labour will drive up the cost of labour which will push up the cost of goods. The result will be unchecked inflation. Maintaining Pentworth's economy and controlling inflation means that as much as possible of every euro printed by the government and circulated has to be clawed back in taxes to finance government spending, which itself had to be kept on a tight rein."

"Does that also mean the banks keeping a tight rein on the amount they're salting away due to their ruinous charges?" Cathy had enquired mischievously.

The banker had not been amused.

Cathy opened her front door saying, "Good morning, Mr Kelly. Don't say you've blown last week's print-run on your mistresses already? You'll have to learn not . . ." but she never completed the sentence.

It was not Vernon Kelly on her doorstep but a tall, unsmiling black-eyed brunette wearing a businesslike skirt and an expensive silk blouse. Four morris policemen were standing behind her.

"Oh," said Cathy, taken back. *Where have I seen that face before?* "I'm sorry. I thought you were Vernon Kelly and Diana Sheldon."

"Good morning, Miss Price," said Vanessa briskly. "I'm Vanessa Grossman – Miss Sheldon's deputy." She held out a document. "And this is a warrant, signed by the Chairman of Pentworth Council. It's an order that empowers the requisitioning of all your computer gear and printing equipment."

Cathy read the warrant and stared in disbelief at Vanessa and her escort of morris police. "But why?" she asked. "What's wrong with the present arrangement? I've always done everything at the drop of a hat."

"Amateurish," said Vanessa curtly. "Your equipment could be stolen, and it's most inconvenient and inefficient having to bring a mobile generator around here for every printing job. I've suggested that a proper government printing unit is set up in Government House."

"But what about electricity?"

"An electric power system has been installed in the basement – a bank of car batteries that will need recharging only once a week. I'll give you an itemised receipt when we've finished." She signalled the morris men who pushed past Cathy into the house.

The removal of Cathy's Macintosh equipment was fast and efficient. Vanessa knew exactly what she was looking for – and that was everything. Under her directions the morris men disconnected the file server, removed interconnecting cables – even pulling them out of the LAN ducting that had been installed beneath the floor boards of Cathy's bedroom. They emptied her stock cupboards, clearing out all her software manuals, complete with distribution diskettes and CD-ROMs. Vanessa even knew about locking the head on the flatbed scanner before the morris men carried it downstairs to the van. It took two of them to haul her big colour laser printer that was used to print Pentworth's currency. As each item was loaded, she carefully noted the details on a clipboard.

One item puzzled her. She held up the golf-ball-like Connectrix QuickCam miniature TV camera. "What use would a professional graphics expert have for a low resolution thing such as this, Miss Price?"

"Oh – for sending rough sample grabs to customers—" Cathy broke off as a terrible thought occurred to her. She met Vanessa's black eyes and felt that the woman was casually turning over all her innermost secrets.

"Well I suppose I'd better take it. If you would just sign this receipt please."

"You'll need me to set the Mac up," said Cathy hollowly, keeping her voice absolutely calm despite her inner turmoil.

"No – I don't think that will be necessary, Miss Price."

Please! PLEASE, God – don't make me sound pleading!

"But I know all its peculiarities, Miss Grossman."

Grossman? Grossman? Where have I heard that name before? Where have I seen that face?

"A Mac? Peculiarities?" The black eyes regarded Cathy steadily. "We'll manage just fine, Miss Price. If you would sign here, please."

Cathy signed the document as though she had suddenly become an automaton. Vanessa thanked her for her co-operation and left, leaving Cathy sitting on her bed, staring glassy-eyed at her cleared workstation in a state of shock, mouthing a single word expletive to herself, over and over again.

Although Cathy had been brought up in Pentworth she had never considered herself as having roots in the town or being part of its society. It was somewhere to run her business, and her CathyCam website. In the case of the latter, it could be sited anywhere in the world because the Internet had made Marshall McLuhan's global village a reality. If her identity had ever been discovered, she would've had few qualms about moving and setting up elsewhere. She and Josh had often discussed the possibility.

But everything was different now. She was no longer a cripple – a prisoner of a wheelchair. The exciting possibility of leading a normal life lay before her even if she were now a different sort of prisoner behind a strange force wall that might last forever. But at least she was a prisoner along with over 6000 other souls and had become a part of Pentworth whether she liked it or not.

On balance, she liked it. She could now get married, have children: objectives which had once seemed so unattainable that, over the years, she had built up a protective shell of sneering contempt for women who held such ambitions in high esteem. Now, with the seizure of her computer system, even those simple objectives would be snatched away from her and she would spend the rest of her days as a victim of a humiliating shame of her own making that would permit no escape.

There were photographs of her in a sub-directory on the server's hard disk.

Hundreds of computer pictures.

JPEG images that had been automatically cached from the QuickCam camera to the hard disk when they had been sent to her CathyCam website: close-ups of her pouting seductively at the camera while squeezing her breasts together; extreme close ups of her smiling at the camera while running the tip of a vibrator over her clitoris; medium shots of her masturbating furiously.

Although shocking, they were pictures that she could laughingly shrug aside. The pictures were small, low resolution, and hard to say that they were of her because she was wearing her wig in all of them. People could talk, snigger if they wished; the pictures would be a five-minute wonder and then forgotten. Besides, Josh had taught her to be proud of her body, and since then she had never made any secret of her sexuality. She had once screwed her milkman for the sheer hell of acting out a cliché, and she got some free cream into the bargain.

But there were other pictures that would not be dismissed. Pictures that had been taken one weekend after she and Josh had snorted some high class coke; pictures in which she had finally given in to Josh's demands that they vary their love-making on the understanding that he would stop if he was hurting her.

Cathy sat perfectly still, submerged in a searing acid bath of the most terrible, agonising shame.

There were ten such pictures. Not taken with the relatively low-resolution 256-colour QuickCam, but by Josh using the timer on his digital camera. They were all pin-sharp, high resolution, and full screen. They had not been sent to the website because they readily identified her – she hadn't been wearing her wig – her face twisted in pain or laughing ecstasy in all of them.

She was still sitting in her bedroom fifteen minutes later. Unmoving, but this time with uncontrolled tears coursing down her cheeks.

She had come to a decision.

She had to destroy those computer files.

If she failed, she would destroy herself.

Eleven

At sixty-two, after a long and undistinguished career in local government, Dennis Davies never expected to achieve happiness. He had never married; there was no one in his life with whom he was sufficiently intimate to send boxed, padded birthday cards.

Everything was different now. The Wall had made him one of the happiest men in Pentworth. He was the town librarian with virtually the entire second floor of Government House as the new home for his beloved books.

Dennis saw himself as a latter-day Ptolemy I, the Egyptian ruler who founded the great library at Alexandria. He was close to heaven, and would be even closer once the team of carpenters were finished. They were cheerfully and noisily cannibalising any suitable furniture they could lay their hands on to make professional-looking rows of shelves that would eventually be home for the half million or so books that had been handed in and were still coming in.

The volumes filled hundreds of cardboard boxes and tea chests that were stacked to the ceiling and piled in the corridor. It was a pity that at least ninety per cent of their contents were paperbacks, but at least they were books – real books – not the ridiculous music CDs and movie video cassettes that he had been obliged to sell or rent out in the old town library. A public lending library with a noisy barcode-reading cash register indeed! Well – at least that particular piece of nastiness had been consigned to a warehouse. Long may it remain there.

Once the bulk of the cataloguing was complete, Pentworth Library would be the repository of Mankind's knowledge – a vast shrine of Britain's cultural heritage, although just how much cultural heritage was enshrined in the countless chests crammed with Mills and Boon romances, or wobbly piles of paperbacks by both the Folletts, was debatable. Fiction was having to take a back seat; for the time being his staff of five assistant librarians were busy writing index cards for the non-fiction donations. The task would take months despite the overtime they were working to take advantage of the long hours of daylight. The trouble was that there was such a desperate shortage of labour, and his requests that the library be provided with electric lighting for the coming winter had been refused.

"Mr Davies?"

Dennis looked up from his desk. A tall, lean man in a white tracksuit stood before him. Wide-set eyes. He had seen him before on several occasions. Malone introduced himself without producing his warrant card – this wasn't police business.

Dennis beamed. "Ah – yes – of course, Mr Malone. What can I do for you?"

Malone explained that he wanted to use his spare time for a research project. A history of the area – the origins of its culture and folklore.

The librarian was delighted. "It's lucky indeed that we're now open for sensible hours, Mr Malone – six days a week – the way public libraries always used to be. Something I insisted we go back to. Luckily, the old library's reference section was very strong on the subjects likely to be of interest to you. The books are all in order on the shelves but not yet indexed. It will take many weeks. We're so short of staff."

Malone assured him that he would manage and that he would put reference books back on the shelves in their correct locations rather than burden the staff.

"That's very good of you, Mr Malone. I'm sure I can trust you."

"Police work if anyone wants to know what I'm doing, Mr Davies. My colleagues don't understand my interests. A hard-drinking lot but one needs to keep one's mind occupied these days without television."

Dennis was understanding. There was a sudden burst of hammering. "I'm afraid the library won't be a conducive place for study for another two to three weeks. I could arrange for you to have a small desk in the far corner . . . And I've got some screens . . ."

Malone was profuse in his thanks.

"When would you like to start?"

"Now, if possible. I've a couple of hours before I'm on duty."

Malone spent the first thirty minutes familiarising himself with the library's layout. He was returning a book on Celtic customs to the shelf when he became aware of a tall brunette looking through the computer books. She sensed his interest and looked up suddenly before he had a chance to look away. He smiled and nodded. Malone was not used to cold, hard stares from women. It unsettled him, particularly because he had a vague feeling that he had seen her before. Her wedding ring and engagement ring hadn't been bought from QVC, and silk blouses like that weren't available south of the Thames. When she left he drifted over to Dennis's desk.

"Who was the tall brunette that was in here just now?"

"Ah – that was Miss Vanessa Grossman. Fourth floor. She's the Town Clerk's deputy. Married, I think."

The name meant nothing to Malone. "Just wondered. I'm sure I've seen her face before somewhere."

"Strange you should say that, Mr Malone," said Dennis. "But I thought exactly the same when I first saw her."

Twelve

"*H*ands off the Wall! Hands off the Wall!*"
A noisy, bustling hot evening in Market Square. A line of blackshirts kept the chanting crowd away from the main entrance of Government House. There were additional units of morris police on hand in case the mob got out of hand, but the crowd of about forty did no more than chant in unison and wave their placards.

Well organised and well rehearsed, thought Malone from his usual table outside the Crown, a glass of beer and a clipboard in front of him. The brew was excellent and there seemed little danger of it running out because barrels of the stuff were being unloaded from a dray. He had never seen the new barrels before. A clever invention: one man could roll several times his own weight and change direction with ease; and they were stable and safe when stacked on end. The waiter served a family at a nearby table: beers for the parents, soft drinks for the children. His idea to scrap bars and have waiter service only at tables in pubs and clubs was working well. Families went out together and under-age drinking was no longer a problem.

Anne Taylor pushed her way through the bystanders with Vikki and Sarah in tow. She bullied her reluctant charges into unfurling a banner made from a sheet and holding it aloft. They stayed with a small group of demonstrators in the middle of the square who seemed anxious to keep clear of the main mob in case of trouble. Her group included several older citizens whose placards endorsed the sentiment expressed in Anne Taylor's embroidered message: "THE NEW LIFE IS THE GOOD LIFE! LEAVE THE WALL ALONE!"

They were the genuine protesters, thought Malone, returning Anne's wave. It was understandable that many elderly people liked the new order with its simplification of what was becoming an over-complicated society. And there were many who approved the strict enforcement of law and order. But the Wall, with its enforced separation from loved ones was the cause of much pain. After nearly four months it seemed that Anne Taylor had decided that life without her husband wasn't so bad. But for Malone, who had not seen his daughters since a school concert in March, the separation was a continuous, nagging ache made worse by the dreadful thought that they might not exist any more – that the whole world had ceased to exist and that Pentworth had become a surviving microcosm of what had been a planet with its teeming billions. Perhaps Pentworth had been allowed to survive as some sort of celestial zoo.

Bob Harding's view was more upbeat. In several question and answer talks on the radio, he had pushed his view that the real world was still there. The chances were that the army had surrounded the Wall on the outside and created an exclusion zone. Malone was not convinced; his gut feeling was that the real world no longer existed.

The clatter of a gig drawn by a pair of greys intruded on his depressing reverie. It dropped off two of Prescott's farm hands who joined the chanting mob. Malone noted their names on his clipboard. St Mary's struck seven, which was the signal for the council meeting to start.

Thirteen

D r Millicent Vaughan was an iron-haired, iron-willed lady of fifty-four who had been the head of the largest general practitioners' group in Pentworth. She was now in charge of the reopened cottage hospital and had overall responsibility for health in the community. Her tough stance on food hygiene and her army of food inspectors backed up by morris police had won her enemies. A farmer who had persistently flouted the strict animal feeding regulations had had his farm confiscated.

David Weir did his best to listen attentively to her delivering her report to the council, but the racket outside the courtroom-cum-council chamber was a distraction and so was Ellen. She looked particularly lovely. She had restyled her hair, bringing it forward so that her rich, dark tresses partially hid her face to give her a sultry, seductive look that suited her admirably.

Millicent concluded with: "To summarise, the general health of the population has actually shown a marked improvement since the Wall was established. Pure drinking water, good sanitation, and wholesome food are still our best defences against epidemics."

"Thank you, Dr Vaughan," said Prescott expansively, feeling very pleased with himself. At the beginning of the meeting he had comfortably overturned a censure motion by Ellen Duncan for his treatment of Brad Jackson and his gang. His tough stance on law and order had wide support. He had also pushed through an enabling measure that empowered the council to introduce revoked or repealed legislation if it were in the interests of the community, and he had also persuaded a majority to accept the setting-up of a proper radio studio in Government House – a measure Prescott had been particularly keen to push through, arguing that the relocation would release a telephone line and provide a more suitable, more professional environment than Bob Harding's workshop.

Prescott looked around the gathering at the long table that was always set up in the courtroom for council meetings. "I take it then that the revised food rationing allowances are not having adverse effects on health?"

"We seem to have the balance about right, Mr Chairman," Millicent replied. "I've been checking in the library. Compared with the Second World War, the allowances are quite generous, although, as we know, they're causing some irritation in the town towards the farming community."

That was an understatement. The initial resentment among the town-dwellers towards the food producers was widening to open antagonism as the new controls filtered through; in a small community, their effects were felt quickly.

It was early summer – an awkward time before main crops were ready and when livestock was being fattened for the winter rather than slaughtered. The problem was compounded by the need to restrict the cropping of early vegetables to provide the following year's seed stock. The healthiest potatoes were going into storage. The food glut of earlier in the year when surplus livestock had been slaughtered to conserve feed was long past, although there was still plenty of EU grain. Grain that had shown signs of deterioration had been sent to the brewery. Milk supplies had been curtailed to make butter in the absence of sunflower oil supplies for the manufacture of margarine. The heat was making it impossible to keep semi-skimmed milk for more than a day, and delays in the supply of ammonia had prevented the new ice-making plant getting into full production. Some early attempts to salt beef and pork for long-term storage had gone wrong and over 200 tonnes of food were ordered to be destroyed by the hygiene inspectors. The relearning of the old skills in food storage was proving a painful process, and too many problems were piling up for Pentworth's tiny working population to tackle efficiently.

Some food was plentiful: the Pentworth House bakery with its methane-fired ovens had been expanded to cope with all the community's bread needs, but essential measures taken by the council's food sub-committee had led to a scarcity of meat, poultry and diary produce with the result that town-dwellers suspected that farmers and growers were withholding supplies. Conversely, the country believed that the town was getting the lion's share of the services. Most houses in the town were now back on a pumped water supply from the old water tower whereas many outlying areas still relied on standpipes or neighbours with boreholes. The previous day there had been an incident in which a wagon delivering lambs to the abattoir had been waylaid by a town gang. The lambs had vanished and the wagon driver beaten-up.

"I should have fifty tonne of sugar beet ready next week," commented a grower.

"The low sugar diet has actually been beneficial," said Millicent. "The dental care team have reported that the condition of children's teeth is improving. Just to round up, we have not encountered any cases of vitamin deficiency in adults or children. We now have a small unit producing a broad spectrum of antibiotic cultures – barely sufficient for our immediate needs, but we're coping. Councillor Duncan's contribution of effective herbal medications has been inestimable. Thank you."

"Hands off the Wall! Hands off the Wall!"

"Points arising?" enquired Prescott.

"Yes," said Ellen promptly. She nodded to the blackshirts guarding the exit. There were several of the stone-faced security men around the courtroom. "Any chance of you asking your blackshirt thugs to knock off the row outside?"

"Peaceful demonstrations are a part of the democratic process," said Prescott genially. "I'm sorry if you find that inconvenient—"

"I find it inconvenient not being able to hear."

"And they are not thugs, Councillor. Nor are they *my* mine, *and* they are not blackshirts. But they will see what they can do." Prescott nodded to one of the guards who left the chamber. "Councillor Baldock?"

"You said that there have been ten births since the Wall," said Dan Baldock, a prickly pig farmer who heartily detested Prescott. "Is that above or below average?"

"Below average," said Millicent.

"How many pregnancies started since the Wall?" asked Prescott.

"Six that we know of."

Ellen looked surprised. "Six? Isn't that low? Point one of one per cent of the population?"

"We're don't have a full year to go on as yet," said Millicent uneasily.

"OK, then. So double your figure. That's still damned low."

"But it's too early to draw conclusions. There are normal peaks and troughs in any given period."

"How many deaths since the Wall?" asked David Weir.

"Twenty-two," Millicent replied. "Five due to accidents and seventeen due to illness or natural causes."

"So the population is going down?" Ellen queried.

"It's too early to see a trend," Millicent replied.

"Well I can. Twenty-two dead. ten born. That's a trend."

Millicent lowered her voice when the chanting from the square quietened. "You have to take social factors into account. There was little employment before the Wall and high house prices which led to an exodus of young couples to Chichester and Portsmouth."

"In other words, we don't have enough breeding pairs," said Baldock bluntly. He grinned. "I don't mind becoming a third partner in a breeding trio. Or even in a quartet."

"Three mother-in-laws, Dan?" queried a councillor. "You can't even get on with one." He added when the laughter subsided, "But you'd think that with all this fine weather and young girls going around wearing next to nothing, there would be an explosion of pregnancies."

"Conception rates tend to decrease in the face of uncertainty," Bob Harding commented thickly through his hayfever.

"The death rate will go down," said Millicent. "The overall health of the community is good. At least four of the twenty-two deaths since the Wall were due to smoking-related causes. We won't be seeing much of that in the future."

"Quite a few people I know are growing tobacco," said Baldock smugly. "And other substances."

"And we could have an epidemic that could wipe us all out," Harding observed. "It's an important issue but idle speculation. Doctor Vaughan is right. There's little point in debating this, Mr Chairman – we have insufficient data to spot trends."

Prescott nodded. "It would be sensible to ask Dr Vaughan's Pentworth Health Authority to keep a watching brief on the situation and report back. Is that OK with you, Doctor?"

"We're doing that anyway, Mr Chairman."

"Next item," said Prescott. "Councillor Harding's proposal to breach the Wall."

Harding needed only five minutes to fill in missing details in his plan. "As for wasting petrol," he said, "we won't be using that much, and we might as well use it as have it evaporating away."

"Such a move might be regarded as a hostile act by the visitors," a councillor ventured when Harding had finished. "They could retaliate."

Ellen snorted. "And what about their act in putting the Wall in place? Wasn't that a hostile act? If they are that advanced, then it behoved them to determine what effect on the populace their actions might have. They didn't do so, therefore we have the right to at least try to breach the Wall if it's possible."

Outside the chanting of crowd became louder and more aggressive.

"Hands off the Wall! Hands off the Wall!"

After ten minutes' heated discussion, with the sounds outside degenerating into a near-riot as the protesters tried to break through the morris police cordon, Prescott said that he was considering vetoing the plan.

Ellen went on the attack. "On what grounds, Mr Chairman?"

Prescott was smoothly confident. "On the grounds that the safety and well-being of Pentworth and its people are paramount. Who knows what weaponry the visitors have in their Silent Vulcan? The thought of the terrible retaliation that they could use against us doesn't bear thinking about."

"Nor does the thought of doing nothing!"

There were nods of assent around the table.

"Listen to them outside," said Prescott. "They actually like the Wall. As a democratic body, we should heed the voice of the people. Go against them and all hell could break loose. What chance do thirty morris police stand against the majority?"

"It's now nearer fifty morris police," David muttered.

While Prescott was talking, Ellen slipped her hand under her hair. Her fingertips found the slide switch on the tiny flesh-coloured hearing aid transceiver that Malone had given her. Before the meeting she practised switching the radio on and off and therefore had no difficulty sliding the switch to the "on" position. The miniature set's microphone was held in position by a hair slide.

"Voice of the people, Mr Chairman? A majority? Or do you mean a mob that's been put together to *sound* like a majority?"

"You have ears, Councillor."

"So have I," Malone's voice whispered in Ellen's ear. "Getting you loud and clear. Give a cough to acknowledge."

Ellen coughed. "Ah . . . You mean your estate manager and his family, Mr Chairman? They're a majority, are they?" She paused. "Then there's Harry Coleman, your gamekeeper and his two sons . . . They seem to be yelling the loudest. Of course, they're being helped by Harry Coleman's sister, her husband and their two boys. Matt, the eldest works for you, does he not?" Another pause. Ellen had everyone's attention. Prescott made no attempt to interrupt but sat smiling benignly at Ellen.

She continued, "And there's Rupert Mates who also works for

61

you. A one-man mob in his own right, that one." She went on to recite details of the rest of the mob. She spoke clearly and succinctly, using effective pauses to count off all of the names on her fingers and detailing their association with Asquith Prescott. By the time she had finished, he was no longer smiling but regarding Ellen, stony-faced.

"There *are* genuine protesters out there," Ellen continued. "Eight to be exact. None of them creating any fuss. But every one of that yelling mob depends on our Chairman either directly or indirectly. The noise outside is not the voice of the people. It is the baying of a rent-a-mob hired by our Chairman because he fears that if an assault on the Wall succeeds, it would be the end of his power." She was about to add that power was the one thing Prescott craved above all else, but decided that she had said enough.

David was the first to speak when Ellen sat. "I think, Mr Chairman, that we should take a vote on whether or not to sanction the assault."

Prescott gave a dismissive gesture. "If you care to ignore my concern for the well-being of our community, then so be it . . . In view of Councillor Duncan's comments, I would add that I've never made any secret of my concerns and have expressed them on many occasions to my friends and colleagues. That many agree with me and have turned up to express their views is hardly surprising and I'm astonished that Councillor Duncan has read so much into it. I could ask her to withdraw her remarks but fear that I'd be wasting your time and my time. Very well – let's vote. All those in favour?"

Prescott lost by three votes.

He smiled blandly in defeat, saying that that was the way of democracy – that sometimes the elected representatives of the people went against the wishes of the people. Inwardly he was seething because the setback meant that he would be forced into doing another deal with Adrian Roscoe and his Bodian Brethren.

Fourteen

M ost of Prescott's supporters melted away when they received news of the vote. There were only a handful left by the time Ellen and David emerged from Government House, and many of the morris police had stood down. Ellen was in a jubilant mood.

"Three votes! *Three!* For the first time that bastard has been stopped in his tracks."

David put his arm around her as they went down the steps. "Don't forget that moving the radio station to Government House gives him effective control of it," he warned.

"Bob Harding was complaining about the room it took up in his workshop."

"True," David admitted. "But it should be fully independent, which it can't be if it's in easy meddling distance of Prescott. *And* he's got that damned enabling vote through to bring back old laws."

"Where they're appropriate, David."

"And who decides what's appropriate? The council, or Prescott acting on behalf of the council?"

They strolled across the square to where Malone was sitting outside the Crown.

"You're right," said Ellen. "I've let a relatively minor victory overshadow everything else. The main problem is that Prescott has legally taken over as executive officer. His idea of having an office in Government House was neat. He's not actually usurped Diana Sheldon as Town Clerk, but she dare not do anything off her own bat – not with Prescott in the building."

There was a burst of cheering behind just as Malone rose to greet them. Suddenly his expression changed. "Stop him!" he roared.

Before Ellen and David had a chance to react, Malone had leapt clean over his table and was streaking across the square to intercept Brad Jackson. The delinquent had an upraised kitchen knife in his hand and was racing towards Prescott who had just left Government House. Malone's second bellowed warning spurred the nearest blackshirt into action. He thrust Prescott aside just as Malone threw himself at Brad Jackson to bring him down.

"Die, you bastard! Die!" screamed Brad Jackson.

Malone's action was partially successful; the knife was sweeping down in a lightning arc that had been aimed at Prescott but the force of Malone cannoning into the assailant spun him around so that the long blade plunged into the blackshirt's chest.

There was a near panic and screams as Malone and the would-be assassin rolled down the steps. By the time the police officer had pinioned Brad Jackson to the ground and secured his wrists behind his back with a cable tie, several blackshirts had poured from the building and bundled Prescott inside. Nelson Faraday was yelling into a radio. Millicent Vaughan had hurried from the building and was on her knees, cutting away the injured guard's shirt from around the jutting knife before she risked withdrawing it. She knew from the murderous blade's length, angle and position that it had penetrated deep into the man's heart.

"Jesus Christ," David whispered as he and Ellen stood transfixed. The entire incident had happened in less than five seconds.

"He had to die!" Brad Jackson sobbed as Malone dragged him to his feet. "Him and everything he stood for!"

Malone's caution was ignored; his prisoner kept repeating that Prescott had to die.

"Except that your victim wasn't Mr Prescott," Malone observed, handing him over to three morris police. He helped clear a path for an ambulance that spirited the injured man and Millicent Vaughan to the hospital. Prescott emerged from Government House flanked by two blackshirts. The attack had shaken him badly.

"Mr Malone . . ."

"Mr Chairman?"

"Thank you. Your prompt action saved my life."

"Not prompt enough, sir. That man looked badly injured. If you will excuse me, I'd better collect a few statements while events are still fresh."

Prescott nodded and returned to the security of Government House.

Malone tore sheets from a large notebook he had taken to carrying and took statements from several witnesses at his table outside the Crown, leaving David and Ellen until last. His witnesses moved to other tables to listen to the Radio Pentworth news bulletins from an outside speaker.

When Malone was through, he stacked the sheaf of statements and placed them inside his notebook before turning his attention to the beer that David had bought for him. He drained the glass in one long swallow. "Christ – I needed that. Thanks, David."

"My pleasure. Another?"

"Better not. I've got a mountain of paperwork to get through as a result of this little episode."

"Surely it'll be an open and shut case?" Ellen queried.

Malone shook his head. "Open and shut cases don't reduce the paperwork – just the detection process. The real problem is going to be Brad Jackson's inevitable sentence. Pentworth is hardly geared for coping with long-term prisoners."

"Prescott said much the same thing to me the other day," said Ellen.

The music playing over the speaker faded. The presenter adopted a sombre note to report that Robert Vincent, the Government House security officer injured in the stabbing incident earlier in Market Square, had died in hospital. "We will observe a three-minute silence as a mark of respect," the presenter concluded.

The radio fell silent.

"Well," said Malone laconically. "There's one thing about the Wall – it simplifies filling in the witness availability forms. The new hairstyle suits you, Ellen."

Ellen looked taken back for a moment before she realised what Malone was referring to. "Oh – I'd forgotten it." She removed her hair slide, slipped her hand under her hair to her right ear, and glanced around the square. No one was watching. She seemed to remove an earring.

"I found this, Mike. I think it must be police property."

Malone deftly palmed the object with its attached microphone and slipped it into his pocket. "So it worked?" he asked.

Ellen nodded. "Like a charm. It was my naming of all Prescott's rent-a-mob cronies that swung the vote."

Malone gave a faint smile. "So you had an accomplice?"

"I rather think I did. I ought to thank him."

"Using police radio equipment for unauthorised purposes is an offence under the Wireless Telegraphy Act."

"I think I'm missing out on something," David observed, but not missing that Ellen had used Malone's Christian name.

"An earpiece radio transceiver," said Malone drolly. "A nifty little surveillance tool. It's good of Ellen to hand it in."

David grinned when he realised what had happened. "No wonder

Prescott looked so stunned. And to think I put your little recital down to a brilliant memory."

"So Operation High Hopes is going ahead?" asked Malone.

David looked puzzled.

"The operation to breach the Wall," Malone explained.

Ellen thought she saw Malone give a conspiratorial wink and couldn't help smiling.

"In a week's time," said David, feeling that he was still missing something. That's how long Charlie Crittenden needs to get my showman's engine running." He frowned. "Why Operation High Hopes?"

"An old Frank Sinatra song," said Ellen, smiling broadly. "About a ram that kept butting a dam. No one could make that ram scram; he kept butting that dam."

"Memorable lyrics," said Malone drily. "But the ram did succeed."

Fifteen

The atmosphere in the library in the morning was different. Dennis Davies' staff were too shocked by the previous evening's killing to concentrate on their work. They all knew the blackshirt security man personally and would have started a collection for his family had it not been Farside. The other topic was general disbelief that anyone should want to kill Prescott after all he was doing for the community.

"He's working fifteen hours a day," Dennis growled, breaking up a gathering around the drinking water dispenser. "Which is a damn sight more than you're all doing."

"Keeping them hard at it, Mr Davies?" asked Diana Sheldon.

"Good morning, Miss Sheldon," said Dennis, turning around and giving Diana a warm smile. That she was a frequent visitor to the second floor to check on progress added to his self-esteem. He had spent several weeks nerving himself to ask her to have a lunchtime drink with him and would probably spend several more weeks doing the same.

Diana took the librarian aside. "I've come to ask a big favour, Mr Davies. I appreciate that you're having to catalogue the books on an as-they-come basis, otherwise you're forever having to shift crates around, but could you concentrate on getting all the law books indexed and shelved please."

"Well, of course. We've got all the original books from the old library shelved."

"I was thinking in particular of Judge Hooper's donation of his library. The judge has just had a meeting with Mr Prescott. They are most anxious that all his law books should be available to the court."

"Court?"

"I'm sorry – I should've explained. We're going to use the new council chamber downstairs as a crown court for the trial of Brad Jackson."

"Ah – yes – of course. I quite understand, Miss Sheldon. I'll make an immediate start."

Diana thanked him and looked at her watch as she turned to leave. "Your new assistant is starting today. I told her to be here at eleven o'clock."

"I'll need all the extra help I can get," said Dennis. "What is that young villain to be tried for? Manslaughter?"

"Murder," Diana replied. "Murder *and* treason."

Dennis returned to his desk and wondered what his new assistant would be like. Perhaps after a year or so they'd let him take part in the interviews. His present team was willing enough, but none were capable of using their initiative. The Wall had certainly stimulated the desire for books but the trouble was that it had also brought full employment; well-educated personnel were at a premium.

The Wall had also led to the abolition of political correctness in the work place. The sudden chorus of wolf whistles and catcalls made Dennis look up. The carpenters had stopped work and were treating the woman approaching Dennis's desk to a barrage of appreciation – their principal gesture being a hand clamped over the biceps of a raised forearm.

Cathy Price deigned to ignore them. She stood before Dennis's desk and flashed him a warm smile that had his virginity yearning to self-destruct. She was dressed in a white pleated skirt, a white sleeveless T-shirt, and looked game for tennis – or anything.

"Hallo, Mr Davies – I'm Cathy Price – your new assistant librarian."

The only way Cathy could get a job in Government House was to settle for the lousy pay working in the library. She had been put through the hoops with two interviews the previous day and had to have her picture taken in the Photo-Me booth that had once stood in Woolworths. The work, which Dennis showed her once he had introduced her to her new colleagues, was writing out catalogue index cards.

"Boring but essential work," said Dennis when he had shown Cathy her desk. He stood over her, his eyeballs falling down her T-shirt and burning up like re-entering satellites. "And rewarding." He nodded to the long rows of wooden filing cabinets with their rows of miniature drawers. "We've forgotten just how efficient card indexes are."

Cathy smiled. "Oh, definitely. Multiple-user access, updating is dead easy with hardly any training required, and they possess unlimited non-volatile random access memory that doesn't need as much as a milliwatt of power to maintain it. Best of all, card indexes never crash and they don't get bad sectors or read/write errors."

"Quite so," said Dennis, wondering what on earth she was talking about.

"Oh. Does Mike Malone work here?" Cathy had spotted the police officer emerge from behind his screen. She caught his eye and exchanged a friendly wave.

"Mr Malone does a lot of research here and is not to be disturbed," Dennis warned.

The moment she was alone Cathy examined her clip-on identity badge and was convinced that it had been produced by the inexpert use of her scanner and laminating machine. It meant that they had got the Mac working and she suffered a misery of embarrassment at the thought that someone might have found her shameful pictures. Her hope lay in the fact that she had not linked the pictures directly to the viewer software for automatic display; a lot of tedious mouse-clicking was necessary to view the files.

She had no clear plan in mind as to how she would set about searching for the Mac, but at least she was in the same building with it.

Sixteen

Bob Harding was in his workshop putting the finishing touches to his plan to breach the Wall when the intercom buzzed.

"Young lady to see you," said Suzi tartly. "Vikki Taylor. A schoolgirl. Country. She works in Ellen Duncan's shop in her spare time."

"Yes – I know Vikki. What does she want?"

"She has some questions on astronomy."

"What's wrong with the library?"

"They haven't put all the books on the shelves. A homework project I suppose."

"You'd better show her through."

"I think a chaperon might be a good idea."

"Nonsense. I'm sure Vikki will be very well-behaved."

Despite his impatience to finish his plan, Harding gave Vikki a warm welcome when she entered his workshop. "Come in, Vikki. Come in. Sorry about the mess. Find a seat." He looked closely at her. A long, pretty print dress that suited her with matching cotton gloves. An incredibly pretty girl.

She looked around the workshop. "I thought the radio station was here, Mr Harding?"

"It's been moved to Government House. New studio on the top floor. Don't you listen to the news?"

"Sorry, Mr Harding."

"Did you come alone, Vikki?"

"Yes, Mr Harding. Why shouldn't I?"

"It's just that some country folk come in for abuse in the town. But mostly those bringing in food supplies."

"A carter delivering blocks of ice shouted something but I didn't take any notice."

"Good for you. How are your parents?"

"Mum's fine. Dad's Farside."

"Yes – I'd forgotten. I'm sorry."

Vikki shrugged. She perched on the edge of a chair. Her gaze kept returning to Harding's homemade Newtonian telescope, staring through the opening in the roof. The scientist usually cranked the sliding panels open in the evening when the sun was low.

"Now then," he said affably, not showing how much his visitor's luminous green eyes disconcerted him. "How can I help you?"

"It's very kind of you to see me, Mr Harding." She came straight to the point. "I need to know about Sirius."

"A school project?"

"A project," said Vikki. She hated lying.

Harding smiled. "Perhaps we'd better start by your telling me what you know about it."

"Only that it's a star like our sun, and that it's called the Dog Star."

"Nothing else?"

"No."

"Actually it's two stars, Vikki. There's Canis Major – the Larger Dog, and Canis Minor – the Smaller Dog. Sirius is the brightest star in the sky. With all this humidity, it's just about the only star we can ever see these days. It gets its name from Sirius, a dog that belonged to Orion – the Greek god of hunting." He broke off. "Aren't you going to make notes?"

"I can remember everything."

Harding wagged an admonitory finger. "Always make notes when undertaking research, Vikki. Anyway, Sirius was held in high esteem by the ancient Egyptians. Its appearance just before sunrise marked the annual flooding of the Nile."

"How far is it?"

"Roughly ten light-years. Quite close in celestial distance terms, which is why it's so bright. Light travels at three hundred thousand kilometres per second, so you'll need a long piece of paper to write down all the zeros."

"Would it be possible for me to look at it through your telescope please?"

Harding glanced at his watch. "We might just catch it before it sets." He quickly adjusted the telescope's azimuth and elevation handwheels, fitted a deep field eyepiece and sighted on Sirius. He sat Vikki in his seat and showed her how to operate the controls. She stared without speaking at the disappointing, fuzzy point of light while working the handwheels to keep the star centred in the field of view as it sank towards the rooftops.

"Why is it moving so fast?" she asked at length.

"It's not – what you're seeing is the earth's rotation."

"Does it have planets, Mr Harding?"

"It's part of a binary system with a white dwarf, but if you mean Earth-type planets – we don't know with absolute certainty if any stars have planets like those in our solar system. We know from the perturbations of many stars that they have invisible companions, so it may be that solar systems like ours are common. But we don't know what sort of planets they are." He paused and added, "If you were an astronomer on a planet of Sirius with our biggest and best telescope, you'd be able to see the effect of Jupiter on the sun's motion, but that would be all. You wouldn't be able to see Jupiter, and certainly not the Earth."

"It's gone," said Vikki abruptly.

"You were just in time to catch it. Within a couple of weeks it'll be rising and setting with the sun, so it won't be possible to see it at all. You've heard of the dog days of summer?"

Vikki looked up from the telescope and nodded. "July and August. The hottest months of the year."

"That's right. The ancients believed that the combined strength of the sun and Sirius produced madness in dogs and people. The so-called dog days. The days of summer madness."

Seventeen

Summer madness, thought Malone.

He had been tasked with drawing up the police duty rosters for the assault on the Wall and therefore his dubbing of the enterprise as "Operation High Hopes" stuck.

As a keen student of human folly, he watched the final preparations with amusement tempered by depression. His capacity for logical thought, by which he set such store, told him that the scheme to breach the Wall would not succeed; if the outside world, the real world – not Farside, with all its resources, couldn't break in through the Wall to end Pentworth's isolation, what chance did Pentworth, with its limited resources, have of breaking out?

The police officer was sitting on a stile on Duncton Rise, wearing white shorts, and wishing that he'd thought to bring a hat or sunshade for it was blisteringly hot. His location was nearly the highest point within the Wall and one which afforded him an excellent view of the activity in the field below – a meadow bisected by the Wall – where there were twenty cars and a few light trucks, strung out in a line with their front bumpers nearly touching the Wall. There were about a hundred people sitting about in family groups or stretched out on the grass. Children were taking part in games organised by an impromptu play leader, and the catering volunteers were tending a large charcoal barbecue. The tea urns contained a share out authorised by Government House of Pentworth's precious supply of tea bags. This was deemed a special occasion. There was the usual food inspector present to ensure that the chicken quarters were properly cooked. For this special day, food rationing had been suspended.

The smell of charcoal, grilled chicken and freshly baked rolls wafted up the windless slope to Malone's lookout point. Bread and circuses, he reflected. He raised his binoculars and watched Asquith Prescott, resplendent in a spotless white safari suit, and Bob Harding in conversation. The field had been selected for the main assault on the Wall because it had a metalled Forestry

73

Commission road that ran downhill and at right angles into the
Wall. The road ended abruptly at the Wall. Beyond the line of
strung-out vehicles lay not the familiar, gloomy stands of Forestry
Commission conifers, packed tight to make them grow straight as
they clawed quickly upwards seeking light, but the image of the
glacier-chilled open steppes of 40,000 years ago. Further south,
beyond the invisible Wall, was a wooded valley – the beginnings of
the mighty deciduous forest that would spread across this landscape
as the ice receded.

Malone levelled his binoculars at a family group. The slim, elegant
figure of the mother was Vanessa Grossman – the brunette who had
given him the iced-shoulder treatment in the library. She was sitting
on a carefully spread blanket, looking cool and detached in neatly
creased slacks while her husband struggled with the task of keeping
two small children content and clean while they raided a picnic box.
Vanessa watched them, laughing occasionally at hubby's antics to
keep grubby fingers away from his trophy wife. Her poised manner
intrigued Malone. It was as though she had decided that whatever
the outcome of the attempt to destroy the Wall, she would be a
winner.

An insistent drone caused Malone to look up. It was Harvey Evans'
microlight aircraft approaching from the north. The tiny biplane was
on fire-watch patrol, ready to summons the fire appliances if any
barbecue looked like it was getting out of control. Pentworth lived
in dread of fire.

The squelch opened on Malone's radio. "Sector 7 reporting."

"Go ahead, Sector 7," said Malone into his speaker-microphone.

"All vehicles in position. Engines off."

"Received, Sector 7. Remain on standby." He added for the benefit
of Bob Harding in the field below, "Sector 7 confirming all vehicles
in position, engines off."

Malone was acting as a police radio repeater, relaying messages
between all the sector marshals and Bob Harding's sector marshal
below in the command sector. UHF radio did not work well in hilly
regions, therefore Malone's coordinating presence on high ground
was essential.

He ticked the sketch map on his clipboard. The bold circle around
Pentworth that depicted the Wall was divided into ten segments like
processed cheese wedges. In response to radio appeals over the last
three days, virtually every vehicle-owner had driven to the various
mustering points around the town where they had been briefed,
issued with typed instructions, and directed to specific sectors.

Four-wheel-drive cars, pickups, tractors and off-road vehicles had been despatched to the more inaccessible sectors, and town-owned saloon cars sent to easy access points. This achieved a degree of trouble-avoiding segregation between town and country but the overall result was that there were now 392 assorted vehicles distributed around the Wall's thirty-kilometre perimeter, waiting to begin the assault.

Sector 4's marshal, the last to report, confirmed that his group was ready. Malone passed the information to Bob Harding. He saw a puff of smoke and steam rising above the trees to the north and added that David Weir's showman's engine had turned off the main road."

"Excellent! Excellent!" enthused Harding. "How long before it gets here?"

Malone gauged the progress of the clouds of steam and smoke shouldering through the foliage from the unseen machine. "It's left the main road, Mr Harding. It should be with you in about fifteen minutes."

"You better get the drivers ready."

"High Hopes command – all sector marshals," said Malone into his radio. "All drivers to their vehicles. Do not start engines yet."

The last acknowledgement was received just as "Brenda" appeared through a break in the trees. The huge machine, spewing smoke from its tall stack, with Ellen Duncan standing crouched over the steering wheel and Charlie Crittenden beside her, was making good progress along the Forestry Commission road.

Malone studied the rust-encrusted machine through his binoculars. It was a sorry-looking sight. Charlie and his family had concentrated on getting the mighty engine mobile and had made no attempt to smarten it up other than to polish its pipe work and brass nameplate, which glinted in the bright sunlight. The great boiler-mounted dynamo had been removed and the rotting remains of the full-length canopy stripped away. The entire clattering, hissing monster, its massive rear wheels crunching and ripping at the sun-softened asphalt as they thrust the ponderous bulk uphill, was a mass of crimson patches where red oxide primer had been applied to bare metal. Stuffing-box glands on the slide-valve steam chests screamed dangerous jets of superheated steam that turned to huge clouds of water vapour in the humid air. Incredibly, considering the state it was in, the improbable behemoth was moving at a purposeful speed up the gradient.

Charlie's grown-up sons, Gus and Carl, were perched on an

improvised fuel trailer behind the engine. The trailer was laden with anthracite beans and a water tank. They had long-handled shovels at the ready to feed coals into the roaring firebox.

David Weir was standing on the narrow platform behind Charlie, clinging to a corroded canopy support and wondering if giving way to Ellen's deadly mixture of cajoling, sexual blackmail, and plain old-fashioned threats of physical violence in her determination to drive "Brenda" to the command sector had been such a good idea. In truth, there was very little he could deny her. Despite "Brenda"'s size, the gearing reduction in the worm-drive steering ensured that little effort was required to turn the steering wheel, although it required about fifty turns for the steering chains to swing the huge steering yoke that the front wheels were mounted on through a full lock.

Bob Harding's plan was simple: to use brute force to overload the Wall and possibly destroy it. The Wall was known to use energy economically – only enough was called upon to repulse an attempt at penetration, and only where it was required. Therefore it might be possible to overload the system and so bring about a catastrophic failure.

"Afterall," he had told the council meeting when he had outlined his plan. "We're dealing with engineering. Advanced engineering, admittedly, but not magic. A determined Roman legion could overrun a machine-gun post."

Malone focused his binoculars on Ellen and decided that old jeans cut down to shorts, and halter tops made from knotted blouses had to be the sexiest garments ever devised. The sulphureous smell of burning anthracite was a poignant reminder of his last outing with his children when he had taken them on a trip on the old steam locomotive of the Bluebell Line.

In the meadow, mothers dashed forward and grabbed their off-spring when the showman's engine breasted the rise and emerged from the trees, picking up a little speed as it started downhill. Children and adults lined the road, watching wide-eyed as the strange vehicle from another century crunched to a shuddering standstill when Charlie spun the handwheel to wind the wooden brake shoes on to the rear wheels. He wound down hard to hold the ponderous vehicle on the slope. It was stopping for only a few seconds, therefore chocks weren't deemed necessary. Steam hissed deafeningly when he dropped the boiler pressure. Some drivers had got out of their vehicles to witness the arrival and were ordered back behind their wheels by the marshal.

Prescott and Harding cautiously approached the machine when Charlie signalled the all clear.

"Is this thing safe?" Prescott enquired.

David laughed and jumped down. "Safe? No tax, no insurance, no MOT, dodgy brakes, about five turns play in her steering wheel before the chains take up, and an uncertified boiler."

"No lights and no horn," Ellen added.

"And a woman driver," said Carl, and immediately regretted it because Ellen's aim with an anthracite bean was unerring.

"All things considered, our 'Brenda''s the most lethal vehicle in Pentworth," David concluded.

"But we ain't broken no speed limits," said Charlie, jumping down so that only Ellen remained aboard. He was pleased with himself and the result of his family's efforts to get the great engine working again. Gus and Carl, their faces and arms streaked with grime, were grinning broadly. Without waiting for instructions from their father, they worked the crank handle that dumped hot, smoking ash and clinker on to the road, and set to shovelling coals into the firebox.

"I don't think you need get up much steam, Charlie," said Harding. "The gradient should've given you a fair turn of speed by the time you reach the Wall."

Charlie eyed the 200-metre downhill stretch of road between "Brenda" and the Wall. "Map says the road goes uphill on the other side. And I'll want a bit of speed to get away from all those cars when we bust through. I'll use power."

Harding nodded in agreement. "OK, Charlie. If you do go through, let's hope you don't run into a Farside army tank."

"Mr Crittenden," said Prescott.

Charlie regarded the landowner with poorly disguised distaste. He had had many brushes with Prescott and Pentworth Town Council before the Wall. It was a different story now that his skills were appreciated. "Mr Prescott?"

"You're not to take any chances. If anything goes wrong, you're to jump off that thing."

The traveller jerked his thumb at "Brenda" and folded his brawny arms. "Sitting up there and running the boiler at three-quarters working pressure for the last couple of hours has been chancy enough. I reckon I can look after myself, Mr Prescott. OK, everyone. Let's get going. Off you get, Miss Duncan."

At that moment a rich, stentorian voice boomed across the meadow. "The Wall is the will of God! Hell and damnation await those who seek to thwart His will!"

Adrian Roscoe had emerged from a public footpath near where the road disappeared into Wall. He was holding a loudhailer to his lips and leading a group of thirty of his "solar sentinels", as he termed his followers, all dressed in spotless white gowns with the cowls pulled forward. They all carried heavy staffs which they handled in a businesslike manner.

The loudhailer swept the gathering. "We have come forth to oppose and thwart the pestilential forces of evil, witchcraft and Satanism that are at work in our community!" With that, Adrian Roscoe sat cross-legged on the road and bid his followers to do likewise. They were all young and disciplined; the three morris police on duty in the sector would be no match for them.

Prescott viewed their appearance with well-disguised satisfaction tempered with concern at the sort of favour Roscoe would require in return for this strong turnout.

All activity ceased. The children stopped playing, the caterers stopped doling out grilled chicken quarters. All eyes were on the improbable group sitting in a line across the road with their backs to the Wall. It was a measure of Roscoe's increasing support among the town people that several exchanged waves and shouted greetings with the monk-like figures.

Malone checked his map and found the footpath that Roscoe had used to reach the field. He was about to warn the sectors that there might be a delay when "Brenda" unexpectedly lurched forward. Her sudden movement was the result of the actions sixty years before of the man who had last parked the showman's engine in a field where she had been allowed to rot before David had rescued her. The long-dead showman had wound the brake handwheel as hard as possible to jam the brake shoes on to the mighty rear wheels. For sixty years the brake shaft had borne the torsional stresses. And now Charlie's jamming on of the brakes on the incline had turned the invisible hairline cracks in the shaft into a fracture.

The breaking shaft sounded like a pistol shot and the brake shoes fell away from the wheels. Charlie gave a cry and lunged for the boarding grab handle but was knocked aside by the trailer. He would've been run over had Carl not grabbed him and yanked him clear. Gus chased after the runaway engine and he too was forced to veer away by the trailer. David uttered a cry of fear. He tried to start after Ellen but was forcibly restrained by Prescott and Gus.

"Gotta let her go, Mr Weir," Charlie panted. "Ain't nothing for it. If she keeps it on the road, she should be OK."

Malone realised that something had gone seriously wrong. The plan was for Charlie Crittenden to drive the engine into the Wall. Certainly not Ellen. He trained his binoculars on her. From this position he couldn't see her face but he could guess at her terror.

The showman's engine had started rolling in such a leisurely manner that Ellen didn't fully appreciate what had happened other than that the giant machine was moving and that she was alone. But within seconds it had picked up speed and was accelerating rapidly. The mighty rear wheels pounding and grinding – the spinning flywheel a terrifying presence beside her, coal flying off the bouncing trailer. She tried to wind on the brakes but the handwheel spun free, and "Brenda" was moving faster than it had at any time during the long, slow journey from Temple Farm. It was veering to the left. She frantically spun the steering wheel clockwise to compensate. The slack in the steering chains, which had been a joke at eight kilometres per hour, was no longer funny.

"Get out of the way!" she screamed at Adrian Roscoe and his followers who were sitting in the clattering engine's path. Even at this distance his intense blue eyes shone with icy hatred.

Malone came to an immediate decision and seized the initiative. "High Hopes Command – all drivers!" he barked into his radio. "Start engines now! Start engines *now*!"

392 hands reached for as many ignition keys and the engines of 392 vehicles spaced along the thirty-kilometre perimeter of the Wall roared. The drivers sat tense, a passenger beside each one twisted around to watch the raised white flags of the marshal in each sector. A slight blackening of the Wall in the command sector indicated that the driver of a Commer van had forgotten his instructions not to move until the flag fell.

Ellen's frenzied correction of "Brenda"'s yaw caused the machine to swing to the right. That veer she also over-corrected with the result that the clattering engine swung from side to side as it careered downhill, but she managed to keep it on the road. When she had first driven the thing the evening before, Charlie had impressed on her the importance of never allowing it on to uninspected ground because there was no vehicle in Pentworth capable of pulling it clear if it ever got stuck.

"Get out! Get out!" she yelled at the group sitting in the road. She stood and waved frantically but the terrible jolting forced her to sit.

It was hardly necessary to attract their attention; the sentinels were staring in disbelief at the clanking, thundering apparition bearing down on them, their faces white with fear. Two of them jumped up despite their leader's bellowed admonitions to remain steadfast in face of Satan.

"Brenda" was thirty metres from the group when they decided as one that remaining steadfast in the face of several tonnes of hurtling cast iron and bronze was not a sensible option. They ignored their leader and scattered like chaff in a wind tunnel. Adrian Roscoe remained seated. He raised the loudhailer to his lips and hesitated.

"I can't stop!" Ellen screamed, spinning the steering wheel to keep "Brenda" on the crown of the road.

With the thundering, titanic forces of hell and damnation only fifteen metres away, the cult leader's beliefs underwent a sudden and profound revelation – namely that the word of God, even when amplified by a loudhailer, wasn't going to stop this monster. He scrambled to his feet and leapt clear. Ellen caught a glimpse of his searing eyes as she swept past. The Wall was straight ahead, a truck each side of the road, passenger faces staring at her awesome approach.

"High Hopes Command – all sectors," said Malone calmly into his microphone. "*Go! Go! Go!*" He repeated the pre-arranged order three times.

The marshals' flags went down. 392 drivers gunned engines and slipped clutches. Nearly 1000 tonnes of steel and glass surged forward into the Wall, driven by the irresistible combined forces of 150,000 shaft horsepower.

Most people had seen the curious, blackening effect when they pressed a hand against the Wall. But what happened next provoked gasps of astonishment and dismay for it was as if a huge black shroud was springing from the ground and climbing to the sky under the assault from the massed vehicles, their spinning tyres throwing up blue smoke and clods of turf as they strained in impotent rage against the unknown forces opposing them.

Malone's view of the adjoining sectors was obscured by trees, but the Wall made visible climbed high above the foliage like a rising curtain of black ink soaking into tissue paper. He stood and stared about him, seeing the terrible curtain as a huge circle ten kilometres in diameter, rising higher by the second.

Harvey Evans, piloting his microlight at 2000 feet above Pentworth Lake, had the most stunning view of all. Hardly crediting his senses, he banked and flew in a tight circle, and so witnessed the entire thirty kilometres of the mighty wall of night rearing up, huge, black and terrifying. For the first time he was confronted with the true scale and the awesome nature of the mighty forces that were holding Pentworth trapped.

Malone, normally unflappable, was so overcome that he had to sit abruptly. The screams of a terrified child carried clearly up the slope.

At that moment the charging showman's engine hit the black barrier square on like an unstoppable iron tornado . . .

And disappeared through it.

Eighteen

For several seconds the group standing on the crest of the rise were struck speechless at seeing the impossible happen.

"She's done it," breathed Harding at length. And then, jubilantly, "By God – she's done it!"

Prescott could think of nothing to say. Ellen's disappearance meant that his months of glory and prestige were over. David Weir saw the incident in a different light: his beloved Ellen might be lost to him. He uttered a cry of anguish and ran down the road.

Malone broadcast a general call to all sector marshals that the operation had been a success and gave the order for all vehicles to stop.

The black curtain collapsed and once again the bleak Farside vista of the primeval steppes of post-glacial Europe came into view beyond the Wall.

Malone was loping down the steep slope with long, easy strides when he saw David running down the hill with Harding and the others following. Without slackening his pace, he radioed the command sector marshal by name and ordered him not to allow anyone near the spot where the showman's engine had disappeared. The morris policeman dropped his flag and ran across the meadow to intercept David. Drivers and passengers piling out of the vehicles heeded the yells of the morris police and remained a respectful distance from the road. Even Adrian Roscoe and his band of sentinels stayed clear. His acolytes looked to their leader for divine guidance that was not forthcoming. Both Roscoe and his loudhailer were lost for words.

David Weir cannoned into the marshal. They struggled briefly but David managed to break free. With the morris man in pursuit, he continued his frantic dash down the road towards the spot where Ellen and the showman's engine had disappeared. What happened next brought them both skidding to a halt, staring in disbelief.

The Wall was blackening where it spanned the road. "Brenda"'s rear wheels appeared, and the rest of the showman's engine followed.

The ponderous machine was being pushed slowly, but inexorably backwards by the Wall's unknown forces. Ellen, white-faced, was sitting, holding the steering wheel. She tightened her grip as the Wall's stupendous thrust caused the engine to slew sideways so that its wheels grated and screeched on the road, forcing up rucks of asphalt.

And then silence. The Wall's blackness cleared. The sudden hush was broken by the slamming of truck and car doors as drivers and passengers came running. The marshal allowed David to approach the great engine. The gathering crowd formed a semicircle that watched in silence as David shinned up beside Ellen and carefully separated her petrified fingers from the steering wheel's handle. She was staring straight ahead, not speaking, not moving until David coaxed her to stand and then helped her to the ground. She moved stiffly, like an automaton, hardly acknowledging his presence.

Bob Harding pushed eagerly through the crowd with Prescott and Malone close behind. "Ellen? What happened? What did you see?"

"Can't you see she's in no state to answer questions?" David snarled.

"It's all right, David. I'm OK." Ellen tried to disengage David's protective arm from around her waist and then felt in need of his warmth and security when she saw the circle of faces staring at her in silent hostility. Adrian Roscoe had worked his way to the front of the crowd. His ice-chip blue eyes burned into her reason. She concentrated on Bob Harding's friendly concern. "I didn't see anything," she said slowly. "Just fog . . . Dense, dense fog. It was freezing and yet . . . And yet I could sense a terrible heat very close."

"*Mekhashshepheh!*"

No one seemed to hear the curse except Ellen. It seemed to materialise from all around her. An enclosure of hate that offered no weak point as a means of escape.

"Jesus," said Charlie Crittenden. "Look at that new paint! It's all blistered!"

Harding looked at "Brenda" and saw that the patches of fresh primer on the showman's engine had crazed and bubbled as if a blowtorch had been applied to them.

"The witch has challenged the works of God, and God has shown her the cauldrons of hell for her blasphemy!" Adrian Roscoe trumpeted.

Ellen didn't hear him. All she was aware of was the night; flickering torches held high; grotesque shadows dancing on thatched buildings huddled around a medieval town square; a lurching dogcart bearing a manacled, terrified young woman, followed by a crowd chanting:

"Death to the witch! Death to the witch!"

She needed David's arm around her because at that point searing flames seemed to be leaping about her, tongueing and darting into a spark-filled night sky. Agonies racked her body, and before her was Adrian Roscoe, his gaunt features twisted into a mocking sneer of triumph as he plunged more burning brands into the bundles of brushwood at her feet.

Nineteen

The following day Ellen and David were finishing lunch at Temple Farm while listening to a report on the radio about the proceedings that day of the trial of Brad Jackson for murder and treason. Ellen and David had been too busy the day before to listen to the news.

"Treason?" said Ellen in surprise. "Why treason?"

"God knows," said David. "At least he's pleading guilty to murder. At least we weren't on the steps of Government House, otherwise we'd be called as witnesses . . . But treason? Some devious plan of Prescott's making, I suppose."

There was a rap on the kitchen door. Dan Baldock had ridden over to see David. The waspish little pig farmer made a few comments about the abortive assault on the Wall, but remained standing awkwardly on the threshold and declined to come in despite David's invitation.

"It's country business, David," he said, glancing at Ellen.

David laughed. "Ellen's country, Dan – she's growing about two hectares of herbs. Come and try a cup of her tea."

Baldock looked sheepish and sat at the kitchen table. "Sorry, Ellen. Don't mean to be rude. It's just that I always think of you as town."

"What's the problem?" asked David, pouring his guest a cup of yarrow tea.

"Bill Croft got hijacked about three hours ago. He was on his way to the government food depot with five tonnes of spuds. The town mob who turned him over said that he had plenty more that he was holding back."

"Is he OK?" asked Ellen.

"Yeah. There was no beating up this time. He didn't resist. One of the town gang had a shotgun."

"This is starting to get out of hand," said Ellen worriedly.

"It *is* out of hand," Baldock replied.

"There's been nothing on the radio," said David.

"A lot doesn't get on the radio since the studio was moved to Government House," said Baldock acidly. "I always said that it was a mistake. I'm calling a meeting at my place – eight o'clock this evening. About a dozen tenant farmers and growers. More if there's interest. The inaugural meeting of 'the Country Brigade'. We need to set up some sort of rota system so that farmers making deliveries have protection from these townie troublemakers."

David frowned. "But after that last incident, Mike Malone said he'd look into supplying a morris police escort for major deliveries."

"He did," said Baldock shortly. "And his plans got the chop."

"By whom?" asked Ellen.

"He wouldn't say. Are you coming?"

"You'll have to choose another name, Dan. 'Country Crimewatch' or something not too emotive. 'The Country Brigade' sounds like a vigilante gang."

"A wishy-washy name ain't no good," said Baldock stubbornly. "We've got to show the townies that we mean business – that we're not to be messed with. As I said, all we need for starters is a rota system so that farmers delivering produce don't get set on."

"I'll be along," David decided. "But don't count on my support for setting up a vigilante gang."

Baldock rose. "See you this evening, David. I'd better be off. Got a lot of calls to make."

When they were alone, Ellen asked David if he had been withholding food supplies.

"Now why should you think that, m'dear? Temple Farm is primarily a training centre."

"Because I'm damn certain you've got a lot more chickens than the twenty-five you've registered. There were six eggs in that omelette. The ration for one person for a week is seven."

"So I've got a few extra chickens? What of it?"

"And Dan Baldock has got a few extra pigs; and Bill Croft's family don't go short of veggies. And farmers are doing a bit of trading with each other. How come you've got a whole leg of cooked pork in your meat safe when you haven't got any pigs?"

"It's lamb. I've got a three-legged sheep."

Ellen wasn't amused. "Does it occur to you that maybe the town people have got a point with their gripes about farmers?"

"Well look at all the perks they're getting," David countered. "Doctors on call in a few minutes; water laid on; several public telephones. This area was promised a phone weeks ago. We're still waiting. They get daily collections and deliveries of mail whereas we only get mail when the refuse collectors decide to come around. Sometimes the bread delivered to local shops is two or three days old. I know Diana is doing her best, but – forgive the crudity, m'dear – the country is sucking a hind tit."

Ellen didn't want to argue. "I suppose you're right. I ought to be getting back. Thomas won't speak to me for a month as he's missed out on his dinner and breakfast, and my helpers are incapable of doing a stroke unless I'm there."

"I'll get the trap."

"I'll walk. It's a lovely afternoon."

"I'll come with you."

"You're supposed to be helping Charlie bring 'Brenda' back."

"He'll manage without me. I prefer your company to Charlie's."

They left Temple Farm thirty minutes later with Ellen setting a brisk pace, showing no sign of her ordeal of the previous day. David questioned her again about what she had seen when she seemed to have broken through the Wall, but she merely reiterated what she had said before – that she had seen nothing but thick, freezing fog during those few moments of disorientation and confusion.

She glanced longingly at the concealed entrance to her cave as they trudged uphill, holding their breath and noses when they passed through the ginkgo tree's primary assault zone. The ancient tree was flourishing in the heat and humidity, thrusting upwards and extending the range of its awesome olfactory offensive. Contrary to expectations, Ellen's apprentices were at work among the herb crops, doing essential daily battle with Dutch hoes to keep weeds in check.

The first thing Ellen noticed as they approached her home through the rear garden was that the still-room door was partially open.

"I know I locked up yesterday," she said, quickening her pace.

The reason for the door's position was immediately obvious: the timber around the lock was splintered where the mortise had been jemmied open.

"Oh, no," she said. "Someone's broken in."

"Haven't got any exotic drugs in stock, have you?" David asked.

"Of course not." Ellen tried to pull the door open but it had been partially torn off a hinge and was jammed. David lifted the door and eased it open. It felt strangely heavy. Ellen's sudden scream of anguish caused his eardrums to sing in protest. One glance at what she had seen was enough. He quickly pushed the door shut and swept his arms around her, holding her tightly.

"For God's sake," he muttered as Ellen tried to push him away. "It might not be Thomas."

"Of course it's Thomas!"

"Let me deal with it."

"He's my cat—"

"Ellen—"

Ellen exploded. "For Chrissake, David! Will you stop treating me like a child!" She disentangled herself from David's grip and dragged the door fully open. She stared in silence until the horror of what was before her wrested a sob from the depths of her being.

Thomas was nailed to the inside of the door – crucified upside-down, wire nails driven through his throat, pelvis, paws, and even his tail, holding him in an inverted black T position in a ghastly parody of St Peter's fate.

Ellen knelt, touched him gently under the chin. His lifeless amber eyes regarded her with a "breakfast is late" expression that she knew so well. Above his pinioned tail, written in his blood on the door, was the legend:

EX2218

Ellen straightened and took in every detail of the terrible scene, ignoring David's well-meaning attempts to turn her away until he stood forcibly between her and the macabre spectacle.

"Let me bury him, m'dear," he said gently.

She pushed him aside, stared at the lifeless cat for some moments, and shook her head.

"You must. *Please*, Ellen."

But she would have none of it. Thomas had been her friend, companion and target for good-natured abuse for eight years and she wasn't going to fail him in this last office, although she did allow David to pull the nails out with a claw hammer. She gathered up the pathetic bundle and held him close for a few moments, not speaking, her back to David so that he wouldn't see her tears.

The rest she performed mechanically, hardly knowing what she was doing as she buried her pet with his feeding bowl in his favourite summer spot under a nearby apple tree. A few moments' contemplation of the sad patch of disturbed soil was enough. She returned to the house without a backward glance, masking her grief with composure, and sipped the mug of tea that David had made. She leaned against the still-room wall, watching as he wiped the blood and its grisly message from the door, and reset the hinge and mortise lock with longer screws. He was unable to completely obliterate the hateful message, so he found a tin of emulsion paint and gave the door a quick coating with a roller. Ellen remained silent as he put the tools away and regarded her thoughtfully, knowing that a warm, sympathetic approach would not be well received – not just yet. She allowed him to steer her into the shop's workroom and sit her at her workstation.

"Who would do such a thing, Ellen?"

"How should I know?"

"I think you do."

She shrugged. "I can't help what you think."

"What does 'EX2218' mean?"

"How should I know?" she repeated and avoided David's gaze by switching on the radio and pretending to listen to a report on the Government's plan to make more lamb available.

David stood over her. "It's what those vandals sprayed on your shop window last spring. You painted over it but it showed through." He hesitated before continuing. Being blunt with Ellen was not without risk. "Don't treat me like an idiot, m'dear. You know perfectly well what it means. The sickos that did that to Thomas, did it for a reason. Obviously a perverted reason. What frightens me is that you could be next. So . . . I'm going to stay here and take as much smelly stuff as you want to give me, but I'm not budging until you tell me everything. Start at the beginning. Start now."

Ellen opened her mouth to blast David but held her fire when she saw the determined light in his gaze. He was easy-going, but only up to a point.

"So tell me what 'EX2218' means," pressed David.

"Exodus," she said quietly. "Chapter Twenty-two, Verse Eighteen."

"Which is?"

"'Thou shalt not suffer a witch to live.'"

"Good God."

"Actually the original Hebrew for witch was '*Mekhashshepheh*' – 'sorceress'. The Pentworth May Day shout. Not quite the same as witch. And as a result of that translation thousands of men and women have suffered unspeakable tortures down the ages."

"So who thinks you're a witch?"

"I don't know."

"I'm going to call you an unpleasant name, Ellen, and to hell with the consequences."

After a pause, Ellen said, "If I tell you, I want your word that you won't do anything about it without my say so."

"I don't understand, m'dear. How can I promise—"

"You can promise me not to do anything!" Ellen snapped. "Now *promise!*"

"Very well," said David with great reluctance. "I promise."

She regarded the farmer steadily. "In that case, I'll tell you because I trust you to keep your word." She paused, gathering her thoughts. "This was a very different sort of shop when I took over from my mother. That was ten years ago – long before you bought Temple Farm. She called it 'the Wicca Basket'. 'Wicca' is an Old English name for 'witch'. My mum sold spells, potions – white witchcraft stuff. All pretty harmless, but it wasn't what I wanted to sell. Still, I couldn't change things overnight. Money was tight and mother had built-up a regular clientele that provided the sort of turnover I couldn't ignore. So I changed things gradually. I ran down her stock of witchcraft publications and suchlike and started introducing proper herbal remedies. In fact I only got rid of her books on the occult recently by donating them to the library . . ." Her voice trailed away.

"Gradually changing a business is a sensible approach," David commented to encourage her to continue.

"One of mother's bestselling decoctions was what she called 'witches' tea'. Yarrow and other stimulants mostly, but it included a dangerous alkaloid made from the seeds and dried roots of Angels Trumpets – datura. It has similar properties to LSD. It's an ancient anaesthetic. The Egyptians dosed their patients with it before drilling holes in their skulls, and the Incas sedated human sacrifices with the stuff. Satanists use small quantities to stupefy new recruits. It's supposed to help witches not feel the cold when dancing naked in the woods in winter, although God knows how they stay awake. Some TMers like it because they really do think they're flying."

"Good grief. Is it legal?"

"Oh yes – so long as kids don't cotton on to its properties. You could buy datura plants in any garden centre, although they're tricky to grow. I've always got a few in the greenhouse."

"Those shrubs that produce what look like ugly great marrow flowers?"

"That's them. I use tiny amounts in my more powerful sedatives. Anyway, just after I took over, a woman came in for some witches' tea. A large amount – fifty grammes – which I sold her because mother charged £2 per gramme. It was virtually the last of her stock.

On the packet were strict instructions on its usage. The warning about not mixing it with alcohol was printed in red. Two weeks later I'm in a coroner's court in Yorkshire giving evidence. The woman had topped herself with a cocktail of all the witches' tea I sold her and a bottle of vodka."

The radio presenter introduced a studio discussion on the Wall assault. Ellen stared at the radio and shook her head. "I was cleared of all blame. After all, the woman had misled me, and there were very precise written instructions and warnings on its usage."

"So who was she?"

"Adrian Roscoe's wife. I had no idea at the time. Roscoe had only just taken over Pentworth House and I had never met him. It turned out that she had come down from Harrowgate to plead with him for a reconciliation . . . without success."

David covered Ellen's hands with work-hardened palms. "And you've blamed yourself ever since . . ."

Ellen looked him in the eye. "You should know me better than that, David. Of course I haven't. I had no idea that she wanted to kill herself. And even if I had known, she would've found a way. I've never blamed myself . . . But that hasn't stopped Roscoe from blaming me because he found out at the inquest that his wife had been pregnant with his child. She hadn't told him. I suppose she felt that for a reconciliation to work, it had to be because he wanted her and not just because she was expecting a baby . . . He really hates me and called me a witch to my face in this shop, in front of customers. And you saw his behaviour yesterday."

"But he's never done anything like this before?"

Pain flickered momentarily as Ellen thought about Thomas. "Nothing as serious as this – no. But with his neurosis about witches and witchcraft, he's blaming me for Pentworth's present troubles."

"In that case, I'll go and confront him now," said David with grim determination.

"God protect me from protective males," Ellen muttered. "You will do nothing of the sort. You promised me that you would do nothing. I'm holding you to that, David."

"And I'll keep my word so long as you're not in danger." He added hurriedly before she had a chance to object, "The damnable thing is that Roscoe has such wide support. I heard one of his orations a couple of weeks ago in Market Square. As usual, he was raving about the asteroid belt being a planet destroyed by the wrath of God and how we would be next. The majority were with him. Hecklers got shouted down."

"He likes big audiences. That's why he never proclaims his message outside the town."

"A news update," said the radio presenter in a matter-of-fact voice. "The trial of Brad Jackson for treason, the murder of Government House security officer, Robert Vincent, and the attempted murder of our Chairman, has just ended. Jackson, who pleaded guilty to the murder and attempted murder charges, but not-guilty to treason, was found guilty of the latter. The jury took only ten minutes to reach their verdict after a summing-up in which Mr Justice Hooper reminded them that the huge weight of corroborative evidence of several witnesses as to what Jackson said immediately before he carried out the attack in Market Square was sufficient to remove any element of hearsay. Also he continued to make statements on his intentions after the attack despite being cautioned by the police.

"Judge Hooper sentenced Jackson to death by hanging and urged the establishing of a court of appeal to review the verdict and sentence. A government spokesman said that the judge's comments would be considered. In the meantime arrangements would go ahead to carry out the sentence as soon as is practical."

Ellen and David stared at each and the radio in mutual shock.

"For God's sake," David muttered. "I don't believe it . . . Hanging! That can't be right. The reporter has made a mistake."

"I don't think so. Prescott got those enabling measures through that give him virtually unlimited powers."

"But the appeal court would be certain to overturn the sentence."

"What appeal court? You heard the radio. It doesn't exist."

"But – Goddamn it – they can't bring back hanging!"

"They? You mean *we*, David. What powers we haven't given Prescott, he's grabbed." Ellen's expression was one of troubled foreboding. She added quietly, "What's happening to us, David? What's happened to Pentworth? It's like a summer madness is taking over."

Twenty

Cathy's instinct when she walked into Market Square the next morning to start work was to return home. She stared at the turmoil in dismay and wondered why there had been no mention of it on the radio. There was a gathering of about fifty jubilant citizens yelling for Prescott and waving placards bearing his picture while chanting his name. Some had even climbed on the stocks to sing their praise of Pentworth's beloved Chairman. The loudest were two thickset men holding a banner declaring that: "JACKSON MUST HANG".

"It's OK, miss," said a friendly voice. "We've got everything under control."

Cathy turned. A white-bloused morris policeman, a veritable giant of a man holding a staff, was grinning at her. He was wearing a crash helmet instead of the customary straw hat. She returned his smile. The morris police were well liked. They were firm but fair. "What happened?" she asked.

"Some troublemakers turned up. Relatives of Brad Jackson and a few others. Mostly country. We've sorted them." He looked down appreciatively at Cathy. He had seen her before – always pretty as a picture in her short, pleated skirts and sleeveless T-shirts. Good enough to eat, he reckoned.

Cathy thanked him and mounted the steps to Government House. She noticed a shredded placard on the ground whose message appeared to have been "PRESCOTT – MURDERER". A cleaner was mopping up what may have been a pool of blood outside the Mothercare shop. One of the windows fronting a display of reconditioned pushchairs and secondhand baby clothes was cracked. In the entrance lobby, several blackshirts were marshalling a small group of sullen detainees for an appearance in the courtroom before a magistrate.

"I seem to have missed the party," she remarked to Dennis on entering the library. There were no catcalls and wolf whistles to greet her entrance. She looked around in surprise. "Where are the chippies?"

"Our carpenters have been given another job," said Dennis curtly, nodding to the windows that overlooked Government House's tiny quadrangle.

Cathy crossed the library and looked down. She guessed that the embryo structure taking shape on the patch of grass was a scaffold. She shivered inwardly and could think of nothing to say. Her colleagues were busy at their desks even though there were still a few minutes to go, and her boss seemed in no mood to talk. There was nothing else for it but to start work.

Malone strolled in an hour later and nodded to Cathy as he passed her desk. She had given up trying to find out what he was researching. He took books from so many different sections that it was impossible to pin down his interests. Nor did he encourage visitors behind his screen, and he always had an opened Ordnance Survey map of the area ready to spread over his work to study closely when she had been near his desk.

Cathy dipped her pen in the ink bottle and started work. She had spent a week now, numbing her brain with the crashingly boring work of writing out library index cards with the horrible lampblack and water ink. She was beginning to give up hope of locating her Macintosh computer in Government House. There was a limit to the number of times she could pretend to get lost and wander into offices, and out again with apologies. The top floor, the adminstration level together with the radio studio and newsroom, was strictly out of bounds; the two blackshirts guarding the top of the stairs were there in response to Prescott's paranoia about security since the attempt on his life. No one was allowed on the top floor who had no business there.

She was half-dozing because an old acquaintance she had met in the Crown the evening before had kept her awake most of the night with his not unwelcome demands, when a shadow fell across her desk. She looked up into the brooding eyes of Nelson Faraday.

"Good morning, Mr Faraday." She sat up straight so that he couldn't see down her T-shirt. The other girls among her colleagues found the head of Government House security attractive. He always chilled Cathy's blood.

"Davies said you could find some books for me."

"With or without pictures, Mr Faraday?"

Faraday's lips curled into an icy smile, but his eyes were hard and unforgiving. "Books on hanging. I've been given a new job."

Looking up the Dewey Decimal Classification and finding entries in the card index saved Cathy having to think of an answer to that. She crossed to the shelves, found two books, and tossed them on her desk in front of Faraday. "They are the only ones we have catalogued at the moment."

"Executioner – Pierrepoint," mused Faraday, thumbing through one of the books. "An autobiography by Albert Pierrepoint. Sounds like he'd be more of an expert on the guillotine than the noose."

"I wouldn't know," Cathy replied, wanting rid of him. His nearness turned her blood to liquid nitrogen.

"Ah – he hanged the last woman to be executed in England. Ruth Ellis – pretty."

"I'm delighted you've found some pictures."

"OK – I'll take them."

"You'll need a ticket."

"And you need a fuck."

Cathy smiled beguilingly. "My partner last night provided three. That's two and a half more than I expect you could manage, Mr Faraday."

Faraday stared speculatively down at her. "Has anyone ever told you you've got nice tits?"

"Only people who get on them."

Faraday turned and left without another word, leaving Cathy wondering if her put-downs had been wise. She suddenly cursed herself for her stupidity when it occurred to her that had she played up to him, she might have found out where her Mac was installed. It was beginning to look as if she would never find it.

Her break came in the afternoon when Dennis issued her with a pocket torch and sent her on an errand that involved her hunting through dusty file boxes and cabinets in the archives of a local solicitor in search of a duplicate set of the deeds for Pentworth House. After an hour she found the folder – a huge binder fastened with ancient ribbons that disintegrated when she lifted it out of the filing cabinet. Yellowing hand-copied documents in beautiful copperplate script dating back to the fourteenth century, and maps of the Pentworth House estate cascaded on to the floor. Cathy returned to Government House with the deeds in a new box file and was told to take it to Diana Sheldon on the top floor.

The blackshirts at the top of the stairs allowed her to pass once they had checked on their Handie-Com radios that she was on legitimate business. She followed their directions to Diana Sheldon's office but took opportunities to get "lost" on the way. None of the hot little offices she entered had her Mac system. The door leading to the radio station suite was locked. There was nothing for it but to make her way along the corridor to her correct destination.

"Oh good, Cathy," said Diana smiling, rising from her chair and taking the box file. "You found them. The Chairman will be pleased. How are you settling in downstairs?"

"Well – it's a bit boring – writing out millions of index cards," Cathy replied, glancing curiously around. Four women were pounding mechanical typewriters. Vanessa Grossman was busy at a photocopier. She glanced at Cathy and accorded her a curt nod. There was no sign of the Mac in the crowded outer office. In fact none of the offices she had entered would have had room for the computer system; space was already at a premium throughout Government House, obeying the law that states that a bureaucracy will expand to fill the space available for its storage.

"We could do with you up here to work your computer system after all," said Diana ruefully. "It's not as simple as we thought. We got into an awful mess doing the ID badges. In the end Vanessa helped out but she's not used to Macs."

"A frightening machine," Vanessa commented, intent on her photocopying. "A law unto themselves."

Diana smiled at the comment. "Don't listen to Vanessa. She managed a print-run of food coupons but I really can't spare her. Would you be interested in a transfer? We'll need you when we start on the identity cards."

"Yes – I would, very much. Will it take long? I think I'll go mad in the library."

"Well – about a week. The library indexing has been given priority during the long daylight hours – our centre of knowledge and all that. You wouldn't be able to dress like that up here, though. I'll have a word with staffing resources." Her antique telephone jangled. "Oh – I've been waiting for this call. Would you take the file into the Chairman for me, please, Cathy. Just knock and enter."

The chill was the first thing Cathy noticed when she entered the Chairman's office. Air-conditioning!

"Shut the door," said Prescott irritably without looking up from the document he was reading. "Don't let the summer in."

Cathy stood uncertainly by the door, wondering what to do. Prescott was too preoccupied to notice her. He was muttering angrily to himself. The document was a petition from a group of local solicitors and other worthies calling on the government to establish a court of appeal. He suspected that His Honour Judge John blasted Harleston-Hooper was behind it. They must have been up half the night drafting the thing. Damn the man! Hooper's job was to hear serious cases and pass sentence – not meddle in politics. Prescott was tempted to scribble "refused" on the petition but Hooper's co-operation was essential. If the unthinkable happened and the Wall disappeared overnight it was important to show that all his actions had been in the light of Hooper's judicial rulings. Of course, Hooper had guarded his arse by calling them opinions but that could always be argued as a misunderstanding. Prescott sighed and opted for political delaying tactics. He noted on the petition for it to be considered at the next full council meeting and tossed it in his out tray. He looked up at Cathy and his eyes widened, the tiresome Judge Hooper momentarily forgotten.

"The deeds of Pentworth House, Mr Chairman."

"Ah. Excellent." He held out his hand. "Cathy Price, isn't it?"

"Yes, Mr Chairman."

Prescott's hungry gaze had all five items of Cathy's clothing and her shoulder bag strewn on the carpet by the time she had crossed the office to the ornate desk. Unable to resist exercising control and not realising the dangerous game she was playing with this man, she bent lower than necessary when placing the box file on the desk.

"Thank you . . . Cathy. Ah – yes. You're the Cathy Price who regained the use of her legs recently after an accident as a kid?"

Cathy straightened, pulling her shoulders back, aware that the pleasant coolness in the room and the piquancy of some gameplay with the most powerful man in Pentworth had caused her nipples to harden. "Yes, Mr Chairman. That's me. Actually it was my sense of balance that I'd lost. There was nothing wrong with my legs. You see?" She hitched up her skirt, not overtly high or for long enough for the gesture to lose its successfully contrived quality of coltish innocence, but high enough to show that her panties were transparent. She had the dubious satisfaction of seeing a sudden gleam of lust in Prescott's eyes before the hem fell.

"Indeed I do, Cathy. And very lovely legs they are too, if you don't mind my saying."

Cathy's cheeks dimpled prettily. "Not at all, Mr Chairman. Thank you."

"And thank you, Cathy."

She turned to leave but he seemed anxious to detain her. "That's your computer, isn't it?"

Surprised, Cathy turned and saw her Macintosh with its scanner and laser printer set up on a desk in an alcove at the far end of the office. "Why, yes, Mr Chairman" she said, hoping that her voice sounded calm. "Is it behaving?"

"So far as I know, it is. More useful here with electricity laid on than at your place, eh?" Prescott turned his attention to the contents of the box file. "Thank you, Cathy. That will be all."

"Everything OK?" Diana asked, replacing the telephone's headphone on its hook as Cathy entered the outer office.

"Yes. Fine. He was quite pleased." It would be foolish not to mention what she had seen, so she added, "My old Mac seems to have been given a place of honour."

The older woman gave a conspiratorial smile. "The Chairman was dead set against the idea, but there was nowhere else to put it. We simply don't have the room. But when Vanessa said that it might be best if it had an air-conditioned environment and that she had tracked down a new air-conditioner, he changed his mind."

"I'd better get back to the grind," said Cathy. She hesitated, her mind racing. "You said about a week to get a transfer. Any chance of speeding that up? It's terribly boring work downstairs."

Diana looked doubtful. "I don't think so. But I'm sure you'll come up and help out with the Mac when we start on the identity cards. We're going to need at least seven thousand."

"Yes, of course, I'd be only too pleased."

A week! Shit! Someone was certain to discover the terrible secrets on the file server's hard disk before then.

Outside in the corridor Cathy saw a door marked "WOMEN" and decided to grab the chance of using a real toilet. All the cubicles were empty. She used one and afterwards relished the luxury of being able to wash her hands in clean, hot running water and dry them on an ironed roller towel. They certainly looked after themselves on the fourth floor.

A glance around before leaving and she spotted a ceiling hatch above the cubicle she had used. Without hesitation, she shinned on to the partition and pushed. The hatch swung open easily. Cathy's arms had always been strong; she had no difficulty lifting herself into the suffocatingly hot roof space and carefully closing the hatch. She spread her weight across several ceiling collar-beams and waited for her heart to stop pounding before risking a quick inspection. The strips of daylight showing under the eaves merely illuminated the underside of the frost-spawled roof tiles. The torch revealed a cavernous loft, not cluttered with junk but home to a curious mixture of ancient and modern plumbing, and piles of bat guano like a range of miniature slag heaps whose peaks disappeared into the gloom.

She flashed the torch up at the roof trusses and saw huddled masses of bats. They were hanging about, waiting for dusk, twittering and fidgeting anxiously at the light. The dozens of long-eared, furry Mr Spocks didn't worry her; Hill House had its fair share and they now enjoyed greater protection than ever, such was their importance in keeping Pentworth's burgeoning insect population in check.

A hundred doubts taunted Cathy once she had taken stock. Climbing into the roof had been on an impulse, a seized opportunity although she had no clear plan in mind. The blackshirts at the top of the stairs would be certain to notice that she hadn't returned. On the other hand, why should they? They probably didn't know what her precise business had been; she recalled that they had showed little interest in people leaving the top floor. What about Dennis? Would he check? There again, the chances were that he would assume that she had decided to skive off work for the rest of the afternoon and her pay would be docked accordingly.

Two chattering girls entering the toilets intruded on her worries. It was the same during the rest of that long, boring afternoon: an intermittent stream of coming and going. Barely had the nearby header tank stopped gurgling and it was off again. The staff flushed the toilets every time without giving a thought to the stream of jingles on the radio exhorting the populace to save water, not that the many householders in outlying areas who had to fetch their drinking water from stand pipes had much chance to waste it.

At 4 p.m. by her watch, Cathy decided to risk a cautious exploration of the loft. She rearranged her keys in her shoulder bag so that they wouldn't jingle, and moved carefully along the collar-beams while holding on to roof trusses. After a drink of water from the header tank she flashed the torch around and found an old horsehair mattress that had escaped target practice by the bat colony. She positioned it near the hatch and stretched out. Sleep was out of the question, of course. She was too keyed up and there was the constant muffled rattle of typewriters, the clatter of horses and wagons from the square, and the hammering of the carpenters in the quadrangle at work on their grisly structure.

It was the silence that woke her. The typewriters and hammering had ceased. The strips of light under the eaves were now faint glows through which the bats wheeled and dived for another night's frenzied feeding. Cathy sat up and listened intently. She could hear voices from within the building. She edged around a mountain of guano towards the gable ends of the roof that fronted Market Square, where the voices were loudest. As near as she could judge, she was now over Prescott's office. Two men: one of them definitely Prescott's booming voice; the other had a rich, deeply resonate quality. The third voice sounded like Diana Sheldon but she couldn't be sure.

Cathy remembered seeing a short offcut of plastic drain pipe. She found it and applied one end to the lath-and-plaster ceiling between the collar-beams, and her ear to the other. The mystery male voice was instantly recognisable as Adrian Roscoe because she had heard him preaching his strange gospel around the town on a number of occasions. She could not help a little shiver of fear when she recalled his wide-eyed proclamations about the evils within Pentworth and how God would ensure that the Wall would remain in place until such abominations had been cauterised from society by society. After the extraordinary events of the last few days, perhaps there was a grain of truth in his crazy accusations. Certainly more people were beginning to believe him. Two of Cathy's neighbours had urged her to hear him speak. They were an ordinary, level-headed couple who were now fervently convinced that terrible evils must be at work within Pentworth for the Lord to take such a drastic step.

Roscoe's compelling voice was not raised now, but even with the aid of the pipe, she was unable to make out what they were saying, other than to catch the odd word here and there.

Twenty-One

"It seems to me to be a very sensible idea, Town Clerk," said Prescott, treating Diana to an Edsel radiator smile. "Father Adrian has already shouldered a considerable burden by providing the security staff for Government House at no charge to the taxpayer. And just look at the string of cases his estate court has already dealt with: fines for just about every misdemeanour under the sun. Bound to happen when you've got over fifty workers on your patch."

Diana had to lean forward to study the list of cases that Adrian Roscoe's unofficial court had "tried" – Prescott's desk lamp was the only light in the office. A fifty euro fine for leaving the milking shed unattended was the heaviest sentence. "So all these fines have been accepted voluntarily?" she asked.

"They have to be," Roscoe replied. "The manorial court as it stands has no powers of arrest and prosecution. It's like a club imposing fines on its members for petty infringements of the rules. But we've had some serious offences recently. Offences that warrant immediate arrest."

"How serious, Father?"

"Yesterday a baker's assistant was caught smoking some homegrown stuff near a methane tank breather valve. There could have been a major explosion. The bakery could've been destroyed."

"In which case he or she should be tried in the magistrates' court here," Diana pointed out.

"True. But we have to find a way of cutting out all the bureaucratic rigmarole, Town Clerk," Prescott replied, maintaining a bland smile that cloaked his mounting irritation at the way his usually compliant chief executive was behaving. "The food control officer is complaining that cases are not being properly prepared. All the adjournments are creating a backlog so that her proper job is suffering. So, what I want you to do, Town Clerk, is go home and burn some midnight oil to word an emergency regulation to reintroduce the powers of arrest and prosecution that Pentworth manorial court used to have, so that they can deal with cases on a proper footing."

"Such powers would have to be confined to within the curtilage of the Pentworth estate," said Diana cautiously.

"Yes, yes."

"If there had been an explosion, a case of criminal negligence would have to be heard in a higher court than a manorial court or even the magistrates' court."

"We have a crown court set up under Judge Hooper, Town Clerk," said Prescott acidly. "It's already dealt admirably with a murder case. I see no harm and many benefits in putting the old powers of the Mesne Lord of the Manor of the Pentworth Estate on a proper legal footing. All the documents you need are in those deeds."

Diana could see much harm and no benefits in such a move. It simply made no sense – it would be easier to appoint a solicitor as a public prosecutor as and when needed, but she sensed the danger in raising further objections. Perhaps a quiet word with Judge Hooper . . . She stood, gathered up the box file and its contents. "I'll do my best, Mr Chairman."

Prescott beamed magnanimously. "Thank you, Town Clerk. Where would we be without you? Perhaps you'd like me to call in on you later this evening? See how it's coming along?"

Diana flushed and smiled for the first time since the strange meeting. "Yes – thank you, Mr Chairman. I'd be pleased to see you."

Roscoe chuckled when he and Prescott were alone. "You seem adept at keeping her sweet, Asquith."

"I'm getting a little tired of keeping her sweet," Prescott growled. "Since Judge Hooper's ruling gave me the green light to do almost anything I choose in the interests of the community, I think she senses that she's no longer so important. She was a virgin, you know. Fifty-five years old and still a virgin. Can you credit that?"

Roscoe steepled his bony fingers. "So I get powers of arrest and prosecution. But only within the curtilage of the estate. That's not what I want, Asquith, and you know it's not. It doesn't address the problem of that abomination of Satan's daughter we're nurturing to our breast."

Prescott grinned and snapped his briefcase open. "I didn't give the Town Clerk all the documents I found in the deeds. Take a look at this." He unfolded a half-imperial vellum that bore the coat of arms of King James I. It was headed in bold, cursive script:

An Acte against conjuration witchcrafte
and dealinge with evill and Wicked Spirits

"The King James Witchcraft Act," Roscoe commented. "It became law in 1604 and is no longer on the statute books. What use is it to me?"

"Damned useful if I use my democratically bestowed and legally backed powers to allow the Act back on to the statute books."

"On what grounds?" Roscoe enquired.

"In the interests of preserving religious harmony in the community following a spate of outrageous acts of desecration committed against the Anglican church, the Catholics and Methodists etcetera. There was a case only last year, you recall – chickens sacrificed in St Mary's churchyard. Big uproar. These things happen from time to time and they cause a lot of upset and unrest. People still take such things seriously. I would be failing in my duty if I didn't take steps to outlaw such vile practices if they got out of hand."

The whole thing was beginning to sound bizarre beyond belief, even to Roscoe's warped mind.

Prescott smiled smugly at his visitor's expression. "And you, my dear Adrian, have a Parliamentary order demanding that such measures are taken." He removed another document from his briefcase and placed it in front of Roscoe. It was handwritten. "Please be careful with it."

Like the Witchcraft Act, the letter was written on vellum. Roscoe read it without touching it. It was addressed to the Lord of Pentworth Manor, dated 12th December 1646. The seventeenth-century spelling and handwriting conventions made reading the letter difficult, but its overall message was unequivocal: the writer called upon the Church, the Lord of the Manor of Pentworth and the good people of Pentworth to exercise vigilance in the hunting down of witches and other such evils, and bringing them to face the justice of God and the King.

Roscoe came to the signature and looked up at Prescott, his compulsive blue eyes alight with suppressed excitement. "Matthew Hopkins – Witch-finder!" he breathed. "This is fantastic, Asquith!"

"I thought you'd be pleased. Note the seal. There's no doubt that it's genuine. This town is awash with former antique dealers. If the document is challenged, a whole string of expert witnesses could be produced to testify as to its authenticity."

Roscoe had reservations. "A conviction of witchcraft carries the death penalty – that means the case would have to be heard before Judge Hooper?"

"Of course . . ."

"Witnesses giving evidence under oath. There is a massive weight of evidence against that woman that she is a witch and that she must hang, but I have no evidence that she has pursued her vile craft on my land. Therefore I cannot see how I can bring a prosecution." His eyes burned into Prescott. His voice rose to the beginnings of that maniacal rave that could hold an audience entranced. "There can be no question of perjury! No lying under oath before the Almighty! No using the tools of Satan to defeat Satan!"

"Calm down, Adrian. No one is suggesting that you do anything of the sort." Prescott searched the papers in his briefcase to produce another rabbit in the form of an indian ink and water colour map that was coming apart along its creases. He positioned it carefully on his desk.

"These old documents are quite fascinating," Prescott continued. "Pentworth House estate was double its present size in the seventeenth century. No doubt the transfer of the land documents are in the original deeds – but they'd be held by the National Trust. They're not in Pentworth. As these deeds stand, a goodly chunk of Pentworth, including North Street and Ellen Duncan's herbal shop and flat, come within the boundaries of Pentworth House."

Roscoe studied the map and the enlarged Pentworth Estate highlighted in pink watercolour. There was a fanatical light shining in his eyes when he looked up. "This means we've got her," he breathed. "We've got the daughter of Satan! She's ours!"

"Yours – *if* you can make your charges stick," said Prescott carefully. "Much depends, of course, on the incidence of sacrilegious acts against churches that force the government into bringing in legislation to deal with witchcraft. If you follow me." He chuckled at his deviousness in using this madman's insanity to his own ends without risk to himself. "I think this calls for a little celebratory drink in the Crown, Adrian."

Twenty-Two

C athy waited ten minutes after she heard the two men leave the office, to be certain that they were unlikely to return. She dropped from her hiding place into the women's toilets and used the light from the torch to wash her face, dust herself down as best she could, and have a drink. She was too scared to feel hunger. She listened carefully at the door. The radio station was on the same floor and it now operated around the clock.

The corridor was dimly lit by emergency lights, as was Diana Sheldon's office. Thankfully Prescott's office was not locked; she guessed that security relied on lockable filing cabinets and the presence of the blackshirts. The air-conditioning unit startled her by coming on with a soft humming when she entered Prescott's office – probably controlled by an infrared body heat sensor to save electricity, but she didn't have time to hunt for it. Getting the Mac up and running was her first and only priority. She positioned her torch, switched the system on and was immensely relieved when the monitor's LEDs glowed and she heard the muted whir of the server's hard disk cranking up to speed.

Cathy started work, unaware that four floors below, her unwitting triggering of the air-conditioning unit had been noted.

The night security blackshirt sitting behind the front reception desk looked at the slave ammeter in annoyance. At night the needle normally hovered just under ten amperes – the average load needed to run the corridor and lobby lights, and the radio station, but it had suddenly jumped to indicate a twenty ampere drain on the uninterruptable power supply batteries in the basement.

"Look at that," he moaned to Nelson Faraday. "Our beloved Chairman's air-con is on the blink again. It's supposed to switch off and stay off when his office is empty."

Faraday was standing in the entrance, talking to the two blackshirts guarding the front door while keeping an eye on Prescott and Roscoe who were drinking at a table outside the Crown. Prescott's two armed blackshirt bodyguards stood at a discreet distance. By the flickering light from the candles on each table Faraday could see that Prescott and Roscoe were looking pleased with themselves, and wondered why. He turned and looked enquiringly at his colleague manning the desk. "How do you know it's the air-con unit?"

"Ten amps over norm. Nothing in the building pulls that sort of load. The air-con played up last week when you were off duty. I went up and tried to fix it and it wouldn't go off. It flattened the UPS batteries. Our Chairman went ballistic in the morning. So did Supplies because we needed the big jenny for a recharge when it wasn't booked to us."

Faraday grinned and looked at his watch. "So long as there's enough juice for the telly and video recorder in the muster room. It's a good "un tonight. Pity you're on duty."

"The UPS batteries will run flat just as it gets interesting," said the blackshirt cheerfully. "The Chairman's been in all day so they've taken a caning."

Faraday scowled and left the building. Prescott and Roscoe had finished their drinks and were standing, shaking hands. They broke off at his approach.

"Mr Chairman," said Faraday respectfully. "I'm sorry to disturb you, sir, but the duty officer thinks that your office air-con unit has come on."

"Just so long as you haven't tried to switch it off," said Prescott testily.

"No, sir."

"Just as well. Damned temperamental thing. I suppose I'd better go up and take a look at it."

"I'll do it if you like, sir."

"You'll do no such thing. I seem to be the only one that understands it. Anyway, there're some papers I want to collect."

"You'll be in touch, Asquith?" said Roscoe, moving off.

"Just as soon as the Town Clerk has done the necessary," Prescott replied.

The two men exchanged final goodnights. Prescott entered Government House, nodded to the blackshirts, and started up the stairs. He turned and looked speculatively at Nelson Faraday.

"How about that extra responsibility you've been given. Nelson? Any problems?"

Faraday gave a confident grin. "All the gen I needed was in the library, Mr Chairman. It'll all go smooth as clockwork. The carpenters will be finished tomorrow. I ordered knock-down construction – in case it's needed again."

"Sensible, but let's hope it won't be." Prescott glanced at his watch. "You'll be late for the video, Nelson."

"I'm on duty tonight, sir," Faraday replied, wondering who was leaking information to the old bastard.

"Since when has that ever stopped you?" Prescott smiled smugly, pleased to have put one over on his security chief, and headed up the stairs without waiting for a reply.

Twenty-Three

Deleting the website QuickCam photographs was easy. Cathy merely had to click on the appropriate icon and navigate through the verification messages warning her that such actions would delete all the files in the directory and did she really want to do that?

But the ten shameful photographs that Josh had taken required a different approach. To ensure that they were properly erased meant zeroing the tracks on the hard disk that the images had occupied. This would prevent a knowledgeable computer buff such as Vernon Kelly from using the Mac's data recovery utilities to rebuild the files. It was a slow but totally data-destructive process.

With the ninth image zapped, she loaded the tenth, and, as with the others, she avoided looking at it while she steered the mouse pointer along the tool bar. Why had she given in to Josh? It wasn't as if she had enjoyed it, and it had hurt despite his assurances.

Her whole body went rigid with terror when she heard footsteps outside the office. She had barely enough self-control to blank the screen and switch off the torch just as the door was thrown open and Prescott entered the office. He snapped on the ceiling lights and strode across the office to the air-conditioning unit. He dropped the inspection flap, tinkered with the controls, and swore when he could find nothing wrong.

Perhaps it was the mythical sixth sense that told him that some-thing was not right about the room for he straightened and turned slowly to meet Cathy's terrified gaze. They stared at each other for timeless seconds.

"What the hell are you doing here?"

Cathy's lips moved but no sound came out at first until Prescott had advanced across the office and was towering over her. "Sir . . ." She struggled to form a sentence. "This . . . This is my computer—"

Prescott spun the swivel chair to face him and planted a hand on each armrest, trapping her. His face was twisted with rage. "*Was* your computer!"

"Was my computer," Cathy mumbled, unable to tear her eyes away from Prescott's hard stare.

"So why are you here?"

In her panic she could think of nothing other than to blurt out the truth. "There are some private files on it that I wanted to delete."

"*Liar!* You thought you'd print some money or food coupons!"

"No, sir—"

The stinging blow across the cheek rocked Cathy back, knocking her hand against the keyboard. Any keystroke was enough to knock out the screen blanker. The monitor glitched and burst into life to a full-screen display of the last of the dreadful pictures – pin-sharp in over 70,000 livid colours.

Prescott stared at the accusing image and at Cathy in turn. He was genuinely shocked and for a moment seemed to share her inability to form a coherent sentence. "You . . . That's . . . It's . . ." And then it came out: "You filthy, disgusting whore!"

"It's not me—"

He seized her right hand and thrust it against the screen. The image was life-size – there was no mistaking the amethyst ring on Cathy's third finger. Her T-shirt ripped when he yanked her towards him so that their faces were centimetres apart. "You filthy, lying little slut! It is you, isn't it?" He shook her hard. Cathy's eyes filled with tears. She looked away and nodded, clutching at her T-shirt across her chest.

"Do you know what the punishment is for that sort of thing?"

"No, sir."

As it happened, nor did Prescott but that was beside the point. Cathy cringed when he brought his hand up again but he realised that he did not need violence to compound the woman's terror, and allowed his arm to fall to his side.

"When was it taken?" He had to raise his hand and repeat the question.

"About a year ago." Tears of humiliation, shame and pain streamed down her cheeks.

Prescott could think of nothing to say. Judge Hooper had warned him that he had no jurisdiction over crimes committed before the Wall was in place. It was Cathy who resolved his dilemma.

"Please, sir – I'm terribly sorry for what happened. I was half-drunk at the time. Please don't tell anyone, I beg of you. I'll do anything—"

"For God's sake, stop whining!" Prescott snapped, still undecided and momentarily distracted by the sight of Cathy's breasts as she tried to wipe her eyes while holding the torn T-shirt in place. He slapped her hands away. "So you're sorry?"

Cathy nodded. His change of tone gave her hope. And then he was idly brushing her nipples back and forth with his knuckles, moving to each one in turn, then pulling to make them harden against her will. She kept her eyes averted from Prescott's calculating gaze.

"And ashamed?"

Another nod. He pinched her hard.

"Speak up!"

"Yes, sir."

"How many more pictures are there like that one?"

"Just that one, sir. I've deleted the others."

"How many were there?"

"Ten."

Prescott stared down at the frightened woman and took his hand away from her breasts. "Well I don't want this sort of filth aired in my courts. And you say that you want to redeem yourself. Did I understand you correctly?"

Cathy's "Yes, sir" was uttered with only the slightest hesitation. She expected Prescott to demand some sort of sexual gratification from her and was prepared to take that hateful route if she had to.

Prescott nodded. He had an idea in mind. "How do you feel about doing some community service?"

The question surprised Cathy and gave her hope. "I'd be pleased to, sir," she stammered.

"Very well then. But first you'd better get rid of that picture."

Cathy's hand shook. She had trouble controlling the mouse and brought up the wrong menu twice, but she eventually managed to delete the incriminating picture.

"Is that all?"

"Yes, sir."

"No more pictures?"

"None, sir."

"Switch the thing off and come with me."

It gratified Prescott that the power he was exercising over this lovely young woman was such that there was no need for him to hold her arm as he strode along the corridor; she followed meekly behind, and made no attempt to escape.

The blackshirt keeping watch outside the muster room stiffened to attention at their approach. He gave a double warning rap on the door but Prescott's brisk entry was too quick for Faraday to grab the remote control and zap the movie playing on the VCR.

"Good evening, gentlemen," said Prescott amiably, beaming around at the six heavies who were jumping to their feet from the circle of armchairs around the television. "Don't worry about your tape, Nelson – I've brought you something much more interesting. This delightful young lady has been somewhat naughty of late and is anxious to carry out some community service to redeem herself. Is that not right, Cathy?"

Cathy sensed a trap. She nodded without looking up. She gripped her shredded T-shirt across her breasts, having no idea how many men there were in the room and lacking the courage to raise her eyes to find out.

"This is most important, gentleman: you all observed her follow me in here of her own free will and without any coercion on my part. Is that not so?"

There was a chorus of assent from the blackshirts as they gathered around, their eyes feasting hungrily on the young woman. Prescott steered her gently by the shoulders into the centre of the circle and patted her affectionately on the bottom. "You're here of your own free will, aren't you, Cathy?"

This time Cathy looked up and saw Faraday sneering at her. "No!" she cried, and lunged for the door. Faraday grabbed her and pushed her into an armchair. A blackshirt clamped a huge hand over her mouth to stifle her scream. Two more grabbed her flailing legs.

"Now then, Cathy," said Prescott affably. "All your community service involves is for you to entertain my troops for a couple of hours."

Faraday laughed and announced his intention of pulling rank on his colleagues by being first.

Prescott lowered himself into an armchair to watch. He was pleased with his little ruse. It promised to provide an interesting finale to what had been an interesting day.

Twenty-Four

Bob Harding was disappointed by the failure of David Weir's showman's engine to breach the Wall, but he was not deterred. He had spent several nights in his workshop industriously converting a fanciful design to a working model. He loved model-making, particularly at night when all was quiet and he could work undisturbed now that Radio Pentworth had moved. Tonight he finally managed to get the model working and was so pleased by the results that he forgot all about time until Suzi decided to flush him out.

He was too intent on his work to hear her creep up behind him. She slid her arms around his rounded shoulders, nibbled his earlobe in a manner that could earn her a prison sentence in some Gulf states, and advised him that his habit of working all night by the light of a low-wattage car bulb instead of going to bed with her was becoming a distressing habit that could result in both of them going blind.

Harding chuckled and kissed her palms without turning around. "I *have* been neglecting you, darling."

"You certainly have," Suzi scolded. "To think that I imagined that you were working on another worthy project to ease the drudgery of day-to-day life in Pentworth, and instead I find you playing with a toy submarine."

Harding lifted the model out of the big, mud-filled aquarium, rinsed off the silt in a bowl of water, and placed it on his bench. It rested on a pair of skids made from a wire coathanger. "It's not a toy submarine. It's a model submersible. What do you think?"

Suzi examined the curious device. The body appeared to be a 400-gramme food tin. Attached to the nose was a double-spiral auger device. It had stabilising fins, a small, wire-caged propeller at the stern, twin hydroplanes and a rudder. The control box was connected to a motorbike battery and consisted of a computer-type joystick, several buttons, and a digital ammeter. It was connected in turn to the submersible by a two-metre length of lightweight cable.

"It looks like a tin of baked beans with an attitude problem," Suzi declared.

His wife's perception impressed the scientist. "Actually, the Mark 1 did have an attitude problem, but I think I've fixed that with larger hydroplanes."

"Mark 1!" echoed Suzi. "You mean that this is the second one?"

"Third, actually," Harding admitted sheepishly. "The first one was a cardboard mock-up – a design concept. Watch."

The scientist lowered the model into the aquarium. It was slightly negatively buoyant so that it sank slowly into the opaque silt. Just before it vanished, Harding operated the control box so that the model's twin-auger nose appeared, sliding down the inside of the glass and held against it by the slow-turning propeller.

"And now it'll burrow into the settled silt. Watch."

The model submersible tilted down and started driving into the sediment, powered by the contra-rotating augers and the thrust of the propeller. It disappeared for several minutes and came bobbing to the surface when the scientist toggled a switch to release some ballast weights.

"Clever," said Suzi. "Do you think Prescott will sanction the cost of building a full-size version for you to play with?"

"It won't have to be very big," said Harding. "Just large enough for one man. I've already got a liquid gas container earmarked for the main hull. That's most of the cost taken care of."

"So you're going Silent Vulcan hunting? What will you do *if* you find it?"

"Well – talk to the visitors, of course. Once there's a physical contact, it ought to be possible to talk to them through a transducer or something similar."

Suzi still looked unconvinced. "Supposing they don't understand English?"

Harding sighed and patted her hands. "We have to make contact first. Once that's established, a system of communication can be worked out afterwards. But the all-important thing is to make that initial contact."

"Which they haven't done?"

"No."

"So their shoving umpteen tonnes of steamroller sideways wasn't them making contact, or at least making a point?"

The scientist reflected that his wife could be remarkably obtuse at times.

Four hundred metres away in North Street, Ellen woke up, sensing that something was wrong. She shouldn't be awake; she had drunk a strong cup of her "night" tea to be certain of a good night's sleep.

Then memories of that tragic day swarmed back and she knew what was wrong. There was no reassuring weight on the bed; no Thomas craftily stretching and thrusting in his sleep to be assured of more than his fair share of bed space.

Alone and desperately miserable, wishing she had stayed another night with David at Temple Farm, and filled with wretchedness and foreboding, Ellen let herself sink into an unashamed flood of tears for her beloved pet.

Twenty-Five

The van pulled up outside Hill House. The rear doors were flung open and Cathy was pitched on to the road by two laughing blackshirts. Her panties and shoulder bag were tossed after her as she lay sprawled, sobbing in pain and humiliation, her face bruised, her skirt and T-shirt in shreds. One of the blackshirts stamped on the floor of the van. Its engine revved and it screeched off into the night.

Cathy climbed shakily to her feet. The bruising and grazing from the fall were nothing compared with the pain of the few steps needed to reach her E-Type Jaguar, still parked in her drive. She clutched it for support. Her mind was already blotting out the unspeakable horrors of the last two hours. In so doing, it was also sapping her reason.

The touch of cold steel and glass was contact with an old friend. When she couldn't walk, the Jaguar had given her more than freedom – the power under its long, phallus-like bonnet had been a stallion-like assertion of her energy and driving sexuality in a society that sought to deny such emotions in those confined to wheelchairs. Suddenly she wanted the protection of the Jaguar's steel womb around her. She wanted a blaring stereo and speed in which she could retreat into her own secure world and shut out the terrors of reality.

She found her keys and fell behind the steering wheel, savouring the cool feel of vinyl against her thighs after so many months. No courtesy lights had come on when she had opened the door. The battery had been taken, and they would've siphoned off all the E-Type's petrol but for the steep slope it was parked on that had prevented the tank from being emptied.

Starting the car was the next problem but she had done so on many occasions when the battery was flat. Provided the alternator was turning over, it would power the fuel pump and so prime the carburettors. She slipped into neutral, released the handbrake and allowed the car to roll out of her drive and gather speed as it coasted downhill. Thankfully there was a moon, just as there had been the last time she had driven it; she had no difficulty avoiding the kerb.

With 200 metres to go to the foot of the hill, she snicked the shift into second and engaged the clutch. The V-8 engine churned sluggishly, its crankshaft impeded by sump oil that had turned to goo.

Please, please, dear God – make it start . . .

The engine wheezed and popped, its valves sticking, allowing unburnt fuel into the exhaust manifolds. The SU carbs were suddenly fully primed; two cylinders caught, then a third, then all eight. An almighty backfire that woke the neighbourhood and the engine was running lumpily; a heady, deep-throated but erratic roar, threatening to stall.

The terrible memories of her ordeal slipped away as Cathy concentrated on nursing the neglected engine, slipping the clutch to minimise load and keep the revs up. She had run out of hill therefore it was essential to keep the engine running – there was no way of restarting it if it stopped. It had settled down to a steady note by the time she was turning south on to the A285 so she risked shifting into third.

Next the lights. Two pure white halogen beams lanced through the humidity – pointing the way to freedom and salvation.

The stereo. A tape was still in the player. The lyrical pounding of Dire Straits – "Telegraph Road". Old yet timeless. The music mounting to a crashing crescendo of perfection that allowed no room for ugly memories. She pushed the throttle pedal halfway to the floor. The Jaguar bounded forward. Wind sucking through the window, lashing her hair, pulling her mouth into a smile, and then a laugh as her right foot went down hard. Friendly, welcoming emotions spawned by speed and music and the comforting roar of the engine crowded in, driving out the terrors, bringing warmth, love she had never known and always craved. The touch of a loving partner; a baby's gurgling laughter – secure in its bonding with its mother. And always the divine speed, and yet more speed until the E-Type's speedometer needle was hard on the stop . . .

The A285 runs almost dead straight south out of Pentworth for five kilometres, ending in an abrupt ninety-degree left hook to avoid the pair of massive four-metre-high granite and brick piers that had been built for Seaford College's wrought-iron gates.

Two hundred metres further on was the Wall.

But Cathy never reached the Wall because she did not make that left hook.

The charging Jaguar continued in a straight line, arrowing across the grass. It hit and destroyed the left pier of Seaford College's gates. The left pier in turn destroyed the Jaguar. And both destroyed Cathy.

Twenty-Six

S everal days later, Prescott shook hands with each of the great and the good of Pentworth as they filed out of his office. The deputation included a Baptist pastor, the rector and several deacons, Father Kendrick, Adrian Roscoe, and a motley collection of lay ministers of both sexes from the wide variety of churches and chapels in Pentworth and its environs. They clattered down the stairs, most of them loud in their praises of Asquith Prescott and how lucky they were to have a leader prepared to take swift, decisive action when the circumstances warranted.

The only member of the party who wasn't happy was Father Kendrick. The Catholic priest had tried to raise another matter during the meeting, namely the question of Brad Jackson's appeal, but Prescott had brushed the priest's concerns aside with the time-honoured phrase beloved by politicians of how it would be "inappropriate for me to comment" on the setting up a court of appeal until the council had considered the matter.

"And *please*, ladies and gentlemen," had been Prescott's parting admonition to the party. "Not a word about this until the government's official announcement."

Prescott returned to his desk, looking pleased with himself and regarded his executive officer. "Well, Diana – I think I handled that rather well."

"Very well," said Diana non-committally, completing the notes she had been taking.

"Do I detect disapproval?"

Diana regarded him with unusual coldness. There had been an undercurrent of rumours in the building about Cathy Price's suicide. Ugly stories about a party in the blackshirts' muster room. She had tried to dismiss the rumours as idle gossip, particularly as none of them involved the Chairman, but there was one aspect that rankled: that he hadn't kept his promise to visit her that night, and he had offered no apologies the following morning.

"I don't think new legislation is necessary," she replied. "The existing laws dealing with criminal damage and trespass are more than adequate."

"Adequate? Churches being desecrated left, right and centre? The very cornerstone of our society under attack."

Diana didn't think a few dead chickens scattered around church-yards at night posed much of a threat to society. "What difference will new legislation make if they're not being caught under existing laws? It's a policing problem."

"It might make the scum carrying out these acts think twice if the penalties are stepped up," Prescott growled. "Tough penalties work. How many times have we had to use the stocks? Twice – that's all. Pilfering, shoplifting, street crimes are almost unheard of now. I want something in place by the end of the week. Something with teeth to keep the churches off the government's back. We can't afford to ignore pulpit power."

Diana protested that drafting new legislation on such a matter could take days.

"I agree," said Prescott, plonking his feet on his desk. "So let's take Judge Hooper's advice and use old legislation with all the wording and definition donkey work done for us. All the case law and precedents in place."

"What legislation?"

"Now what could adequately cover what's been happening?"

"It might be possible to extend the Town Police Clauses—"

"There's an old act that meets all our requirements . . ."

"Which is?"

"The James the First Witchcraft Act of 1604," Prescott answered, and chuckled richly at Diana's expression.

Twenty-Seven

S arah unrolled the condom and subjected it to a critical examination. They were made by a garden-shed entrepreneur by dipping a glass former in latex tapped from ficus elastica plants – the popular rubber plant – that were flourishing outdoors and growing into respectable trees. An edict issued by Government House the week before had banned the manufacture of condoms but that hadn't stopped the entrepreneur – just made him richer because he had put up his prices.

She partly inflated the condom and watched for the slightest sign of deflation.

"For fuck's sake get on with it," moaned the youth she was sitting astride in a patch of tall fronds of Ellen's asparagus ferns. "Ellen will go ape if she catches us."

Sarah rolled the condom into place. But unlike the condom, the boy's penis had suffered some deflation so she expertly aroused its interest with short strokes back and forth over the glans with one hand while running her thumb up and down the underside with the other hand, ending each return stroke by squeezing the base of the penis to trap the blood.

The boy lay back with his eyes closed. "Fucking hell, Sarah – you've got a fabulous pussy."

"I haven't started yet, you pillock."

"What are doing then?" He tried to tip his head forward but Sarah knocked him back.

"Wanking your corpus spongiosum."

"My what?"

"Sorry – don't know its proper name. The big vein under your cock."

Eventually the boy's erection was as good as it was likely to get at this stage. Sarah was an old hand at this business and knew that he would stiffen in his resolve to please her once she got the thing in place and her vaginal muscles got to grips with the problem. She smeared saliva on her vulva, eased her hips forward and down, working his glans back and forth to spread the juice about a bit before the final positioning and sinking down.

They both groaned in unison. Sarah began pumping her hips, slowly at first and then with increasing frequency as the boy's penis swelled rapidly to its full potential. She leaned forward, taking her weight on one hand while vigorously stimulating her clitoris with the other. She climaxed almost immediately with this beat-the-dreaded-PE technique she had patented, but the boy spoilt the moment by trying to kiss her and fondle her breasts. He received a sticky fingered slap for his temerity – Sarah hated intimacies when she was screwing. She straightened and leaned back, eyes closed, while making circular motions with her hips to increase the pressure on her clitoris.

She opened her eyes and gasped when her second orgasm came, and then opened them wide because Malone, kitted out in tight shorts and sweatshirt, was jogging along the nearby path. She ducked down but knew the police officer had seen her.

"Bugger."

"What's up?"

"Shut up. Keep still. I'll do the talking."

"What talking!" The boy writhed but Sarah kept him pinned down.

"Hallo, Mr Malone."

"Good morning, Sarah."

Sarah was in no position to pull her skirt down from around her hips so she contented herself by sitting tight with her hands folded demurely in front of her crotch, school blouse and tie crisp and neat. Her companion took one squint up at the figure against the sun and clapped his hands over his face to hide his agonies of embarrassment. He groaned in despair.

"Sorry if I interrupted anything, Sarah. I've come by to see Ellen if she's in."

"I think she is. I hope she is." Sarah paused, and decided that introductions were in order. "This is Detective Sergeant Mike Malone. This is a friend, Mr Malone."

"I guessed he might be."

The hapless boy gave another groan and wished a hole would open and swallow him. In a way his wish was being partly granted because Sarah was gripping him with Rottweiler tenacity to prevent his escape and keep him still.

"Isn't he supposed to be gardening?" Malone enquired. "No. No. Don't answer that. Sorry to have disturbed you both. I'll be on my way. Carry on." He turned and disappeared through the trees.

"Christ," said Sarah wistfully as she began pumping again. "Isn't he just gorgeous? He really is the most shagable bloke I've ever met." She added by way of encouragement, "I reckon his is bigger down than yours is up."

"I should be getting back to work," the boy complained.

"I haven't finished yet." She lifted her hips just a little too high and squeezed just a little too hard with the result that her companion's now unenthusiastic pecker was expelled from its prison with a soft plop. "Oh for Christ's sake!" she complained, looking down at the wretched object. "What fucking use is that to man or beast?"

But Sarah, ever resourceful, determinedly ground herself back and forth on the hapless lad's flaccidity to build an erection of sorts that provided two orgasms of sorts.

"Anyway," she said, standing and stepping into her panties. "What *is* your name?"

"I've fucking forgotten," moaned the shattered boy.

Twenty-Eight

There were loud cheers from the crowd when Prescott stepped on to the platform erected beside the water hyacinth sewage treatment plant. His two blackshirt bodyguards, armed with a shot-gun each, stood behind him, their eyes alert, scanning the throng.

The secondary treatment plant had been built on a flat area of common land south of Pentworth. It was a very simple structure that consisted of a long, brick-built tank, 200 metres long, 10 metres wide, but only 300 centimetres deep. Floating on the 2000 square metres of formerly foul water was a magnificent carpet of water hyacinth – half a million of the impossibly blue flowers, giving off a wonderful scent as they fed greedily on the pollutants in the water, purifying it and growing at a prodigious rate in the process.

"In Florida they call the water hyacinth the 'beautiful nuisance'," Prescott's voice boomed over the loudspeakers after he had wel-comed everyone to the simple opening ceremony. "It spreads at a tremendous rate, choking waterways if it's not kept in check. The wondrous spectacle you see here are the progeny of a few plants cultivated by an enthusiast to keep his aquaria clean. By this time next year the government hopes that three more such treatment works will be completed." He looked quizzically at a man in overalls. "All ready, are we?"

"All ready, Mr Prescott."

"Very well, ladies and gentlemen. I declare the Rother Water Hyacinth Treatment Plant open!"

The crowd gathered around the discharge valve as it was opened and cheered lustily when sparkling, clean water gushed into a culvert that bore the water into a ditch. A man at the other end of the long tank opened a valve to admit polluted water at the same rate to maintain the level. When the out-flowing water became discoloured, both valves would be shut to allow the hyacinth to work on the new charge of polluted water. Prescott held a tumbler in the outlet stream and raised the full glass above his head so that everyone could see it. The water was so clear, it was almost invisible.

"Looks good!" he declared, and sniffed the tumbler's contents. "Smells good!" He drank the water in one long swallow. "And, by golly – it tastes good!"

It was an effective theatrical gesture, though the purpose of the treatment plant was not to provide drinking water, but to ensure that water returned to ditches and waterways was pollutant-free.

Prescott returned to the microphone to tell the crowd how hard the government was working to improve their lot. He said his farewells and hurried back to Government House in his methane-powered, armoured Range Rover to a meeting with Vernon Kelly. The chairman of the bank group was being entertained by Diana Sheldon in his office. He brushed aside Prescott's apologies for being a few minutes late.

"Miss Sheldon and I listened to the opening on the radio, Mr Prescott. A worthy project, I must say."

"A *cheap*, worthy project," said Prescott, settling at his desk. "Just a big, shallow tank with an inlet valve and an outlet valve. The biomass of the dead hyacinth will be used to produce alcohol. Unfortunately not all government projects are so cheap, which is why we need a loan." Prescott refilled his guest's sherry glass, poured one for himself, and added, "But we can't afford the extortionate interest rates being charged by the banks."

Such plain speaking made the banker uncomfortable. "I hardly think four per cent is extortionate, Mr Chairman."

"It is when you're paying out a paltry one per cent on deposits," Prescott replied. "And grabbing most of that back in trumped-up, invented bank charges."

"We have an unexpectedly high level of deposits, and the banks have few outlets for investment."

"In other words, we need to get the economy moving?"

"Yes – but the opportunities are so limited, Mr Chairman."

"Well you haven't missed any opportunities to raid your customers' deposits to keep the banks' economy moving," Prescott observed.

"The banks are just like any business making a charge for its services," Kelly replied.

"Not like any business, Mr Kelly. All businesses present invoices – you just swipe the money straight out of accounts."

"We try to be of benefit to our customers—"

"We've got a scheme in mind that will benefit everyone," Prescott interrupted. He placed an unusual telephone on his desk. The base unit and handset were a glossy moulding in green, but in place of buttons, there was a lever-operated plunger that fitted neatly into a recess.

"Selby Engineering produced that," said Prescott. "Moulded papier mâché, would you believe. Smart, eh?"

Kelly, mystified, agreed that it was.

"A modern version of the old-fashioned hand-cranked phone," said Prescott. "Making automatic phones is beyond our capabilities, but Tony Selby says his company can make manual switchboards to serve over a thousand lines. And he's confident that he could gear-up production to make one thousand five hundred phones like this one over a three-month period."

"One thousand five hundred phones?" Kelly queried, a little less mystified now.

"One for every household and business plus a stock of spares."

"Well, if it can be done," said the banker cautiously, masking his astonishment. "It would certainly generate the revenue."

"A free service like the kiosks," said Prescott pointedly. He held up his hand to silence the banker's protests. "If it's free, we would have no trouble recruiting pensioner volunteers to man the switchboards. A free service means no staff tied up in disputes over bills, or chasing unpaid bills or bogged down in accounting. The benefits to the community would be incalculable – particularly in rural areas. A telephone system requires hardly any energy to run. A small methane-burning generator would be all that's necessary to keep the exchange's batteries topped up. Once the network's up and running, maintenance and operating costs would be reasonable. Around eight full-time staff. But the installation costs will be high. We can use many of the existing lines, but our plan for a free connection and phone installation for every dwelling and business is going to be expensive to set up."

"I'm surprised we've got the cable," Kelly commented sourly.

"It's amazing just how much copper wire there is in a washing machine motor. Kilometres of the stuff. We need to crop some pine plantations to free up some Forestry Commission land, so we'll have plenty of poles. A surplus in fact."

"You seem to have thought of everything."

"Good planning," said Prescott smugly. He had omitted to mention that the only reason the service would be free was because Selby Engineering had said that it would be difficult to make reliable billing meters, and manual logging would be cumbersome, therefore he had decided to make political capital out of the problem.

"Except you haven't thought through how to finance it," said Kelly pointedly.

"I have in mind an undated loan at a fixed two and a quarter per cent. Interest repayments only. Like building society permanent interest bearing shares."

Kelly had no taste for a loan at a derisory rate of interest that would never be paid off. He began to see what was behind Prescott's thinking. He was losing support in the rural areas. This way he would be going some way to redress the grievances of the country at the expense of the banks. What Kelly didn't realise was that Prescott's plans went even deeper than that. The new exchange would be sited in the Government House annex that was being built by knocking through into Mothercare. Manual exchanges allow for easy eavesdropping and would tighten his grip on the community.

"You don't look too happy," said Prescott.

"There are other ways for the government to raise money."

"Such as? And you can forget bonds."

"Well . . . Get the radio station to take ads, then privatise it. You could do much the same with the bus company, the laundries, water and the supplies centre – the post offices."

"Yes – but those services are paid for out of people's income taxes, transaction taxes and property taxes. We'd be selling them something they already own."

"It's been done before," said Kelly.

Prescott looked doubtful. "Well – perhaps it's something to think about in the long term. In the meantime I'm keen to get the phone service off the ground."

"I will have to bring the matter up at the Joint Banks Committee meeting."

"Ah, yes. I hear their credit card scheme is nearly complete."

"All it needs is the government's green light," said Kelly cautiously, scenting trouble.

"I can't see that being withheld, Mr Kelly," said Prescott expansively. "And think what a boost a phone system would be for credit card sales. Telephone ordering. Confirmations of purchases, etcetera. You could even close a few branches and go in for telephone banking. Of course, I don't wish to anticipate the reaction of the Joint Banks Committee but I should imagine that they'll be only too delighted with my proposals."

Kelly gave a noncommittal grunt. Prescott beamed and raised his sherry glass. "Let's drink to the success of both our schemes, Mr Kelly. Your papier mâché moulded credit cards and my papier mâché moulded telephones."

Twenty-Nine

The first thing Malone noticed as he jogged into Ellen's rear garden was the fresh coat of paint on the inside of the open back door. Hardly out of breath despite the long, uphill slog, he bent to examine the door and was puzzled. It had certainly been in need of repainting, but not with emulsion. Also no attempt had been made to scrape away the original paint where it was cracked and lifting. Nor had the jamb or the outside of the door been repainted although it needed it. He doubted that Ellen was slapdash – quite the opposite, he considered.

He saw a paintbrush bristle embedded in the fresh paint and teased it out with a fingernail for a closer look. It wasn't a bristle, it was a fine, short black hair that one would expect in a small watercolour brush. But no one in their right mind would repaint a door with an artists' brush. Besides, the flat finish on the door had been achieved with a roller. Then he discovered more of the black hairs, and that new screws had been used to reset the mortise lock.

Some chewed-up holes in the middle of the door caught his attention. Obviously fresh because they were filled with the emulsion and not grime like some of the cracks. When he stood back he saw that the holes formed an inverted T pattern.

In his remarkable mind he formed an impression of the horror that may have taken place here. An impression that hardened to a certainty when his gaze swept the garden and he saw a patch of recently disturbed soil beneath an apple tree, a spade leaning against the tree, and a few drops of what could be dried blood on the doorstep. The clincher was the legend "EX2218", just discernable under the new paintwork when he held the door at a certain angle to catch the light. The fear that he had been nursing for Ellen's safety for so long became a hard knot.

"Hallo!" he called out in a loud voice, and rapped hard on the door. "Hallo! Anyone at home?"

He went through the still room to the workroom just as Ellen came through from the shop. She was wearing a white laboratory coat and little else judging by the tantalising gaps between the straining buttons. Her initial surprised expression, tinged with fear for a fleeting moment, changed to a genuine warm smile.

"Hallo, Mike. Checking on my lousy security? I have to leave the door open to let some air through. Especially when I'm brewing up eye of newt and tongue of bat." There was bitterness in her voice as she gestured to a stainless-steel catering urn that was simmering on a charcoal burner.

"How are you, Ellen?" As he expected, there was no sign of the cat feeding bowl he recalled seeing on his last visit.

"Fine. Fine. Keeping busy. So what is this nice surprise in aid of? Business or pleasure?"

She didn't look fine. The rich lustre seemed to have gone from her hair. Her wonderful eyes were drained of their customary vitality and yet, to Malone, nothing could impair her loveliness.

"Bit of both, really," he replied. "I've come to crave some information and a favour. Hope you didn't mind me coming up the back way. It's quicker than going round the town."

"No – of course not. It's lovely to see you. How about some tea? The water's boiling. I'll go and shut up shop for a bit." She was gone before Malone could object.

"I don't want to interfere with business if you're—" He began when she returned.

"What business?" she interrupted.

"Oh." Malone was nearly lost for words. "Like that, is it? I would've thought you'd be inundated."

"I am. I'm working all hours keeping the hospital dispensary supplied. But I don't get so many customers through the door now. Not town, anyway. Country – yes."

The answer added to Malone's mounting concerns for Ellen's safety. "Why is that, do you suppose?"

"Sorry, Mike. I'm forgetting my manners. You look whacked. Grab a seat."

Malone sat. He repeated his question while Ellen busied herself at the urn.

"It's hardly surprising really," she replied, working the plunger on the burner's air reservoir. There was a hiss of escaping compressed air. The charcoal glowed white. "The town has the hospital on its doorstep – dishing out my medications at a subsidised price. Also town people can check with the dispensary from phone boxes before making a trip. Country folk don't have that advantage. They've got used to coming to me, so they keep coming to me." She paused. "And these idiots sacrificing chickens in church porches and churchyards don't help. Years ago my mother used to run this place as an occult shop. Quite a few people still remember it. The radio said that another church had been vandalised in the night."

"A private chapel at Tillington," said Malone. "The usual blood, feathers and bits of chicken scattered about. Which is one of the reasons why I'm here. Do you have any idea who could be behind these attacks, Ellen? The chapel was the ninth. The thing's getting out of hand."

Ellen shook her head. "I've no idea at all, Mike. There was a wart-charmer in Chiddingfold but that's Farside and I think she died a year or so back. I think it's bored kids out to make trouble. The summer is a quiet time for witches and Satanists – most of their rituals are around the spring and autumn equinoxes. These childish outrages don't make sense at the best of times – even less so at this time of the year."

Malone was silent. He had formed a bored kids theory and discarded it. The desecrations were too well-organised. Every church and chapel was being picked off, some getting repeat visits.

"My turn, Mike. What's this favour you're after and do you have to wear a policeman's cap to ask it?"

"'Fraid so. It's about Dan Baldock's Country Brigade."

Ellen placed two mugs of tea on the workstation and sat down. "What about it?"

Malone was sidetracked by Ellen tipping some greyish powder into her mug. "What's that?"

She smiled wanly. "Don't worry, Mike. It's a salicylate I've extracted from willow. Aspirin in other words. A bit rough but it works. I've got a headache you could stuff and mount. So what's worrying you about the Country Brigade?"

"David's on the general staff?"

"A stupid name for a committee."

"A dangerous name for a committee, Ellen. 'Country Brigade' is a dangerous name, too. These things can become self-fulfilling. So far they've stayed within the law by acting as a deterrent with their presence on delivery wagons. I've heard that they're holding a full meeting on Sunday evening. I'd like to be invited. To go openly to advise them in a friendly way as to what is legal and what isn't. I don't want to see any of them get into trouble with the law – not with the way it's being administered now."

"Brad Jackson's parents are members," said Ellen thoughtfully.

"I guessed."

"Do you think Prescott will hang him?"

"I don't doubt it for a minute. The scaffold is finished and has been tested with a goat."

"God help us all," Ellen muttered.

"Have a word with David, please, Ellen. I'll give my word not to reveal who was there. OK – policeman's cap off."

"In that case, what was really behind Cathy Price's death?"

Malone didn't like the question but was careful not to show it. There were aspects of Cathy's supposedly accidental death that troubled him deeply. His hunch was that she had been driven to suicide.

"I was off duty at the time. All I know is what was in the radio report. That she'd been drinking heavily at a private party, and took it into her head to go for a drive after she'd been dropped off outside her house."

"Was there alcohol in her blood?"

It was the first thing Malone wanted to know when he learned the tragic news, but Government House had vetoed the expense of a post-mortem. "I'm sorry, Ellen, I know it sounds like a cop-out, but I really can't comment before the inquest."

Ellen sipped her tea in silence for a few moments. "I never really got to know her. But she enjoyed life, even when she was disabled. Since then she's had so much to live for. She was a good driver and she knew the A285 well."

Malone had visited the scene of the accident on the morning after the accident. There were no skid marks to indicate that the Jaguar had braked – it had driven in a straight line off the road. The manager at the garage where the car had been serviced, now converting government-commandeered vehicles to run on compressed methane, had produced an MOT test certificate copy and service reports that showed the car to have been in excellent condition. "If it wasn't suicide then it must've been an error of judgment," the manager had commented. "After all, she hadn't driven for several months."

Malone drained his mug. "This is good tea, Ellen."

"Another?"

"Please."

She took his mug to the urn and rinsed it in a squirt of hot water, standing with her back to him.

Malone thought of a way of steering the conversation. He didn't want to hurt Ellen but it had to be done. He chuckled. "Remember the time I made tea in here that night when those brats painted that message on your shop front?"

"How could I forget?"

"EX2218," Malone mused. "I had no idea what it meant at the time. It looked like a telephone extension number."

Ellen didn't answer. She stood with her back to him, hands knuckle-white clutching the edge of the worktop, head bowed. He sensed rather than heard her tears and came up behind her.

"Ellen . . ."

Her reaction to his tentative touch took him completely by surprise. She spun around, pulled him close and buried her face against his sweatshirt in a futile attempt to suppress the powerful, shuddering sobs that welled up from her very core. His arms enfolding her were a warm, protective cocoon that allowed her to slough off her control, to shed her customary assertiveness and let her emotions follow a natural course. She cried. For how long she knew not, and cared not, for this strange man seemed to be a source of unselfish strength that she could draw on.

"Mike . . ." she said at length. "They killed him . . . They killed Thomas . . ."

"I know." His voice sounded distant and yet soothing. "You don't have to say anything."

"How do you know?"

"I'll tell you later."

"Tell me now – please, Mike."

They stood entwined, hardly moving, other than Malone's gentle stroking of her hair as he explained how he had deduced what had happened. That he was actually holding this divine creature, her every contour pressed against him, the scent of her body, her hair, filling his very being, made it difficult for him to concentrate on what he was saying. "As for that logo sprayed on your shop front, I racked my brains at the time as to what it could mean. I *had* to know because it frightened you so much and therefore it frightened me. I found the answer on my bookcase. In the Old Testament. And some digging in the library turned up that Hebrew curse. *Mekhashshepheh*. The May Day shout. I've heard it said since then. Always directed at you."

Ellen drew away slightly and looked up at him, the first time he had seen her face since he had held her. There was wonder in her eyes. "You've known? All this time?"

"Yes."

"And the curse? You've heard it since the May Day carnival?"

"Yes."

"I thought I was imagining it."

"I had to find out. I was worried sick about you. I still am."

Malone had other pressing worries; Ellen was still clinging to him – her breasts a disturbing pressure. His excellent control over his mind did not always extend to his body. He tried to ease back a little but she tightened her grip. To Ellen, that this remarkable man had been sharing something with her for several months enhanced the wondrous sensation of warmth and security she was experiencing in his arms.

"Ellen . . ." He traced her temple with his finger. "I've been running. Sweating. I must stink to high heaven."

"You smell wonderful, Mike." Before he could reply, she pulled his head down and kissed him, and the last remnants of her grief flowed from her like an ebbing tide. Her face became alive with a knowing smile. "And you feel wonderful, too."

"I ought to be going . . . You're busy . . ."

"I'd like you to stay a little longer." Ellen underpinned her desire with another kiss, longer, her questing tongue shredding Malone's reason, her hips moving gently against him.

"Ellen . . . It wouldn't be right – especially with the state you're in."

"It will be perfectly all right – especially with the state you're in."

Malone abandoned his rule about avoiding laughter and joined in. He scooped his arm under her thighs and picked her up without any apparent effort. "I seem to remember carrying you in here like this on that night, Miss Duncan."

Ellen relaxed, relishing his strength. This was something David would never do for fear that she might see it as an attempt to undermine her equality. Right now she was in favour of some serious undermining. She pressed her forehead against his temple and said mischievously, "Carrying me off the street is one thing, Mr Malone. But you'd never get me up the stairs."

Malone proved her wrong.

Thirty

Nelson Faraday did a good job.

Millicent Vaughan was not at her best having been dragged from her bed at 4 a.m.. She finished her examination of Brad Jackson's body that had been dumped on a stretcher beside an open coffin, and dropped her stethoscope into her bag. She wrote out a death certificate, signed it, and held it out to Prescott.

"Asphyxiation," she said curtly. "I'll send authenticated copies when I've finished my night's sleep."

"Thank you, Doctor," said Prescott. His fingers shook slightly as he took the form. "Please invoice Government House a hundred euros for your professional services."

Millicent could think of nothing to say without the risk of losing her self-control. She snapped her bag shut and looked around at the macabre tableau, illuminated by the harsh glare of a single floodlight. Every detail in the quadrangle of Government House would be etched into her memory for the rest of her life. Father Kendrick, clutching his missal, staring at Prescott, his pyjama trousers showing beneath his surplice; two ashen-faced witnesses; two blackshirts lifting the body into the coffin and screwing the lid down; a third taping everything with a camcorder. Towering over them was the high platform of the scaffold that Faraday was perched on, sitting swinging his legs, looking pleased with himself. Higher still and almost lost in the glare was the cross-beam with its rope hanging down through the open trapdoor.

She turned and went through the doorway that led to the lobby. Prescott followed her, trailed by his bodyguards. "I'm sorry it was such short notice, Milly. But this way, doing it twenty-four hours early, we nip any trouble in the bud. There was to have been an all-night vigil starting this evening. It could've led to trouble."

Millicent made no answer. She crossed the lobby and went down the steps into the dawn-lit, silent square. A blackshirt was holding the bridle of a pony harnessed to a cart, waiting to deliver the coffin to the executed youth's parents.

"If you need an escort home—"

"No!" said Millicent, stopping abruptly and turning to face Prescott. For the first time she had looked at him properly and saw something she had never seen before. His face was drawn with anxiety, as though the grisly event they had just witnessed had brought home to him the nature of the irrevocable step he had taken and its likely consequences.

"It would be wise—"

Milly gestured contemptuously to the hovering bodyguards. "I have nothing to fear from the people of Pentworth, Mr Prescott. Either from the town or the country. And please, don't ever again call me Milly." She turned and walked across the square, her heels echoing on the flagstones.

Prescott watched her for a moment. He turned to enter Government House and had to step aside for the two blackshirts bringing out the coffin. They slid it on to the cart, closed the tailgate quietly, and climbed aboard – sitting on the coffin. The driver flicked the reins and the cart set off in silence. The pony's feet were muffled with sacking and the cart's wheel rims were bound with rubber strips cut from old tyres.

Faraday appeared with a notice. "Just pin this on the door and that's the end of the matter, sir."

Thirty-One

M alone was in the library, reading a book on the origins of morris dancing, and trying to stay awake having worked a double shift, when his senses were sharpened by the sound of a diesel engine vehicle pulling up outside and doors slamming. Books were usually delivered by cart and managed to arrive without a lot of shouting.

Dennis Davies watched apprehensively as Malone approached his desk, thinking that the police officer had thought up some more questions in connection with Cathy Price. He had nothing to add: she had been sent on a fourth floor errand and that was the last time he had seen her alive, although he had heard that she had carried out the errand. She had seemed her usual self at the time.

"You don't normally have books delivered by truck, Mr Davies?" Malone queried, moving past the librarian and looking out of a front window.

"No, indeed," said Dennis, joining Malone at the window.

Below was a battered pick-up with a cargo of shotguns. Some sporting guns in smart cases but mostly they were farmers' working guns that had never seen a case since purchase. The vehicle had blackshirts guarding it while colleagues were unloading two firearms security lockers bearing Sussex Police logos.

Deeply concerned, but not showing it, Malone went downstairs to the lobby where Nelson Faraday was holding a clipboard while checking the contents of an ammunition box. Blackshirts were carrying shotguns into the lobby and dumping them on the floor.

"Looks like it's going to be quite a shooting party, Mr Faraday," Malone observed. "But it's still a while to the Glorious Twelfth. Out-of-season pheasant pie will make a nice change. Mind if I come?"

Faraday glanced at Malone and turned to harangue a blackshirt who was checking that a 12-bore was unloaded. "I said I wanted every one checked *before* they're brought in!"

"No point," said Malone. "They've all been checked at the nick."

"I'm busy, Malone."

"Glad to hear it, Faraday. I wouldn't like to think of you hanging about with nothing to do."

Two blackshirts came through the door carrying one of the Sussex Police firearms lockers.

"This is the one with the Sterling submachine-gun and the magazines, Mr Faraday," a blackshirt reported.

"One can't help wondering what Sussex police want with such a weapon," Faraday commented.

"It was handed in by a member of public just before the Wall appeared," said Malone.

Faraday ignored the police officer.

"Let me guess," said Malone. "Our Chairman has issued a directive that the armoury is to be transferred here?"

"Perceptive of you, Mr Malone. We have better security here than you have at the police station. And as Mr Prescott is the firearms issuing officer, it makes sense to move everything here. If you will excuse me – I'm busy."

Malone jogged to the police station, where Russell Norris, one of the original police constables, was on duty. He showed Malone the strongroom – which had been piled high with seized and impounded weaponry, mostly shotguns – was bare. There were craters in the walls where the steel cabinets had been jemmied free.

"What the hell was I supposed to do, Mr Malone? They came in mob-handed with a seizure warrant signed not an hour ago by Mr Prescott. I phoned his office and they called back to say that the warrant was genuine and that I was to co-operate. I tried calling you."

"I'd left my radio on charge," said Malone, his face impassive as he surveyed the stripped armoury. "Even the CS gas has gone."

"They were thorough," said the morris policeman ruefully. "They've had everything away, including that Sterling. They were in and out in fifteen minutes." He grinned and pulled a police baton from his breeches. "They didn't find this, though."

"I feel better already," was Malone's droll reply.

Thirty-Two

Anne Taylor looked at the envelope in dismay. "Oh, no."

Vikki paused in her task of checking the tyre pressures on her bicycle. "What's up, Mum?"

"I've a horrible feeling that this is Pentworth's first junk mail." She peeled open the envelope carefully so that it could be reused. Its contents confirmed her fears. It was a letter from her bank. Mounted at the foot was an embossed papier mâché credit card with a small-print interest rate that spelt big profits. The letter said that the government were to allow ten per cent of bank deposits, frozen when the Wall appeared, to be converted to Pentworth euros.

"Ads on the radio, more money in circulation, and now credit cards," she sighed. "We're going back to all the bad old ways."

Vikki started pumping her rear tyre. "Maybe I could become a double-glazing salesman when I leave school?"

"I really think you should give today a miss, Vikki," said Anne anxiously, bending the credit card back and forth while wishing that Vikki would use her left hand properly. To continue to ignore such a wonderful gift from God was wrong.

"But it's Saturday, Mum."

"You worked yesterday *and* the day before."

"I promised Miss Duncan that I'd be in everyday that she needs me now school has broken up," Vikki replied, stowing the bicycle pump. "She's got a lot on her plate. Sarah's working all hours, and besides, the radio said that the town was quiet."

"I don't believe anything I hear on the radio any more," said Anne emphatically. "With the hanging this morning, there's bound to be trouble." She succeeded in tearing the credit card in half.

"A day early, Mum. No one would've had time to organise anything."

"But a *hanging* . . . Dear God, and to think that I thought the Wall was a good thing."

"We all know it was Brad Jackson that raped Debbie French

138

last year," Vikki replied, mounting the sports machine. "He had it coming to him."

Anne wondered what was happening to the liberalism she thought she had impressed on her daughter. "You'll be back by two?"

"I thought I'd go and see Sarah after I'd finished. She hates being back with her mother."

Anne raised no objections. She had sensed that Vikki had been wanting to tell her something for several days and hadn't pushed her. Boy problems, she thought. Understandable that she'd rather confide in a close friend. "All right then, Vikki. Give Sarah my love. And bring back a fresh loaf. Yesterday's delivery was stale, and I'm out of flour. You'll need a box." Anne went into the house and reappeared with a Tupperware container. Most goods were supplied loose and shoppers had to provide their own containers. Household refuse was now a thing of the past; and all organic waste went on compost heaps.

Vikki crammed the box into her saddlebag.

"Come straight home if there's the slightest sign of trouble," said Anne worriedly.

"I will. "Bye, Mum – and please don't worry. I'll be OK." She blew Anne a kiss and pedalled into the lane.

As it happened, Radio Pentworth had been telling the truth. The town was going about its Saturday morning business, although there was an impressive turnout of hard-faced blackshirts in Market Square, looking hot and uncomfortable in riot gear. A sprinkling of morris police were chatting with home and allotment growers and even helping them set up their market stalls and unload handcarts. Any likely trouble arising from the vigil outside Government House planned by the Country Brigade had been spiked by the early morning news report that Brad Jackson had been executed at 4.30 a.m. – a day early. His distraught parents had passed a message to their supporters saying that his body had been delivered to them.

Nelson Faraday at an upstairs window in Government House focused his binoculars on Vikki as she cycled along the opposite side of the square, her golden mane tangling provocatively around her face; sunlight catching the fine hairs on her slender legs, a short skirt riding up, lifting off bronzed thighs in the breeze. A foul cocktail of lust and hatred surged and heaved in him like a backing-up sewer. So many scores to settle with that cock-teasing little bitch and her friend, Sarah Gale, who had kneed him in the groin during the May Day celebrations. The Gale girl was a slut, but he reckoned that pretty little Vikki Taylor was still a virgin. He reckoned he could tell – breasts still pert, arse tight and clenched.

Not a virgin for much longer, bitch! And when I've smashed away your tightness, I'll turn you over and start again – show you what real pain is.

The finale was him staring into those green eyes, wide with terror, as he fitted the noose around her neck. She was sixteen now which meant that as from midnight, when the new law had come into force, she could be hanged. Which side for the knot? People's bodies were slightly asymmetrical – heavier on one side than the other, particularly women. One breast was always larger than the other. The knot went on the opposite side so that the imbalance helped with a good, clean break of the vertebra at the knot. Get it wrong and they danced, usually pissing and crapping themselves, making it necessary to grab them around the thighs, lift and jerk down hard to break the neck. With Ruth Ellis old Albert Pierrepoint had used a spyhole to watch her taking a bath in her cell at Holloway Prison. No need to spy on Vikki fucking Taylor – he would know where the knot should go. Or maybe he would deliberately botch it? A drop too short for her weight so that she strangled to death? Yeah – why not?

He checked that his Handie-Com's selective calling tones were correctly set and pressed the PTT key.

"Go ahead," said Roscoe.

"She's arrived for work."

"Excellent. I'll get busy."

Yes, thought Faraday, returning the radio to his pocket. She would most assuredly hang.

Vikki turned into North Street. The high wall of Pentworth House on one side of the narrow street and the shoulder-to-shoulder houses and shops on the opposite side stirred a sense of foreboding in her. The atmosphere in North Street was always dank, even on sunny days like today, but now it seemed even colder and the gloom more oppressive. The stares of passers-by were hard and unfriendly.

"Country scum!" a passing carter sneered as she was wheeling her bicycle into Ellen's shop. She had learned to ignore such insults, although it was worrying that perfect strangers seemed to know who was country and who wasn't. The town had become worryingly clannish.

"Good morning, Vikki," said Ellen brightly. "Tea's ready. Today I'm going to show you how to use the pill press Tony Selby made me."

The girl was astonished by the transformation in her boss. Ellen's hair brushed and shining, a freshly ironed white coat, some make-up, and she was actually smiling – something Vikki hadn't seen for several days. "Has Thomas come back?" she asked, glancing around the workroom as she pulled on a pair of plastic gloves. She had been so concerned about the missing cat that she had put a card in the window.

"Oh – he'll turn up when it suits him," said Ellen dismissively. "He's done it before. I've decided that there's no point in worrying about him."

"Probably taken up with someone else," said Vikki, matching Ellen's mood. "We've got a cat like that. Fickle as a February freckle, my mum says."

"Let's hope she doesn't teach anyone else to say it."

"She didn't want me to come in today."

"Because of the hanging?"

Vikki nodded. "Mind you, it was no more than that Brad Jackson deserved. Everyone says so."

"Everyone does *not* say so," said Ellen severely. "I don't say so, for one. And there're a lot of people that agree with me. I was going to take part in the vigil in Market Square tonight."

Vikki sipped her tea. "But I thought all the townies were in favour, Miss Duncan? Brad Jackson being country."

"Yes – well I'm not a so-called townie, any more than you're so-called country. God – I loathe this moiety that's evolved. We're a tiny community facing a massive crisis – the last of humanity, for all we know – and yet we're turning against one another."

"We're not the last of humanity," said Vikki with uncharacteristic conviction that took Ellen by surprise.

"And what makes you so sure, young lady?"

Vikki seemed to regret having spoken so emphatically. Ellen repeated her question. The girl made no reply but stared into her mug. Ellen started wheedling. She was a tenacious wheedler.

"Because I was told!" Vikki blurted in exasperation.

"By whom?"

"The visitors."

Ellen opened her mouth to speak and fell silent. She could see that the girl was distressed. She pulled a chair close to her and put an arm around her shoulders. "Do you want to tell me about it?"

As it happened Vikki had been aching to talk about her strange summons to the lake by the visitors. Sarah had been understanding, but Vikki wanted an adult to talk to. Mother would've worried about her daughter having religious visions. Ellen was always a sympathetic listener but Vikki was no longer confident of a friendly hearing from the older woman.

"You'd think I was lying, Miss Duncan."

"That I know you could never do, Vikki. You always tell the truth as you see it. So tell me in your own time. There's no hurry."

The story of Vikki's nocturnal summons by the visitors to Pentworth Lake came out. A little disjointed – Ellen had to ask her to go over some points until the account was complete. There was one omission: Vikki could not bring herself to tell Ellen about her regenerated left hand.

Thirty-Three

"For God's sake, Adrian. Can't it wait? Does it have to be today of all days?"

Prescott was more than deeply concerned, he was scared, but he did his best to conceal this from Roscoe. That morning he had received two death threats. The crude letter that had been sneaked into the lobby didn't worry him too much, but the phone call from a public telephone box did. The caller knew the codeword for the operator to put the call straight through to his office, and had disappeared by the time two blackshirts had raced to the kiosk.

The cobalt-blue eyes regarded Prescott steadily. "It is for God's sake that it has to be today," he said coldly. He held out a sheaf of papers across Prescott's desk. "I want this arrest warrant signed and I want seven men to execute it. *My* men, Asquith. Let us not forget that. I'm not leaving without them or without your signature on this warrant."

"You don't realise what a powder keg we're sitting on," Prescott protested. "This coming right after the hanging—"

"The situation is of your making," Roscoe replied curtly. "The hanging was nothing to do with me. The Witchcraft Act came into force at midnight. I will have to account to God for every minute I delay in bringing that whore daughter of Satan to justice."

"This will all blow over in a week. Surely God will understand a delay?"

Roscoe's gaze hardened. "I do not presume to second guess the Almighty. As your new regulations stand, this warrant has to be signed by you. You drafted the regulations, Asquith."

Prescott inwardly cursed Diana Sheldon and Judge Hooper, wishing that he'd spent more time going over the wording of the order. The judge's advice had been that warrants dealing with serious matters had to be issued by the elected government. The Town Clerk had drafted the legislation accordingly. It all seemed sensible and logical at the time. The trouble was that he hadn't thought through the consequences. Those consequences were now a white-gowned figure, arms folded, intense blue staring down at him, waiting for him to speak.

"I can't sign your arrest warrant just yet, Adrian. Maybe by next Tuesday or Wednesday—"

"I will not tolerate any delay!" Roscoe snapped. "It has to be now! We have a deal. I've provided you with a trained force and used my influence and powers of oratory to support you all the way! I even risked my life and the life of several brethren sentinels to stop that foolish attempt on the Wall of God!"

"It'll mean keeping her in custody over the weekend. She's not going to go anywhere. So, please, Adrian—"

"I will not be thwarted in my duty to God!" Roscoe's voice came close to a scream of rage. He pulled a Handie-Com from a gown pocket. He raised the radio to his mouth, his finger resting on the PTT key. "Very well then, Asquith. If you can't stick to a deal, then neither can I. I will order the closure of the Pentworth House bakery."

Prescott was trapped. The whole community depended on Roscoe's bakery. Not only were the methane-gas-fired bread ovens non-polluting and kept going around the clock by three shifts of Roscoe's now skilled bakers, but most of Pentworth's stock of EU grain had been moved to Pentworth House's silos, behind Pentworth House's high walls. If the unthinkable happened and the bread stopped, he would be facing trouble from the town *and* the country, and he couldn't count on the loyalty of the blackshirts in a showdown because Roscoe had stepped up their entertainment facilities in Pentworth House.

He thought fast, groping desperately for options but there were none. He was beaten. There was nothing for it but to hold out his hand for the warrant.

"You'll have to sign each copy individually," said Roscoe, handing him the papers. "This new paper's too thick to use carbon paper."

Prescott thumbed through the documents one by one, not reading them, signing and stamping each copy in turn at the bottom. "Seems a lot of copies," he muttered.

Roscoe shrugged. "Don't blame me for your creaky bureaucracy, Asquith." He took the papers and smiled thinly. "Thank you. This puts our relationship back on an even keel and you can be assured of my continuing support in the trials that lie ahead. Following God's path is never easy. Good day to you, Asquith."

He turned and left, sweeping imperiously through Diana Sheldon's office, ignoring everyone until he met Nelson Faraday halfway down the stairs. The blackshirt chief was looking resplendent in his favoured head-to-toe black garb, his crimson-lined black leather cloak fastened at his throat by a gold chain, his cavalier boots gleaming.

"Get your men ready, Nelson."

"He signed, Father?"

"Both warrants. We have the witch's infernal acolyte as well."

The sudden gleam in Faraday's eyes matched his boots.

Thirty-Four

"**M**r Malone," welcomed Dennis Davies. "You received my note?"

Malone propped himself against the library counter. He had been on duty for eleven hours and was exhausted. "I did indeed, Mr Davies."

"I have the book right here. I knew I'd seen it. I came across it quite by chance when going through the crates." The librarian placed a well-used book on the counter. Its plain buckram binding was worn, the endboards hanging by threads. "*The End of the Witches*, Farrow Press, 1924. It must be quite valuable. Please be careful with it."

"But with respect, Mr Davies, this isn't the book I was after."

"I've had to put the *History of Witchcraft in England* on the lost books list. Probably stolen by whoever's been carrying out these atrocities. I hear they sprayed runes or something on the gates of Pentworth House last night. Shocking when you think of the trouble Father Roscoe goes to keep us supplied with his delicious bread and milk. But this book contains a great deal of source material on witchcraft trials that was used in the missing book. It seems appropriate in view of the Witchcraft Act that's just been promulgated. I thought it might be of interest to you."

Malone was puzzled. "Witchcraft Act? What Witchcraft Act?"

"Why, the James the First Witchcraft Act that's been resurrected to deal with all these despicable acts of desecration. The proposal has been on our Government Notices board for some days now. Quite fascinating, really. James the First was a strange man. Before his time. Anti-smoking, you know . . ."

But Malone didn't listen to the librarian's views on James I. His tiredness forgotten, he strode to the noticeboard, so crowded with overlapping government announcements and information leaflets as to render it useless, and hunted through the dozens of documents. "Where is it?" he demanded.

Dennis joined him. "It must be here somewhere. I remember reading it before it was pinned up. Ah, yes – well hidden."

Drawing-pins scattered on the floor as Malone yanked the stapled sheaf of close-typed sheets off the board and started reading. The mass of sections and clauses made little sense, but the preamble said enough to cause his pulse to quicken in alarm.

"Good God," he said at length. "There's been nothing about this on the radio."

Dennis rescued the drawing-pins. They were an important part of his life. "There are so many government orders and notices issued these days. I suppose reading them out would—"

"When does it come into force?"

"It's already in force. It came in at midnight . . . Mr Malone – don't forget your book."

But Malone had gone.

Thirty-Five

Ellen was at a loss when Vikki finished her account. A dream. It had to be. But a sleepwalking dream? Was it possible to sleepwalk three kilometres across country at night in a dream? Yet it had to be so because Vikki would not have invented the incident about her being picked up and taken home by a morris police patrol.

"You *do* believe me, don't you, Miss Duncan?"

Ellen patted the girl's knee. "Yes – I believe you, Vikki. No one would go wandering that distance at night without good cause or coercion." She looked quizzically at the girl. "Did they say why they've come here, of all places?"

"Sort of. But I didn't understand what they meant."

"What concerns me is what the visitors said about sending a man."

"They didn't say so in so many words. As I said: pictures kept sort of forming in my mind. But it was a man."

"Did you see his face?"

Vikki struggled to remember and shook her head. "Sort of. All mushy and vague. I think I would recognise him if I saw him but I couldn't draw him or describe him."

"And they implied that he was some sort of saviour?"

Vikki's forehead creased. "Well – not as such. It was just an impression I got. But what was clear was that he wasn't ready. That's what they said – he wasn't ready." She looked steadily at Ellen. "But he will come. That I do know."

Both women jumped at that moment at a loud crash from the shop as the front door burst open. Boots on the hardwood floor. Voices. Vikki jumped up in alarm when Nelson Faraday marched into the workroom followed by blackshirts in riot gear, carrying batons. The security chief was dressed as he had been on the night of the Pentworth House party when he had tried to rape her.

"What's the meaning of this!" Ellen demanded furiously, thrusting

148

herself between Faraday and Vikki. "What the hell gives you the right to come storming into my shop like this? Get out!"

"These give me the right," Faraday replied, waving the warrants. "Eleanor Rose Duncan and Victoria Taylor. You are both under arrest and will be taken from this place to another place where you will be charged with being witches engaged in the making of potions, spells, and the uttering of blasphemies and other evil deeds to summons the devil and his disciples from hell. Contrary to the Witchcraft Act of 1604. OK – take them."

Vikki gave a scream of terror when two blackshirts grabbed her and pinioned her arms behind her back. Ellen's response was to snatch up her black-handled herb knife, but Faraday was too quick for her. He grabbed her wrist and twisted savagely, causing her to whimper in pain and the knife to clatter to the floor. He picked it up and pressed its point under Ellen's chin while two blackshirts held her and a third seized her around the thighs to prevent her kicking.

Faraday increased the pressure under Ellen's chin with the knife point. He yanked Vikki closer to him by her hair with his other hand and smiled at the look of abject terror in the young girl's green eyes. "Now, Miss Duncan. You can either come with us and not give us any bother, or you can watch while we take it in turns to fuck and bugger this pretty little bitch to within a centimetre of her life. Which is it to be?"

Despite the knife point, Ellen's aim was good. The glob of saliva caught Faraday full in the face. He released Vikki and wiped it away, following through with a savage swipe across Ellen's cheek that drew blood. Her head went back but she didn't utter a sound. Faraday glanced around the workroom and pulled a cork from a bottle. He jammed the cork on the tip of the knife and held it in the glowing embers of the charcoal burner until the pungent fumes of burnt cork filled the workroom. The blackshirts looked on with interest. Their boss was remarkably inventive as they and Cathy Price had learned.

Faraday turned to Vikki and tore her blouse open, pulling it down hard so that it was wrapped around her arms at the elbows. Ellen had imbued her with courage for she made not a sound, not even when Faraday used the knife to cut through her bra and rip it away. He paid no attention to her exposed breasts but turned his attention to Ellen. Ripping her lab coat open all the way down took more effort. Buttons bounced and skittered across the floor. All she was wearing underneath were thin cotton panties. The blackshirts stared lustfully at her breasts and the shadow of her pubic hair as Faraday jerked the coat down around her arms. He used the burnt cork to draw a large, bold cross on his victims' chests, nipple to nipple, throat to navel. He stepped back to admire his handiwork and grinned at them in turn.

"You'll need all the protection you can get. OK. Enough messing about. We'd better round up some evidence and get going. Mustn't keep the magistrate waiting."

A small crowd of gaping onlookers was forming along North Street as the unlikely procession set off with Faraday leading the way, blackshirts flanking Ellen and Vikki, stumbling along with prods from behind. Vikki's head was bowed, tears splashing on to the road, but Ellen was steadfastly upright, returning the accusing stares of onlookers, willing them to avert their gaze which many did.

"Witches!" someone hissed. "Her all along. Just like her mother."

They were a hundred metres from Ellen's shop when Malone arrived, running from the direction of the town with three morris police struggling to keep up. Malone sized up the situation quickly and realised that there was little he could do against eight men. He spoke to the morris police and they fanned out across the road, staffs held level to form a barrier.

The procession halted with Malone and Faraday confronting each other.

"Good morning, Mr Faraday," said Malone affably, not looking at Ellen.

"Out of our way, Malone."

The police officer shook his head sadly. "You'll never make a policeman, Nelson. Arrests should be kept as low-key as possible. Public displays like this are most undesirable and certainly illegal."

Malone pushed past the blackshirts and stood before Vikki. He pulled her blouse over her shoulders and drew it closed.

"They're my prisoners, Malone! You'll leave them alone!"

The police officer gave the terrified girl an encouraging smile and tucked her blouse into her skirt, noticing that she was wearing plastic gloves. He moved in front of Ellen. Faraday pulled back his cloak and produced a .45 revolver. He levelled it at the police officer's head but didn't pull back the hammer. A mistake because Malone missed nothing.

"You leave them alone, Malone!"

Malone ignored the threat. He drew Ellen's white coat closed and fastened it with the two remaining buttons.

"For God's sake, Mike," Ellen whispered. "He's mad – he'll kill you."

"You do as I say, you scum!" Faraday howled, tightening his finger on the trigger.

"It's a magistrate's committal hearing," said Malone quickly and quietly. "Who's your solicitor?"

"Harry Sheldon – Diana Sheldon's father. But he's very ill."

"I'll have a word with her and Vikki's mother. I'll do what I can and see that the shop's secure."

Ellen nodded. Malone moved clear of the procession and signalled his men to the kerb. He turned to face Faraday, seemingly unconcerned by the gun levelled at him. "Just like to see that everything's orderly on the streets, Nelson. Can't have displays like that. Most improper. Carry on."

Faraday lowered the revolver. As he did so, Malone moved with astonishing speed, spinning his body on one foot and bringing his other foot around in a blurred arc. The trainer connected with Faraday's hand, sending the revolver spinning into the air which Malone caught deftly. Faraday gave a cry of pain and clutched his wrist. Malone's warning look to the blackshirts as he hefted the .45 was enough for them to remain frozen. He moved closer to Faraday and lowered his voice. "If these women come to any harm in your custody, Nelson, you had best relish each morning that you wake up and find yourself alive because there won't be many of them left. You won't know where or when the end will come, but come it will, and very soon. Trust me."

With that he broke the .45, ejected its shells into his hand, and pocketed them and the gun.

Faraday's face was pale. The speed and deadly accuracy of the kick combined with Malone's calm, almost matter-of-fact tone had frightened him. His wrist felt as though he had tried to stop a train with it.

"That gun's been issued to me, Malone."

"I'll look after it until you've learned how to handle them. Best to use two hands with S and W .45s, Nelson. Their kick can dislocate a shoulder . . . My kick can dislocate a life." Malone gave an icy smile. "See you in court."

Thirty-Six

M alone reflected that Dan Baldock was a better organiser than he had supposed. The barn was packed with about a hundred farmers, and their families for this third full meeting of the Country Brigade. They were angry, all wanted to have their say about their grievances but Baldock kept good order from a rostrum that consisted of scaffold boards laid across oil drums. David Weir, looking haggard with worry, and two other members of the brigade's so-called general staff were sitting at the table.

None of those crowded into the barn were remotely connected with Prescott. Two of his tenants had turned up at the beginning of the meeting, claiming that they were dissatisfied with their landlord, but they had been escorted off the farm. Several youngsters were patrolling the outside on the lookout for spies.

Malone and Anne Taylor were sitting in plastic chairs in front of the rostrum. Anne's eyes were red-rimmed from crying that day but she was now composed, sitting with her hands folded on her lap, her grief over the arrest of her daughter temporarily forgotten as she listened to Brad Jackson's mother recount the harrowing events before and after her son's execution.

Malone knew Freda Jackson. It was inevitable considering the number of times her eldest offspring of six had had brushes with the law. She and her common-law husband scratched a meagre living from two hectares of downland that her great-grandfather had claimed nearly a hundred years ago. A small, tired-looking woman as a result of years of hard work and too many pregnancies. To Malone's surprise and gratification, she had spoken in favour of allowing him to be present at the meeting, describing him as a decent bloke even if he was a policeman.

"They just banged on the door and dumped his coffin on the step," she was tearfully telling the gathering. "No by your leave or nothing. *And* they wanted me to sign a receipt for his body."

There were murmurs of indignation.

"Can you imagine how Will and me felt? Five in the morning.

152

Poor Brad being hung a day early . . . We didn't have a chance for any last prayers or nothing." She dug into a pocket of her jeans and held up a scrap of paper. "And today we get this – a bill for his coffin!" Her tears became a flood. She was unable to continue so Baldock guided her into David's care. She sat at the table sobbing quietly to herself with David offering what comfort he could.

"So that's the way things are," said Baldock grimly. "We've been patient." He raised his voice. "We've put up with having our goods seized! We've had hygiene inspectors ordering the destruction of livestock on a whim. We've been accused of withholding supplies! We've been set upon! Beaten up by townies! They killed Freda's boy and dumped his body on her doorstep! And now they've arrested Ellen Duncan and Vikki Taylor on crazy, trumped-up charges of witchcraft!"

Each point was greeted with a chorus of angry shouts.

"So we take a vote on it! All those in favour of stopping all food supplies to the town!"

There was a loud roar of approval and a forest of hands went up. Malone was immediately on his feet, signalling for Baldock's attention. Their brief conference ended with Malone jumping nimbly on to the stage, and Baldock holding up his hands for silence.

"Right," he said when uproar had subsided. "Mr Malone would like a word."

Malone's commanding presence was sufficient to still all conversation. "Nothing I can do or say and nothing you can do or say can reverse the terrible wrong that was done to Mrs Jackson's son," he began. "But what we can ensure is that such a thing doesn't happen again." He glanced at David and Anne in turn. "I'm sorry to have to say this with Vikki's mother and David Weir present, but Ellen and Vikki face the death penalty if they're found guilty."

"What's this got to do with the Country Brigade?" someone called out from the back. "We were set up to defend the rights of farmers and growers."

There were a few noises of assent.

"Upholding your rights and freedom means little unless you're prepared to uphold the rights and freedom of others," Malone replied.

"Yeah – the word is that you applied to the magistrate at the hearing this morning for Ellen and Vikki to be held in police custody, Mr Malone. So don't go bleating about rights and freedoms to us."

David spoke for the first time. "That was Jeff Dawson, wasn't it?"

A stocky figure pushed his way to the front. "Yeah. It was me."

"You've got it wrong, as usual, Jeff," said David. "Mike applied for police custody for Ellen and Vikki to prevent the blackshirts holding them. Ellen had a terrible bruise on her cheek from the blackshirts that arrested them. The magistrate didn't like the look of it, so she agreed. Vikki and Ellen are being looked after by a WPC and the morris police at the police station and will be during the trial."

Dawson shrugged. "So I got it wrong. I still say it's nothing to do with the Country Brigade."

"It's got everything to do with us," said Freda Jackson suddenly. She left the table and stood beside Malone, facing the crowd which immediately granted her a respectful silence. "Can I speak, Dan?"

"Go ahead, Freda."

She stared angrily at the sea of faces. "When my Brad was put in the stocks, Ellen Duncan was the only one that faced up to Prescott and got him released. She got the keys and done it herself. Undid the lock and freed him. The square was crowded with people all yelling and jeering at Brad. She didn't think nothing for her own safety – she done what she thought was right." Her scathing gaze roamed over the crowd. "Pete Linegar. You told me yourself that Ellen's medicine was the only one that helps your Dawn with her fits. What will happen to her if Ellen's hung like they hung my Brad? Mary – what about that time when you was on your back in agony with sciatica? Who was it who came up with a painkiller that worked? Ellen Duncan. A lot of us here owe a lot to Ellen. And as for Vikki Taylor, what harm has she ever done anyone? As sweet a kid as you could wish to meet. Just sixteen years old and those bastards want to see her hung.

"Mr Malone's right – I know Brad was no saint – but he didn't deserve to die and nor do Ellen and Vikki. If they do because we've done nothing, then we'll be as much to blame as them that did it." She glared at the audience, ready to meet any challenge but none came. She thanked Baldock and returned to her seat.

"Freda's right," said Baldock. "We have to do something about Ellen and Vikki. The question is, what?"

"We could storm Government House," said Jeff Dawson. "A thousand of us should do the trick. Clear out the whole rotten nest and release Ellen and Vikki at the same time."

The idea of direct action had wide appeal.

"That sort of thing is best discussed by the general staff," said Baldock with a warning glance towards Malone.

154

"It's best not discussed at all," said Malone bluntly. "There are now over eighty blackshirts. Your shotguns and cartridges which you handed over to the police, and police firearms are now in an armoury on the top floor of Government House."

"That's right," said someone at the front. "My brother had the job of converting a storeroom into a strongroom."

Malone mentally photographed the speaker with the intention of having a word with him afterwards. "You'd be cut to ribbons," he continued. "Yes – I know that there are fifteen shotguns that haven't been handed in or seized, but what use would they be against the blackshirts with plenty of cartridges and even some semi-automatic weapons? It would be carnage."

"Government House would burn nicely, Mr Malone."

David spoke up. "And what good would that do? Yes – I know how aggrieved many of you feel about the lack of services in rural areas but on balance Pentworth has a reasonably well-run administration under Diana Sheldon. I know her – I've complained to her often enough on your behalf – and I know that she's doing her best to redress many of your problems. The enemy is Asquith Prescott and Adrian Roscoe. They're the reason why Ellen and Vikki are in such danger."

"So we assassinate the bastards!"

"Something Freda's son tried," said Malone drily. "Those two have plenty of protection now. Prescott doesn't move anywhere without two armed bodyguards, and his Range Rover has armour plating inside."

"Thank you, Mr Malone," said Baldock, a sarcastic note in his voice. "We have a motion to put to the meeting. All those in favour of the Country Brigade giving priority to Ellen and Vikki, please raise your right hand."

There was a solid show of hands.

"All those against?" He counted the showing. "And ten against. The motion is carried. But what worries me, Mr Malone, is that you haven't come up with any ideas on how us pussies are going to hang a bell around the cat's neck."

"Let's worry the cat sick by doing nothing for the time being," said Malone wryly. "The trial of Ellen and Vikki doesn't start until Monday and will probably last three or four days. Once it's underway, we'll have a better idea of what to do."

"A cop out," Dawson sneered. "First you say you want to do something positive and then you're against doing anything. Let's face it, Mr Detective Sergeant Malone – you're a policeman first and foremost. You took an oath to uphold the law and that's why you're here. Prescott's tame monkey."

Malone regarded the stocky man dispassionately. "The laws I swore to uphold did not include persecuting people for witchcraft and the hanging of innocent people, or even guilty people. I will promise you this much, Mr Dawson, I will have a plan to prevent Ellen and Vikki meeting the same fate as Freda's son. And if I have to resign from the force to carry it out, then I will do so."

Thirty-Seven

Nelson Faraday lay sprawled on his bed in Pentworth House nursing a bruised wrist and a bruised ego, and saw no reason why Claire Lake, the blonde who was doing her best to please him, shouldn't be the target of his venom. He grabbed her by the hair in frustration and jerked her tear-stained face up to his.

"How long have you been here? A year now?"

She nodded.

"Long enough to learn how to do it properly. For fuck's sake, no wonder your husband ditched you."

"I'm sorry, Nelson. I'm doing my best." And then she was crying again.

Faraday was tempted to hit her but this one was useful in the dairy and was one of Father Roscoe's favourites. "Well keep trying," he muttered.

The girl went back to her task. The trouble with her, as far as Faraday was concerned, was that she was too old. Twenty-five/twenty-six – at least ten years too old, although she looked younger. He closed his eyes and imagined that she was Vikki Taylor. Soon he wouldn't have to do any imagining. The problem was that it was going to be a proper trial like Brad Jackson's trial. The judge had nit-picked over every bit of eye-witness evidence as though he wanted the little bastard to get off. But this case was different. It would be convulsed with argument and counter argument. The evidence against the Duncan woman and little virginal Vikki Taylor might not stand up. Faraday had been in enough courts to know what was good evidence and what wasn't.

He twisted around so that he could open a drawer in his bedside cabinet where he kept his private papers. He managed it without interfering with the girl's ministrations, and removed an envelope. Inside was a Polaroid picture of the witch's black cat nailed to her back door. A neat job that he hadn't been able to resist photographing with the last exposure in the pack. Luckily Father Roscoe didn't know about it. "Do whatever is necessary to frighten her, Nelson,"

157

had been his instructions. Well he had certainly done that. And this photograph, handled right, was evidence – good, solid evidence that would ensure Vikki fell into his clutches.

He had an idea and pulled Claire's head away. "Forget it," he said shortly. "You're worse than useless." He tossed some keys at her. "Those fit the witch's shop. There's a handwritten card taped inside the window about a lost black cat. Go and get it."

Thirty-Eight

There was no sign of His Honour Judge John Harleston-Hooper's acerbic sense of humour as he surveyed the hot, crowded little courtroom over his half-moon spectacles. Ellen Duncan sitting beside Victoria Taylor in the dock. The older woman gripping the brass bar, the girl keeping her hands out of sight. Both staring at Adrian Roscoe, resplendent in a pure white gown as he addressed the jury. The women were certainly bewitching. But witches? Ha!

The trial of Brad Jackson had been straightforward enough, quick but properly conducted – he had seen to that. That the penalty for Jackson's crimes had been death wasn't his fault: politicians decided penalties. But this case was Kafkaesque. A seventeenth-century Act of Parliament being used in the twenty-first century. An act that had been deemed absurd in its day and repealed in the eighteenth century, now back on the statute books as a result of all manner of convoluted legal gymnastics in which he had played an unwitting part. He bitterly regretted the opinion he had provided Prescott regarding the almost unlimited powers of a colonial governor. A terrible mistake. He could picture the lord chancellor pacing up and down his office when this confounded business of the Wall was over.

"What the devil were you thinking of, Hooper? Didn't it occur to you that there's a huge difference between the conferring of the powers of the Crown and Parliament on a colonial governor – someone who has been carefully selected for the post from hundreds of well-qualified people – and such powers being assumed by an ambitious, social-climbing nonentity like Asquith Prescott?"

Right now the ambitious, social-climbing nonentity was sitting on a reserved bench, his florid features impassive as he listened to Roscoe droning on in his opening address about the evils within Pentworth and how it was the Christian duty of every man and woman to cauterise the evil – banish it back to hell whence it came.

Prescott was seething with anger, not only at Diana Sheldon for electing to defend the women, but at the way Roscoe had duped

159

him over the arrest warrants, but more than that – he was frightened. Badly frightened. Dear God – two women in the dock, not only on absurd charges, but facing the death penalty if found guilty. One of them a sixteen-year-old! The very last thing he wanted. His hope lay with the jury: six men, six women. The number of challenges from Diana Sheldon to arrive at the present mix had taken up the entire morning. All twelve faces devoid of expression. He told himself that they couldn't convict – that they wouldn't convict. He studied their faces in turn, searching for clues as to what they were thinking during Roscoe's rant, and found nothing.

Chanting outside: "HANG THE WITCHES! HANG THE BITCHES!" Not his supporters. He'd asked Faraday to move them away from Government House. The blackshirt chief's men had moved some of the demonstrators. Now they were back. Not loud. But loud enough to carry through the courtroom's gaping windows to maintain Prescott's cold sweat. The blackshirts were loyal to Faraday, and Faraday's loyalty was with Adrian Roscoe. God dammit – he should've created his own security team.

And why hadn't there been a word from Vikki Taylor's mother or Ellen Duncan's supporters? No deputations; no demonstrations – nothing. What the hell was going on? He was uneasy. The courtroom was too crowded. Had everyone present been checked for concealed weapons? Another ten minutes and he would return to the safety and blissful cool of his air-conditioned office.

Roscoe turned to Judge Hooper. "That concludes the opening for the prosecution, Your Honour. I will now introduce the exhibits – the accoutrements of witchcraft – that were removed from Ellen Duncan's shop at the time of her arrest."

Judge Hooper nodded to Roscoe to proceed. He glanced at Diana Sheldon, sitting at a separate table with David Weir. It had worried him that the Town Clerk was defending and he had expressed his misgivings to her in his chambers. She had pointed out that Ellen Duncan and Vikki Taylor had appointed her and that there could be no clash of interest because the judiciary and the town council were supposedly quite separate. Her forthrightness had surprised him – she was no longer the mouse-like daughter of his old friend, Harry Sheldon.

Someone had supplied her with a bulging wallet of handwritten notes on witchcraft. Obviously not her work, the way she was working her way through them – often soliciting David Weir's opinion on handwriting. It all smacked of no proper preparation, although whoever had done the research donkey work had been busy.

A serious case carrying the death penalty and no silks defending or prosecuting – something that had also worried him during Brad Jackson's trial.

The other damnable thing was that he knew the prisoners but what could one do? In a small community like Pentworth, everyone knew everyone. As a governor of St Catherine's, he had presented Victoria Taylor with a special prize for bravery when she was twelve. Ellen Duncan provided him with a monthly medication that worked wonders for his gastric problem. The whole wretched business had placed him in a legally dubious position and he resolved to make life difficult for those who had engineered this absurd situation.

Witchcraft indeed.

The only consolation, if it could be called that, was that under Prescott's absurd legislation, responsibility for sentencing the accused, if they were found guilty, rested with the Mesne Lord of Pentworth Manor – Adrian Roscoe.

Diana rose, looking neat and professional in a close-fitting cashmere skirt and top. Prescott looked away from her withering stare.

"Yes, Miss Sheldon?"

"Your Honour. The prosecution has made much of an obligation placed on the Lord of the Manor of Pentworth over three hundred and fifty years ago by the so-called Witchfinder General Matthew Hopkins in which he called on him and the people of Pentworth to hunt down and bring witches to justice.

"As a result of painstaking research in the library, which Your Honour will appreciate is our only source of information these days, I have a list of several references by reputable historians in which they assert that Matthew Hopkins was not what he claimed. Of particular interest is a summary by Ivan Bunn, which I wish to read out with Your Honour's permission."

Roscoe spotted the judge's sudden interest and was on his feet. "Your Honour – historians bicker and argue among themselves as to what is fact and what is fiction or myth." He picked up the vellum letter signed by the witchfinder. "We have several depositions from experts stating that this letter is undoubtably genuine."

"I don't think Miss Sheldon is disputing the authenticity of the letter, Mr Roscoe – merely the credentials of the writer. Go ahead, Miss Sheldon."

Diana quickly scanned through some handwriting clarifications of Malone's copious notes on Ivan Bunn's findings and began reading aloud:

"'Matthew Hopkins started his witch-finding activities at

Manningtree, Essex, early in 1645, assisted by John Stearne and Mary Philips. At the time Charles the First was on the throne, but was preoccupied with the English Civil War and not effectively ruling the country. Some sources claim that Hopkins had been commissioned by Parliament to discover witches. However no names or authority are mentioned, and there are no records of a commission being granted to him. Most historians now agree that this claim is probably incorrect and that his role and title were self-appointed. Even the use of the title "Witchfinder General" is doubtful. It only appears once and that is on the frontispiece of his book *The Discovery of Witches* (London 1647). Everywhere else in the book and in all other contemporary records he is referred to as "witch-finder". In reality both Hopkins and Stearne were probably self-appointed Puritan zealots with a fixation and fear of witchcraft who set themselves the task of discovering witches and bringing them to justice under the Witchcraft Act of 1604.'"

Judge Hooper held out his hand for Diana's document. "And your list of library citations, please."

The court usher passed the papers to the judge who glanced through them quickly. "Interesting . . . Your researcher appears to have been busy." He looked up. "Mr Roscoe. If these references are substantially correct – and we have some respected historians cited here – it may put your prosecution in a very different light." Roscoe rose to object but the judge continued. "I would like to study these sources, therefore court is adjourned until 9 a.m. tomorrow. We'll have an early start and beat the sun."

"My God," Diana muttered to David who was exchanging smiles and waves with Ellen as she and Vikki were escorted from the dock by a woman police constable. "I do believe we're going to get a dismissal."

Thirty-Nine

A drian Roscoe did not share Diana's optimism. He dined that evening in his apartment in Pentworth House with Nelson Faraday as his guest.

"The trial is going according to plan, Nelson," he said, his eyes glittering in the candlelight. He had refused to broach the subject until Theta had brought in the brandy.

Nelson was puzzled. "According to plan, Father? I thought things went badly today?"

The cult leader gave a dismissive wave. "Hooper is difficult, but what judge isn't? He is bound by the law as it now stands and he knows that the trial has to continue. If he does anything silly, then we appeal to Prescott, and Prescott orders a retrial and appoints another judge. Prescott doesn't want it to come to that – he wants a proper judge presiding."

Faraday chuckled. "He's livid over the arrest of the Taylor bitch."

Roscoe swirled his brandy in the crystal balloon. Only ten bottles left. But there'd been a good crop of cherries, so maybe it would be possible to make some. "Understandable. He fears that a sixteen-year-old on trial will rebound on him. But he underestimates the strong feeling in the community against witchcraft. The jury is with me, and that's all that matters. The trial should be over by Friday. I shall sentence them here on Saturday, and we will carry out the sentence on Saturday night."

"Saturday night, Father? But the traditional time for hanging is always early morning."

Roscoe smiled thinly and produced a typed carbon copy, which he handed to Faraday. "A detailed schedule for you, Nelson. Those old titles which Prescott dug up show that Market Square is part of my estate so I can't see any legal problems there. And, of course, such an event at night by torchlight will be much more dramatic. So much more memorable, and it will steer those who've had their minds poisoned back to the path of righteousness."

Faraday came to the procession details halfway down the page. "This is going to take some organising, Father. Torches will have to made. We'll need—"

"And who better than you to organise it, Nelson?"

"Setting the scaffold up in the square won't be a prob—"

"Read on," Roscoe interrupted.

Faraday read on and came to the last paragraph. He stopped reading and raised astonished eyes to his host.

Roscoe was pleased with his reaction. "What do you think?"

"Fantastic, Father. Really fantastic. A brilliant idea."

"Quite. I take your point about the traditions surrounding hanging, but there are even earlier traditions when it comes to the destruction of Satan's apostles that are worthy of consideration."

Forty

"Members of the Jury," said Judge Hooper the following morning. "Yesterday the prosecution made much of the fact that the Witchfinder General had tasked the Lord of the Manor of Pentworth with bringing suspected witches to trial." He gestured to a pile of books before him, their pages flagged with marker slips. "But the balance of probability is that Matthew Hopkins was a private citizen, with no royal warrant and no parliamentary commission to hunt for witches. He and his assistants acted off their own bat in the hunting and bringing to book of witches under the Witchcraft Act of 1604 – which they did with great zeal from around 1645 to 1647.

"However, the fact that Matthew Hopkins acted privately does not have any bearing on the legality of this prosecution. The act is extremely intricate but what we can glean from it is that the people, local justices, mayors, and lords of manors in particular had, or I should say 'have', a clear duty to bring suspected witches to trial. I've decided therefore that this trial should continue. Yes, Mr Roscoe?"

Not even Roscoe was a good enough actor to completely suppress his smirk of triumph as he rose. Ellen and Vikki, who had had their hopes raised after their meeting the previous evening with Diana Sheldon, looked utterly crushed.

"Thank you, Your Honour, said Roscoe. "I will now go through most of the various accoutrements of witchcraft that were removed from Ellen Duncan's shop at the time of her arrest."

"That the items on display belong to my client is not in dispute, Your Honour," said Diana.

"Exhibit One," said Roscoe, selecting Ellen's black-handled herb knife from a tray loaded with labelled exhibits and holding it up. "A witch's athame. Their ceremonial dagger."

The usher passed the knife to the judge who commented, "I have a similar knife at home, Mr Roscoe."

Roscoe smiled benignly as the knife was passed among the jurors and then back to him. "It is used by witches in their blasphemous

165

practices, Your Honour. It is representative of the phallus in the rite of cakes and wine. It is dipped ritually into the chalice. The dripping wine symbolises semen, the chalice is the female genitalia. Together they represent the sexual union of male and female."

"I use mine to chop onions."

Several jurors actually smiled at that and the usher got busy with a handkerchief.

"I think the old sod's on our side," Diana whispered to David.

"You thought that yesterday."

"Exhibit Two. Belladonna," said Roscoe, holding up a small green bottle. "Witches drop it in their eyes to dilate the pupils and so make themselves more attractive to demons with whom they wish to have sexual intercourse."

"It's proper name is atropine, Mr Roscoe," said Judge Hooper shortly. "I've got several of those bottles in my medicine cupboard. There's a herbalist in this town who prescribes controlled doses for my indigestion. She makes them from deadly nightshade. It works marvels, and for several of my friends, too." He paused and added regretfully, "Not too effective in matters of the occult, though. Neither they or I have ever been approached by demons with improper suggestions."

Several jurors and court officials laughed outright. Ellen managed a meagre smile but Roscoe appeared unmoved. Next he produced a box of black candles and a black silk scarf, both of which received similar derisory treatment from the judge. The last exhibit was more serious – a small cardboard box containing coin-like medallions bearing pagan runes and symbols.

"Witches arrange these hellish devices around their pentagram during their profane rituals," Roscoe declared. He started reciting the function and purpose of each item but was interrupted by the judge requesting that he examine the box. There was silence in the courtroom as Judge Hooper peered at each medallion in turn. Eventually he looked up and glared at Roscoe. "These are nothing but charms from a charm bracelet, Mr Roscoe."

"With respect, Your Honour – each one of those devices has a special pagan significance—"

"And here's the original bracelet," said Judge Hooper, fishing out a slender gold bangle from the box. "Ah – the catch is broken. No doubt that's why the charms are kept together in this box."

"They are all pagan artifacts," Roscoe insisted calmly.

"Well of course they are. That's the whole point of charm

bracelets." The judge glanced around the courtroom. "Does anyone have such a bracelet?"

A woman juror put up a tentative hand.

Judge Hooper grinned. "Ah, you're wearing one. May we see it, please?"

"Does Your Honour want it admitted as an exhibit?" the clerk of the court demanded frostily.

"Hardly necessary, Clerk," the judge replied. He took the juror's bracelet from the usher and examined it, comparing its charms with those in the box. "Would you believe it, I've found four identical charms," he announced. "No doubt there are more."

Diana rose. "Your Honour, all the exhibits the prosecution have produced so far have been mundane household objects. Unless he is about to produce a levitating broomstick and a long black, pointed hat, the defence requests that they be ruled as inadmissable."

"I can't do that," said Judge Hooper, hiding a smile. "But it's likely that I'll have something to say on the matter in my summing-up."

Roscoe produced his first witness who claimed he had bought a packet of witches' tea from Ellen's shop some years before but he couldn't remember exactly when.

"But the label definitely stated witches' tea?" asked Roscoe. "Are you absolutely certain?"

"Absolutely," agreed the witness. "I remember telling the wife that it would make a good present for her mother. And she got mad at me and started throwing things."

"Let's see what else you can remember about the label," said Diana when it was her turn to cross-examine. "Can you remember the name of the shop that was printed on the label?"

"Well – it would've been Earthforce, wouldn't it?"

"I don't know," said Diana drily. "I wasn't there. It could've even been called the Wicca Basket—"

"That's it! The Wicca Basket. Remember it clear as a bell now. Spelt W-I-C-C-A. Even I can spell wicca proper."

"Your Honour," said Diana. "I shall be producing documentary evidence showing that the Wicca Basket, spelt as the witness says, was the name used by the shop's previous owner, Miss Duncan's mother. Miss Duncan changed the name to Earthforce when she became the owner."

"Yeah – but it was her that sold it to me," said the witness pointing to Ellen. "And it definitely said witches' tea on the label."

"Have you ever bought Earl Grey tea, Mr Street?"

The witness was nonplussed. "What?"

Diana repeated the question.

"Yes – but not from her."

"But you have bought it?"

"Well – yes. I like it. Can't get it now, more's the pity."

"When you used to buy Earl Grey tea, did you buy it from Earl Grey?"

Witness perplexed. "No – dunno where his shop is. I used to get it from Mr Patel who owns our local Mace shop."

Roscoe next called Harvey Evans. The former police inspector was an old hand in court and gave his full details after taking the oath without being prompted. But in all his years, he had never been so apprehensive on entering the witness box as he was now.

"You are a keen microlight pilot, Mr Evans?" was Roscoe's opening question.

Evans' apprehension deepened. He avoided looking at the dock. "Yes."

"You used to fly around this area a great deal before God put His Wall in place?"

"We don't know who or what put the Wall in place, Your Honour," said Diana, rising.

The judge nodded. "Rephrase your question please, Mr Roscoe."

"You used to do a great deal of flying around this area?"

"Yes."

"Low flying?"

"Yes."

Too many leading questions for Judge Hooper's liking but it had come close to having to subpoena Harvey Evans to get him into court, therefore he decided not to intervene.

"You have related to a number of people that you once saw a woman dancing naked at the Temple of the Winds."

Evans remained calm. He had never revealed Ellen's name as the dancer to anyone. Roscoe was shooting in the dark. "Yes," he said at length.

"Did you recognise her?"

God – if only he'd kept his mouth shut in the Crown. "Yes."

Diana rose to ask if the questions were relevant on the grounds that the Temple of the Winds was not part of the Pentworth estate and never had been. Roscoe countered that the questions were relevant as he intended to show. Judge Hooper allowed the examination-in-chief to continue.

"So who was this naked woman dancer, Mr Evans?"

More for the benefit of Ellen than the court, Evans replied, "I can state quite categorically, under oath, that I have never disclosed the name of the person."

"I can understand your discretion, Mr Evans," said the judge. "But the prosecution seem to think it important. Is the lady in court?"

Evans, realising that he was trapped, could only nod.

"If you would point her out, please."

Levelling a finger at Ellen seemed a worse betrayal than uttering her name. "Ellen Duncan," he answered reluctantly. "But I couldn't tell if she was dancing. She *seemed* to be dancing about. There's a difference – particularly when you discover that you've been sunbathing on an ants' nest."

"Pure conjecture," said Judge Hooper severely.

Roscoe smiled. "So . . . she was naked and she was dancing. Thank you, Mr Evans. No more questions."

Diana rose to say that she did not wish to cross-examine.

Dennis Davies, looking grave and uncomfortable, was the next prosecution witness to take the stand. He gave the oath and agreed that he was the chief librarian. Diana frowned when he was called and whispered urgently to David.

"Mr Davies," said Roscoe. "You have received many thousands of books in answer to government appeals for donations?"

"About half a million volumes. It's going to take weeks to catalogue them all."

"Have you received entire libraries or collections?"

"Yes."

"How many?"

"Three significant collections."

"Would you detail them, please."

Dennis glanced at the judge. "The largest collection were the law books donated by Mr Justice Hooper. Then there was a science-fiction collection of about two thousand paperbacks." He hesitated. "And Ellen Duncan's remarkable collection of books on the occult, witchcraft and black magic."

The jury were noticeably surprised.

"What is so remarkable about it?" asked Roscoe.

"It's an extraordinary collection. It contains some rare volumes such as the *Book of Shadows*, and a complete set of the *Equinox* – an occult magazine published by Aleister Crowley between 1909 and 1913, and all of his other works including a first edition of his *Book of the Law*."

"*Aleister Crowley*, members of the jury," said Roscoe, spitting the name with venom, "was the most notorious Satan worshipper that has ever damned the face of this planet. He called himself the Great Beast 666 – the creature from hell referred to in the Book of Revelation." He turned to the witness. "You will, of course, be destroying these infernal works?"

The idea of destroying books appalled Dennis. "The collection may be the only complete set of Crowley's works in existence. They are—"

"They are the works of Satan!" Roscoe thundered, his eyes blazing with the intense blue of Cherenkov radiation. "It's unthinkable that Pentworth has the only complete set! And that daughter of Satan sought to spread the obscene word of her Prince of Darkness master by putting those books in the library where they would poison the minds of all decent men, woman and children and turn them against God! Is it any wonder that the Almighty has damned us with His Wall? And we will remain damned for eternity unless we destroy this evil that we are nurturing to our innocent breasts!"

Judge Hooper had to use his gavel to stop Roscoe's outburst. He spelt out in blunt terms that he would not tolerate such behaviour in future. Roscoe bowed and apologised, looking pleased at the impact his tirade had had on the jury. Several were now staring at Ellen with a mixture of loathing and contempt.

"Is there any doubt," Roscoe continued, "that the collection is the property of the accused or is it possible that it came from someone else?"

"None whatsoever. I collected it myself from her flat over her shop with a handcart after she told me about it. A wooden crate."

"Thank you, Mr Davies. No further questions, Your Honour." Roscoe sat, pleased with his witness and even more pleased with Diana's shaken expression. She rose.

"No questions, Your Honour."

The rest of the day's hearing consisted of a string of witnesses that Roscoe had unearthed, all of whom testified that Ellen had sold them books on potions and spells *after* she had taken over the shop. Diana did her best to challenge their memories but what little success she had was overshadowed by a witness who produced a belated exhibit – a ten-year-old receipt, signed by Ellen, for several witchcraft publications.

At 4 p.m. Judge Hooper decided that everyone had had enough and adjourned the trial until the next morning.

Diana angrily gathered up her papers, stuffed them in her briefcase and marched out of the emptying court with David following in her wake.

Outside, blackshirts and morris police kept the placard-waving group back as the Commer van returning the defendants to the police station nosed out of the narrow entrance that led to Government House's stables. The demonstrators were a small group but they compensated for their size with a barrage of insults and catcalls. Some managed to bang on the side of the van. David ran after it, waving frantically, and was rewarded with a brief glimpse of two frightened faces at the rear windows before the vehicle sped away. He joined Diana at a table outside the Crown and ordered two ciders.

"I'm sorry," he said lamely.

She shook her head. "It's not your fault. Ellen should've told me."

"How was anyone to guess that her handing over a crate of her mother's books that had been kicking around for years could have such repercussions?" David complained. "I mean – it's so damned absurd. I've donated some Inspector Frost whodunits to the radio drama group. R. D. Wingfield is the equal of Agatha Christie at keeping one guessing. I enjoy his books, but does that make me an advocate of murder?"

Diana regarded David steadily. "Is there anything else I should know? Anything at all? It doesn't matter how inconsequential it may seem."

David wondered if he ought to tell her about the crucifixion of Thomas but decided that there was no point. There was no evidence as to who had carried out the terrible act, and making unfounded accusations would be unlikely to help Ellen's case.

"I can't think of anything offhand," he said.

"I just have this uncomfortable feeling that something's being held back from me. Something vital that Roscoe knows . . . Well . . . I shall have to give both my clients a good grilling this evening."

Her assertiveness surprised David. But he was constantly being surprised by the change in Diana Sheldon over the months. She was no longer the shy, retiring woman he remembered when he had first joined the town council. "Give Ellen my love," he said. "I only wish to God I was allowed to see her."

"She understands. Not even Vikki's mother is allowed to visit. I think that's hard. The poor kid's scared out of her wits. Still – at least they're being well looked after."

Their drinks arrived. They were silent for a few moments as they quenched their thirst.

"Roscoe worries me," Diana said at length. "When he first started with all those silly exhibits, I thought he was going to blow his case. But he was merely playing all his weak cards first. He's doing well for someone with no legal training. He's a shrewd operator."

"He's a bigot," said David bluntly.

"A bigot with a following. Have you noticed how the jury always seem to perk up when he speaks?"

"It's his voice. Appropriate in his case that it should be as rich as a fruit cake."

"Perhaps. It makes me very uneasy. And there's something else that worries me . . . So far he hasn't come up with a shred of his so-called evidence to implicate Vikki Taylor. There's an exhibit in an envelope that he hasn't referred to yet. So what sort of nasty rabbits has he got up those monk's garb sleeves for us tomorrow?"

It was as well for their chances of a night's sleep that Diana and David didn't know just how nasty Roscoe's rabbits would turn out to be.

Forty-One

M alone knew he was being followed but was not unduly concerned, nor did he make any attempt to shake off his pursuer. There was little point because he was decked out for his daily jog in his fluorescent-striped white tracksuit and was as conspicuous as a chimney sweep on a glacier – especially now that a crescent moon had risen.

The mysterious figure had been following him across country for two kilometres. Young, whoever it was because they had been able to keep up reasonably well even when he had put on a spurt – it was the pursuer's panting that had been one of several giveaways. By the time he was skirting Pentworth Lake he decided to allow whoever it was to catch up. Few people in Pentworth were in as good physical shape as he was, therefore they were unlikely to be in any condition for a scrap. Also the pursuer was much smaller than him. A clump of trees and shrubs ahead would serve his purpose. He veered towards them.

The runner did likewise, losing speed on the slight rise, breathing hard, skirting the trees, stumbling on roots, and then saw Malone about a hundred metres ahead, standing quite still under a willow – probably taking a pee – the safety chevrons on his back showing up clearly in the moonlight.

The runner slowed to a walk, and then crept towards the still figure. At ten metres the follower seemed uncertain and stopped, peering at the quarry under the willow and looking furtively around before moving closer and then calling out in a tentative whisper.

"Mr Malone?"

"Right here," said a voice from close behind.

The pursuer gave a yelp of surprise and spun around. Malone was standing, arms folded, not two metres away, and was naked.

"You frightened me," the girl gasped.

Malone had spoken to her on only one occasion but he remembered the educated voice. "Good evening, Claire. Claire Lake, isn't it? One of Adrian Roscoe's Pentworth House dairy maids. If I recall, you were collecting information on children in the area on the morning that the Wall appeared."

"Yes."

"A clever move by our Adrian," Malone observed. "Supplying free milk to children. It won him and his looney brethren a lot of support, and solved the problem of what to do with the stuff."

The girl continued to gape at the naked man.

"You're a great disappointment to me, Claire. It's taken you six months to decide to follow me in order to have your wicked way with me. But I must warn you that I'm no pushover – I'll put up a struggle."

Consorting with naked men in the woods at night was outside Claire's experience. "I wanted to see you, Mr Malone," she stammered.

"Well you're certainly doing that." He moved past her and removed his underpants from inside his tracksuit that he had hung from the willow. He pulled them on, the girl watching bug-eyed as a formidable battery of male artillery disappeared under white cotton. "You must forgive me for taking off all my kit, Claire. I usually insist on keeping my underpants on during a first date, but being white, you would've seen them." He donned his tracksuit and sat down, patting the grass beside him. The girl accepted the invitation.

"So you knew I was following you all along?" she asked.

"Your breath control needs work. Your dark pants and top were effective enough but you forgot that lovely blonde hair. And slapping at mozzies now and then wasn't a good idea."

"But I was a long way behind you."

"They emit telepathic screams when they die."

Claire gave a little laugh that failed to cloak her nervousness. "I used to have good breath control when I did a lot of running. This was the only way I could think of talking to you – by getting permission to go out jogging. There are so many eyes in the town."

She glanced uneasily around at the hungry stomach of the waiting woodland shadows.

"And it has the advantage of making it impossible for those blackshirt heavies to follow you," Malone added. "They're all pretty well out of condition. So what's on your mind, Claire? Let me guess. Being a member of the Bodian Brethren is losing some of its charm?"

"It was wonderful when I first joined. I felt secure. Wanted. And Father Roscoe seemed the kindest man in the world."

With a little prompting from Malone she went on to recount a story of an unhappy marriage, being abandoned by her husband, losing a baby that she had ached for, and a drift into homelessness, hopelessness, and alcohol before she saw the brethren's recruiting Winnebago in Brighton and fell under Roscoe's influence.

"He gave me a job in the dairy and then promotion because he said I was a good organiser. There was company. Real friendship. Everyone sharing their problems. I didn't even mind the sex – sometimes three or more altogether. Sometimes just girls together; sometimes a mixture." She hesitated. "God forgive me, but I got to enjoy it, Mr Malone, and never felt used because it was like everyone was sharing their love around. I began to realise the way things really were underneath last Christmas. One of the girls hung some mistletoe in the temple. Father Roscoe went mad, really mad. He said that we had a witch in our midst and that the punishment he would mete out was nothing compared with God's punishment we could all expect unless whoever did it came forward. Ella owned up. She was stripped in front of everyone and whipped by the chief sentinel – Nelson Faraday. Do you know him?"

"I know him," said Malone tonelessly. He was listening to, not only the girl's story, but paying close attention to her voice – registering every little hesitation and change in timbre, and even the occasional unconscious shudder and catch in her throat – audio clues, almost impossible to fake, that told him Claire was telling the truth.

"It wasn't a hard whipping," she continued. "More ritual, but it was terrifying at the time. Then there was the Wall and we all had to work twice as hard. There were all those security men to look after. Then when they became blackshirts, Father Roscoe wanted the girls to keep them sweet. There was no feeling of love after that. Some of them are OK, but they're mostly brutes. One girl had a nipple almost bitten off. Another ran away and hid in the park. They used the hunt hounds to track her down. You know that the Chiddingfold and Leconfield Hunt have got their kennels in Pentworth Park?"

"Yes," said Malone. "I do know. Do you know what happened to Cathy Price?"

"Well – not much. Some of the blackshirts were boasting about what had happened . . ."

"Tell me."

"I don't know any details. Something about her going to a party in the blackshirts' room in Government House. I didn't know her – only heard her name – but for her to go looking for them – to seek them out deliberately. Mr Malone – she must've been a real nympho. I heard a blackshirt telling a mate what he'd missed . . ." She shook her head. "I don't believe them . . . They're all mouth, some of them."

Malone did believe and said nothing. He stared through the trees at the lake and the patterns on the water made by clouds drifting across the moon. Bats flitted in ghostly silence over the water. The plaintive cry of a nightjar. He thought about Cathy Price, the terrible scene at the gates of Seaford College and the speed she must have been travelling at when her Jaguar hit the stone pier. "Tell me about Nelson Faraday," he asked at length.

There was no faking the girl's sudden stiffening. "He's the worst," she said quietly. "When I first met him I was physically attracted to him . . . I must've been mad. Now my blood freezes whenever he touches me – thinking that his hands hanged that boy . . . just as they'll hang Ellen Duncan and Vikki Taylor. Roscoe wants Ellen Duncan and Nelson wants Vikki. He likes them young. He likes the youngest-looking girls to dress-up in schoolgirls' uniforms . . . To shave themselves . . ." She gave an involuntary shiver.

"They'll have to be found guilty first," Malone said casually.

"That's bound to happen – the way that Vikki Taylor grew a new hand."

Malone gave no outward sign that he was shaken but Claire sensed it and turned to him. "Didn't you know about her hand?"

"I knew," said Malone grimly, thinking fast. "I didn't know that Roscoe knew."

"That was my fault. It was just after the Wall appeared. I saw her getting out of her swimming pool using two hands when I was delivering milk . . . God – if only I'd kept my stupid mouth shut."

There was an uncharacteristic urgent note in Malone's voice when he spoke. "*If* Ellen and Vikki are found guilty, they'll be handed over to Roscoe for sentencing and for carrying out the sentence. Do you have any idea of what he's planning?"

"No . . . No – wait a minute. Some of the sentinels had to make torches in the workshop yesterday."

"What sort of torches?"

"Procession torches. Sacking wound around the end long sticks and left to soak in old engine oil. About a hundred of them. The girls were complaining that they couldn't get the smell of oil off their hands."

"Anything else?"

Claire shook her head.

"Can you find out? Faraday's certain to be the organiser."

She remembered the bedside drawer in Faraday's room that was full of papers. But he kept his bedroom door locked. "Well . . . I could try."

"You must, Claire. Do you know the Temple of the Winds?"

"Yes."

"Go jogging tomorrow night – tonight, that is, as it's gone midnight. Meet me there at eleven. Can you make that?"

"I'll try."

"Don't make any attempt to contact me if you can't. I'll wait an hour and I'll be there at eleven the night after."

"I'll be there tonight," Claire promised. She tilted her watch towards the moonlight. "I ought to be getting back . . . They said I could be gone a couple of hours." She looked uncertainly at Malone.

He smiled and touched her cheek. "Thank you, Claire. OK – go ahead – I'm still listening."

The girl looked puzzled.

"You want to tell me the real reason why you followed me, and I'm listening."

Claire's expression changed to that of surprise. "Can you read minds?"

"That would be useful. Sadly, I have to rely on less reliable clues."

"I'm six weeks pregnant," Claire blurted. "May God forgive me, Mr Malone, but I don't even know who the father is, but the chances are that it's Nelson Faraday." She suddenly seized his hand and gripped it with passionate intensity. "It doesn't matter who the father is – I want this baby. I want it so very much, but not with the Bodian Brethren, and not with Nelson Faraday claiming it as his. Please, Mr Malone – will you to help me escape?"

Forty-Two

Malone's four hours of sleep got the better of him. He actually had to pause a couple of minutes outside the police station to get his breath back.

"You're bright and early, Mike," observed WPC Carol Sandiman, looking up from her typewriter when he went in. She glanced at the duty roster. "Four hours early."

"Early – yes. Bright – no. Good morning, Sandy. Marry me, my beloved – I need a woman to keep my shirts as white as your blouses."

That the police officer found Mike Malone quite devastating made it difficult for her to sound severe. "I turned you down last week. Don't you ever give up?"

"How are our detainees?"

"So-so. I took them their breakfast half an hour ago."

"I'd like to see them please. Ten minutes."

"You know that would be in breach of the court order. Only their lawyer—"

"We were ordered to keep them in a secure place. I ought to check that it's secure. Ten minutes, Sandy. No one's due in for an hour, and you never saw me nick the keys."

"Mike – I shouldn't."

"I'll allow you to subject me to relentless sexual harassment for five minutes a day for a week."

"Ten minutes a day for a month."

"Done. You drive a hard bargain, missy." Malone pecked her on the cheek and took the keys from her desk drawer that she had obligingly opened while studying her typing.

He climbed the stairs to the disused two-bedroom flat on the third floor that had been hastily prepared for the prisoners, the double-glazed windows framed with heavy gauge chainlink fencing on the outside. He turned the double mortise key, calling out as he entered, and locked the front door behind him.

"Mike!" Ellen in a dressinggown rushed into the tiny hall and

178

threw her arms around him. She tried not to cry as she kissed him and clung to him with a strength borne of desperation and misery. "Mike – by all that's wonderful – I thought you'd deserted us."

Malone smiled at Vikki who was standing in the doorway, wearing a long nightdress, looking pale and distraught. "That I would never do. I've only got a few minutes, Ellen, Vikki. Are they looking after you?"

They went into a small sitting-room. A few sticks of 1980s furniture, cluttered with old magazines. Ellen sat beside Malone on the narrow sofa and held on to his arm, pressing her cheek on his shoulder, marvelling at the strength that flowed from this man.

Vikki looked at them uncertainly. "Do you want me to go to my room?"

"This especially concerns you, Vikki," said Malone, motioning her to an armchair. She sat and regarded him – her ordeal had not robbed her lovely green eyes of their bewitching quality. Malone noticed that she kept her left hand resting on her lap, fingers half-clenched, seemingly lifeless. Her man's watch with its broad leather strap completed the illusion that the hand was artificial.

"They've got little enough on me," said Ellen. "But nothing on poor Vikki. Why is she here? What has she done?"

It was as Malone had guessed. Ellen knew nothing about Vikki's left hand, even though they had been thrown together for several days. It was hardly surprising: after over a decade, the girl was adept at not using it properly or drawing attention to it.

"I think Vikki has something to tell you, Ellen. Isn't that so, Vikki?"

The girl flinched away from Malone's penetrating gaze and looked down, her long hair hiding her face.

"Vikki. I haven't got much time. Diana Sheldon will be along soon. It's essential that she and Ellen know everything so that Roscoe can't spring any surprises."

Silence.

"Please, Vikki."

Her answer was a tear splashing on to her treacherous hand.

Malone rose and knelt beside her. He took hold of her left forearm and lifted it gently. She offered no resistance. "It's all going to come out, Vikki. Let it be now with people who love you, who want to help you – don't let it be something that feeds Roscoe's hate."

For a confused moment Ellen had to reorient herself to be certain that it was Vikki's left arm that Malone was holding and that it was the fingers on her left hand that were opening one by one. She sat

179

stunned and speechless with shock as Vikki looked up and stretched out both hands to her.

"I'm sorry, Miss Duncan. I'm terribly sorry. I should've told you but I didn't know how to."

A dozen questions tripped over each other when Ellen eventually managed to speak.

"The visitors did it," Malone interrupted. "They sent their spyder device into her bedroom when she was asleep. They did the same for Cathy Price – restoring her sense of balance."

"When?"

"The night before the Wall appeared. Is that right, Vikki?"

The girl nodded.

"The visitors!" Ellen exclaimed. "It doesn't seem possible. I mean . . . Well – how could they? Grow a new hand?"

"The Wall doesn't seem possible," said Malone. "But it's there sure enough."

The girl surprised them by standing, an air of uncharacteristic defiance in her stance as she looked at them in turn. "It *was* the visitors who gave me my hand. They told me they did it."

It was Malone's turn to express astonishment. "They did what? How?"

"They called me to the lake to talk to me." Vikki raised her voice, something she rarely did, to speak with resolution and passion. "They told me where they've come from, and that they're preparing a man to come amongst us. And that I was to prepare the way for him!"

Forty-Three

When he left the police station Malone was surprised by the number of horse-drawn wagons converging on Pentworth. There was always a goodly amount of vehicles making deliveries but these wagons had no cargo other than grim-faced men, women and children.

By 9. a.m. Market Square was filling fast with country workers disembarking from tractor-drawn trailers – carefully hoarded stocks of diesel fuel being used illegally. Two morris police were issuing summonses which were promptly torn up.

There was no shouting, no disorder. It was all well organised. Malone found Dan Baldock in the front line of the silent phalanx that had formed across the square facing Government House. Confronting them were two uneasy blackshirts armed with shotguns.

"We have to do something to show Ellen and Vikki that they're not alone, Mr Malone," declared the pig farmer. "This is as good a way as any of showing Prescott that he can't do this."

"The enemy isn't Prescott," said Malone.

"Any sign of your plan?"

"Not yet. But I give you my word I'll have something within twenty-four hours. In the meantime, it's imperative that you retain control here."

Baldock grunted. "They've all been briefed – a silent, non-violent protest."

Not *that* silent, because the Commer van bearing the prisoners had arrived. As it turned into Government House the two faces at the rear windows were greeted with cheers and waves.

A group of counter-demonstrators arrived waving their placards calling on the destruction of the witches who had brought so much misery to the community. The new arrivals gestured and shouted catcalls at the stony-faced Country Brigade, but without eliciting a response.

"See what I mean?" said Baldock. "You do your bit. We'll do our bit. And if you don't come up with something by this time tomorrow, then we will start doing our bit with a vengeance. Twenty-four hours, Mr Malone."

Forty-Four

Vikki watched in amazement as Brenda Simmons, the head of her year at St Catherine's, had to be virtually frog-marched, protesting loudly, into the witness box by two blackshirts. The school teacher ignored the usher by refusing to take the oath.

"Mrs Simmons," said Judge Hooper severely, glaring frostily at the reluctant prosecution witness. "If you do not take the oath and answer counsels' questions, I will hold you in contempt of court."

Brenda Simmons was a small, spry greying woman in her mid-fifties. "I have nothing but contempt for any court that puts people in the dock on charges of witchcraft. Particularly schoolgirls. I've never heard such nonsense and I refuse to recognise this ridiculous charade as a court of law."

"This ridiculous charade has the power to impose an unlimited fine," said the judge drily, polishing his spectacles. "And if you can't pay it, all your assets may be seized, *including* your house and land."

Support for the judge came from an unexpected quarter. Vikki brushed aside Ellen's restraining hand and jumped to her feet, clutching the bar with her right hand. "*Please* do as he says, Mrs Simmons! *Please* – I beg of you!"

The judge passed no comment on Vikki's outburst. He replaced his glasses and stared coldly at the witness. She seemed to be wavering. She suddenly seized the bible and card from the usher and recited the oath. Her answers to Roscoe's opening questions establishing her identity were spat out.

"Your Honour," said Roscoe. "I wish to introduce two more exhibits that were taken from Ellen Duncan's shop and flat following her arrest."

Diana was on her feet to protest that the defence had not been given a chance to see the exhibits. Roscoe assured the judge that he could, if required, produce witnesses to testify that they had been removed from the accused's premises.

"Very well. Please continue, Mr Roscoe."

A card made from a cereal packet was passed to the witness. "Will you read what it says on that card please," Roscoe requested.

"'Kelloggs Cornflakes. Packed full of goodness to start your day the Kelloggs way.'"

"The other side, Mrs Simmons."

"'Lost. Much loved large black cat. Sometimes answers to Thomas. Always used to answer to sound of a tin opener. Reward. Apply Vikki Taylor – Assistant Manager.' And it's been signed."

"Do you recognise the signature?"

"Yes."

"Whose is it?"

"Vikki Taylor's."

"Thank you."

On a nod from Roscoe, a covered easel was set up in the well of the court. Roscoe removed a Polaroid picture from an envelope. "If it pleases Your Honour, this photograph is rather small therefore it has been enlarged to poster size so that it can be seen properly by everyone."

Judge Hooper was about to observe that everyone was capable of examining even a small photograph if it were passed around but was interrupted by a chorus of shocked gasps when the cover was whipped away from the easel. The juror with the charm bracelet screamed in anguish.

The colour poster was made from nine sheets of A4 paper that had been Scotch-taped together. It was a picture of Thomas's crucifixion but it was upside-down so that the wretched cat was the right way up – large wire nails driven through his throat, outstretched paws, pelvis and tail. His yellow eyes open, looking straight at the camera so that they appeared to be staring directly and accusingly at every individual in the courtroom. Blood trails going upwards. Ellen gave a sob of torment and buried her face in her hands. She was comforted by Vikki – a poignant mingling of blonde and dark hair.

"Cover it up!" Judge Hooper snapped. He turned angrily on Roscoe. "I will not have my court turned into a theatre. If you have exhibits, they will be admitted and taken around in the correct manner."

Roscoe bowed and apologised. "I merely wished to bring home to the jury the fiendish practices that have been perpetrated in this community, Your Honour. It seems that not even a witch's familiar is safe from their diabolical rites."

Diana bounced up but Roscoe's resonant voice rose to its full volume as he held up the original Polaroid and pointed at Ellen.

"This picture was found in that accursed woman's flat! Not only does she think nothing of butchering her pet cat to appease Satan, but's she proud enough of her terrible deed to take a photograph!"

The courtroom was already in an uproar when Ellen threw herself at the bar and screamed out, *"That's a fucking lie, you callous bastard! You planted that picture! That's how David and I found Thomas! Nailed to my back door!"*

David was on his feet. "She's telling the truth! We found Thomas like that after we returned to the shop! Ellen could never do such a thing! She loved that cat!"

Judge Hooper banged his gavel repeatedly but Ellen kept up a stream of invective directed at Roscoe, who seemed content to remain seated while bedlam erupted around him. He noticed that most of the jurors were still unable to tear their eyes away from the easel, even though the picture was now covered. Vikki and the WPC were unable to restrain Ellen so two blackshirts bundled her out of the court on Judge Hooper's orders. Her sobbing protests could still be heard in the distance when order was restored. The judge refused Diana's request for an adjournment and rebuked David for his outburst. He regarded Roscoe with evident distaste.

"If you have a witness to testify as to where that picture came from, you'd better call him or her now, Mr Roscoe."

"Indeed, Your Honour. I have a witness. But one can only wonder why the accused had a card put in her window about her lost pet if she already knew of its fate. Unless she wished to cover up that she—"

"You will call your witness and save your conjectures for your closing address to the jury!" the judge snapped and told the jury to disregard Roscoe's comments.

Brenda Simmons, looking bewildered by the storm that had raged around her, was asked to step down for a few minutes. Nelson Faraday was called. He took the oath and testified that he had found the Polaroid photograph in Ellen Duncan's bedroom. Diana did her best to shake him in her cross-examination but he stuck doggedly to his account.

"You'll have to call me to refute that," David whispered to Diana when she sat.

"Look at the jury," she whispered back. "Do you think they're going to believe you? You're her lover, for God's sake."

Brenda Simmons was recalled to the witness stand and reminded that she was still under oath. She gave Vikki an encouraging smile.

"How long have you known the accused?" asked Roscoe.

"About four years. More so this last year since she's been in my year."

"A model pupil?"

"There's no such thing. But Vikki is a good-natured, even-tempered girl. Somewhat impudent at times." The witness stared coldly at Roscoe. "Anyone who thinks she's a witch is a religious looney, clean out of their skull."

Judge Hooper let that pass.

"Is she different from other girls in any significant way?"

"I've never ever known her to arrive at school on a broomstick. She prefers a bicycle."

"Physical differences," said Roscoe woodenly, ignoring the ripple of nervous sniggers.

"If you mean her artificial hand – no – she's no different. She never lets it interfere with school activities."

Oh, God – here we go, thought Diana.

"You seem convinced that the accused has an artificial hand."

The witness looked confused and glanced at Vikki who was staring down. "Well – yes. She lost her left hand in an accident years ago. It's common knowledge except that we don't talk about it."

"So you've seen her stump?"

Vikki shuddered and kept her eyes downcast.

"Yes."

"When?"

"Several times, if you must know!" the witness retorted.

"When was the last time?"

"Earlier in the year when she was having trouble with a new hand. I helped her—"

"Mr Roscoe," Judge Hooper interrupted. "As the witness said, it's common knowledge that Victoria Taylor lost her left hand in a terrible accident as a child, so I see no purpose in these questions."

There were nods from the jurors.

"As Your Honour pleases," said Roscoe graciously. "If it is common knowledge, then I have no further witnesses."

Judge Hooper glanced at the wall clock in some satisfaction. 11.15 a.m.. Allow thirty minutes for lunch, and a thirty-minute limit on counsels' summings-up and it might be possible to clear up the case by evening. It was all down to the jury, of course.

"But I do have a final exhibit, Your Honour. The accused's left hand."

Vikki looked on the point of fainting.

"What the devil are you blathering on about, Mr Roscoe? How on earth can an artificial hand be evidence in this case?"

David closed his eyes and muttered a silent prayer.

"It is vital evidence, Your Honour – I assure you."

Judge Hooper glowered at Roscoe. "Very well." He turned to the dock and, in a kindly voice, asked Vikki to remove her left hand.

She stared back at the judge, her eyes glazing with shock. "I can't remove it, sir – Your Honour."

"Very well. Allow her to come forward."

Vikki refused to accede to the WPC's whispered instructions. There was a heated altercation.

"What's the problem now?" Judge Hooper demanded.

"She won't leave the dock, Your Honour," said the police officer.

Vikki and Judge Hooper stared at each other. "I can understand your embarrassment, Miss Taylor. I do sympathise, but if you can't or won't remove your hand then you will stand right there." He pointed to the area in front of the clerk's bench but the glaring match continued. The silence in the courtroom was total.

Diana rose. "Please do as his honour says, Vikki."

"No!"

The WPC had no wish to use extremes of violence. She took Vikki by the arm but the girl responded by grabbing hold of the brass bar with her right hand.

"I don't have to show anybody anything!" Vikki shouted.

The woman police officer prised open Vikki's fingers to pull her away but the girl's next action provoked a stir of astonishment that had even Judge Hooper forgetting himself to goggle in amazement. Vikki had suddenly lashed out and was clinging with grim strength to the bar with her left hand.

"It's a real hand!" cried the WPC, jumping back as if stung when she tried to open Vikki's fingers.

"*Yes!*" Vikki screamed, fighting to hold back her tears. "It's real! Look!" She tore off her gloves, held up both hands and opened and closed her fingers. "The visitors gave it to me! They chose me! I am their chosen one! They came to me and gave me my new hand because they are sending a man to be among us! He will rise from the swamp and I am to prepare the way for him!" With that her control dissolved and she fell into the WPC's arms, her whole body trembling, and convulsed with weeping.

Roscoe's quick thinking turned this extraordinary and wholly unexpected turn of events to his advantage. He strode into the centre of the court, his gown swirling, and levelled an accusing finger at the sobbing girl.

"The witch has condemned herself with her own confession!" he boomed. "She is summonsing an abomination – a nameless obscenity – that will rise up from the black swamps of Hades to claim his reward from this evil sorceress, this daughter of Satan! And in so doing, they will plunge us further into the dark age of hell and damnation. As a consequence, God's punishment of the Wall will endure for as long we ignore the word He gave us in Exodus – Chapter Twenty-Two, Verse Eighteen! 'Thou shalt not suffer a witch to live'! They must be destroyed!"

Forty-Five

Judge Hooper was pleased. It was 1.45 p.m. and he was halfway through his summing-up to the jury. Following the remarkable business with Vikki Taylor before lunch, Roscoe had declared that he had no more witnesses or exhibits, and Diana Sheldon had called only two witnesses: Detective Sergeant Malone and Ellen Duncan. At least Miss Sheldon got on with it and didn't indulge in theatricals, although one had to admit that Roscoe's theatricals were effective.

Malone had testified that he had seen Ellen Duncan's shop being subjected to criminal damage on the day before the Wall had materialised. Also he had expressed an interesting theory that the visitors were responsible for Vikki's astonishing growth of a new hand – a theory that also covered Catherine Price's cure.

When cross-examining, Roscoe had managed to implant in the jury's mind that it was odd that the only people to have seen this miracle-performing crab-like device had been the two defendants, plus Malone, and Cathy Price – now deceased. Moreover, there had been no reported sightings since March.

Ellen Duncan, now back in court, had apologised for her language and behaviour and recounted how straitened circumstances were when she had taken over the shop meant that she had to rundown her mother's old stock rather than dump it. Her mother had never been a witch, although she had had a passionate interest in the subject. Ellen maintained vehemently her own interests had never included the occult, and that palaeontology was her great passion.

She had to brush back her tears when she related how she and David Weir had discovered Thomas crucified to her back door, and that she hadn't told Vikki or the police because she didn't want to attract attention or more vandal attacks.

Roscoe had refused to cross-examine, and had aroused the judge's wrath by stating that the Bible the accused had sworn on had been defiled and demanded that it should be burned.

If he was angry then, Judge Hooper thought as he addressed the jury, he's certainly going to be incandescent at my closing remarks:

"Finally, Members of the Jury, we come to possible feelings of disbelief, or even revulsion, that you may be experiencing that such archaic laws have been revived. You must set aside any such feelings; whether we like it or not, the law exists, which it is your duty to uphold by deciding whether or not the accused have broken it. You must reach your decisions on the basis of the evidence you have heard and not allow your feelings concerning the possible inappropriateness of the law to influence your decisions.

"You may feel repugnance at the thought that a pretty sixteen-year-old girl is facing death by hanging if you find her guilty. You must put such feelings out of your mind and decide your verdict solely on grounds of the evidence you have heard.

"Similarly, with Ellen Duncan, you must not be swayed by the fact that her considerable skills and knowledge of herbal medicine makes her one of the most valued members of our community, particularly under our present bizarre circumstances. You must put such feelings from your mind and consider your verdict solely on the basis of the evidence you have heard."

It was all nonsense, of course, the judge told himself. The checks and balances inherent in the jury system were that juries refused to convict those accused under harsh or unjust laws. And telling the jury not to think about something was like the kids' game in which a player could have a chocolate provided they didn't think about unicorns. It was impossible to win because it was impossible not to think about unicorns when trying not to think about them.

"Thank you, Members of the Jury," Judge Hooper concluded. "You have been most patient these last three days. Will you please retire to consider your verdicts."

Forty-Six

By 4 p.m. the atmosphere in Market Square while the jury were retired was electric. Prescott stood at his office window taking in the scene below. The numbers of demonstrators on both sides had swollen. The way in which the ranks of farmers stoically ignored the jeers of the hanging brigade spoke of a high degree of organisation and discipline, strengthening Prescott's feelings of deep foreboding.

To one side of the entrance to Government House was a queue waiting to be admitted to hear the verdict. Among them was Anne Taylor accompanied by Father Kendrick. She and the priest had spent many hours of the last three days praying for Vikki's salvation.

Roscoe appeared and was immediately surrounded by a throng of admirers. Genuine admirers. Ever since the abortive assassination attempt, Prescott had become progressively more concerned for his own safety and restricted his public appearances to a few seconds at unexpected times. He had even got Selby Engineering to fit steel plates around the rear passenger seat of his methane-powered Range Rover. The hoisting of a flag from the flagstaff on top of Government House whenever he was in had been abandoned.

In his hot little anteroom that served as his chamber, Judge Hooper had just decided that he would allow another thirty minutes before sending a note to the jury saying that he would accept a majority verdict when word came from the bailiff that they had completed their deliberations.

The courtroom was packed when the jurors filed into their box. Not one of the six men and six women as much as glanced at Ellen and Vikki in the dock.

Judge Hooper swept in and took his seat. The clerk approached the jurors and asked their foreman to stand. The woman who had provided her charm bracelet rose and looked nervously from the judge to the clerk. She was holding a slip of paper.

"Your Honour – we have a statement that we wish to read out."

"You are here to give your verdicts," Judge Hooper ruled. "No more – no less."

The woman foreman looked frightened but she was determined to see this through. "In that case, we refuse to offer any verdicts at all."

There was a long silence. Judge Hooper could find the entire jury in contempt. Fines. Prison sentences. The spectre of a retrial. A shambles that could be easily avoided by acceding to the jury's request. "Oh, very well if it makes you feel better. Read your statement."

The clerk of the court looked aggrieved.

The foreman cleared her throat. "We the jury, have done as requested and considered the charges against the accused solely on the evidence presented. But we deplore the application of such legislation and urge clemency and that a court of appeal should reexamine the cases."

"That's your statement?"

"Yes, Your Honour."

Judge Hooper nodded to the clerk. "Carry on, clerk."

"Please answer this question yes or no," said the clerk coldly. "Have you reached verdicts on which you are all agreed?"

"Yes."

"Please answer guilty or not guilty. To the charge of practising witchcraft and other evil things, do you find the defendant, Eleanor Rose Duncan, guilty or not guilty?"

"Guilty."

"To the charge of practising witchcraft and other evil things, do you find the defendant, Victoria Taylor, guilty or not guilty?"

"Guilty."

The crowded courtroom erupted in a fury of whistles, cheers, and screams of anguish. But for the prompt action of a blackshirt, Anne Taylor would've hurled herself at the jury foreman. She had to be dragged from the courtroom screaming.

Judge Hooper's gavel banging had no effect on restoring order but blackshirts bursting in with shotguns at the ready most certainly did. Their presence inflamed the judge. "Get those men out of here!" he fumed.

The blackshirts withdrew once order was restored and the turmoil showed no signs of starting again.

"Eleanor Rose Duncan and Victoria Taylor," said Judge Hooper. "You have been found guilty of the charges against you and will be placed in the custody of the Pentworth Manorial Court for sentencing and the carrying out of any sentence the manorial court deems appropriate."

He rose and left the courtroom hurriedly, having no wish to witness the travesty of justice that was certain to follow. The clerk formally closed the session and he, the usher and bailiff followed the judge.

Nelson Faraday entered, flanked by the armed blackshirts that the judge had just shooed from the courtroom. He was wearing his black outfit; the blackshirts were carrying chains and neck irons.

"Thank you for looking after our prisoners," said Faraday to the WPC. "We'll take over now."

Ellen and Vikki appeared to be in a trance as the blackshirts clamped the neck irons in place.

"You can either walk or be dragged," said Faraday indifferently. "It makes no odds to me either way."

They walked, led like dogs, to the main entrance and blinked uncertainly in the bright sunlight. Roscoe was on hand, recording the moment of his glorious victory over the massed forces of Hell with a camcorder. There was an angry murmur from the Country Brigade but Dan Baldock's leadership was strong enough for them to obey his signals to remain calm. A few jeers from Roscoe's supporters but generally the mood of the crowd was sombre.

For Ellen the sight that confronted her was the culmination of all her nightmares. It was a large dogcart harnessed to a black horse. At the front of the cart was a waist height crossbar. She had to remain strong for Vikki's sake so she climbed behind the bar and calmly allowed herself to be shackled to it by the wrists. Vikki received the same treatment so that the two women were standing side by side.

The driver touched the horse's flank with his whip and the dogcart moved off on its short journey to Pentworth House. Roscoe and Faraday fell into step behind it.

"Congratulations, Father. I never thought I'd see this moment."

"I must confess, Nelson, that there were moments when I thought the same."

Faraday stared lustfully at Vikki. Like Ellen, the girl was gripping the crossbar with both hands to keep her balance as the cart swayed and jolted on the uneven flagstones.

Roscoe noticed the look. "You will save your lusts for the scourging, Nelson."

"But—"

"I have given orders that they are to be looked after by three shifts of female sentinels. No male is to go near their quarters. Don't worry, Nelson – you will be able to give full vent to your feelings on Saturday night."

Forty-Seven

N elson Faraday was the only one who didn't appear to enjoy the party in Pentworth House's ballroom to celebrate Roscoe's victory. He glowered in turn at Roscoe, now the worse for drink as he lolled on a couch with three adoring girls in attendance, and at the disorganised dancing of the revellers. He had been looking forward to this moment. Something he had worked hard for and now he was going to have to wait a few more nights. By 9 p.m. he had had enough. He grabbed a bottle of wine and went to his room, his departure watched by Claire Lake, who slipped away ten minutes later to prepare herself for the horrors that lay ahead.

Faraday was half way through the bottle when there was a tentative tap on his door.

"Come in."

The door opened and the vision that stood coyly in the doorway nearly caused the bottle to slip from his fingers.

Claire had done a good job. She had started by binding her chest so that there was little hint of her breasts under the tight schoolgirl's pinafore dress. It was white, with fine blue stripes, its chest pockets trimmed with white linen. Some of the lower buttons were undone to show a pair of grubby knees. Her tie was badly knotted and slightly askew. Her blonde hair had been plaited into two tight bangs which she had stiffened with wire so that they stuck out at an absurd angle. Completing the ensemble were white ankle socks and black buckle shoes, and a lollipop – an immature apple on a stick – which she sucked on while eyeing the black-clad figure on the bed.

Faraday grinned. "Who the fuck are you?"

"My name's Jennifer, Mr Faraday."

Faraday knew perfectly well who she was but this little one had never entered into these games before.

"Well come in, Jennifer, and lock the door."

Claire did so and stood beside Faraday's bed, looking down at him, her eyes large and innocent as she sucked noisily on the lollipop.

"I've been a naughty girl, Mr Faraday. I've been sent to you for punishment."

"So what did you do that was so naughty?"

The girl shrugged her shoulders back and forth – a perfect imitation of a mixture of childish indifference and defiance. "I put all my knickers in the laundry so I haven't got any to wear."

"That was very naughty of you, Jennifer." Faraday slipped his hand under her dress and stroked her thigh, reaching higher to her buttocks to establish the truth of her statement. He thought he felt a tiny tremor of fear. So much the better if she were afraid. But why should she want to play this little game now when she had always refused before? He was about to ask her but was distracted by the noises she made with the lollipop. They irritated him. He took it from her and placed it on his bedside cabinet.

"Are you going to take my lollipop away, Mr Faraday?"

"I've got a much nicer lollipop for you to suck, Jennifer."

"Have you, Mr Faraday?" She gave a little clap of anticipation.

Christ – this one is good after all, thought Faraday, making room for her on the bed. She knelt and he told her what he wanted her to do.

"Ooo! Mr Faraday. That would be really naughty of me. Are you sure it'll be all right?"

That she wasn't so good at doing what he wanted didn't matter this time; any expertise on her part would've spoilt the illusion. He took a swig from the wine bottle with one hand and pushed the other between her thighs and moved it up. She was smooth, perfectly smooth – just the way it should be . . . A smoothness that could come only from a very recent shave . . . He closed his eyes and groaned.

Forty-five minutes later Claire was at Faraday's hand basin, one foot on the rim, determinedly washing away all traces left by his loathsome presence. Satisfied that she was as clean as she was ever likely to be, she turned and surveyed him, stretched out, naked, snoring gently, the empty wine bottle on the floor. As she had hoped, the noise of her washing had not woken him, therefore what she had to do next was unlikely to disturb him.

Her heart was thumping wildly as she opened the drawer in the bedside cabinet. Some old letters; a packet of unpleasant photographs featuring young girls; a passport – a singularly useless document now. And then she found it: a typed carbon sheet of instructions with pencilled ticks against the various points. Halfway down was a strange schedule. It was the timetable for the scourging of the two prisoners – exactly what she was looking for. It detailed the time the procession would set off from Pentworth House, the time of its arrival at the bizarre site chosen for the scourging, and the time of arrival at Market Square for the terrible finale.

The room swam at the horrors of what was spelt out in such matter-of-fact terms. She wanted to be sick, but she forced herself to re-read the timetable several times to be certain of committing its horrors to memory. She put everything back as she had found it and left the room, pausing only to glance at Faraday and contemplate the appalling wound she could inflict on him. But there were enough complications in her life as it was, and she had much to do.

In the relative security of her bedroom, she wrote down the entire timetable, virtually word for word. A part of her brain that was divorced from reality guided her hand as she penned the details of the final scene in Market Square.

That done, she unravelled her plaits, unwound the bindings from her breasts, and changed into her running kit, zipping the scourging timetable into an inside pocket.

"I don't know how you do it, these hot nights," said Helen when Claire appeared. Helen was the main gate duty officer.

Claire smiled. "I'm putting on weight."

"Why don't you jog in the park?"

"The trees scare me in the moonlight and I scare the deer."

Helen laughed and opened the gate. "Two hours," she warned.

Claire thanked her and set off at a steady pace. She glanced at her watch and saw that she was in good time for her rendezvous with Mike Malone at the Temple of the Winds.

Forty-Eight

M alone's first call early the next morning was Temple Farm where David made him welcome and brewed-up some chicory coffee which they sat sipping in the kitchen while David studied the scourging timetable. It was a copy Malone had made the previous night when he had returned to his digs after his meeting with Claire. He had burned the original.

"Incredible," David muttered, looking up at Malone. There were dark hollows under the farmer's eyes from lack of sleep.

"Not that it's much consolation," said Malone. "But they're not being abused at the moment. Roscoe's keeping them in guarded quarters."

"But they can't do this!" David exploded. "It's barbaric – inhuman."

"They can unless we stop them," said Malone. "Which we will. Roscoe's sufficiently unhinged to do anything now, and Prescott's terrified out of his wits at the power Roscoe has acquired. I've heard that his signing of Vikki Taylor's arrest warrant was a ruse that Roscoe pulled off."

"Meaning that Ellen's arrest was OK?" said David bitterly.

"Meaning nothing of the sort. Listen, David. I've got a rough plan worked out. But before we go ahead, there's one thing that we must agree on, and that is that you and I should be the only people who know the full details. There'll be as many as thirty people involved. What they know has to be on a need-to-know basis. That's as much to protect the plan as to protect them if it goes wrong. Are we agreed on that?"

David considered and nodded. "That seems sensible. So what have you in mind? An ambush?"

Malone pulled a large scale Ordnance Survey map of the area from his pocket and spread it on the table. His finger traced the route from Pentworth House to the scourging site.

"An ambush in the town is out of the question because the procession will be too bunched up. With eight armed blackshirts, they'll probably have the dogcart surrounded at all times." Malone pointed. "That's our best place – where they will be forced to string out."

They discussed Malone's embryo plan for several minutes. David Weir was a good, clear thinker and had several excellent ideas so that the plan was soon much less embryonic. Malone started on a list of needs. It turned out to be a worryingly long list.

"Procession torches are no problem," said David. "We've got about thirty for lambing and working at night on broken-down machinery. Charlie makes them and they burn for about two hours." His eye went down the list. "Look, Mike – it's Thursday. We've only got today and tomorrow, and most of Saturday to pull this thing together. You've got a lot of people to see so take my pony and trap."

Malone's inclination was to refuse – to be seen driving a trap would be out of character, but if his visits were successful he would have a lot of gear to shift, so he accepted.

They went to the stables and harnessed up the trap.

"What's your first port of call?" David asked once Malone was installed.

"A visit to our intrepid round-the-world yachtsman. Your job is to get over to Dan Baldock to stop the Country Brigade going off at half-cock."

"How much should I tell him?"

Malone thought hard. "You know him better than I do, David. But he strikes me as the sort of man I'd rather have with me than against me in a scrap."

David nodded. "You're right. Dan Baldock is a prickly, nit-picking bastard, but I'd trust him with my life. I'll ride over to see him this morning."

Malone released the handbrake and was about to flick the reins when David pointed out that there was something important he had forgotten. Malone's ego took a knock. He was confident that his plan covered all the major points. He looked questioningly at David.

"If we succeed," said the farmer, "it won't be the end of the matter. We might have to hide Ellen and Vikki away somewhere safe. Perhaps for several weeks until something is done about Roscoe and Prescott. Prescott doesn't worry me so much. He's sensitive to political pressure. With even Diana Sheldon turning against him by defending Ellen and Vikki, he's certain to be feeling that his position is being undermined. But after watching Roscoe in court, I'm convinced that he's insane. He'd rather die than agree to any compromise. If he gets control of Pentworth, then God help us all."

"You're right," Malone conceded. "We'll need somewhere secure to hide Ellen and Vikki. We'd both better give it some hard thought."

He flicked the reins and the pony moved off. As he drove away from Temple Farm, turning over David Weir's words, it occurred to Malone that what they were planning was more than just a rescue – it could well be the opening shots in a bloody revolution.

Forty-Nine

Ten years previously, Roger Dayton's reaction to an enforced early retirement as director of a major yacht chandlery business in Chichester had been to fulfill a lifelong ambition by renting out his house and paddock for two years and sailing around the world with his wife and cat. His fifteen-metre yacht didn't do any sailing now but sat on blocks in his paddock, its winter home that now looked permanent.

He was a cautious man and subjected Malone's warrant card to a detailed study before handing it back. He was short, stocky with a slow manner of speech. An unlikely long-distance yachtsman.

"What can I do for you, Mr Malone?"

"The government order calling for the surrender of all firearms and explosives didn't make it clear that the order also covered marine pyrotechnics – rockets, flares, and so forth. I'm sorry to inconvenience you, sir. But the oversight is entirely our fault and there is no penalty attached to their retention, provided you surrender them."

The sailor grunted. "I should think not indeed. This way."

Malone followed him into a spacious garage occupied by a vintage Bentley. The sailor pointed to three steel fireproof safety lockers. "There they are. Help yourself. They all fall out of date this season. I was going replace them but for that damned Wall."

Malone opened one of the lockers. It contained a selection of lethal-looking rockets and flares. "You say, out of date, sir. But they'd still work?"

"Sure. It's just that it's not worth putting your life at risk for the sake of replacing five-year-old rockets."

Malone picked up one the rockets and feigned interest. It stood his height. "I've never seen such things before, sir. How on earth do you launch them?"

"Easy. Just yank the safety ring to release the ignitor lock, then pull the lanyard and whoosh – they fire immediately. No messing about with wet matches and blue touch paper in a Force Eight."

"They look fearsome things."

Dayton chuckled. "They are. They can climb to about two thousand metres. But they're safe enough to launch. You can hold them upright by the stick to launch them. A small rocket fires first to lift the thing clear of the vessel, and then the main rocket kicks in. The long cartridges are hand-fired parachute flares."

"Thank you, sir. Perhaps you'd kindly give me a hand with these lockers."

"I certainly won't. The order didn't say anything about handing over expensive lockers. They stay. The contents are yours."

Fifty

M alone took the rockets and flares back to Temple Farm in the trap, returning in time to catch David saddling up a horse for his visit to Dan Baldock. He helped Malone unload the pyrotechnics and hide them in an outhouse.

Malone's next call was on Bob Harding. The scientist was alone in his workshop with his hayfever and a supply of handkerchiefs, spending his lunch break tinkering with his model submersible. He listened to what Malone had to say and his red-rimmed eyes lit up in eager anticipation.

"Thank God – we're actually going to do something. A disgusting travesty of justice. I thought it was going to be some sort of mock trial at first. I can't believe how naive we've all been to let Prescott and those Bode's Law loonies run amuck with their crazy beliefs. If there is anything I can do . . . Anything at all."

"There is, Mr Harding."

"For God's sake call me Bob – everyone does."

Malone outlined his plan, but stuck to his need to know policy. The scientist's animated expression changed to one of deep concern as he listened.

"Mike – it's suicide – even ambushing at that point along the procession route. One blackshirt behind the cart with a pump-action shotgun will make mincemeat of all of you, and you won't be able to muster enough men there to be certain of overrunning him."

"You're right, Bob. But I wasn't thinking of a fire-fight. It's the last thing we want. We have only a few shotguns anyway. We need something that's quick and effective."

"Like what?"

"Like a gas attack."

The scientist regarded Malone steadily. His voice was low when he replied. "You're joking – no, you're not joking."

Malone explained the nature of the gas he wanted and its radius of effectiveness. When he had finished, Harding was deep in thought.

"It might be possible, Mike . . ." he said at length.

"How about the ingredients?"

"You'd be surprised at what I can lay my hands on in this town. The problem is not so much the ingredients, it's the mixing and filling. How much will you need?"

"I was hoping you'd tell me."

"Well . . . At a guess, around thirty one-kilo bomblets ought to do the trick. Two problems: what do we put the stuff in, and how do we launch them? Some sort of spring gun? A modified clay pigeon gun?"

"That's not such a bad idea," said Malone.

"It's a crap idea. It'll take an age to launch enough bomblets to do the trick – you're going to have to fire clusters of them."

"I've got a launching device in mind, so leave that one to me. You've got enough on your plate."

"OK. So what do we put the stuff in? The containers have to be fragile enough to burst on impact, yet strong enough to withstand handling and being launched."

Both men fell silent.

"Got it," said Harding softly. He rose abruptly and disappeared into a storeroom. After a few minutes rummaging he returned with a glass flask. It was globular with a slender neck and a flattened bottom. "Old-fashioned one-litre acid bottles," he said, passing the flask to Malone. "Like miniature carboys. I bought them at a junk sale some years ago. Never have found a use for them."

"How many have you got?" Malone asked, turning the vessel over in his hands. The glass was thicker than a laboratory flask.

"A case of twenty-four. Actually, the more I think about, the more I realise that they'd be ideal. They can withstand about five bar pressure. It wouldn't be too much trouble to make up some seals and pressurise them so that they go off with a bit of a bang when they burst. It would certainly help with the dispersal, but you'd have to be careful handling them. Wind's going to be a problem. At night the air at the highest point in the dome – over Pentworth Lake – tends to cool. As it descends, it displaces air away from the lake so that night breezes tend to blow away from the lake. The reverse of what happens in the daytime. But it'll swirl and eddy – get some of your gas back in your face and you could end up looking rather silly."

It was a good point. Malone made some notes. He snapped his notebook closed and thanked the scientist.

"I'm only too pleased to be doing something."

"Can you have them ready by tomorrow?"

Harding smiled. "They'll be ready. Make sure you save one for Roscoe."

Malone stood and picked up the flask. "I'd better take this as a sample." He shook the scientist's hand. "Thanks, Bob. I've a few more calls to make."

It was only five minutes from Bob Harding's shop to the Pentworth Museum where Malone found the curator, Henry Foxley, at work in the basement making notes of the contents of his crates. He had less space for storage now that one end of the basement had been partitioned to provide a room for the telephone switchboard. Malone's request surprised him.

"Gas masks, Mr Malone?"

"Last year you staged an exhibition of World War II memorabilia. I seem to remember a tableau – several tailor's dummies dressed up in 1940s clothes and wearing an assortment of gas masks."

"Well – yes – we've got about a dozen. But they're well over half a century old – the rubber's perishing, which is why we keep them out of the light. The filter elements must be useless by now. What possible use could they be to the police?"

"We may need to use them as patterns to get new ones made. You'll get them back, sir."

Malone left the museum fifteen minutes later carrying a bulging cricket bag that was even older than its contents. He dumped it in the trap and was about to climb aboard when:

"You usually jog everywhere, Mr Malone."

He turned. The speaker was Diana Sheldon, her expression impassive. "Good afternoon, Miss Sheldon. I'm rounding up clobber that might be useful to the police."

She nodded to the Copper Kettle tearoom. "They do an excellent pot of nettle tea and homemade biscuits, Mr Malone. Won't you join me?"

Malone was pushed for time but it was obvious that the Town Clerk had something important to say. "I'd be only too delighted, Miss Sheldon."

He left her thirty minutes later and decided to postpone weighing up what she had said until some other time. His next call promised to be his toughest assignment of all. The entire operation depended on the willing co-operation of the next person on his list.

Fifty-One

It was a little after 6 p.m. and the sun had lost most of its spite when Malone returned to Temple Farm. He tethered the pony to the water trough and went off in search of David Weir. He found him in a large paddock riding a grass mower hauled by Titan. The big Suffolk horse had no difficulty pulling the hundred-year-old machine, even though the grass-cutter bars were at their lowest settings. Charlie's boys were raking the clippings from the scalped field into heaps and dumping them in a row of chicken folds. The occupants, hardly believing their luck, fought and created a clucking uproar over the bonanza. David relinquished his saddle on the mower to one of the boys and joined David.

"Fresh-mown grass," he said. "Best chicken feed there is. We'll have eggs with yokes the colour of sunsets for a week. How did it go?"

Malone grinned. "We've got our gas bombs and a delivery system."

In the kitchen over chicory coffee the two men exchanged accounts of their day, although Malone made no mention of his meeting with Diana Sheldon.

"Dan Baldock's with us all the way," David reported. "He's going to pick a group of the best lads and start drilling them tomorrow."

"Good actors?"

"All farmers are good actors otherwise they'd never survive visits by VAT inspectors . . . Or the pollution and husbandry hygiene inspectors that we have to put up with these days."

Malone smiled and produced the empty flask that Harding had given him. "Our bombs. Twenty-three of them. Not only can Bob Harding find some effective ingredients, but he can pressurise them so that they explode on impact. Only a small explosion but enough to help disperse the contents. What we have to come up with is some sort of double rack system to mount them in."

David took the flask and examined it critically. "That won't be any problem. Some sort of framework made of tubing. They'll slide easily. I'll get Charlie on to it first thing. He's a wizard at making lash-ups."

"Any thoughts on the rockets?"

"They're easy," David replied. "I actually had to fire a couple once in my younger days when I was crewing for my partner in the Fastnet. Plastic waste pipes with extension cords on the lanyards. No problem."

"Won't the tubes melt?"

David grinned. "Probably – but the rockets will be gone by the time they do. They only have to be used once."

"Which leaves the question of where to hide Ellen and Vikki when we've rescued them."

David looked pained. "Ah. I was coming to that. I could've kicked myself right after you left for not thinking of it before. I know an absolutely ideal place, but we can't risk going there until after dark."

Fifty-Two

A drian Roscoe's team of sentinels waited until the area outside Mothercare in Market Square was in shadow before starting work. Twenty of them rode into the square on a heavy goods wagon, all stripped to the waist and wearing shorts instead of their usual gowns. They split into two teams and set to work with pickaxes, lifting flagstones and breaking up two areas of asphalt, each about a metre square and separated by five metres.

The manager of Mothercare bustled out to remonstrate with the gang's foreman, arguing that they were digging too close to his shop. A small knot of curious onlookers gathered. Four blackshirts appeared to assure the shop manager that the holes were being dug in the right place and that everything would be restored on Sunday morning. The manager returned to his shop in a huff and the gang continued work. Once through the hardcore they started digging two holes. In less than an hour they were down two metres, which their foreman decided was enough. Lying the length of their wagon were two massive baulks of timber – each about six metres long. They had been intended as replacement roof purlins for Pentworth House but Roscoe had decided to use them for a more sinister purpose.

Diana joined Prescott at the window of his office and watched as the sentinels assembled an A-frame and used it to manoeuvre the end of the first timber to the rim of its hole. They hauled on a block and tackle and the timber began lifting to the vertical.

"Certainly doing a proper job of it," Prescott commented.

"Mr Prescott," said Diana coldly without preamble. "I want you to accept this letter. I've lodged copies with the bank and with my friends."

Prescott took the envelope. "What is it?"

"It's a formal statement saying that I will work for the good of the people, but I will take no part in the organisation of what I consider to be illegal activities. Nor will I permit any departments under my jurisdiction to take part in or contribute to such activities."

Prescott was expecting something of the sort. Relations between them had been particularly strained since she had opted to defend Ellen and Vikki.

"What's been happening is hardly illegal, Diana. Judge Hooper's ruling—"

Diana's self-control came near to breaking. She snapped, "Judge Hooper's ruling, as you insist on calling it, was a counsel's opinion. Nothing more. It carried no legal authority. It was a sensible analysis of the law and how it might be applied to the circumstances in Pentworth. But you treated it as some sort of carte blanche to do exactly as you pleased. I went along with you at first because you did focus on dealing with all the immediate problems in a sensible manner. I was confident that when the Wall went, as I'm sure it will and soon, that parliament would retrospectively endorse everything you have done. But never in a thousand years will parliament endorse the setting up of a private police force, the return of capital punishment, witch-hunts, mock trials for witchcraft, and now this ultimate obscenity: public burnings at the stake!"

As if to underline her point, the first stake dropped into its hole with a dull thud that sent a tremor through Government House.

"I have a clear duty to maintain religious harmony—"

"Harmony!" Diana laughed bitterly. "Oh, that's rich. That really is. Who was it who instigated all those attacks on churches? That's your idea of preserving religious harmony, is it?"

Prescott wondered how much his chief executive officer knew. Quite a lot or she was bluffing. But Diana Sheldon wasn't given to deception. As they stared at each other, he wondered what had happened to the quiet, self-effacing woman he remembered. But everyone had changed, including himself.

"I'll tell you something, Prescott," said Diana, addressing him by his surname for the first time. "When all this is over, not only will you be facing criminal charges, but I will help Brad Jackson's parents bring a civil action for the unlawful killing of their son. And the same applies if anything happens to Ellen Duncan and Vikki Taylor. The level of damages will be astronomical. You'll lose everything – your land – the lot. That's if you live, because you've brought this community to the brink of a civil war."

"You're being over-dramatic. The Country Brigade are nothing but a disorganised rabble. They've done very little so far."

"*That* in itself," Diana replied, "suggests a high level of organisation. Perhaps you saw their restraint during the trial as a sign of weakness. I saw it as a sign of strength. If they so choose, they could starve out the town." She paused and regarded Prescott with icy contempt. "I only pray to God that your bodyguards do their job well and you do survive, Prescott, so that I'll see you in the dock." She turned and left the office.

Vanessa Grossman was in the outer office, ostensibly working late on an urgent audio typing task, in reality listening to every word of the conversation between Diana and Prescott over her headphones because she had flipped Prescott's desk intercom to conference mode when she had last used the Macintosh computer. She was the only one who had mastered the Mac – having free access to Prescott's office was proving very useful. She bade Diana goodnight as the Town Clerk hurried by, her face pale and drawn.

Vanessa experienced that sexual pulse-quickening tension of a lioness closing for the kill. It was a heady, addictive drug that she had been deprived of for many months. But it was too early to go for a fix just yet. Getting the timing right was part of the thrill of the pursuit of power.

From his office Prescott watched Diana leave Government House.

Another dull tremor shook the building as the second stake dropped into its hole.

Fifty-Three

M alone nearly dropped his blazing torch when he saw the mural of the charging woolly mammoth. He muttered an uncharacteristic expletive and spent a few minutes studying each of the remarkable cave paintings in turn. His attention kept returning to the 3-D mammoth.

"Amazing," he said. "Unbelievable."

David chuckled. "You're the third person to see them in forty thousand years since the artists sealed this cave. They used the shape of the rockface to give a three-D effect."

The police officer reached up to wedge his torch into a fissure and stood back to take in all the vivid hunting scenes. He shook his head. "To think that they've been here all those centuries . . . All of human history has passed them by."

"Puts everything in perspective," David remarked.

"How did Ellen find this cave?"

David's reply was an approximation of the truth. "She said at the time that she'd spotted an anomaly in some aerial photographs taken by Harvey Evans from his microlight."

"Well, thank God you both had the sense to keep quiet about it. I would've trumpeted such a find to the heavens."

"So what do you think?" asked David.

"I think it's bloody marvellous."

"As a hiding place for Ellen and Vikki."

"That's what I meant," said Malone. He looked up at the torch. It was still burning brightly. "Well that's something; the place should've filled with smoke by now. Air must be getting in through natural fissures in the rock. They're going to need light around the clock but we can't risk them using torches – smoke might escape from somewhere and be noticed."

"I've thought about that," said David. "A decent-sized truck battery and a fluorescent camping light will do the trick. I've got a couple. They draw hardly any current. Selby's have converted my small jenny to run on methane, so providing a recharged battery once or twice a week won't be a problem."

"We can't risk too many visits," Malone warned.

"I'm often out at night with torches chasing sheep," David pointed out.

"Even so, we're going to have to stock this place with plenty of food and water to last them at least two weeks – longer if possible. Roscoe will have us watched – you can be certain of that."

"OK – a pair of fully-charged truck batteries should last them a couple of weeks. That's a long time, Mike. They'll need toilet facilities."

"Can you get hold of a chemical loo and some chemicals?"

"I've got an Elsan."

Malone moved to the far recess of the cave. "We could rig it up it here with a screen."

David crouched and examined the floor. "It seems dry. A bit of carpet wouldn't come amiss. A few sticks of furniture . . . A charcoal stove . . . Wash basin . . . We could make this quite comfortable for two women."

"For three women," Malone corrected.

"Three! Who's the third one?"

"Our informant. I've provided her with a guarantee of safety. We have to do it, Dave. She's taken a bigger risk than all of us – the rescue wouldn't be possible without her. She's pregnant and she's terrified that she'll lose her baby if she's beaten up. She's already lost one."

David knew better than to ask who she was. "Fair enough," he agreed, and started writing a list of their requirements with Malone adding suggestions. "I could use the big wagon tomorrow night," the farmer decided. "Do the whole thing in one fell swoop and take back a few sheep in case I'm seen." He looked around the cave and managed a joke despite the grimness of the situation. "One thing that might appeal to Ellen. There can't be many people who can boast of having forty-thousand-year-old paintings on their living-room walls."

They doused the torch, left the cave and emerged into the moonlight. The entrance was now overgrown with gorse bushes; David had planted cuttings from some nearby shrubs several months before and they had taken well. He positioned the hurdle in the opening, and the two men levered the heavy clod of turf back into position and tamped it down.

"The beds and furniture will all have to be dismantled first," David commented.

Malone thought of the times he had jogged past this spot without noticing anything amiss.

The two men set off for Temple Farm, not speaking. As they tramped downhill, Malone glanced back at the great sandstone scarp of the Temple of the Winds – brooding and silent in the ethereal moonlight. He was not superstitious but it seemed that the scowling gargoyle face was angry at the pleasures the two conspirators were seeking to deny it.

Fifty-Four

The next day was Friday – the day before the executions were due to take place and the last full day for plans to be finalised. The lack of communications made matters difficult as did the need to make it appear that everyone was going about their normal work. Seemingly casual meetings by passing wagons and what looked like idle chat between drivers were serious discussions with ideas and instructions being passed to and fro.

Malone sauntered into the police station, even though he had taken a couple of days' leave, exchanged gossip, and purloined an extra PMR radio with a charged battery on his way out.

At Temple Farm Charlie Crittenden tested his two bomb racks, fashioned from soldered lengths of garden furniture aluminium tubing. It was a pig to solder but the racks had to be made of aluminium. A few modifications to make sure the controls worked perfectly took up most of the morning until he was satisfied. Like everything Charlie made, the end results looked efficient and businesslike. He sorted out the tools he knew he would be needing to install the racks and waited for Carl's return with the wagon.

Bob Harding had spent the night filling the twenty-three gas-bomb flasks in his workshop. He had rigged up a charging system of tubes so that the cocktail of ingredients could be gravity-fed into the flasks without risk of the particles escaping. To be on the safe side he had worn a mask and goggles. Each flask was filled three-quarters full to allow room for compressed-air – their necks sealed after filling with a tyre valve set in cement. He used a hand pump to charge each flask to a pressure of five atmospheres, having first tested them individually inside a stout box to be sure that there were no flaws or weaknesses in the glass. He carefully tied each finished bomb into a bundle of straw. He had just completed the last one when Charlie Crittenden's Carl called, ostensibly to collect a repaired radio. He backed his cart into the narrow alley beside Harding's shop and quickly loaded the fragile bundles. He paid for the radio, and left, taking particular care to avoid ruts and potholes.

Dan Baldock was rehearsing his procession group when they had to hide. A lookout had spotted Anne Taylor approaching his pig farm. She tearfully begged and pleaded with him for the Country Brigade to do something about the execution of Vikki that was scheduled for the next day.

"There's nothing we can do, Anne," Dan Baldock said quietly, avoiding her red-rimmed eyes. "There's certain to be every blackshirt in the square – they'll all be on duty – armed to the teeth. We've got nothing. It would be a slaughter with no certainty that we'd be able to save Vikki and Ellen. Is that what you want?"

"Have you seen those terrible things they put up in the square? Have you?"

"I've seen them," said the pig farmer heavily. "I'm sorry, Anne. Really I am, but there's nothing we can do."

His heart ached for the anguished mother as she turned away. He offered to run her home in a gig. Her tears gave way to a vehement outburst in which she called him a weakling and a coward, and told him to go to hell.

With the coming of nightfall, David Weir harnessed Titan and set off from Temple Farm driving a large wagon that he used to recover wounded or lost sheep. It had broad wheels which made it ideal for cross-country work. Underneath a heavy tarpaulin were all the items he had listed for the cave the previous night plus equipment that would be hidden at the scourging site.

He was 200 metres from the farm when Titan snorted his indignation as a dark-clad figure darted out of the shadows and climbed aboard the moving wagon.

"Titan doesn't like you, Mike," David commented.

"I've never got on with horses."

"You better make it up to him when we get there or he'll take a lump out of you."

As they neared the cave, Titan laid his ears back and snorted angrily.

"It's Ellen's maidenhair tree," David explained. "A ginkgo. It's flourishing in this climate. Its smell is reaching further as it gets bigger."

"I've encountered it," Malone replied.

They reached the cave. Their sweat as they unloaded the wagon attracted swarms of mosquitoes that made the work a misery but they got all the stuff into the cave. It needed two of them to manoeuvre the truck battery into position. David said that he had checked its cells with a hydrometer, and that such a large

James Follett

unit would last two weeks of continuous use. Two fluorescent camping lights eased their task of clearing debris from the cave floor. They unrolled a carpet and assembled the furniture. The mattresses had to be rolled up to get them through the cave's entrance. An Elsan chemical toilet screened by a shower curtain was rigged up. David had even managed to scrounge a caravan sink and water pump for the "kitchen". Together they prised up some large stones that had been laid 40,000 years previously and dug a small soakaway for waste water. Two charcoal burners and several bags of ground charcoal would serve the occupants' hot water and cooking needs for at least two weeks. There were over 150 litres of drinking water in plastic containers lined along the far wall. Cutlery, crockery, cooking utensils, toiletry items including sanitary towels, linen – a home was found for everything. Finishing touches were cushions, towels, books, old magazines, games, and what clothes Ellen had left at Temple Farm, and clothes donated for Vikki and Malone's informant.

The two men conducted tests with a radio and determined that it worked in the cave and could not be heard outside. They provided headphones because they were less drain on the batteries than the loudspeaker.

After four hours they decided that they had done everything they could to make the cave comfortable. David had even thought of plastic flowers. He knew Ellen's views on the subject but they did brighten up the place. They tested the cooking facilities by brewing some tea and flopped on the beds to contemplate their work.

Malone realised he was dozing off and shook himself awake. "This won't do – we've got all that kit to hide at the site."

David stood, looked at his watch and swore softly.

"What's the matter?" asked Malone.

"It's gone midnight. It's now Saturday. D-Day."

Fifty-Five

There was none of the usual Saturday morning cheery bustle in Market Square. When setting up their stalls the traders had shunned the area near the two grim stakes, standing tall, upright and forbidding outside the Mothercare shop. A blackshirt tried to revive their spirits with, "The Wall will be gone when the witches are gone," but few listened, less still believed him. The stakes were their fears and prejudices about witchcraft turned into a bleak, disturbing reality that was impossible to accept.

Shoppers made their purchases and hurried home. Housewives laden with bread from the bakery at Pentworth House passed through the square without pausing to gossip. The usually crowded tables outside the Crown were virtually deserted.

Shortly after midday a hay wain piled high with bundles of brushwood arrived. The sentinels on the wagon formed a human chain to unload the cargo. They didn't merely pile the bundles up but arranged them in tightly packed layers around the first stake so that the cone of brushwood was firm enough to walk on. The empty wagon was driven off and reappeared two hours later with another load of faggots for the second stake.

The shadows were lengthening when Judge Hooper marched into the square and stood staring up at the stakes with undisguised anger. The blackshirts standing either side of the entrance to Government House saluted him as he strode past them.

"I want to see Prescott now," he demanded of the blackshirt behind the reception desk.

"The Chairman isn't in, Judge," said the blackshirt. "You can always tell if he's in or out by the flag—"

"When will he be in?"

The blackshirt had strict instructions not to disclose Prescott's movements to anyone. "I don't know, Judge."

"Well when he does come in, tell him that that method of execution is illegal. This is England. If witches must suffer capital punishment, it should be by hanging. The barbarities of Scottish law do not apply here. You will tell him that, please."

The judge turned and marched out.

Prescott saw him leave from his office window. He guessed the reason for the visit without the front desk's call to pass the message.

Damn Roscoe! Damn Diana Sheldon! If the burning went ahead she would be certain to reduce her level of cooperation to zero. She was already proving an obstructive nuisance – not by openly defying him, but by her slowness in clearing the backlog of business which she blamed on pressure of work. Urgent matters were piling up. They had had two acrimonious rows that afternoon.

He called the lobby and asked for his Range Rover to be made ready. Dammit – he was getting forgetful – he'd left the intercom in conference mode again.

Vanessa was alone in the outer office, covering her typewriter and just about to leave when Prescott entered. She had judged that the right moment had arrived, and decided to strike.

"Good evening, Mr Chairman."

Prescott muttered a preoccupied response.

"You look all in, Mr Chairman."

"It's been a particularly trying day," said Prescott, glad of even this straw of sympathy from an underling.

Vanessa had rehearsed what she said next. "Please forgive me for speaking out of turn, Mr Chairman. But I think that much of the problem is that you don't have a personal assistant."

"Miss Sheldon is very capable," Prescott replied brusquely, thinking that this usually quiet and always smartly dressed woman *was* speaking out of turn.

"She's the Town Clerk," said Vanessa, standing and gathering up her handbag. "Her first responsibility is to the council as a whole and not to you."

Prescott sank into a typist's chair and glowered at Vanessa. "So your vast experience of business matters tells you that I need a personal assistant, Miss . . . Grossman, isn't it?" His voice was heavy with sarcasm.

"I have some experience of business, Mr Chairman. Enough to tell me that a busy chairman with many responsibilities, such as you have, usually has a gopher to look after them and deflect many non-urgent problems. A good town clerk, such as Miss Sheldon, is, by the very nature of her job, a source of problems, not solutions."

Prescott had been about to interrupt her, but the logic of this woman's statement gave him pause for thought. Vanessa's instinct told her that she had scored a good point and that now was the time to leave. She moved to the door. "Goodnight, Mr Chairman. Oh – if you want to check my qualifications for speaking out of turn, you could always look at my file in the personnel cabinet. It's not locked."

With that she was gone, leaving Prescott alone. He surveyed the desks in the outer office. Most of them had trays overflowing with work, but Miss Grossman's desk was neat and clear – just a few typed letters in the out tray awaiting his signature. Now that he came to think about it, he realised that she always left a clear desk.

He took the day file out of a filing cabinet and went through the most recent flimsies. Nearly all the work that had been processed during the past week bore the initials /VG/ in the document references.

He recalled that she had spent two or three days in his office learning how to use Cathy Price's computer from the manuals, and had succeeded where others had failed. She had refused to give up until she had mastered the machine and all its peripherals. A tenacious, hard-working lady indeed.

Intrigued by her closing comment, he found her personnel file. Vanessa Grossman. Married name Harriman. Thirty-two. Two children. Chairman and principal shareholder of Grossman Properties; Grossman Commercial Holdings; Grossman Estate Management.

My God! *That* Vanessa Grossman!

There had been a furore in the local press over her ruthless business tactics three years previously when she had persuaded her family to let her take over the management of the family's ailing property group. Even the *Financial Mail* had run an article.

After a few weeks in the saddle, Vanessa Grossman had approached several members of the family on an individual basis to say that the group would inevitably fail, crippled as it was by bank debts. They believed her. The books backed her up. She bought their holdings at knockdown prices. Once she had sixty-one per cent, she closed a deal with the banks to convert a percentage of the debts for non-voting stock, and worked her pants off to turn all the group's companies around, which she achieved with spectacular success coupled with some suspicion of bribery behind her securing of planning permission for 500 houses on an old Ministry of Defence site, and a fortuitous fire that had destroyed a disused factory. The insurance investigators had found no sign of arson and their company had paid out. Some friends of Prescott's on the district council had been caught up in the scandal.

He came to her job application form. In the reasons for seeking employment in Government House, she had written in large block capitals: "BECAUSE I'M BORED OUT OF MY F*****G SKULL!"

He could well believe it. To think that she had been working in this office for several weeks and he had hardly noticed her. And he had been almost rude to her just now when she offered some sound advice.

Four floors below, Judge Hooper paused in the bright evening sunlight and decided that he needed a drink. The only other occupant at the tables outside the Crown was a gawky blonde teenager crying into a glass of blackcurrant juice. He could hardly not be moved by the girl's anguished tears while he was waiting for a waiter to appear.

"What's the problem, young lady?"

Sarah looked up, her eyes bloodshot from crying. "They won't let me see her. Those bastards have said no every day. Even today."

"Won't let you see whom?"

"Vikki . . . Vikki Taylor. She's my best friend and I'm not allowed to see her. Not even her mum's been allowed in."

The judge could think of nothing to say.

"If only I could do something for her," said Sarah through her tears. "Anything . . ."

"There's nothing," said Judge Hooper. He moved from his table and sat opposite Sarah. "But perhaps there's one thing . . . One very small thing . . . It might sound silly, but who knows?"

Sarah looked hopefully at him. "What?"

"What's your name?"

Sarah told him.

The judge gestured to St Mary's. "You could pray, Sarah. You could pray for Vikki *and* Ellen."

He half expected the girl to dismiss the idea out of hand, but instead she stared at him while wiping her eyes.

"Vikki always went to church . . . She used to moan about it, but she always went."

"Well then . . ."

Sarah stood. "Yes . . . That's what I'll do. There's nothing else now, is there?"

"No," said the judge sadly. "Nothing else." He hesitated. "If you're going now, Sarah, and if you don't mind, I'd like to come with you."

Sarah nodded. "I'd like that."

Together, the unlikely pair made their way to the church.

Fifty-Six

It was over a week since Ellen and Vikki had been arrested. In that time they had got to know one another; to understand each others' moods, to know when to speak and when to remain silent.

It was 6.30 p.m., dusk was closing in and now was a good time to be silent. Each was sitting in her respective armchair in the little living-room of the apartment in Pentworth House that was their prison. They tried not to look at the window and the message of the failing light.

The door opened abruptly – there was no lock because there were always at least three girl sentinels on guard outside. The chief female sentinel entered the room. Her name was Helga. A woman Vikki remembered from the party at Pentworth House.

"You will remove all your clothes and put these on," said Helga, holding out two black, sleeveless gowns. "You can keep your shoes on. Leave your clothes here. You won't be needing them again – they will have to be burned separately."

The two women complied. Helga's eyes feasted greedily on Vikki's nakedness just as they had done so on the night of the party when she had helped pin Vikki down for Faraday's attempted rape.

Helga turned to the three female sentinels waiting outside. "OK. Let's go."

There were no fastenings on the garments; the two women held them closed as best they could while being shepherded along the corridor. They were ushered into the ballroom with its huge picture of Johann Bode. At the head of two long benches filled with sentinels Adrian Roscoe was standing on a low dias. He was wearing a gown of the purest white linen, arms folded, his blue eyes burning unbridled hatred down at the two women as they were thrust before him. Ellen stared him straight in the eye, not allowing her gaze to shift to the grim sight that she had noticed on first entering the hall. It was a butchers' block standing on four sturdy legs to one side of Roscoe. Imbedded in the block's sycamore end grain was a meat cleaver – its blade gleaming and looking razor-sharp.

Vikki kept her gaze directed at the floor. She had lived with terror for a week now; by concentrating hard on the pattern of the parquet floor, she could stand still without trembling, showing no outward sign of the demons of despair and fear that were tormenting her while she waited to wake up and find herself in her lovely little bedroom that her beloved daddy had prepared for her, with its electric curtains, her arms around Benji – her cuddly bear, and the life-size poster of Dario at the foot of her bed. Dario would rescue her. Dario would leap out, despatching her enemies with his assegai. Dario could do anything except, perhaps, save her sanity, which was teetering on the edge of the abyss after a week of mental torture.

"I was going to sentence you in the Solar Temple of the Bodian Brethren," Roscoe announced, his rich voice rolling around the hall. "But to do so would be to profane it with your vile presence."

"I haven't brought you any presents," said Ellen spiritedly. "It's too early for Christmas and I've no idea when your birthday is."

Roscoe looked taken back at first until the joke sunk in. His smile was slow but genuine; Ellen's defiant attitude added to the piquancy of what would happen next. He gestured to Vikki. "You gave this one a vile present, did you not?"

"What the hell are you talking about, Roscoe?"

"Yes – I'm talking about hell . . ." And then his face was contorted with fury. "The place from whence you summoned creatures to give your acolyte a new left hand!" He seized Vikki's left forearm and held it up. "This abomination! Confess that you arranged this!"

"Roscoe," said Ellen tiredly. "Your insanity has drilled too deep for you to listen to any rational explanation from me."

The cult leader nodded to one of the benches. Four male sentinels seized Vikki. They unfastened her watch and strapped her left wrist down on the chopping block. She gave a little gasp of fear, the first sound she had uttered, and stared at Roscoe – her green eyes listless, unseeing. The sentinels stood back. One looked on with interest, one closed his eyes, the other two looked sick, particularly when Roscoe jerked the cleaver from the block and swung it aloft.

"You either confess or you leave here with this hand hanging around your neck." He smiled and added, "You'll have to wear it for the rest of your life."

Vikki saw the older woman's indecision and cried out, "No, Ellen! You mustn't! You mustn't!"

"Very well," Ellen snapped. "I confess to being a witch! Is that what you want?"

Roscoe lowered the cleaver. "Drop your gown," he ordered.

It needed only a shrug for the loose garment to fall around Ellen's ankles. She held Roscoe's gaze so that she would see the slightest flicker of interest in her body. It annoyed him: he wanted to study her closely. He gestured to a sentinel holding a camcorder's viewfinder to draw nearer.

"Lie on the floor on your stomach, arms and legs outstretched in the shape of an X, palms down, your head near my feet."

Ellen did so.

The cameraman circled her on his knees.

"Repeat after me. I confess to profaning Almighty God by consorting with Satan . . ."

"I confess to profaning Almighty God by consorting with Satan . . ."

Roscoe stepped down from the dais and walked around Ellen. He could now look at her without being disconcerted by her gaze. This was the moment he had dreamed about – having this magnificent creature supine at his feet. But the intense surge of exhilaration he had been expecting never materialised.

"And summonsing his demons . . ."

"And summonsing his demons . . ."

It continued in that vein for several minutes; Roscoe reciting a litany of accusations of archaic religious crimes which Ellen repeated in a flat monotone.

Chanting started outside. "We want the witches! We want the witches!"

Roscoe controlled his rage and frustration. Even lying naked before him, her face to the floor, he felt that the woman was gaining in stature and dignity at his expense. She was looking down on him; sneering at him. "Stand up," he said curtly. "Put your gown on." He turned away to avoid her gaze as she climbed to her feet. But instead of donning the gown, she stood quite still, legs slightly apart, one hand over her mons pubis, but not to cover herself. Her fingers were moving slowly and sensually, mocking him, an enigmatic half-smile playing at the corners of her mouth – willing him to look down.

"I said, *put your gown on*, you filthy harlot!"

Still with that infuriating half-smile, Ellen drew the gown up and slipped her arms through the openings. She managed to make even that simple movement seem tormentingly sensual. Roscoe motioned to the sentinels to release Vikki's straps. They looked relieved to do so.

Roscoe stared at his two victims in turn. It was his turn to smile. Control was back with him. "My turn with the jokes, ladies. Your carriage awaits you."

Fifty-Seven

If Vanessa Grossman was surprised at Prescott's visit to her
tastefully restored mansion on the southern outskirts of Pentworth,
she didn't show it, whereas her husband was astonished.

Vanessa's gaze went from the armoured Range Rover in her drive
to Prescott, flanked by his usual retinue of two armed blackshirts.
One of them had forsaken a shotgun for the Sterling submachine-gun.

"A business matter, Miss Grossman," said Prescott awkwardly.
"It's so difficult discussing such things at the office."

"Those hoods stay outside," said Bernie Harriman firmly, looking
over his wife's shoulder. "They'll terrify the children."

Prescott gestured to his men to return to the Range Rover. Vanessa
ordered her husband to put their two children to bed and showed
Prescott into a huge kitchen lit by a methane lamp. In the office
she always looked neat in smart, businesslike clothes, and now she
even managed to look sharp in gardening jeans. The kitchen was not
merely tidy, but well organised – most of one wall taken up with
home-dried spices, their jars bearing indian-ink labels. She made
small-talk while making tea. Everything she would need to serve
the tea she placed on the kitchen table in advance.

She sat opposite Prescott when she had finished. Poised. Confident. Very different from her demeanour in the office.

"This is excellent tea, Miss Grossman."

Vanessa regarded him thoughtfully, her black eyes giving nothing
away. She had expected a move from Prescott following their little
tête-à-tête at the office, but not quite so soon. "You've praised it at
the office often enough but I suspect that that is not the reason for
your visit."

"I want to apologise. You gave me some sound advice at the
office. I fear I may have been a little rude in my reply. I had no
idea who you were. Vanessa Grossman of the Grossman group. You
should've said."

"OK. Apology accepted with thanks."

"I would also appreciate some advice."

If there was a gleam of triumph in Vanessa's eye, Prescott didn't see it. "You might not appreciate my tendency to be outspoken, Mr Prescott."

"I'm sure I would. I'm worried about the general organisation of the admin in Government House—"

"It's taken you long enough," Vanessa interrupted. "It's a shambles now that all the empire-builders have got their feet under their respective tables. The Town Clerk should've been much tougher with them."

Prescott nodded. "For some time now, I've felt that matters have been getting on top of Diana Sheldon."

Vanessa decided that now was the right moment to apply a little pressure to get the talk moving but keep control with her. "That's right, Mr Prescott – you've been shagging her."

Prescott was taken back. "Well – I hardly think—"

"Why don't you get to the point? Diana Sheldon has rebelled. She won't do your dirty work and you think I will. Do I get ten out of ten and a free day ticket to Legoland?"

The woman's fathomless black eyes unsettled Prescott but he pressed on. "You have considerable management experience. Do you think she should take early retirement?"

Vanessa raised an eyebrow. "And lose a person who's capable, provided she's not too overloaded or in a senior management position where her conscience is troubling her? That's not efficient use of human resources, Mr Prescott. Diana Sheldon is excellent middle-management material. If I were in your position, she would be my choice to run the supplies department. It's an important job and she'd be a damn sight better than the clown that's running it at the moment."

"She would never accept being demoted."

"Demoted? Who said anything about demotion? Supposing the government wants to turn the supplies department into an independent agency? The Pentworth Supplies Agency. She could be appointed its director/chairman for eventual floatation. There's no reason why not. It buys in, it sells or rents out. It could flourish on a five per cent margin if the deadwood is kicked out. With a fat share option and a salary linked to turnover, Diana Sheldon would be a fool not to accept it. Particularly as she's unhappy in her present job."

"It's an idea," Prescott admitted.

"I come up with solutions, Mr Prescott – not more problems."

"Which is why I'm offering you her job," said Prescott bluntly.

Vanessa laughed, scenting victory. But, as always, victory had to be on her terms. "Town Clerk? Forget it."

"But—"

"Call the position Director of the Civil Service, pay me treble what Diana Sheldon was paid, and I'm your man."

The stunning gall of the woman was amazing. "Well – I hardly think—"

"I'll save you a hundredfold my salary. I'd scrap the ludicrous departmental budget system for starters. Give a department a budget and they'll spend it. The compartmentalised budgetary system bedevils all organisations because the prestige of department heads is based on what they spend, not on what they save or what they're worth. Also you'll have someone to do all your dirty work. I've no equal when it comes to stabbing people in the back, and churning out everything-in-the-garden's-lovely press releases. I'm a source of solutions, Mr Prescott."

Prescott left Vanessa Grossman's house ten minutes later. He settled into the cushions of the Range Rover, sandwiched between his bodyguards, feeling very pleased with himself. He now had his very own tame Lucrezia Borgia.

Meanwhile Lucrezia was listening to the news on the kitchen radio. The crazy farce with the so-called witches was going ahead. She had no feelings concerning the fate awaiting the two women. Vanessa saw matters in terms of smart political moves or bad political moves. There were strong feelings against Prescott in her own social circle. The honeymoon period between the government and the people of Pentworth was nearly at an end, therefore it might be possible to exploit Prescott's weaknesses to her advantage. Her heartbeat quickened. The much-needed adrenalin rush that she hadn't felt for a long time stimulated other needs. She mounted the stairs, intent on sneaking up on her husband as he bathed the children.

Looking after their two children was a job Bernie Harriman was used to. The success of their marriage centred around their deal that Vanessa should work because she made serious money while he kept house. Vanessa loathed housewifely and motherly activities. But since the Wall, her humdrum clerical job in Government House had tapped very little of her dynamism and none of her driving ambition that stemmed from a family background that set little store by the abilities of a mere girl. As a result she'd had to watch in silent rage as her two incompetent older brothers set about driving the family business to the brink of ruin.

She put her arms around Bernie Harriman and sank her teeth sensually into his shoulder. It was a signal that she hadn't used for many months since her enforced separation from her office.

"Hallo," he said, turning around, grinning in anticipation. "What's got your juices flowing?"

She kissed him hungrily, ignoring the children. "Congratulate me."

"For what? Some sordid deal you've done with Prescott?"

"First step in a takeover battle. I'm in need of a lot of congratulating tonight, so get them packed off to bed ASAP. You're looking at Pentworth's next big white chief."

Fifty-Eight

The forecourt of Pentworth House was bathed by a floodlight. The waiting dogcart was guarded by a circle of six blackshirts armed with shotguns, and two more on horseback keeping back a group of about fifty men and youths – the yob, bomber jacket and shell suit element of Pentworth society. Nelson Faraday, looking like a black bat, was standing on the dogcart talking to the driver sentinel. Seeing Sarah Gale hanging back near the open main gates reminded him that he had a score to settle with that little cock-teasing bitch, but it would have to wait for another day.

Sarah was dressed and made-up to look at least eighteen. She had decided to accompany the procession, keeping in the background but determined to see out every horror so that she could bear witness against those who had abused and murdered her beloved Vikki. Either that or she would systematically kill them – she knew not how but she was bitterly resolved that she would do it.

The youths stopped their chanting and broke into cheers when the main door swung open. Roscoe appeared with Ellen and Vikki following, clutching their gowns closed. Their escort of sentinels was unnecessary; the two women walked erect to the dogcart. A wooden case containing shotgun cartridges had been placed in position as a step at the tailgate. The two women climbed aboard the dogcart. Vikki hesitated when she saw Faraday but accepted coaxing forward from Ellen. They stood side by side at the crossbar, staring straight ahead as Faraday manacled them by the wrists. This time they had to endure leg irons shackled to the floor planks by short lengths of chain. Their gowns fell open, provoking a chorus of whistles and catcalls.

"Hey, Nelson! Looks like we're gonna see a nice burning bush tonight!"

"Two burning bushes!"

The yells of laughter were silenced by a glare from Roscoe, who had also mounted the dogcart. He had hoped for a larger crowd; but it was a three-kilometre walk to the scourging site; doubtless there would be many more in Market Square for the burning. The route had been announced on the radio two hours earlier. He raised his bony arms in a gesture of supplication.

"God-fearing people of Pentworth!" he boomed. "You are not here merely to witness the destruction of these loathsome enemies of God! Before that, you are to take part in their scourging – in the driving out of the demons that have possessed them so that their black souls have a chance of redemption at the moment of their deaths! The male life essence of righteous ones is poison to demons! It sears them with fires more powerful and more enduring than those of their master! We will take these women to the place of their scourging where all men true to God will help drive out the forces of evil and eternal damnation that have seized the bodies of these witches, and send them back from whence they belong! Having saved the souls of these miserable wretches, we will then bring them back to burn their Satan-defiled bodies just as we burn diseased wood cut from a tree in order to save the tree! It will not be a pleasant task but God never made his path easy to follow. But God will be with you, pouring His strength into your bodies for what must be done this night. And when it is done, He will remove the Wall, for Pentworth will be purified! Let us march!"

A ragged cheer accompanied Roscoe as he climbed down from the dogcart. Faraday lit and handed out torches to eager hands. The box of cartridges and spare torches were placed in the dogcart and the tailgate closed. The two mounted blackshirts went ahead and the procession moved off with Roscoe walking at its head. Ellen and Vikki had to grab the crossbar as the dogcart lurched and bumped over the cobbles.

The phalanx filed through the gates and detoured through Market Square so that Ellen and Vikki saw the two massive stakes and their surrounding cones of brushwood. The two mounted blackshirts stayed in the lead, followed by Roscoe, and then the dogcart flanked by the sentinels and the blackshirts. Bringing up the rear was the noisy band of youths and young men. There was a group of six among them led by a gangling youth that tried to get to the front of the procession for a better view of Ellen and Vikki but were shooed back by the blackshirts.

A few people came out to watch but not the cheering crowds that Roscoe had expected. No people spilling off the pavement for the mounted blackshirts to clear. The men stared up at Ellen and Vikki, and looked away in embarrassment. A woman rushed out of a house and snatched away a small boy.

From his flat over the Catholic church hall on the corner of Market Square, Father Kendrick watched the procession's approach. The gangling youth was leading a small choir singing "We're going to a gangbang! We're going to a gangbang!" to the tune of "We're on Our Way to Wembley"; they seemed to have little trouble remembering the words. Some of the gangling youth's mates were among the bystanders; he persuaded them to join the procession, jeering at the doubters that they were frightened of not being able to get it up.

As the dogcart drew level with Father Kendrick's flat, Vikki looked up and saw the priest at the window. She actually smiled, the light of the blazing torches reflected in her green eyes, and made a brave attempt at a wave as best the chains would allow. The Catholic priest was deeply moved. He gave the sign of the cross and offered a fervent prayer for the salvation of both women. In the answering of that prayer he had a small but important part to play.

He climbed to the disused housekeeper's flat on the fourth floor and entered the living-room. It faced south. He opened the window and leaned out, holding a penlight infrared laser pointer. The half moon broke through wispy clouds, providing plenty of light for him to identify the dark hump of his target some two kilometres distant. He aimed the pointer at the target and sent dot-dot-dot-dash three times – the letter V in Morse code. He allowed a pause and sent six dashes. Another pause and then two dashes. He repeated the sequence three times.

Fifty-Nine

At that range the laser beam from Father Kenrick's pointer could not damage Carl Crittenden's eyes but the tiny point of light was bright enough for him to see it at the Temple of the Winds without his binoculars. He read two sends of the message to be certain and called down from the branches of a tree on the heavily wooded slope above where the great sandstone slab protruded from the hillside: "They've just left Pentworth House, Mr Weir. Six blackshirts on foot and two on horseback."

"Thanks, Carl – you'd better come down now." David turned to Malone. "Just as your informant said, Mike. She's certainly worth looking after."

Carl dropped out of the tree just as Dan Baldock with two burly stable lads dressed as blackshirts joined David and Malone for their final briefing. Carl, David, Baldock and Malone were completely swathed in black, even to the extent of black cotton gloves. David opened a tin containing a homemade mixture of lampblack and oil which he used to black all their faces except the two stable lads.

"We haven't got long," said Malone. "Let's go over what everyone has to do."

The six men talked for five minutes. They shook hands all round and melted silently into the trees. Malone's position behind some gorse bushes afforded him a good view of the track where it emerged on to the plateau. He lay prone, the weight of the .45 he had taken off Faraday pressing reassuringly against his thigh.

A thousand worries crowded in on him as he waited; the main one being that the two mounted blackshirts wouldn't scout ahead. Had the Country Brigade been too successful in establishing that they would be taking no action to stop the executions? That concern was banished when he heard the sound of hooves coming up the track. The others would have heard them, too. A few moments later the two mounted blackshirts appeared. They reined in their horses in the middle of the moonlit plateau and scoured the area with powerful halogen lanterns, their questing beams whipping back and forth above Malone, stabbing white light into the trees.

"Look, darling – if I say you take your knickers off, you take your bloody knickers off!"

Both beams swung as one to a narrow avenue through the trees towards the sound of the angry voice.

"Did you hear that?" asked one of the blackshirts.

"We'd better flush 'em out."

Don't dismount! Malone prayed, training his revolver on them. *Don't dismount!*

"Hey. Who's there!" yelled the indignant voice in the woods. "Bloody peeping Toms! Fuck off, you perverts!"

The blackshirts spurred their horses towards the trees. Malone's relief was like a blanket lifting, particularly when the riders broke into a canter.

The piano wire strung between two trees caught both blackshirts almost simultaneously across their chests and swept them off their saddles. The two stable lads dressed as blackshirts leapt from cover and grabbed the horses reins to calm them and prevent them returning riderless to the procession. They were skilled horsemen and had the nervous creatures under control within seconds. David and Baldock snatched the shotguns from the saddle holsters and covered the two winded men as they climbed to their feet.

"One sound!" Malone snarled. "One sound – and your headless ghosts will be haunting this place for years to come." He was standing legs slightly apart, clasping the heavy .45 in both outstretched hands in the correct manner to minimise kick so that he could be sure of getting in two fast, accurate shots with the intention of wounding them if they tried to escape.

The blackshirts put their hands up without being ordered. Malone told them to lie down on their stomachs, hands behind their backs. Carl secured their wrists with cable ties and bound their mouths using a generous amount of wide gaffer tape. Malone had even thought to provide mouth tubes in case the men had colds and were unable to breath through their noses. Carl and Baldock yanked the prisoners to their feet and marched them into the woods at the points of their own shotguns. They were back five minutes later looking pleased with themselves.

"They have a tree each but seemed most ungrateful," Baldock reported.

"Break a leg," said Malone to the stable lads as they mounted and returned the shotguns to the saddle holsters. One was pushing a flesh-coloured earphone into his ear, looping the wire behind his ear and under his collar so that it could not be seen. "Stay clear of the radius of the torches," Malone continued, "and listen out for my long burst of carrier."

The riders acknowledged, wheeled their horses expertly around and disappeared down the track.

David called from the edge of the plateau. He was pointing down and to the west. Carl, Malone and Baldock joined him and watched the distant points of flickering lights moving along the valley. The torches were clustered close together and were about a kilometre away.

"OK, back to your positions," said Malone. "I'll join you just before they get here."

David, Baldock and Carl vanished into the wooded shadows. Malone trained his binoculars on the cortège. He picked out the sentinels, easily distinguished by their white gowns. The one at the front without a torch was probably Roscoe. Altogether there were fifty-eight torches. That meant a crowd of about forty – less than he had anticipated. He was uncertain whether it would be an advantage or disadvantage. The armed blackshirts were sticking close to the dogcart. As it drew nearer he could see Ellen and Vikki more clearly, standing together, manacled to the crossbar and pressing against it to keep their gowns closed. Seeing the two hapless, innocent women subjected to such humiliation and mental torture made it difficult for him suppress his hatred towards Roscoe. The man was insane, but only clear thinking and decisive action was going to resolve this miserable situation. Hatred could wait.

He switched on his radio, made sure it was set to channel 41 – a frequency never used by the police – and sent five bursts of carrier. It was the signal for the seventh member of the rescue team to get ready to join them. The prearranged four burst acknowledgement came back immediately. Then the procession was lost to sight behind some trees.

Malone darted a little way down the narrow track and stopped, listening intently. After a few minutes he heard the faint strains of a lusty but ragged rendition of "Onward Christian Soldiers" and his heartbeat stepped up as he switched on his radio again. The five bursts of carrier and the acknowledgement was the signal to the approaching seventh member to begin his attack. There was no turning back now. Harvey Evans in his microlight biplane-bomber would be closing in. Malone raced back up the track, crossed the plateau, and plunged into the woods.

"US Cavalry and the Apaches are on their way!" he called and dived down beside Carl.

The four pulled their gas masks over their faces and waited, eyes trained on the spot where the cortège would appear. They could all hear the uproar of the approaching procession now. Some of the party were yelling the words of the hymn, drowning out those who were singing.

The blazing crowns of the torches carried by the lanky youth and his boisterous, whooping gang came into view first. The blackshirts had given up trying to keep them behind the main phalanx.

"Oh, leave them alone," Roscoe had ordered. "At least they provide a carnival atmosphere."

The gang had been a pain, yelling and screaming, pausing occasionally to stand in front of the dogcart and gesture suggestively by jerking their hips and elbows back and forth for the benefit of the dogcart's passengers. One of the new recruits that the lanky youth had picked up on the way had a ghetto blaster perched on his shoulder, with fully charged batteries, judging by the volume of the Bee Gee's "Stayin' Alive!" that belted from its twin speakers when he switched it on, adding to the uproar.

And then Roscoe and Faraday appeared, striding confidently ahead of the dogcart towards the centre of the plateau. But the procession had not strung out to negotiate the narrow track as the conspirators had hoped; four of the blackshirts had stayed close behind the dogcart. Malone sent a long burst on his radio and almost immediately there were the sounds of shouts and screams from further down the track. A shotgun boomed.

"Trouble below!" yelled one of the mounted stable lads, riding fast on to the plateau. "Need help!" He wheeled his horse around and disappeared down the track. Two of the four blackshirts followed the horseman at the double.

Malone thumped Carl on the back. The young man jumped to his feet and streaked off, a razor-sharp hunter's knife clutched in his right hand. He kept to the shadows as best he could but there came a point when he had to break cover and risk being seen. His job was to hamstring the horse drawing the dogcart. One of the concerns that Malone and David had had about the Temple of the Winds as the site of the ambush was the danger of the horse bolting and taking Ellen and Vikki over the edge. Malone had suggested his shooting the horse with the .45 but a reconnoitre and a study of the angles showed that there was a very real danger of hitting Ellen and Vikki. As much as Carl loved horses, he had volunteered for the job.

At that moment, just as Malone was about to fire a parachute flare, everything started going disastrously wrong.

Sixty

C arl's restricted field of vision through the round windows of the grotesque gas mask was one thing that the planners had overlooked – a shortcoming that was to trigger a sequence of disasters. He tripped on a rock and fell as he was about to dive under the dogcart. A sentinel saw him and yelled. Before Carl had a chance to recover, two more sentinels threw themselves on him and a fourth whipped out a shotgun from under his gown.

Malone's view of what happened was obscured by the dogcart's wheels. He saw something of the commotion and heard the horse neighing. He assumed that Carl had carried out his task and fired the flare. It climbed lazily into the sky and burst into life – a burning magnesium sun hanging from a parachute, turning night into day as well as giving a good indication of wind speed and direction.

A small measure of luck for the ambush team was that Harvey Evans in his microlight had seen Carl dash across the plateau of the Temple of the Winds and had turned toward his objective by the time Malone fired the flare to signal the air attack.

Evans was already lined up on his target. He put the tiny biplane's nose down to pick up speed and pulled the lever that released the first cluster of four bomblets. Timing was more a question of instinct than training. Two exploded harmlessly against the sheer sides of the sandstone scarp but the other two hit the rim, sending dense white clouds rolling malignantly towards the lanky youth and his noisy gang of revellers. One whiff was enough to send the lanky youth into paroxysms of abject terror. He sank to his knees, clutching his face, screaming, "I'm blind! I'm blind!"

Others in his party reacted likewise, gagging, clutching their throats, rolling about and thrashing their limbs, their screams lost in the roar of the microlight as it swept low over the Temple of the Winds. Malone, Baldock and David charged from their hiding places, firing flares low over the heads of the crowd to help the panic along.

It was all too much for the horse. The four sentinels hanging on to its reins and bridle, desperately trying to calm it, were shaken off when it reared up. White-eyed, ears laid back, it charged towards the woods but slewed around, throwing its driver clear, when a flare burst in front of it. Ellen and Vikki cried out in terror and doubled up, their arms hooked around the crossbar as best they could. The terrified beast wheeled again and headed for the only clear way out. With the dogcart crashing along behind it, threatening to overturn while shedding its cargo of spare torches and a case of shotgun cartridges, the petrified horse galloped straight for the rim of the sandstone plateau.

Sixty-One

O nce he had passed over the Temple of the Winds and was out
of shotgun range, Harvey Evans put his microlight into a tight
turn, increasing power as he did so to maintain height. He lined up
on the chaos of torches and flares on the plateau for his second run.
The wind screamed through the bomb racks, one fitted each side of
the fuselage.

He had never been licensed for night flying and had never
flown at night, and would never have agreed to this crazy
enterprise but for Malone's tenacity, and the promise of a properly
lit airstrip for his landing. It was one thing to take off from
a familiar field at night, quite another to find it for a safe
landing. Another worry had been that his engine would be heard
– the little air-cooled engine was as noisy as they came; it
seemed inevitable that his first approach would be heard and
that his low-level attack would be greeted by a barrage of
shotgun blasts. Malone had come up with a plan to deal with
that problem, too.

It had taken two hours of cajoling by Malone before Evans
had eventually agreed to take part in the rescue. Yesterday
Charlie Crittenden had visited him to fit the bomb racks, and
mount a lightweight plywood framework on the upper wing that
held four lengths of plastic waste pipe. Sticking out of each
tube was the business end of a marine distress rocket – their
four firing lanyards fitted with wooden toggles and arranged
in a neat row just above his head. He fervently hoped that
it wouldn't be necessary to use them. Launching rockets from
his tiny aircraft was not to his taste. Whereas objects dropped
over the side merely fell, there was no knowing what rockets
would do.

He roared down on the plateau and pulled the levers that released
the second cluster of four bombs. The flasks rattled down the racks.
In the instant that he pulled up, he caught a fleeting glimpse of the

horse and dogcart bolting for the edge, with the two terrified women clutching the crossbar. Sick at heart, he knew that something had gone terribly wrong – the horse was supposed to have been disabled before his attack.

Sixty-Two

When Roscoe first saw the swirling white clouds and his supporters writhing and screaming on the ground, clutching their faces, he ran to the higher ground and raised his arms to calm everyone, but for once no one was taking any notice of him. Several of his faithful sentinels suffered a profound and sudden loss of faith, particularly when the lanky youth staggered towards them, his face a grotesque mask – eyes bulging horribly, his skin blue. His cries that he was blind decided them. Those that had been armed flung down their shotguns to be rid of their weight and took flight down the track, dragging their cowls across their faces to protect them from the now dispersing white clouds. The blackshirts did the same, and when the sentinels and driver, who had tried to control the rearing horse, were thrown clear, they too abandoned all hope and joined the panic-fuelled exodus.

It was two prancing black demons with hideous, goggling gas mask faces that caused Roscoe's courage to fail him. He promptly decided to put his faith in his legs rather than his silver cross. Demons were notoriously ill-informed on occult matters. He didn't know what had happened to Faraday and didn't much care. His only thought was to get away from this hellish place.

Malone yanked off his gas mask, fired two shots at the bolting horse, and was suddenly surrounded by exploding bomblets, showering him with glass. He took a deep breath before the white clouds engulfed him and raced towards the brink in time to see the horse crash lifeless to the ground within five metres of the edge, blood spurting from the terrible exit wound in its head. The careering dogcart slewed around the bulk of the dead horse, pivoting on its hafts. It crashed on to its side, but still had sufficient momentum to drag the horse several metres as it went backwards over the edge.

The cart stopped, its rear wheels spinning, rocking wildly on the sandstone rim, its weight gradually dragging the horse by the one remaining harnessed haft, Ellen and Vikki screaming hysterically, hanging helplessly by the chains of their manacles and leg irons which had saved them from a fifty-metre fall.

Malone threw himself prone and grabbed the dead horse by the harness collar. The slide slowed but didn't stop. His yells brought everyone running, including the lanky youth and his supposedly gassed gang. They all scrambled to their feet and rushed to get a handhold on the dead horse, none of them blind or seeming the worse for wear, other than white dust in their hair and clinging to their clothes, and blue dye on their faces.

One of the mounted stable lads saw what was needed and rode into the woods to retrieve rope and the bolt-cropper from the supplies cache.

Nelson Faraday was dressed entirely in black therefore it was understandable that the stable lad didn't see him. Faraday emerged from behind his tree and watched the fake blackshirt riding away. By the light of burning torches dropped on the ground, he could see what had happened at the brink. He could also see a discarded shotgun. No one saw him creep forward. He had no clear plan in mind but he would think of something once he had a weapon.

Sixty-Three

To his immense relief, Harvey Evans saw that the dogcart had not gone right over the edge, though it was hanging down at a dangerous angle. There were plenty of people at the site trying to make it secure. There was nothing he could do about the situation so he moved on to the second phase of his attacks – to ensure that the exodus from the Temple of the Winds became a rout.

"We'll be taking Ellen and Vikki to a safe house," Malone had told him. "We don't want any blackshirts or sentinels in the area that might take it into their heads to follow us. The whole area has to be cleared."

Luckily the sentinels were easy to spot in their white gowns. A small group were holding a conference at the foot of the track that led up to the Temple of the Winds. None appeared to be armed. They fled in panic towards the relative safety of Pentworth when Evans flew towards them and dumped four more bombs at their heels. The consternation that a mixture of pressurised flour and talcum powder could produce amused him but it was understandable.

Two blackshirts halfway down the track were made of tougher stuff. They stood their ground, one even raised a shotgun, but their courage deserted them when they realised that they had been spotted, and they, too, joined in the panic-stricken flight towards Pentworth.

Evans patrolled the area for another ten minutes, scouring along the valley for any sign of movement. He was tempted to return to the Temple of the Winds to see what was happening but he had to conserve fuel, and he was now close to Temple Farm.

He didn't have to make a pass over the farm to alert the Charlie Crittenden and his younger boys. They had been waiting outside. The moment they heard the microlight's approach, they raced along the recently close-mown paddock, lighting the lane of torches.

Evans' landing was remarkably smooth – like touching down on a bowling green. He brought the machine to a stop, shutdown the engine, and reflected that a lot of work had gone into the paddock to mow it so short, roll out bumps and fill hollows. Gus trotted along the makeshift airstrip dousing the torches and pulling them out of the ground. He and his father hauled on some wheeled chicken houses to park them in the middle of the paddock before turning their attention to Evans.

"How'd it go?" Charlie asked, inspecting his bomb racks.

"A couple of hitches but it looked like everything was being sorted out when I left. Your bomb racks worked perfectly, Charlie. Could you do something about the rockets, please. Thank God I didn't have to use them."

Evans felt better when the rockets had been disarmed and removed from their tubes. Charlie also unloaded the unused bombs and released their charges of compressed-air. The group trundled the diminutive biplane across the paddock to the rick that had been hollowed-out to hide it. The makeshift hanger also housed Evans' supply of spares for the microlight including a spare engine, all of which Charlie had collected when he had installed the bomb racks at Evans' home.

Evans glanced at his watch and noted that twenty-five minutes had lapsed from take-off to landing. It had seemed much longer. He experienced a little twinge of guilt when he realised that he had enjoyed every minute of the bizarre operation.

Sixty-Four

The two stable lads urged their horses backwards. The creatures were jittery at the sight and smell of the dead horse but the voices and confidence of their riders calmed their nerves. The ropes fastened between their saddle pommels and the teetering dogcart tightened. The cart was now secure.

Dan Baldock was the lightest of the group. With the long-handled bolt-cropper hanging from a cord on his belt, he climbed gingerly on to the precariously balanced wagon while others held torches for him. He carefully eased himself on to the crossbar so that he was immediately above Ellen and Vikki, hanging by their leg irons and manacles, their faces white with terror, unable to speak. He appraised the situation quickly and decided to start with Ellen. She was the heavier, her wrists and ankles had suffered the worst abrasions.

"Soon have you have got of this mess, ladies," he said cheerfully. "Can't have you hanging about like this all night, can we?"

He passed a rope around Ellen and secured it with a bowline knot, taking care to position it above her breasts so that it was a snug fit under her armpits.

"OK – lift."

The four men holding the rope heaved.

"Stop!"

The chains were now slack. Ellen smiled her relief at the sudden removal of the excruciating load on her ankles and wrists. The bolt-cropper made short work of the four chains and Ellen was free. Baldock gave the signal and she was lifted to safety. David had a cold chisel and club hammer to break the locks open on the irons.

Baldock repeated the process with Vikki. By the time he had climbed back on to the rim, both women were sitting, clutching their gowns around them, badly shaken, yet smiling happily for the first time in a week. David was making a fuss of Ellen that Malone sensed she found embarrassing. The men held up blankets to screen the women while they changed into underwear, jeans and T-shirts that had been hidden in the supplies cache for them. None of the clothes fitted but they were too pleased to be out of the gowns to complain.

Everyone clustered around near the edge of the sandstone scarp was too preoccupied with the rescued women to notice Nelson Faraday creep forward and retrieve the shotgun.

"This is a decent cart, Mr Malone," said one of the riders. "We ought to try and save it."

"We don't have time – best let it go," Malone replied.

The ropes attached to the horses were released, and the lanky youth and his mates relinquished their grip on the dead horse. The weight of the dogcart dragged it towards the edge. The cart sank out of sight with a loud grinding of splintering wood and finally it and the dead horse disappeared. Two seconds silence and then a loud crash echoing up from the darkness, followed by a series of smaller crashes, and then silence again.

Faraday could scarcely believe his luck when Malone moved slightly away from the main group. He had a perfect sight on him against the moonlit sky. He raised the shotgun and aimed.

"No!"

Startled, Faraday swung the shotgun towards the voice but Sarah was upon him, a kicking, screaming dervish, blonde hair lashing and a bony knee pile-driving into his groin as she tried to wrest the shotgun from him by grabbing it by the barrels.

The first barrel discharged into the air.

The second barrel discharged into Sarah. Over fifty grammes of deer shot hit her in the stomach and hurled her backwards like a discarded peg doll. Malone's charge was stopped by Faraday swinging the shotgun around by the barrels. The stock catching him on the temple. It was a glancing blow but the few seconds of disorientation Malone suffered were enough for Faraday to drop the shotgun and disappear into woods.

"Get after him!" Malone yelled at the stable lads as they galloped up. "Don't for Christ's sake let him get away!"

The two riders plunged into the darkness after Faraday but they had been too busy mounting their horses to see which way he had gone.

"Sarah!" Vikki screamed. Before her rescuers could stop her, she raced across the plateau to the still form of her beloved friend and gathered her into her arms, unmindful of the huge spread of warm blood that was soaking through the front and back of Sarah's clothes. "Sarah!" Vikki kept sobbing. "Oh, Sarah . . . Why? Why?" She rocked her friend's body back and forth, trying to stroke Sarah's hair from her staring, sightless eyes and succeeded only in smearing blood across her face.

David touched her shoulder. "Vikki—"

"You've got to get help for her!"

"She's dead, Vikki . . ."

The distraught girl stared up at the circle of ashen faces that had gathered around. She hugged Sarah's body closer to her and her tears mingled with the dead girl's blood. "Why couldn't you have left us alone?!" she screamed, her voice cracking in hysteria. *"Why?! Why?! Why?!"*

Sixty-Five

It was a little after nine o'clock on Sunday morning. Prescott was sitting behind his desk feeling very relaxed and very pleased with himself, although his expression was grim for the benefit of Roscoe and Faraday. The cult leader was badly rattled by the night's debacle at the Temple of the Winds. Serve the religious loony right for thinking he could get the better of him.

Prescott's intercom key was down, in conference mode, the front panel hidden by some papers, and Vanessa Grossman was at her desk in the outer office wearing audio typing headphones and seemingly intent on some minutes she was typing. He had sent a car for her and she had come immediately. Ten minutes briefing on the night's shambles was all she needed, and she had offered some seemingly sound advice on turning the night's disaster to his advantage.

"So you're claiming three ringleaders, Adrian," said Prescott, making notes. "Mike Malone, David Weir and Dan Baldock . . . Not forgetting the role played by Harvey Evans. Dropping flour bombs . . . hardly illegal and therefore I see no need to issue warrants for their arrest."

Roscoe stopped his angry pacing and stared at Prescott. "They disrupted a legal execution!"

"An illegal execution, Adrian. Hanging is the only legally sanctioned form of capital punishment in England. If you want to use your sentinels to search for the two women – fine – their warrants are still in force. But we leave Malone and the others alone until we have concrete evidence against the Country Brigade."

"Every detail!" Roscoe fumed, resuming his pacing up and down the office. "They knew every detail! How? How?"

"Pentworth House always was leaky, Adrian," Prescott observed.

The cult leader continued pacing, twisting his bony hands together to control his rage while watched apprehensively by Faraday who was decidedly unhappy, his fine leather pants and cloak torn and scratched by brambles from having to alternately flee and hide from his mounted pursuers until he reached the outskirts of the town. He was even more unhappy when Roscoe turned his glare on him.

"Only you and I knew the details! And the whole of the Country Brigade, it seems! How?"

"It's not possible that they knew anything, Father."

"Not possible!" Roscoe thundered. "They unseated Tom and Kes with a wire strung between two trees at the Temple of the Winds! They knew every move we made before we knew ourselves!"

"How many were involved in the planning?" asked Prescott.

"Just the two of us," Roscoe replied, nodding to Faraday. "He had a copy of the timetable and schedule."

"So how many copies were there of this timetable, Adrian?"

"Two! The one I typed, which has never been out of my possession, and the carbon copy which I gave to Faraday!"

"Father – I give you my word, there's no way that anyone could've . . ." Faraday's voice trailed away when he realised something.

"Well?"

"Claire Lake . . ." Faraday breathed. "She was in my room when I was asleep."

"She wouldn't do anything. Claire's a trustworthy girl."

"She got into my room on a crazy pretext on Wednesday night during the party," Faraday answered. "I'd had too much to drink so I let her in. She's usually a prissy little bitch, but not on Wednesday night. When I woke up, she'd gone. She could've gone through my things when I was asleep."

Roscoe picked up Prescott's telephone and was about to ask the operator to put him through to Pentworth House, but Prescott took the headphone from him and replaced it on the hook.

"This is my office, Adrian. If you wish to use the phone, you ask."

"Undermine him at every opportunity," had been Vanessa's advice. "Never call him Father, and never let him try to seize any initiatives. So much the better if he gets angry – angry people are easier to manipulate because your behaviour is controlling their emotions. The centre of an angry person's personality moves outside them for others to control."

Prescott calmly returned Roscoe's glare, his hand remaining firmly on his telephone.

"May I use your telephone?" Roscoe snapped.

Prescott grinned at the capitulation and took his hand away. "Go ahead," he said generously, reflecting on the shrewdness of Vanessa Grossman's advice. She was proving very useful.

Roscoe put his call through and asked for Claire Lake to be brought around to Government House immediately. He listened for a moment, and replaced the headphone. He stared accusingly at Faraday. "The duty sentinel says the log shows that Claire Lake went jogging at her usual time last night and hasn't returned. I want her found, too. Use every blackshirt you've got."

"If you don't mind, Adrian," said Prescott mildly. "*I'll* be the one to decide on the deployment of government resources."

Roscoe was shaken. He started to protest but Prescott cut him short. "As I've said, Adrian, if you want to use your own staff to hunt for Ellen Duncan and Vikki Taylor, that's up to you. But Claire Lake has broken no laws. If she wants to leave your brethren, she has a perfect right to do so. Now, if you don't mind, I wish to discuss what needs to be done next with my head of security. You've had a long night. You look dead on your feet and you're not thinking straight. If you wish to see me tomorrow, call my secretary to fix an appointment. Now go and get some sleep. Oh, by the way – a small point. Have those stakes removed from outside ASAP. Next time you want to put something like that up, you might consider applying for planning permission in the normal way."

For a moment it looked as if Roscoe was going to lose his temper, but he controlled himself, directed a hard stare at Faraday, and swept from the office. The damper denied him the opportunity to slam the door.

Prescott waved Faraday to a chair. "I'm not blaming you in the slightest for what happened last night, Nelson. Under the circumstances, you did extremely well to get away."

"Thank you, sir . . ."

"I heard that Roscoe ran like a rabbit when things started to go wrong."

"He did," Faraday replied bitterly. He paused and added, "There's the girl that got shot—"

"An accident from your account, Nelson. I don't think you need have any worries on that score. The coroner is a personal friend. A sensible man. I'm sure he'll come up with an accidental death verdict. However, much has to be done to clear up this mess. It's important that we tackle everything properly. I'm going to need your wholehearted co-operation and the co-operation of the blackshirts."

"You can be sure of that, sir."

Prescott beamed. "Excellent. The armoury situation is worrying, of course. Five shotguns unaccounted for and a box of a thousand cartridges."

"The search unit I've sent out might turn up something, sir."

"I doubt it, Nelson, but you're right to try. I think you ought to get some sleep, too. You've had a far more hectic night than Adrian. We'll talk tomorrow."

Sixty-Six

P rescott waited for several minutes after Faraday had gone, expecting Vanessa Grossman to come in. In the end he had to go out to her.

"You did well, Prescott," she said. "I particularly liked the touch with getting Roscoe to ask to use the phone. Assertiveness over details is important. His influence is definitely on the wane."

Her patronising tone and that she had addressed him by his surname irritated Prescott but he let it pass. She was proving to be too important for him to risk upsetting her now.

"As for Baldock, Weir, and Ellen Duncan," Vanessa continued. "It would be useful from your point of view if it could be proved that they were members of a proscribed organisation. They would lose their seats on the council, and as it's mid-term, you'd be within your rights to co-opt new members."

"I had thought of that," said Prescott. "You mean proscribe the Country Brigade? All they've done so far is provide extra men on food delivery wagons and dropped flour bombs on an illegal execution party."

"They'll show their true colours soon enough, Prescott. When they do, you must be ready for them. You're going to have to amalgamate the morris police and the blackshirts into a single police force. That'll remove the blackshirts completely from Roscoe's influence – especially if they're given senior positions in the new force – which will have to be expanded considerably to cover the country areas properly. In the meantime, you ought to consider holding discussions with the leading lights in the Country Brigade before proscribing them."

"What good will that do? They're turning into a bunch of terrorists."

"They've got wide support, Prescott. It would demonstrate that you're doing your best to resolve this rift between the town and the country. You'd be seen as the peacemaker. Also, it would be an opportunity for you to see how united they are and just how much authority Dan Baldock holds – to see if he has the clout to agree matters off his own bat or whether he's forever having to go into huddles with his cronies to get their support."

"Perhaps it's not such a bad idea," said Prescott doubtfully.

"I'll get it organised," said Vanessa. She added, "Calling it a peace conference would make you look good."

Prescott was pleased. In Vanessa Grossman it looked like he was going to have a capable administrator, an excellent advisor, and a shrewd PR operator. Well worth her pay. "Fine, Miss Grossman. I'll leave all the details to you."

"I'll need your seal. I'll deal with all the paperwork, which is what I'm good at. You go after hearts and minds, which is what you're good at. A deal?"

"A deal," Prescott agreed, grinning.

Sixty-Seven

Claire moved her rook, carefully examined the chessboard before taking her finger off the piece and announced, "Check!"

"No it's not," said Ellen sourly.

Claire was indignant. "Yes it is. You said that if a rook threatens the king in a straight line—"

"It's not check!" Ellen snapped. "It's bloody checkmate! I was hoping you hadn't seen it."

The girl bounced excitedly up and down in her camping chair. "Hey – I've beaten you at last, Ellen!"

"It's always the same," Ellen grumbled. "I once taught a nephew to play chess, an eight-year-old, and he ended up wiping the floor with me after three days. It's taken you two days."

"Another game?" asked Claire eagerly.

Ellen tipped the chessmen into their box. "I've had enough. One thing you will learn about me in the fullness, Claire, is that I'm a bad loser."

"How about Monopoly so that we can all play?"

Ellen glanced across the cave at Vikki who was staring listlessly at the mammoth mural. "How about a game of Monopoly, Vikki?"

Vikki made no reply.

"Vikki?"

No reply.

"With a face like yours, we'll let you be the boot."

"I don't want to play any fucking stupid games!"

"I will not tolerate such language in my cave!" Ellen retorted.

Claire giggled. Vikki scowled at her and returned her gaze to the painting. The older women exchanged despairing looks. Ellen had had enough. She and Claire had spent much of the two days they had been incarcerated in the cave trying to comfort Vikki in her grief over the death of Sarah. Ellen rose from her chair and confronted the girl.

"Vikki, look at me." The girl refused to turn her head so Ellen forced her chin around. "Now you listen to me, young lady.

We've had two days of this ridiculous sulking and we're both heartily—"

"I'm not sulking!" Vikki snapped back. "How would you like it if your best friend was murdered in front of you?"

"That's a stupid question and you know it is. We both understand how you feel. But this isn't going to help Sarah, and it certainly isn't helping us. Heaven knows how long we're going to be stuck in here, so for God's sake please pull yourself together and try to make life a bit more bearable for all of us."

"It would've been better if they'd let us burn instead of interfering—"

Ellen's answer was a hard slap across Vikki's face that jerked her head back, her eyes wide with shock. "You ungrateful little bitch! A lot of people have taken terrible risks to save your miserable skin, including Claire. They're probably being hunted down now, their families arrested, and God knows what else. Now you make yourself more amenable, young lady, or, I swear, you'll wish you *had* ended up at that stake!"

"That's what I do wish!" With that Vikki burst into tears. She jumped up and threw herself on her bed, her back to the cave, shoulders heaving.

"I don't suppose that did much good," said Claire quietly, a note of rebuke in her voice.

Ellen shrugged. "Maybe not. But it did *me* a power of good."

Sixty-Eight

The terror organised by Vanessa Grossman began quietly enough with a dark-clad figure leaving the Pentworth House bakery just before dawn clutching a loaf that was still hot from the ovens. There were always a few early risers anxious for the first bread of the day; therefore a small queue outside the bakery before first light when the gates opened was not unusual. What was unusual was that the figure did not leave through the gates but vaulted quickly over a safety zone fence, dashed across the grass, and rolled under the main low-pressure methane storage tank that supplied gas to the bread ovens. There were two of the ten-metre diameter tanks supported on brick piles, and a third under construction. The methane was produced from pig manure.

Once out of sight, the saboteur crawled to within a metre of one of the pressure-relief breather pipes – the smell was appalling – and unpacked the components of his incendiary device. It was fiendishly simple, consisting of paraffin wax fire lighters fixed to the underside of the storage tank with gaffer tape. Pushed around the fire lighters were small balls of tissue paper that had been soaked in potassium nitrate – used for curing meat and highly inflammable. Hanging from each fire lighter was a length of fluffy, white cotton string. There was a good deal of debris under the tank: bits of paper, straw, even a few pieces of wood, which he arranged into a neat pile under the fire lighters. Last operation was to light the end of each dangling string and quickly blow the flame out leaving a smouldering point of red at the tip. The strings smouldered at a rate of a centimetre per minute which meant it would be thirty minutes before they set fire to the balls of tissue paper which, in turn, would ignite the fire lighters.

Satisfied that the string fuses were smouldering properly, he wriggled out from under the tank, picked up his loaf, and made sure that no one was about before hopping over the fence and rejoining the shoppers leaving the bakery.

The entire operation had taken less than ten minutes. The saboteur prided himself on his technique. The beauty of his device was its simplicity and that all the component parts were combustible and would be burned. As with all his work, there would no incriminating bits of timer or metal to arouse the suspicions of insurance investigators: everything would be destroyed. All that he had to do now was make a phone call from a phonebox that implicated the Country Brigade. He had worked for Vanessa Grossman before in the days before the Wall. She had paid well then, and tomorrow she would hand over the second half of his fee.

One tiny worry as he tore a crust off the loaf and chewed it while putting distance between himself and Pentworth House: where was he going to get such delicious bread after the inevitable outcome of his mission?

Sixty-Nine

It wasn't so much an explosion, but a huge sheet of flame that ripped the methane tank open and destroyed the second tank in a similar spectacular manner. The resulting fireball climbed into sky, briefly illuminating the entire town. No one was hurt but the ground fire threatened to engulf the nearby grain silos. Pentworth's two fire appliances were on the scene within five minutes, branch pipes dousing the bakery and the grain silos to stop the fire from spreading.

A crowd gathered and an announcement followed on Radio Pentworth to say that the radio station had received a phone call purportedly from the Country Brigade claiming responsibility for the sabotage.

Vanessa Grossman was first to start work on the fourth floor of Government House. She made a cup of tea and listened on her radio to the comments of outraged citizens being interviewed in Market Square, while reflecting that everything was off to a good start. The previous day Diana Sheldon had accepted Prescott's offer as director of the supplies agency with some eagerness – anything to be completely independent of Prescott – and had moved out of Government House by midday.

Vanessa now had Diana Sheldon's old position in Prescott's outer office but not for long: she had earmarked a separate office for herself so that she could plan her intrigues in private. Her intercom buzzed. The lobby desk blackshirt tipping her off that Prescott had arrived. She was getting them trained.

"Bad business, Miss Grossman," said Prescott when he came in. "Who would've thought that that rabble would have the nerve to do such a thing in the middle of the town?"

"Who indeed," said Vanessa handing him a briefing note. "You're due down the corridor in the radio studio in ten minutes. You'll be deploring this cowardly act without overtly blaming the Country Brigade, and calling on volunteers to join the new part-time police reserve."

"What police reserve?"

"The one you'll be announcing on the radio in ten minutes," said Vanessa patiently. "While you're doing that, I'll be fixing up some transport to start shipping our grain out of Pentworth House's silos and getting local bakers geared up to produce bread instead of fancy cakes."

"My God," said Prescott suddenly, as a thought occurred. "This business is going to work to our advantage. Roscoe had a virtual monopoly on bread production."

"Yes," said Vanessa drily. "It had drifted across my mind."

"He once threatened me with closing his bakery unless I played ball with him. Damned impudence."

She removed an imaginary thread from Prescott's safari shirt. One small gesture for a woman; one giant leap for domination. "Well, he won't be doing anything like that again. Now off you go and do your piece, Prescott. Call to arms. Pentworth facing a crisis. You do that sort of thing well." She meant it, and sent him packing.

The other girls came in, chatting animatedly about the bakery explosion. They liked Vanessa and accepted her promotion. That she had children, worried about their schooling, understood the problems of running a family and a job, made it possible for them to relate to her in a way that they couldn't to Diana Sheldon.

Vanessa called the messenger service and sent for Tony Selby, the boss of Selby Engineering. While listening to Prescott, she read a file on the engineering company's resources that Diana Sheldon had put together.

"We don't know, as yet, how the explosion was caused," Prescott was saying. "You can't expect me to comment until we have more information, but the perpetrators of this cowardly act will be caught and brought to justice."

"We had a call claiming it was the work of the Country Brigade," said the presenter.

"Anyone can make a phone call," was Prescott's guarded reply.

Vanessa closed the Selby file and concentrated on Prescott's interview. She rolled a press release blank into her typewriter and rattled out a short statement saying that the Country Brigade had not denied responsibility for the attack, therefore they were under suspicion. She signed it on behalf of Prescott and used his seal. A messenger took it to radio station's newsroom. It was certain to be mentioned in the next news bulletin.

Seventy

Tony Selby was ushered into Vanessa's commandeered office. He was a grave-looking man of about thirty-five. He had taken over his father's engineering business at the age of twenty-three and, in an unusual move for a British company, had promptly borrowed the equivalent of five years' turnover for investment in new machine tools. With new shapers, capstans, lathes, mills, stamping presses, injection moulding equipment and a wide variety of other tools, Selby Engineering and its hundred employees had been able to tackle any business that came their way. Immediately following the Wall crisis they had doubled their staff and turned out solar cooker dishes by the score – from which they had acquired skills in papier mâché moulding. They had followed this with solar water heating panels, methane lamps, and charcoal cookers – all well designed and built to last, and with good spares support, because Pentworth could not afford to waste materials on planned obsolescence. They had even designed and built a pair of twenty-kilowatt methane-powered generators to supply their plant's power needs, and had converted a number of vehicles to run on the gas.

After a few opening pleasantries, Vanessa got down to business. "Mr Prescott is embarking on an ambitious expansion plan for the police."

"Certainly something needs to be done after that business with the bakery, Miss Grossman."

"It's not only the Country Brigade that concerns him, but the fact that such a force would be poorly armed should our Silent Vulcan friends in Pentworth Lake make any hostile moves."

Selby grinned. "I don't think any weaponry we could turn out would be much of a match against the technology that produced the Wall."

"But we must be prepared to meet any threat to the best of our ability," Vanessa insisted. "There's a bag in the corner beside you. Take a look, please."

Puzzled, Selby unzipped the Nike sports bag and took out a

sub-machinegun. The lightweight weapon had an open frame stock made of pressed steel, and a folding butt. "Good heavens. A Sterling. Some years ago we had an overhaul subcontract from Royal Ordnance at Blackburn on a few hundred of these things."

"So you're familiar with them?"

"My chief designer is."

"And there're two loaded magazines," Vanessa added.

Selby opened the weapon and inspected its ejector mechanism. "Where did it come from?"

"A woman handed it in to the police a few days before the Wall appeared. Could you reproduce it, Mr Selby?"

The engineer sensed a joke. "These things are incredibly crude and simple," he commented. "That's the whole point of them. Cheap and nasty. Easier to make than, say, wind-up clocks. About half-a-dozen moving parts to work the blow-back and ejector mechanism via the trigger, a barrel, and that's about it." He put the gun down on the desk and picked up one of the magazines. "As for these things – almost an empty box for the rounds and a coil spring that rams them into the chamber as they're fired. The only difficult bit about the gun itself is machining and heat-treating the barrel. But these are low-pressure weapons, so it's nothing fancy."

"How many could you make?"

Selby met Vanessa's gaze and realised with a sinking feeling that she was serious. He took a steel tape from his pocket and measured the length of the barrel. "We've got enough mild steel bar stock to turn out about two hundred."

"Excellent. That sounds like a sensible number."

"The pistol grip, the sights, even the frame could be easily made from moulded plastic using this gun as a pattern." The engineer paused. "Miss Grossman – we could turn out two hundred Sterling copies with very little trouble but it would completely exhaust our stock of fifty-mill-diameter mild steel bar stock. Forgive me if I'm speaking out of turn, but do you think it wise to expend our limited resources on armaments on such a scale? We'll need that steel for water pumps, generator armatures, hospital equipment – a whole range of socially useful applications."

Vanessa's smile was icy. "You *are* speaking out of turn, Mr Selby, and you are forgiven. Expenditure on defence is essential to maintain peace otherwise there is no point in your socially useful applications."

"But the cost—"

"Can be met by pruning other budgets," said Vanessa, thinking that education and health were having too much spent on them anyway. "But that's not your concern, Mr Selby."

"There's a major problem," said the engineer. "The ammunition. We can mass-produce the cases, the noses – no real problem there. But we can't produce cordite for the firing charge, or the impact-sensitive material for the percussion caps. You're going to need a chemical manufacturing plant."

"I've thought of that, Mr Selby. Who would be best to advise? Bob Harding?"

"I'd certainly start with him."

Vanessa summoned a messenger and sent him to collect Bob Harding. "Right, Mr Selby. Two hundred Sterlings. Let's talk prices. If we can agree, I'll raise a purchase warrant here and now. But I want a batch of at least twenty within ten days, with or without ammunition, and I want them produced under conditions of absolute secrecy."

Selby assured her that only a few trusted employees would be tasked with assembling and testing the finished weapons. He left Government House wondering if Pentworth's little world was going crazy.

Seventy-One

O f all people, Anne Taylor was one person that David Weir could not bring himself to lie to, so he bent the truth to the best of his ability.

"I'm sorry, Anne, but I can't tell you where Vikki is. But I can promise you that she's safe."

"Then you must know where she is."

The green eyes staring at him were disturbingly like Vikki's eyes that had regarded him across the courtroom.

"That's not what I said, Anne."

Anne indicated the bag and a large, threadbare cuddly bear that she had dumped on David's kitchen table. "You can at least see that she gets these. That's Benji – Vikki will be lost without him."

For God's sake, Anne! She's sixteen now!

"I can't, Anne. You would've been seen bringing Benji here, so you'll have to be seen taking him back."

Anne produced a cardboard tube. "Surely you can give her this? It's Dario – a wall poster of a Zulu warrior – she adores him."

"Did she have it in her bedroom?"

"Yes."

"Then put it back, Anne. And the teddy bear."

The mother's shoulders slumped. "You're right, of course. I've had the sentinels around twice now, looking for her. They've turned the place upside-down. What can I do to stop them? I'm alone, there're no phones."

"They've tried it on here," said David grimly. "But there're too many of us for them to be a nuisance. They get escorted around the farm and then kicked off."

"Have the police been around?"

"Yes. They wanted a statement about the shooting of Sarah Gale."

Anne grimaced. "Poor little Sarah. Thanks to you and Mike Malone and the others, it looks like that bastard, Faraday, is going to get away with it."

263

"From what we all saw, it looked like an accident. Sarah was trying to get the shotgun off him. We'll never know if the second barrel going off was an accident or deliberate."

Anger flashed in Anne's eyes. "He would've killed you all if it hadn't been for Sarah! And now he's going to get away with killing her thanks to you!"

"I'm sorry if you think that, Anne. We all told the truth."

The mother was suddenly deflated. "I'm the one who should be sorry, David. I must sound so ungrateful after all the risks you took to rescue them."

"There's nothing to be sorry about, Anne. And you sound as a mother who cares for her daughter should sound . I'm only sorry that I can't tell you anything other than to promise you that Vikki is safe."

"If the police aren't looking for Vikki and Ellen, I would've thought it would be safe for them now."

"Those warrants and those convictions are still in force," said David. "Until they're set aside, they have to remain in hiding. If anything, it's even more dangerous for them now. Have you seen the notices that have gone up around the town?"

Anne looked puzzled. "What notices?"

"Roscoe is offering three thousand euros for information that leads to the recapture of Vikki and Ellen."

The mother looked devastated. "I had no idea."

"He's got the money now that the banks are allowing conversion of ten per cent of cash held before the Wall. At a nice, fat commission of nine per cent, of course."

Anne shook her head sadly. "It all looked so good at first . . . Everyone working together for the common good. A clear distinction between what the state provided and what the private sector provided. The way socialism was meant to work in a market economy before it lost its focus. We all had a sense of community and purpose. Now there's talk of privatising the bus service and the radio station, water, the laundries. It's gone so horribly, horribly wrong."

Seventy-Two

Bob Harding arrived at Government House a few minutes after Tony Selby had left lugging the sports bag containing the Sterling and its magazines. The scientist's eyes were red, his nose running, throat sore. Despite all his precautions when filling the bomblets, some of the flour and talcum powder had got loose and set off his asthma, which was showing no signs of clearing up.

He was shown into Vanessa's office. He congratulated her on her promotion, and she in turn sympathised with his condition. Harding brushed aside her apologies for calling him – he was always glad of a chance for a spot of flirtation with the girls on the fourth floor.

"The reason Mr Prescott has asked me to see you, Mr Harding, is his concern over this morning's terrorist attack, allegedly by the Country Brigade."

"We both know that they wouldn't do that, Miss Grossman."

"Someone planned and carried it out. It smacks of organisation. The Chairman feels that a major expansion of the police force is necessary to forestall further acts and to set the populace's mind at rest."

Bob Harding had no quarrel with that. Helping out with the rescue of Ellen and Vikki from a horrible death was one thing, acts of terrorism such as the attack on the bakery was another.

"He asked me to ask you about the possibility of setting up a chemical plant with the objective of producing cordite and percussion caps for nine-millimetre ammunition. How soon could you get such a plant in production?"

Not, Harding noted wryly, whether or not it was possible to make the stuff, but when. But it wasn't such a crazy idea. He had been toying with the idea of proposing a small plant at Selby Engineering to produce nitrate-based fertilisers and materials for his submersible pet scheme. Air passed through an electric arc would produce a nitrate compound but he would have to mug up. But if the costs of setting up a plant could be foisted on to another budget, it made it all the more likely that his submersible to investigate Pentworth

Lake would get the green light. Like many scientists, Bob Harding had no conscience when it came to getting his hands on funding.

"Well, Miss Grossman . . . It can be done on a limited scale. Luckily nine-mill ammunition doesn't need large quantities of cordite."

"How about raw materials?"

"The basic ingredient of explosives are nitrates which we can extract from thin air. Our atmosphere is eighty per cent nitrogen. When do you want a production facility set up?"

"Yesterday," said Vanessa promptly, and joined in with Bob Harding's laughter.

He rather liked her, but he liked all women, and somewhat rashly agreed that he could get limited production underway within five days.

"One thing you, of all people, should be aware of, Mr Harding," said Vanessa as her visitor was about to leave. "I expect you've been bound by the official secrets acts all your professional life?"

Harding agreed that this was the case.

"Nothing has changed, Mr Harding. These projects are to be kept absolutely secret."

In the afternoon Vanessa kept the messenger service busy. By the time she finished work for the day, she had arranged for the "peace conference" with the Country Brigade to be held in seven days. Also the police recruiting officer had reported that over 200 suitable volunteers had come forward to join the police reserve and that more were expected tomorrow.

A regular army in the making, she thought with considerable satisfaction.

Seventy-Three

Tony Selby didn't waste any time. Back at his factory he went into a huddle in his office with his chief draughtsman/ designer and foreman toolmaker. They dismantled the Sterling sub-machinegun and set to work with micrometers, thread gauges, and vernier calipers to produce a set of sketched engineering drawings of each of the weapon's relatively few component parts. They used their experience and a Brinell hardness gauge to determine the heat treatment that each part required.

An apprentice was given the task of hack-sawing the firm's precious reserves of mild steel bar stock into blanks for the barrels, and he even had enough time left at the end of the day to make a start on rough-boring the blanks through – undersize for eventual reaming and honing to their finished bore size.

Many of the common piece parts such as screws were carried in stock. With a computer-controlled automatic capstan set up and spitting firing pins into its hopper by 4 p.m. and a start made with the shapers to produce male and female moulds for the plastic fittings, Tony Selby was confident that his firm could deliver the first batch of tested Sterlings within four days.

Seventy-Four

E very detail of the peace conference, from the chauffeur-driven government car sent to collect the three Country Brigade delegates, to the long red carpet outside Government House was the result of Vanessa's careful planning. Market Square was filled with a formidable turn-out of 150 well-drilled reservists looking smart in new uniforms – sleeveless white shirts dyed black and black trousers. They were spaced out to make their numbers appear greater than they were, and the two ranks of the fifty-man guard of honour flanking the red carpet were ready to present arms using gleaming Sterling sub-machine guns.

It was a formidable display of power that Nelson Faraday took pride in as he stepped forward and opened the rear door of the chauffeur-driven car. He saluted the three arrivals.

"The three delegates have got friends in the town," Vanessa had told him that morning. "Watch them like hawks, Nelson. I don't want them talking to anyone other than us."

Faraday didn't see how they would have a chance but he agreed to her order.

Dan Baldock's expression was blank as he shook hands with Prescott on the steps of Government House. Malone was as inscrutable as always, but David Weir appeared to be visibly shaken by the unexpected nature of the reception. Sound gear had been rigged. Loudspeakers. Prescott's pious platitudes prattled around the square: need for co-operation between town and country; living together in harmony; common good; blah . . . blah . . . blah . . .

As they were shown through Prescott's outer office, Malone was engrossed in conversation with Baldock and knocked one of the secretary's filing tray stacks to the floor. Papers went everywhere. The mishap embarrassed Malone; he was profuse in his apologies as he and everyone else stooped to gather up the scattered documents.

In Prescott's office there was real coffee served at a conference table that had been set up in the middle of the office. The air-conditioning was working hard, the room pleasantly cool. The coffee was the last of Vanessa's hoard; she had decided that using it for this meeting was a sound investment.

The neat gameplay amused Malone. Prescott would not have dreamed up all this: even down to details such as fresh flowers and jugs of iced water on the table. What had to be Cathy Price's computer system was at the far end of the office. He weighed up the implications of its presence in Government House.

He was even more intrigued and puzzled by Prescott's new chief executive and watched her surreptitiously. He noticed that she paid him the same compliment. At one point, while sipping his coffee, he succeeded in locking eye contact with her, but she didn't flinch away. An interesting woman, he decided, but where had he seen her before or heard her name? He allowed his inscrutability to slip by treating her to a knowing grin when she seated herself at Prescott's desk and prepared to take notes.

Malone unsettled Vanessa. There was something about the searching gaze of those wide-set eyes that suggested he was reading her thoughts. Well – the meeting had served one useful purpose so far, and that was to show that Malone was dangerous. She guessed that he would say little and absorb much.

"Right, gentlemen," said Prescott briskly. "Let's get a few formalities out of way first. Mr Malone, I accept your resignation from the police force with great reluctance. I would like to thank you for the valuable service you have performed for your community, and to say that your job will be held open should you change your mind." Without waiting for an acknowledgement, he went on, "Mr Baldock and Mr Weir. I feel you should follow Mr Malone's example and resign your seats on the council."

"Why?" Baldock demanded. "We've done nothing to disqualify us."

"You both took part in that disgraceful incident at the Temple of Winds."

"We stopped two illegal executions taking place. Nothing illegal about that, Prescott."

"The question of your continuing membership of council will be discussed at the next council meeting."

David observed that it was an academic point because council meetings were rarely held now.

"And, as a fugitive from justice, Ellen Duncan has disqualified herself," said Prescott.

Baldock snorted. "Justice, my arse. Trumped-up charges, a kangaroo court, and sentencing delegated to a religious looney."

"We'll put that down as unresolved otherwise we'll never get anywhere," Prescott ruled. "The first item on the agenda is—"

"The bloody lies you've been putting about saying that the Country Brigade bombed the bakery last week," said Baldock bluntly.

"So you said in the newsletter you circulated to every household," Prescott observed.

"We had to do that because the radio station have hardly allowed us air-time during the day. Middle of the night if we're lucky. I'll give you my word, Prescott, that the Country Brigade had absolutely nothing to do with blowing up the bakery."

Prescott was inclined to believe Dan Baldock. Much as he detested the waspish little pig farmer, he respected his integrity.

"So you stop all these crap discussions on the radio saying that we did it."

"Radio Pentworth is independent," Prescott replied. "The government has no say over its editorial content. If we were to interfere, the programme controller would rightly—"

"Bollocks. You appointed the controller. Now you're planning to privatise the station. You're like a pair of my pigs in shit toget—"

David jumped in. "I think, Dan, if the Chairman were to draw the controller's attention to the need for balance, and if the Country Brigade is given equal studio time during the day, and the right to reply, we would be happy with that."

"I'd certainly go along with that," said Prescott.

Baldock grudgingly accepted.

First concession to the Country Brigade, thought Malone, and noticed that Vanessa Grossman's pencil was moving too quickly for normal writing. Shorthand, he guessed. A business background. A faded, forlorn estate agent's for sale board that he had seen on his jogs kicked his mind into gear. Grossman . . . Grossman Properties! He had her pinned down immediately: Vanessa Grossman – boss of the Grossman Property Group – Chichester – Portsmouth – Southampton. He saw her leaving a courtroom, shunning Meridian TV cameras, racing for a car. The car burning rubber with snappers chasing after it. An aggrieved relative describing her to a TV reporter as a scheming little bleep with a heart of bleep, assuming she had one.

The pieces falling into place enabled Malone to quickly sum her up. A driving, ruthless talent cut off from its power base and looking for new conquests within the narrow confines of Pentworth. Prescott had a considerable degree of political acumen, and even social awareness, but it was nothing compared with the ruthless street-fighting cunning of Vanessa Grossman, now looking cool and self-effacing in a formal skirt and blouse as her pencil flew across her pad.

She sensed Malone's attention and looked straight at him. Malone was angry with himself when he realised that he was unable to hold the duel and turned his attention to Prescott. God dammit! First victory to Vanessa Grossman.

"I hope we've typed your list of demands accurately?" said Prescott.

"Negotiating points," said David.

"Demands," Baldock corrected bluntly. "The order they're in is not significant, Prescott. They're all of equal importance." Which was not strictly true. Before the meeting the three delegates had decided that Prescott's agreement to the first point was crucial to the success of the conference.

"So let's take the first one, Mr Baldock," said Prescott. "An immediate set aside of the convictions against Ellen Duncan and Victoria Taylor, and the repeal of the Witchcraft Act. That's actually two negotiating points, and neither are negotiable."

"The persecution of those two is inhuman, Prescott! Posters all over the place offering rewards for information. It's got to stop!"

"The police are not actively searching for them," said Prescott smoothly. "The reward posters are nothing to do with the government. But that doesn't change the fact that they're fugitives and should give themselves up."

"No active searching?" snarled Baldock. "What fucking planet are you living on? There's hordes of those damned sentinel loonies scouring the countryside for them, descending mob-handed on farms and turning them over. Sometimes going back after thirty minutes and doing it all over again."

"They're acting as private citizens. If they're being over-zealous – exceeding their legal powers – then there is machinery through the courts for dealing with them. I see no point in further argument on your first points."

Nevertheless the argument dragged on for an hour. The Country Brigade appeared to win a concession from Prescott when he said that he would set up a court of appeal to re-examine the case. It was something he wanted to do all along to be shot of the wretched business but Vanessa had suggested that there were political Brownie points to be won if it was seen as a concession.

David was suspicious. "And what about the sentence? Will that be reviewed too if the court of appeal upholds the original verdicts?"

"How can I predict the outcome of a hearing by a court of appeal that hasn't been set up yet?" Prescott countered in some irritation.

"So you want Ellen and Vikki handed over in exchange for no guarantees for their safety?" Baldock summarised.

"I can promise you that they won't be handed over to Father Roscoe in his capacity as the Lord of the Manor."

"I don't trust you, Prescott," said Baldock with his usual candour. "You need the milk and crop production of Pentworth House Farm, even more so now if we don't get something thrashed out today."

Prescott shrugged.

"Let's come back to the first point when all the others are out of way," David suggested. "Otherwise we're not going to make much progress."

A sandwich lunch was served at the conference table and the negotiations lumbered on with Prescott being obdurate on important issues and giving way on relatively unimportant matters. He agreed to reduce the number of food and farm hygiene inspectors by five per cent but refused to curtail their formidable powers, which had cost many farmers dear. A request for a ten per cent increase in compensation for slaughtered livestock was negotiated down to five per cent. Prescott's frequent spouting of his favourite phrase – "I would be failing in my duty to the people as a whole if I . . ." – annoyed Baldock to the point when he felt that *he* would be failing in his duty if he didn't hit Prescott with something large and heavy.

The discussion over civic amenities for rural areas degenerated into a row. Prescott pointed out that the government's long-term plans were an expansion of the telephone network so that every household and business would eventually have a free telephone.

Vanessa made a margin note about that: capital expenditure on social amenities did not figure highly in her priorities.

By 2 p.m. very little progress had been made. A major sticking point was the decommissioning of the Country Brigade's weapons, including the handing over of the box of shotgun cartridges.

"How the hell can we agree to being disarmed when you're refusing to give way on everything, and when you've recruited a militia that's armed to the teeth?" Baldock wanted to know. "And where the hell did those machine guns come from?"

"The word is decommissioning," Prescott pointed out.

"Now we're arguing semantics," said David despairingly.

When the radio station asked for an interim statement for the three o'clock news bulletin, Prescott said that the peace conference was proving useful and constructive; Baldock said that it was proving a time-wasting load of bollocks.

"We might as well come clean now as we don't seem to getting anywhere," the pig farmer declared, glaring across the table at Prescott. "The Country Brigade won't enter into any agreement without a pardon for Ellen Duncan and Vikki Taylor. You agree to announcing that today, and we'll give way on all our remaining points – eight to twelve."

Prescott was tempted: it would break the deadlock, and end the problem of the two women which had worried him sick ever since Roscoe's ruse over the arrest warrants, but Vanessa was giving him a gamma-ray warning glare that didn't escape Malone's notice.

"I have a suggestion to make," said Malone, speaking for the first time. "Let's adjourn for forty-five minutes. I daresay Mr Prescott needs some legal advice, and we need to talk – best done with beers in front of us in the Crown."

He rose to forestall argument. Baldock and David followed suite with alacrity. Prescott shot a questioning look at Vanessa, who was staring indifferently into the middle distance. That meant that she had no objections.

"Perhaps that's not such a bad idea," said Prescott, beaming.

Seventy-Five

A few minutes later at a table outside the Crown, Malone took an appreciative long swallow from his glass and observed that they had minders in the form of more police around the square than were necessary.

David grinned. "Your imagination is in overdrive, Mike. Cheers – this was brilliant idea."

"I was busting for a dump," said Malone. "Guard my drink a couple of minutes." He rose and entered the pub; his colleagues assumed that he had gone to use the toilets, which, according to a sign, were now working.

But Malone had other ideas. He went through the pub, but instead of using the toilet in the pub's stable yard, he shinned nimbly over a locked gate and dropped into the service alley. He had chased enough villains around Pentworth to know his way around the town's maze of backyards, gardens, and alleys. Two more fences, a garden crossed, a fast trot down a another alley, a fence vaulted, and he was rapping on the open door of Bob Harding's workshop.

The scientist's eyes popped in alarm when he came to the door. "Hallo, Mike. How the devil did you get you get past Suzi?"

"By not going past her. Are you alone?"

"No." Harding took Malone by the arm and guided him to a secluded bench near the end of the garden.

"Looks like your hayfever's still playing up, Bob."

Harding grunted. He seemed agitated in Malone's company. "What's the latest on Ellen and Vikki?"

"Still fine as far as I know," was Malone's guarded reply.

"According to the radio, you're one of the delegates at today's conference."

"We've taken a beer break, so I haven't got long."

"You may have been followed here."

"Not the route I took. Selby's are to be congratulated on producing those Sterlings."

"I'm sorry, Mike, but I can't say where they came from, though producing a simple weapon like that is no great shakes for a competent engineering company."

"Let me guess – they'd have to be much more than just competent to make ammunition?"

"Mass-producing ammunition is very specialised," said Harding, clearly unhappy at the question. "I'm talking in general terms, you understand? Nothing specific to Pentworth."

"Of course. So if I wanted to set up a hypothetical production line to make ammo, and I had only limited resources, how long would I need?"

Harding thought for a moment. "Such a hypothetical plant would take at least a month to produce large quantities of suitable ammunition. If you had promised to do it any sooner than that, then you'd be in trouble. And, of course, to make the guns, you'd need to test fire the barrels in a firing jig. That would mean using up all the genuine rounds you happened to have."

Malone stood. "The advice is much appreciated, Bob."

"I don't think you fully understand me," said Harding uneasily. "I said *suitable ammunition*. As a man of integrity, you would, of course, be wholly opposed to shortcuts which result in the limited production of unjacketed lead rounds."

A cold hand stirred Malone's bowels. "You mean dum-dum rounds?"

"Your engineering plant might find it virtually impossible to nickel-jacket your rounds," said Harding. "You might also find that your objections might be overruled by your political masters. I'm sure that that would make you very unhappy."

"Yes," said Malone slowly. "It would." He looked at the scientist and saw despair in the older man's eyes. "So I get overruled. How long would that mean before limited production of soft-nosed rounds would start?"

"Three days," said Harding heavily, and stared down at the ground.

Malone touched the scientist on the shoulder. "Many thanks, Bob. Maybe I'll forget the whole idea." He paused. "Do you still have that spare Spectrum transmitter?"

Harding nodded. "I did as you said and told no one about it. Everyday I pray that the one in Government House will blow its main output transistor, but they're running it on low power into a decent antenna on the roof with plenty of gain. It'll last years."

"Maybe that spare will come in useful sooner or later. Be seeing you."

With that Malone disappeared into the depths of the garden and retraced his route so that he emerged casually from the pub fifteen minutes after he had vanished.

"A policeman was worried about your absence," said David. "We told him that it was due to some homemade vindaloo you'd been experimenting with."

"It seemed more plausible than a quickie with the barmaid," Baldock added.

Malone grinned and finished his drink. "I've been researching non-vindaloo explosives."

"We were talking about Prescott appearing keen to do some sort of deal over Ellen and Vikki," said Baldock, who had long before decided that Malone was clever but weird. "Our guess is that he will if we keep up the pressure."

"He wants to," said Malone. "But Vanessa Grossman is dead set against it."

"I can't see what it's got to do with her," Baldock declared, downing the last of his second beer in one swallow. "She's only the Town Clerk. Better looking than Diana Sheldon, though. Do you reckon Prescott's perching on her nest?"

"I can't see Vanessa Grossman going along with that," said Malone drily. He briefed his two colleagues on who she was.

"For Chrissake why didn't you tell us before the meeting?" Baldock growled.

"I only realised who she was during the meeting."

"Does it matter who she is?" David queried.

"It matters," said Malone. "The whole style of government has changed. All that nonsense with guards of honour and their machine guns with empty magazines was meant to intimidate rather than impress."

"How do you know they were empty?" David asked.

"I'll tell you afterwards. It wouldn't matter if she and Prescott have the same agenda. But I don't think that is the case. I've a hunch that Miss Vanessa Grossman is using us to put the skids under Asquith Prescott."

David couldn't help but laugh at that. "You amaze me, Mike. You'll be seeing Reds under the bed next. She strikes me as nothing but a quiet, efficient young lady sitting taking notes."

"And with more influence than Diana Sheldon ever had," said Malone.

"What makes you say that?"

"Diana Sheldon was never able to wangle herself a telephone in her home, yet our Vanessa's just got herself one."

David was disbelieving. "Now how the devil do you know that?"

Malone grinned. "That little mishap I had in Prescott's outer office resulted in a copy of the Pentworth telephone directory ending up in my pocket. Only two typed sheets. Vanessa's name, address and number has been added by hand as an amendment. She's quieter and more efficient than you think, David."

Seventy-Six

At that moment Vanessa was being anything but quiet. "You've given in enough as it is, Prescott. To go further would be a serious threat to democracy."

"It occurred to me," said Prescott, "that it would be a good idea to go along with the pardon provided Harvey Evans returns to government service with his microlight. That way, they get what they want, and we gain control of the microlight. I'm not happy with the Country Brigade having air power."

Vanessa snorted. "We have nothing to fear from that thing unless you're scared of flour bombs. The Country Brigade don't have the resources to make explosives whereas we will have within a month."

"Even so, I don't suppose Harvey is happy being away from his home and his hives. He's an old friend, Miss Grossman. I owe him that much."

Vanessa thought it an excellent idea – from Prescott's point of view. She poured scorn on it, saying that no democratically elected government could afford to bow to terrorism. Give in on one thing, and they'd be demanding something else. If the Country Brigade wanted power-sharing then they could field candidates in the following year's elections, and if they really wanted a peaceful settlement, then let them demonstrate their supposedly good intentions by agreeing to hand over their weapons.

Prescott conceded that she had a point, although his political instinct was to find room for compromise.

"We'll be forcing them into a corner, Miss Grossman."

"Which is precisely where they belong."

When the meeting reconvened, Prescott told the three delegates that the setting aside of the convictions against Ellen and Vikki had to be conditional on the Country Brigade agreeing to the decommissioning of their weapons.

"In that case," said Baldock, "we've achieved exactly nothing today. We've never got on in the past, Prescott, yet I've always

278

thought of you as having some political savvy. Seems I was wrong. You leave us with no alternative but to start operating sanctions. As from midnight all food deliveries to the town will cease."

Prescott looked indifferent. "We now have a police reserve large enough to cope with all deliveries."

"Touch one potato and we start selective burning of crops."

The only sound in the room was Vanessa moving Prescott's telephone to the windowsill so that she could use it with her back to the meeting. Her demeanour was of someone wishing to make a private call without disturbing anyone, but Malone suspected that this was not the case.

"That would be extremely foolish," said Prescott at length.

Baldock stood – the signal for David and Malone to do likewise. He stuffed his papers into a briefcase and glowered at Prescott. "Who's being foolish here? All we want is for the convictions against Ellen and Vikki to be set aside, and in return you get concessions from us all the way down the line. If you want to play some stupid game of brinkmanship, Prescott, then the Country Brigade will be happy to shove you over a brink of your making." He paused and looked around the big office with its expensive furniture and humming air-conditioning. "You and this whole rotten, corrupt set up you've got here will be wiped out."

Seventy-Seven

The three delegates were silent in the car taking them home. Anything the chauffeur overheard would be certain to get back to Prescott.

A kilometre south of Pentworth they encountered a police road-block.

"What the hell's this?" Baldock muttered as the car slowed.

It was no ordinary vehicle or cart roadside safety check that were now commonplace, but a serious roadblock with a Commer van parked across the road and several police armed with the new Sterling copies in attendance. Three of them approached the vehicle, two stood their distance while one carefully examined the identity cards of the four occupants.

"Just following orders, sir," said the policeman in answer to Baldock's questions. "OK – all in order." He waved the Commer aside.

"Any ideas?" Malone asked the driver once they had resumed their journey.

"None at all, sir. It wasn't here an hour ago." The driver seemed genuinely puzzled.

Roadblocks work in two directions. From its layout, Malone's surmise was that it was intended primarily to deal with traffic entering the town. He had a shrewd idea that its appearance was linked to Vanessa Grossman's phone calls and that it was likely that all the roads into the town were also blocked.

Another kilometre and the driver was forced to slow to pass an angry crowd that had gathered around the Volvo bus that was used for shoppers and schoolchildren. The bus stop it was parked at was a drop-off point for children. Some women were arguing with the driver, others were in a state of near-hysteria.

"Stop the car!" Baldock yelled.

"My orders are to take you to your destinations," the driver protested.

Baldock wasn't interested in the driver's orders. He flung the car door open, forcing the driver to brake and protest volubly as his passengers piled out and ran back to the bus.

"Mrs Lawrence, isn't it?" Baldock queried. "What's the problem?"

The woman, who was the chief remonstrator, turned and looked immensely relieved to see the new arrivals. "Mr Baldock – my Jane and Damian aren't on the bus!"

There was a chorus of exclamations from several other anxious mothers with similar stories about missing offspring. Baldock held up his hands for quiet and asked the bus driver what the hell was going on.

"I called at the school at my usual time," said the driver. "The deputy headmistress came out and gave me this list of kids that wouldn't be taking the bus. I thought maybe they'd gone on an outing or something and that their parents knew. Then I get here and all hell breaks loose."

Baldock looked at the list that the driver handed down. He didn't recognise all the first names, but many of the surnames were familiar enough: they were country names.

The first hostages had been taken.

Seventy-Eight

Harvey Evans entered David's kitchen at Temple Farm a few minutes before 6 p.m. Malone, David, and Baldock looked expectantly at him. He sat at the kitchen table with the three men, his face lined with worry. Music was playing on a portable radio.

"You were right, Malone," said the former police inspector. "The roadblocks are keeping country folk out of the town. My trap was turned back. When I moaned, the so-called police officers were sympathetic but they said that they had strict orders. There was a Mrs Tinnings at the roadblock – worried out of her mind. Her two children haven't come home. Jessie Tinnings, aged seven. And Michael, eleven."

"That makes twenty-two kids," said Baldock grimly, adding the names to a clipboard.

The music on the radio cross-faded to commercials.

"Vanessa Grossman's telephone calls when Dan issued the sanctions ultimatum," Malone commented, adding drily, "You're right, of course, David – she certainly is very quiet and very efficient. Not in the way you meant, I imagine."

"Hostages!" Evans snapped angrily. "Prescott may be a shit, but this isn't like him."

"I did say there's been a change of style at Government House," Malone observed.

The radio presenter announced the six o'clock news. David turned the volume up.

"And we start with an important statement from our Chairman, Mr Asquith Prescott."

"Good evening, citizens of Pentworth," said Prescott, striking a sombre note. "As you know, an important conference was held today between your government and the so-called Country Brigade with the aim of bringing peace to our tiny community. It was our hope that reason and goodwill would prevail, but this was not to be. It is with great regret that I have to inform you that our efforts to find a peaceful solution to our differences have failed.

"Despite numerous concessions from the government, such as our agreement to reduce the number of farm inspectors, and to increase compensation to farmers where livestock has had to be destroyed, the Country Brigade steadfastly refused to discuss any agreement to decommission their arms, and they insisted on an amnesty for their members convicted of crimes. We offered to refer such cases to a court of appeal for review, a reasonable enough move, as I am sure you will agree, but the Country Brigade rejected it out of hand. Finally, and most serious of all, they stated their intention of burning crops if they did not get their way."

Prescott paused. "Given our present circumstances and the very fragile nature of our atmosphere, I know that I do not have to spell out the disastrous consequences of such actions. The thought of burning farms damaging our atmosphere and depriving us of the food that we shall need to see us through the coming winter hardly bears thinking about. Fire is our greatest enemy, therefore our thoughts must immediately turn to the protection of our greatest asset – innocent and vulnerable bystanders in all this – our children.

"We have two fire engines, and a willing team of professional and part-time fire-fighters – capable men and women as they have shown on many occasions, but even they could not cope with a campaign of deliberate burning of farms. The thought of children dying of suffocation in smoke-filled bedrooms in remote difficult-to-reach farms as a result of terrorist actions by a fanatical minority is something we refuse to countenance . . .

"Over half a century ago, the children of England faced a similar threat from such tyrants. As a result, they were moved to places of safety – they were evacuated . . . My late elder brother was such an evacuee. Just as our parents moved us from danger, so we must we must follow their fine example and do the same for our children. We have therefore issued orders that those children most at risk should be placed in the care of families in the town until the danger is over – when the tyrants of the Country Brigade have been crushed. Thank you for listening to me."

David angrily snapped the radio off. "Lies! How can that man spout such downright lies!"

"Not so much lies, but plenty of distortion as a result of some neat wording," said Malone. "Note how Dan's selective burning of crops has become burning of farms. And child hostages passed off as evacuees. A clever linkage with World War Two."

"Have you come to praise Caesar or bury him?" David demanded. "The bastard's holding twenty-two country children hostage!"

"They won't come to any harm," Malone answered. "He would not risk lying when he said that they had been placed in the care of town families – and he certainly can't risk them coming to any harm – that really would be political suicide – for him and everyone riding on his coat-tails. We must act, and fast. My information is that within three days ammunition will be available for those imitation Sterlings. At the moment those magazines are empty. When they do get some ammo, they won't be proper rounds. They'll be made of unjacketed lead because they're easier to make. In other words, dum-dum bullets. No matter where you're hit by one of those things, an artery is certain to be shredded and you die."

The four men were silent for some moments.

"How good is your information?" Baldock demanded.

"Believe me, Malone's information is always good," said Evans with some feeling.

"We have to think also of those poor women who've been shut up in that cave for two weeks," said David.

Malone turned his gaze on Baldock. "When we left Prescott's office today, Dan, your parting words to him were that his whole rotten set-up would be wiped out. I've always been concerned about your tendency for bluntness, and your eagerness for direct action. Much as I dislike many politicians, politics is a great invention because it enables differences to be settled without conflict. But politics has failed. Direct action is the only course open to us now – therefore it must be a course that will achieve our aims with the least spilling of blood." He paused for a few moments before continuing. "We should spend the rest of today and all of tomorrow on planning, and make a decisive move tomorrow night. The time has come for us to go for the jugular. A quick kill."

Baldock grinned suddenly. "Sounds like my kind of talk, Malone."

Seventy-Nine

The spyder surfaced in the centre of Pentworth Lake.

It listened intently. Dusk was closing in. A hungry hedgehog nearby was making an early start on its nightly foraging. There was the snuffling of badgers, leaving their setts with the coming of darkness. The spyder extended an infrared and visible light sensor to a height of several metres and swept the surrounding terrain to ensure that no humans were nearby.

All was clear. The sensor was retracted. There was an eruption of marsh gas bubbles released from the depths of the lake which heralded the sudden arrival on the surface of a coffin-like casket. The spyder towed the casket towards the sandy shore where the bathing beach had been created. The casket was grounded and the spyder left the water to haul laboriously on a fine thread until the casket was several metres clear of the sand, resting on grass.

One control caused the outlines of the casket to shimmer. The spyder waited while the casket vaporised, giving off a thin white cloud that was rapidly absorbed into the atmosphere, leaving the still, naked form of a man lying on the grass. His pillow was a bundle of his clothes.

The spyder placed a probe each side of the man's head and waited until he started breathing. His body temperature rose steadily until it reached normal. The spyder had many checks to perform to ensure that the man's metabolic and nervous system was working properly, which it accomplished in a few seconds. It moved two metres from the man and waited.

Less than a minute elapsed before the man stirred.

He opened his eyes and stared up at the darkening sky. He was confused and a little frightened. A host of vivid memories of bright lights and shapes behind them were at the forefront of his consciousness but were suddenly snatched away as if they should not have been there. Something was telling him to stand. He didn't want to stand; he wanted to lie there, trying to fit the world together in a mind he could not control. But the compulsion was too strong for him to resist.

He climbed to his feet. His balance was unsure at first for there was hardly any feeling in his legs. He thought he was going to fall but there was a sudden surge of strange sensations along his sciatic nerve. The ground hardened to a gritty reality beneath his bare feet; a feeling of his own weight; a pleasant breeze playing on his back, for the humid night air was holding the sun's heat.

His gaze focused on the spyder. Impossible to tell if it were looking at him because it was dark. If it was, where were its eyes? Did it have eyes? But a sensor or something was pointing at him.

Running on the spot now, arms pistoning. A proper run would be nice. And then he was off, racing in a wide, exuberant circle as through relishing being alive. He tripped and fell. The spyder started after him but stopped when the man jumped to his feet, laughing now, and completed the circle.

He stopped before the spyder, breathing easily, wondering how he was doing.

Very well. It has taken a long time but you are ready now.

The words just marched into his head, ready-made, sharp and clear.

What has taken a long time? he wondered.

The answer came as a kaleidoscope-like montage of images, most of them incomprehensible, but every now and than one would stand out with vivid clarity, like a light being switched on and off in a random manner.

You will keep still now.

The man did so, standing perfectly still. The spyder moved closer to him to finish its tests. The machine's makers had been responsible for restoring Cathy Price's sense of balance, and regenerating Vikki's left hand. Those tasks had been relatively straightforward for them because they had been dealing with living tissue and the stimulation of healing and growth systems that Cathy's and Vikki's bodies already possessed.

But Arnie Trinder, the big, good-natured West Indian radio interference investigator, had been drowned for several hours by the time they had recovered his body from the bottom of Pentworth Lake in March. Many billions of his oxygen-starved brain cells had already decayed and so they had to replicate them as best they could. It had been a time-consuming business, even for them. There were gaps in their knowledge about the human brain that had been only partially filled by their second visit to Cathy Price. Areas of the brain controlling Trinder's higher functions, including memory, had been lost.

Trinder's colleague, Nevil Rigsby, had also drowned in the lake. He had been older, less fit than Trinder, and had proved beyond recovery.

There was one test that the spyder did not carry out on the West Indian as he stood in frozen obedience. There was no need because Arnie Trinder no longer had a heart but something much more efficient in the form of thousands of nano-engineered pumps distributed throughout his bloodstream. They worked continuously rather than in surges. His lungs had also been re-engineered to improve their effectiveness at transferring oxygen to his bloodstream. The collagen and other fibres in the muscles throughout his body had been increased so that he was now heavier and stronger than he had ever been. A build-up of extra calcium in each vertebra resulted in an overall increase of forty millimetres in his height.

The visitors had done their best for Arnie Trinder, and in so doing they had modelled him in a manner that they considered would be useful.

He was a big, powerful man, but no longer wholly human.

Eighty

The roadblocks around Pentworth were part of a cordon with police observers occupying every strategic point that provided a good view of the countryside. Many of them had their own dogs.

Malone's surmise that all the groups in the Country Brigade task force could get through the cordon and into the town area via a cutting in the disused Midhurst railway line appeared to be substantiated with his first group. They flitted in pairs along the overgrown cutting and mustered in a tumbledown engineers' hut half a kilometre inside the cordon. There were six of them: Malone, David Weir, Dan Baldock, the two stable lads who had acquitted themselves so well during the rescue of Ellen and Vikki at the Temple of the Winds. The last member was Carl Crittenden.

They changed out of their all-black garb into more normal dark clothes and checked their equipment. Malone was carrying a PMR radio – for use only if the crucial stage of the night's operation had to be aborted. A final confirmation of the separate routes they would be taking to Vanessa Grossman's home and they left the security of the hut one by one. Their timing was excellent – as Carl left, the vanguard of the second group arrived. The plan was to have one hundred men at key locations around Pentworth by 11.30 that night but the task of the second group was to recover the children and return them to their families.

Most of the police force were manning the cordon, therefore the conspirators were not expecting problems in the town. Malone went alone to Vanessa Grossman's house. He took the shortest route so that he was first on the scene fifteen minutes later. The mansion was set back from the road in its own grounds, almost completely surrounded by a screen of leylandii conifers. With the intruder alarm batteries exhausted long ago, the place was a housebreaker's dream. Judging by the lights, the downstairs back room was in use, and a faint glow from around the curtains of an upstairs dormer window was probably a night light in the children's bedroom.

He waited in the back garden, using his body as a screen from the house for the occasional homing flashes of his torch. Baldock was first, followed by David and then the two stable lads with Carl, all moving silently on the unmown grass as they formed into a group.

They conferred briefly and went to work. The two stable lads had been using a suitable farmhouse to practise what they did next. One threw a cricket ball right over the house. The ball was attached to a long length of twine. It thumped down on the lawn. The second lad grabbed it and began hauling on the twine that was attached to a rope. There were a few anxious moments when the rope snagged on the roof guttering but a couple of flicks freed it so that the lads finished at each end of a rope that went right over the house. Two jerks each way to confirm that they were ready and they quickly climbed their respective ends of the rope for a rendezvous on the ridge of the roof. The lightest of the lads carried their housebreaking tools in a haversack to equalise the differences in their weight. They gathered up the rope and moved silently to the dormer window that Malone had indicated. A minute's work with a crowbar was all they needed to force the window and enter the house.

Five minutes passed with agonising slowness before a torch winked three times from the dormer window – the "mission accomplished" signal. Carl remained on watch in the front garden while Malone, Baldock and David went to the front porch. Baldock produced a double-barrelled sawn-off shotgun from his trousers. David held a powerful halogen lamp ready. He had expressed grave reservations about this stage of the operation but had been persuaded that it was necessary. They stood to one side as Malone rapped the door knocker.

A light flickered in the hall. A man's voice. "Who's there?"

"Bernie Harriman – Vanessa's hubby," Malone whispered. He said out loud, "Mike Malone to see Miss Grossman. Sorry to trouble you this late in the evening, Mr Harriman, but it's urgent."

There was the rattle of a security chain being locked into its slide. The door opened slightly and then crashed fully opened with the aid of simultaneous kicks from Baldock and Malone. The three men burst into the house. Bernie Harriman gave an exclamation of surprise and staggered back, blinded by David's lamp. Malone unhurriedly closed the front door. Vanessa should have appeared to see what the commotion was about. Malone slipped quickly into the living-room. Two strides and he jerked Vanessa's arm up behind her back as she was about to turn the crank handle on the antique telephone. She whimpered in pain.

"My temper and your arm are both dangerously close to breaking point, Vanessa," Malone quietly advised her. "You'll have to take my word for the former, but I've no doubt that you are painfully aware of the latter. Give a nod to indicate your willingness to sit quietly and calmly on that settee and I'll release you. Understand?"

She nodded. To make his requirements clear, Malone spun her around and thrust her on the settee just as her husband entered the room at the point of Baldock's shotgun. His face was white, his body shaking in a mixture of fear and rage. "They've got the children," he muttered.

"Sit beside Vanessa please," Malone requested.

Bernie Harriman's answer was to hurl himself dementedly at Malone. Baldock didn't fire. He and Malone had discussed this eventuality and it was decided that Malone should deal with it. The former police officer did just that by stepping nimbly aside. The swing of his arm ended abruptly when the edge of his hand connected with Bernie Harriman's temple. The chop was sufficient to cause him to crumple unconscious on to the carpet. Malone picked him up and heaved him beside his wife who was staring white-faced at the three men. She turned to tend to her husband.

"There's nothing you can do," said Malone. "Best leave him. He'll be OK in about ten minutes."

"What the hell do you want?"

"An extra ordinary council meeting," Baldock answered. "In Government House at midnight tonight. But before then, we wish to restore the status quo. We want a list of the addresses of where Prescott is holding our children."

"Evacuees!" Vanessa snapped.

The answer enraged Baldock. He took a step towards the woman and levelled his shotgun at her. "Don't you play Prescott's fucking semantic games with me, you bitch, or, by Christ, you'll be seeing your kids' ears lined-up on that coffee table!"

Suddenly there was real fear in Vanessa's eyes. "I'm sorry," she said quietly.

Baldock moderated his tone. "I'm sorry we have to do this. Miss Grossman. Our argument isn't with you but that bastard, Prescott. Mr Malone thinks you're an efficient operator. It's his opinion that you'd have such a list with you. Any argument from you that the only copy is at Government House is likely to be disbelieved and even more likely to lead to much grief."

"The desk by the window," Vanessa replied listlessly. "In my briefcase."

David moved to the desk and tipped out the contents of the

briefcase. He found the document immediately. "Eleven names and addresses. Is this it?" He held the paper up.

Vanessa confirmed that it was. "Two children to each address," she said. "Mr Prescott wanted to keep brothers and sisters together."

"Well that was fucking decent of him," said Baldock sarcastically. "And before you use the term evacuees again, the kids that were sent to safety in World War Two were sent with their parents' consent. What Prescott did yesterday afternoon was kidnapping – hostage-taking, pure and simple."

David went out to the front garden and gave the list to Carl. The young man grinned in triumph as he pocketed it. "Looks like it's all going to plan, Mr Weir."

"So far," said David worriedly. "Break a leg."

"Reckon she'll bite?"

"So it seems, Carl. But I'm not happy about this. It's a dirty business."

"It has to be done, Mr Weir." With that, Carl disappeared into the night to rendezvous with the second group, and David returned to the house. Malone was placing the telephone in front of Vanessa.

"Just in case you've told the exchange to block calls to this number, I want you to call them and tell them to put all calls through."

Vanessa regarded Malone in contempt and told him to do something that was physically difficult, even for Malone. He gave her no second chance but went to the door and called out.

"Yes, Mr Malone?" answered one of the stable lads from upstairs.

"Left ear. The eldest."

"*NO!*" Vanessa screamed.

"Hold on that!" Malone instructed. He returned and stared down at the badly frightened woman. "Call the exchange and tell them to put all calls through to here. Hold the phone away from your ear."

Vanessa's hands shook as she held the headphone near her ear and turned the crank handle. An operator answered immediately. "Yes, Miss Grossman?" An elderly woman. Her voice could be heard clearly by everyone in the room.

"I want you to put all calls through."

"How long for, Miss Grossman?"

"Until further notice."

"Very well, Miss Grossman. I go off duty at midnight, so I'll leave a note against your number."

"Thank you, operator."

"Good night, Miss Grossman."

"Good night." Vanessa replaced the headphone on its hook.

"There's a lot to be said for a phone system run by human beings," Malone observed, moving the telephone out of Vanessa's reach. "None of that tedious button-pressing business which I always got wrong."

"I want to see my children," said Vanessa.

"Of course you do," said Malone. "But you'll have to wait."

"Wait for what?"

"Until we hear that *our* kids are safe," said Baldock simply.

The three men made themselves comfortable. Not for a second did Baldock allow his attention or his shotgun to falter from Vanessa. Malone admired her composure. He checked that Bernie Harriman was OK when he showed signs of recovering. A decent man from what Malone had learned. He regretted having to hit him.

"I want to use the toilet," said Vanessa abruptly.

"For a pee?" asked Malone.

"Yes."

Malone left the room and returned with a plastic washing-up bowl and some tissues.

The woman's eyes blazed hatred at Malone. "You expect me to use that with you scum watching?"

"What we expect and what you need are two different things," said Malone boredly. "You either use it or wet yourself. But you're not leaving this room."

Vanessa's husband stirred. She comforted him as he sat up, holding his head. Malone fetched him a glass of water which he drank greedily.

"What happens now?" Vanessa asked.

"We wait," said Baldock.

Eighty-One

Vikki . . .
    Vikki was dozing.
Vikki . . .
The girl's eyes snapped open. She stared up at the roof of the cave, lit softly by the low-wattage bedside lights that Ellen and Claire were reading by.
Vikki. Can you hear us?
It was the same voice in her head that she had heard before when it had summonsed her from her bedroom to Pentworth Lake. But it was stronger – the concepts that formed in her mind as words were much sharper. But Pentworth Lake was not so far from the cave as her bedroom.
"Yes." She said it as an almost mute whisper.
Come to us, Vikki.
"I can't."
The girl was aware of a sensation of puzzlement until she concentrated on her surroundings.
You are trapped?
"In a way – yes."
Vikki turned and looked at her companions. Ellen was already dozing off. She switched off her bedside light and muttered a general goodnight. Claire did the same and Vikki was left in the feeble glow of the low-wattage night lamp that provided just enough light for toilet visits and to relieve the frightening totality of the darkness that would otherwise prevail in the cave. It would be at least ten minutes or more before her companions were sound asleep.
We understand. But you will come to us. He is ready.
"Yes," Vikki whispered to the darkness. "I will come."

293

Eighty-Two

The harsh, discordant jangle of Vanessa's telephone startled everyone in her living-room. Malone glanced at David and Baldock before gesturing to Vanessa for her to answer it. She picked up the headphone and spoke into the horn microphone.

"Vanessa Grossman speaking."

"Miss Grossman," said the operator. "I have a call for you from the public phone box in Silver Square."

"I'll take it," said Vanessa.

"You're through, caller – go ahead."

"Miss Grossman?"

Malone recognised Carl's voice and took the headphone from Vanessa. "Guess who this it?"

Carl chuckled. "The eaglets have landed. They're all in their home nests. All safe and well." The wording of his phrase indicated that Carl was not under duress, although that was obvious from the jubilation in his voice. "It was just like you said – none of the keepers was happy with the situation and they were pleased to see the goods returned to their owners."

"Well done," said Malone with feeling. He looked at his watch. "We're running late. You've got those councillors to deal with now."

"My next calls. They won't take long," said Carl confidently.

"Stress that they must all be in the courtroom at Government House by midnight," said Malone, speaking clearly.

Carl chuckled again. It was an instruction that he was not required to carry out. "I'll do that. See you there."

The line went dead.

"Right," said Baldock, eyeing Vanessa dispassionately, leaning his shotgun against his chair. "Now that that little bit of Prescott nastiness has been knocked on the head, we can get down to business in a more civilised manner."

"What business, Mr Baldock?"

"Malone's our honest broker in all this," he said.

"So broker away, Mr Malone," Vanessa invited, feeling that she was gaining a measure of control over this outlandish situation.

"Firstly," said Malone, more to Bernie Harriman who was watching him with dulled, listless eyes, "your children are in absolutely no danger and never were. We don't operate like that. The chances are that our two men upstairs are playing snakes and ladders with them."

"That I guessed," said Vanessa coolly.

"The plain truth is that the Country Brigade will refuse to enter into any agreement with Prescott. His kidnapping of twenty-two children was the last straw – it's damaged his political standing in this community beyond repair. The Country Brigade are at this minute organising an extra ordinary council meeting to be held in Government House at midnight. We want as many councillors there as possible, including Ellen Duncan. The motion will be for Prescott to resign and for a new acting Chairman to be appointed." It was the Big Lie: the only people the conspirators wanted in the courtroom-council chamber at midnight were Asquith Prescott and Adrian Roscoe.

Vanessa arched her eyebrows. She did it well. "Really? And you think the vote will go your way?"

"We've been busy lobbying the last twenty-four hours despite Prescott's feeble roadblocks," growled Baldock.

"That's not what I asked, Mr Baldock," said Vanessa acidly, very much the chairman of the board now.

Baldock contrived to look uncomfortable with Vanessa's searching eyes on him. "There's still a better-the-devil-we-know attitude to contend with. But if we get Roscoe's vote, it'll be in the bag and we'll have a new Chairman by morning."

"And that will be you, Mr Baldock? As you're Deputy Chairman?"

"Not fu— bloody likely," was Baldock's vehement response. "I never wanted to be deputy in the first place. And I certainly don't want to be Chairman unless I could get away with doubling the transaction tax on beef and abolishing it on pork."

Vanessa permitted herself a faint smile. "You must have someone in mind."

"We have a caretaker Chairman in mind," said Baldock slowly. "You, Miss Grossman."

Malone watched Vanessa carefully but there was no reaction this time. He could guess why: this was her world. A world of poker-faced deals and counter-deals. A world of power-skirmishing where she was at her best in the driving seat.

"Why me, Mr Baldock?"

"You've never been involved in local politics. You're not aligned with any factions. You're a self-made businesswoman. New money. Prescott is old money. You understand the workings of Pentworth's government, and, as a wife and mother, we're unlikely to see from you the sort of Prescott decision-making that has caused so much anguish over the last twenty-four hours."

Vanessa's hard stare gave nothing away. "And you think that Adrian Roscoe will agree to being in the same room as Ellen Duncan, *and* voting the same way as her?"

"He's on the phone," said Malone. "If you did a bit of wheeling and dealing with him first in which you agree to handing over Ellen Duncan to him as soon as you're Chairman – he'd jump at the chance."

"I think I'm ahead of you," said Vanessa calmly. "This is the big catch. As soon as I'm Chairman, you want me to renege on any deal with Roscoe and grant a free pardon for Ellen Duncan and the Taylor girl."

"As the new Chairman, it would be a popular move," Malone observed.

Vanessa smiled icily. "Let's get a few things straight. Firstly, I haven't said I'd take on the job, and secondly, if it goes wrong I lose my present well-paid job. Thirdly, I don't take on any major responsibility with my hands tied by undertakings I may not be able, or wish, to fulfill. If you want me to do this, I'll do it my way. Those are my terms. You either accept them or we don't have a deal."

Malone had warned David and Baldock that this was likely to be Vanessa's reaction; they had decided in advance what they would do.

Baldock rose and held out his hand. "We have a deal, Miss Grossman."

The others stood and shook hands with Vanessa in turn. She remarked that David didn't look too happy but Baldock intervened to say that she would have to persuade Prescott to attend because standing orders required that a councillor subjected to a censure motion should be present."

"I have already thought of that," said Vanessa. "He'll be there."

Once her visitors had left Vanessa ordered her husband upstairs to see to the children. Her first call was to Roscoe. After apologising for disturbing at this late hour she brought all her considerable negotiating skills and charm into play to persuade the cult leader that he was on the brink of a new era that would usher in the formal recognition of the Bodian Brethren in which her first action as the new Chairman would be the handing over of Ellen Duncan. She explained that she had persuaded the Country Brigade to bring the infernal fugitive witch to Government House. His vote was essential to help bring this state of affairs about. Even the witch's vote would have to be used, but that was a matter of expediency and surely he considered that the means justified the end?

Roscoe promised to be at the meeting.

Vanessa's next call was to Prescott. She told him that she had learned of a plot to overthrow him in which all the councillors opposing him would be meeting in Government House at midnight. Prescott was incensed, declaring that no vote could be taken without him being present.

"I don't think they're interested in legal niceties," said Vanessa. "But they can hardly refuse you your vote if you're present."

Prescott said that he would be there and offered to collect her.

Vanessa looked at her watch when she ended the call. Just enough time to get ready. Her pulse was racing. Adrenalin surging through her. It had started out as yet another boring evening, and now she was at the centre of a takeover battle that would see her ambitions realised.

Eighty-Three

On leaving Vanessa's house, after the stable lads had left to meet up with Carl, Malone's first words to his colleagues were: "Much as I dislike clichés, the one about a hook, line and sinker seems appropriate."

"You think she bit?" David asked.

Baldock snorted. "Bit? You could smell her craving for power. Like a sow in rut. Worse than my pigs except their stink is more honest."

"My God – I never thought it would come to us resorting to this sort of thing," said David bitterly. "A putsch."

Malone put his hand on David's shoulder. "I can understand how you feel. Most of us believe that we have decent, civilised standards, but we have to set them aside tonight. We arrest Prescott and Roscoe *and* we knockout the radio station with one blow. OK – let's talk cricket."

The three men made their way into the town, arguing about the relative merits of Pentworth's various cricket teams, and generally giving the impression of having had too much to drink. They kept this up until they reached the centre of Pentworth and then took Malone's back alley route to arrive at Bob Harding's workshop at 11.25 p.m..

As expected, the scientist was tinkering in his workshop. He now had a much-improved working model of his submersible to play with, as Suzi would put it; to experiment with, as Harding would put it. He was surprised but not displeased to have visitors.

"You have to get that spare broadcast band radio rigged," said Malone. "Radio Pentworth goes off the air at midnight or just after. We need to jump in the moment it does with an announcement."

Harding stared at each man in turn by the light of his low-wattage bench lamp. "You'd better tell me what all this is about."

Baldock quickly outlined the bare plans for the night. The scientist paused as he was connecting a dummy load aerial to the transmitter.

He looked at the three in astonishment. "Arrest them all! On what charges?"

"With Adrian Roscoe, it'll be attempted homicide," said Malone. "The same for Nelson Faraday if he shows up. If not, we pick him up later. Likewise with Vanessa Grossman – conspiracy to abduct children. And there's a whole stack of charges against Prescott, including perverting the course of justice and conspiring to cause acts of criminal damage against churches and chapels. The evidence against him is solid – from a reliable source."

"But he doesn't move anywhere without armed bodyguards. It'll be carnage."

"We have a diversion planned that will separate Prescott from his hoods," said Baldock. "And we've enough men infiltrated into the town to secure Government House within seconds. Some are armed but we pray to God that the announcement from here will prevent bloodshed."

"It'll have to be a helluva diversion."

"It will be."

Harding shook his head. "Well let's hope to God that it works." He finished checking the transmitter. "OK – it's fine. My aerial's not so well-sited as the one on Government House, but I've put a ten-watt linear amp in line. No one will notice any difference." He switched on a portable radio.

"And to take us up to the news at midnight," said the Radio Pentworth presenter, "a vinyl recording of Beethoven's *Pastoral* Symphony."

"How very apt," Malone observed.

"So what's in the statement you're going to read out?" Harding enquired.

"That *you're* going to read out, Bob," said Baldock, handing Harding an envelope. "In the next few minutes ten men will be arriving here for your personal protection and that of your wife. We want you to take over as acting Chairman."

Eighty-Four

Vikki was surprised but not alarmed to see that her skin was the same colour as Dario's skin, her breasts much fuller than normal, her nipples dark and prominent. But what held her attention was *it* . . . so dark and slender, vein-laced, rising up, forcing its way into the valley between her breasts with a bewildering, insistent strength. She instinctively knew what she had to do. She squeezed her breasts together against him and began moving them up and down, gently at first and then more quickly to keep pace with his breathing.

She concentrated on lifting herself up and pushing down, using her whole body now, sometimes quickly, sometimes slowly, and all the time revelling in the power she was exercising over this magnificent warrior as she rolled the oiled sleeve of skin back and forth. A glance showed that his eyes were still open, searching the long grass for shadows fleeing from the doomed village that his *impi* had raided, but his lips were parted in a silent grimace, his teeth clenched.

It ended with a sudden warmth spreading across her breasts and between her thighs. She straightened and stepped back, smiling at the Zulu warrior while working the milky fluid into her skin to be sure of absorbing the strength he had given her.

Vikki. Come to us.

The sun went in and the blinding glare on the yellow bush and red soil was no more.

Vikki . . .

She woke with a start from her favourite dream. She hadn't meant to doze. She listened intently. Claire's and Ellen's regular breathing told her that they were asleep.

Come to us, Vikki.

"I'm coming!" her lips mimed in reply.

The glow of the night lamp enabled Vikki to dress in jeans and a T-shirt, and push her feet in trainers without knocking anything over. Lacing the trainers could wait; the voice urging her to go to Pentworth Lake was an insistent clarion call of such intensity that she was sure her two companions would hear it.

Ellen and Claire didn't stir as Vikki arranged her pillows so that it looked as though she were asleep under the sheet. She took Ellen's penlight torch and a bread knife, and ducked into the narrow passage that led to the blocked entrance. David Weir and Malone had sealed the cave's entrance so that it could be opened from inside in an emergency. Sometimes, when she had been feeling particularly miserable over the death of Sarah, or when her longing to be free became a torment, she would often come and sit close to the hurdle that retained the turf covering and listen to the sound of birdsong. Sometimes she had heard people passing by, talking. On one terrifying occasion she had sat in petrified silence as she listened to a group of voices discussing which farmhouse they would be raiding next in their search for the fugitives. They were so close that they must have been sitting on the grass outside the cave entrance.

She listened carefully now in case lovers were nearby or a morris patrol enforcing the curfew for under eighteen-year-olds. A barn owl hooted mournfully but there were no other sounds, so she carefully sprung inwards the hazel wands that held the hurdle in place. Using the bread knife to cut a hole through the turf large enough for her to wriggle through was easier than she expected.

The draughts of night air she breathed seemed to sting with their purity after two weeks shut up in the cave. The sweet air and the realisation that she was now free for the first time since Nelson Faraday had arrested her in Ellen's shop was a heady brew, quickly displaced by the summonsing voice that told her that she wasn't free. Not yet.

She reached through the opening to reposition the hurdle, clenching the penlight torch between her teeth. The turf had to be packed into place in exactly the right position. To be doubly sure that she left no traces she even brushed the grass upright around the cave entrance. A sudden movement out of the corner of her eye gave her a fright until she realised that it was a group of David's southdown sheep that had drifted from the main flock.

Vikki. Come to us.

"Yes," she answered. "I'm coming."

She set off towards Pentworth Lake.

Eighty-Five

It was fifteen minutes to midnight and the PMR radio clipped to the rim of the microlight's cockpit had remained infuriatingly silent. Harvey Evans had been sitting at the tiny biplane's controls for ten minutes, praying that he would receive Malone's 'operation aborted' signal, but the frequency had remained silent. Not so much as a burst of static to open the transceiver's squelch.

A flash of an approaching torch. "Looks like this is it, Mr Evans."

"We'll give it another two minutes, Charlie. Just in case."

Charlie Crittenden grunted and moved away to talk to Gus. There was nothing to do but wait. The microlight was ready, its fuel tank full, the four maritime rockets were in their tubes mounted on the upper wing. Their firing lanyards terminating in a row of wooden toggles dangling above Harvey Evans' head. They were now painted white – unlike the night of the rescue of Ellen and Vikki, there was no moon.

Evans shone his torch on the detailed sketch of Government House's front elevation even though he had memorised every window. His target was Prescott's office on the top floor which would be empty. Any of its three main windows would do. The resulting fire would lead to the evacuation of the radio station on the same floor. There was only one person – the presenter – on duty at night. He had access to a fire escape. If possible Evans would also take out the transmitter's aerial on the roof of Government House, but the real purpose of the attack was to create a diversion that would distract Prescott's bodyguards in the courtroom.

With other diversions planned throughout the town to coincide with his attack, Malone had been confident that the putsch would succeed and, more importantly, succeed without bloodshed. Evans wished that he had Malone's confidence in his flying ability. It was going to be a difficult attack. He would have to come in low over the Crown, aiming the microlight at the target windows, fire the rockets, which would mean taking one hand off the controls during crucial moments, and follow through with a sharp right turn and climb at full power because there was no chance of him pulling up in time to clear Government House's steeply pitched roof. The flares someone in Market Square was supposed to fire the moment they heard his approach ought to make things easier, but the whole operation had been planned in too much of a hurry; its success depended on the smooth dovetailing of too many events with precise timing.

Something was certain to go wrong.

Eighty-Six

The two blackshirts guarding the entrance to Government House brought their staffs to attention when Prescott's Range Rover pulled up outside. Prescott was driving. He and Vanessa were the only occupants of the vehicle.

Malone was peering through curtains of Father Kendrick's flat over the Catholic church hall on the opposite side of Market Square. "Well that's something," he told the gathering behind him in the darkened room when he reported the arrival. "Prescott hasn't got his thugs in tow."

"Our first break," David muttered.

Adrian Roscoe appeared on foot with Nelson Faraday and two gowned sentinels. The cult leader's step was brisk, purposeful. Malone caught a glimpse of his elated expression as he turned to speak to Faraday before the party entered Government House.

"There're all inside," said Malone curtly, turning away from the window. "We'd better get into position."

Father Kendrick held a candle lamp aloft and led the arresting party downstairs into the church hall. They gathered around the heavy oak door that opened on to the square. Malone knelt and peered through the letterbox. The view was restricted – he could see no higher than the second floor of Government House, but he could see the main entrance and the lights on in the courtroom windows on the ground floor, which was all that mattered. Harvey Evans' rocket attack would be the signal for them to rush Government House.

A final equipment check. Malone set the chamber of his .45 revolver to the first of his four remaining rounds. Dan Baldock checked his shotgun. Brilliant white light flared briefly in the hall as David made certain the halogen lantern was working. There were now two additional armed Country Brigade supporters in the party dressed as blackshirts. Their job was to bundle the two blackshirts at the entrance into the ante-room set aside for magistrates. David would use the lantern to temporarily blind the one at the lobby reception desk, who would be overpowered and imprisoned. Once

304

the lobby was secured, Malone, Baldock and David would burst into the courtroom to make the arrests and so bring a speedy and bloodless end to the tyranny that ruled Pentworth.

That was the theory.

Eighty-Seven

Prescott was surprised. "We're the first?" he queried of the blackshirt behind the reception desk.

"Yes, sir. How many are you expecting?"

"It's to be a full meeting of the council."

"There's still ten minutes to go," Vanessa commented, looking at her watch, betraying nothing of her mounting excitement. Within twenty minutes at the outside, Prescott would be deposed and, with the backing of Adrian Roscoe and the blackshirts, she would be the undisputed ruler of Pentworth. There would be changes. Changes such as Baldock and his rabble never dreamed possible. No one got away with manipulating Vanessa Grossman. No one! That was a vow she had made years before when she had used her stockholding muscle to sack her useless older brothers from the board of the family business.

"Ah, Adrian!" Prescott went forward shook Roscoe's hand as the cult leader and his party entered the lobby. "Sorry about the short notice. Didn't know myself until an hour ago."

"The witch is here?" Roscoe demanded, his ice chip gaze sweeping the lobby as though he expected to see Ellen hiding behind a potted plant.

"She will be, Adrian. She will be. Right everyone. We seem to have a few minutes in hand so we might as well spend it discussing how we're going to deal with this skullduggery." He moved towards the courtroom door.

"Sir!"

Prescott paused and looked questioning at the blackshirt.

"I'm very sorry, sir. But we had no idea that you'd be needing the courtroom.

"Nor did any of us. What's the problem?"

"The cleaners have shifted all the furniture out. They've sanded the floor and they're now sealing it."

"That's awkward," said Prescott.

"It's no problem," said Vanessa. "The conference table is still

306

set up in your office, Mr Chairman. We could all get around it comfortably."

"Excellent idea, Miss Grossman." He beamed. "Always ready with a solution, eh?" He turned to the blackshirt. "Send the councillors up to my office as they arrive, please."

The party headed up the stairs.

Eighty-Eight

"Ready, Mr Harvey?"
   "OK, Charlie. Let's go."
Gus ran down the lane of torches that marked the airstrip. When all the brands were burning, Evans started the microlight's engine. It was already warm, so it was running smoothly after a few seconds. He returned Charlie's wave and opened up. As before, he marvelled at the smoothness of the grass runway. The little biplane unstuck after eighty metres and he began a fuel-conserving spiralling climb, the blazing torches of the runway dwindling beneath him. The plan was to leave the torches burning so that they provided a reliable reference point.

He levelled out at 3000 feet and had less difficulty picking out the key features of Pentworth than he had feared. There were enough lights flickering in the windows of houses to mark the lines of the principal streets.

He set course and throttled back. The wind noise dropped, so he switched on his broadcast receiver and jammed the earphone more tightly into his ear. Radio Pentworth was playing Beethoven's *Pastoral*. As always when he heard it, the gentle, lilting music conjured childhood images from Walt Disney's *Fantasia* of brash male centaurs and coy female centaurs gambolling and frolicking across an idealised Hellenic landscape. Pentworth should have been like that. God knows it had had the chance: clean rainfall, a marvellous climate, fertile soil, and a small but balanced, industrious population with more than enough land and skills to support them. They could have created a utopia but they had opted for hell. God willing, everything would change after tonight. He prayed that people would see sense and that there would be no bloodshed.

A tiny point of light below near the dull sheen of Pentworth Lake caught his attention. Lovers perhaps. Or maybe a couple heading back from the Temple of the Winds. The ancient legend that babies conceived on the sandstone outcrop were singled out by the gods for special favours had gained even more credence recently. Of course, those who disdained such nonsense were the same people who listened to the horoscopes that Radio Pentworth churned out each morning.

Still losing height, he swung east until Market Square was on his port wing and about a kilometre distant. He banked hard left, not increasing power so that the turn cost more height, and lined-up on the distant Government House. It was the largest building in the square, therefore easy to pick out. Too easy because it was the only building with electric lighting – the number of windows with lights on was not to his liking but Government House staff had a reputation for being profligate.

It was three minutes to midnight. Losing height a little too quickly, so a shade more power and ease back the control yoke.

The music was still coming through his earphone. No time to switch it off. Besides, the *Pastoral* was a piece of music he loved.

The flare that burst into the sky cost him his night vision, but it was no longer needed, such was the brilliance of the artificial sun it created over Pentworth. Rooftops passing underneath were too low. More power, more yoke, and then he was perfectly positioned at the right height, trading that height for speed at the right rate, Government House swelling rapidly dead ahead.

The girl and boy centaurs now pairing off, dancing joyously together.

The microlight continued losing height as it flew over the dark, silent streets. Evans estimated that he was about level with the top of St Mary's spireless tower. It was as planned when he had spent hours pouring over maps, calculating rates of descent.

The *Pastoral*'s gathering storm. The centaurs anxiously eyeing the fomenting black clouds that hid the sinister workshop of Zeus, waking now, and the biplane droned on towards its target.

A minor god tended an anvil upon which he forged white-hot lightning bolts with a mighty hammer, and tossed them to his master.

Market Square now 400 metres dead ahead. Zeus clutching the glowing bolt, peering down, looking for targets.

The biplane's fixed main gear undercarriage cleared the distinctive chimney pots of the Crown by two metres. Evans increased power and put the nose down. The Durand swooped low across Market Square and climbed as he hauled back on the yoke while piling on the power.

The windows of Prescott's office were zooming straight at him. He aimed for the centre window. No time to worry any more about the lights being on. He yanked on the toggle to fire Rocket 1. It streaked away, trailing fire from its sustainer, sagged a little and then picked up when its main rocket fired. Rocket 2 next and then 3 and 4 together as he jerked their lanyard toggles simultaneously. The launch tubes were arranged in a slight fan pattern so that at least one of the rockets was reasonably certain to smash through a window.

Zeus hurled his first bolt at the ground. A terrible flash, a clap of thunder, and the terrified centaurs scattered.

The first rocket hit the front of the building below the target windows and zoomed crazily up the façade to explode against the roof parapet. Evans didn't see what happened to the second rocket such was his shock when he saw that there were people in Prescott's office, appearing at the windows. Roscoe, Prescott – Faraday opening a sash. And a *woman!* The second rocket had glanced off the roof and hurled itself spiralling madly into the night with the third rocket chasing after it.

Zeus now crazed with jealousy and hatred. Bolt after bolt crashing down. The terrified centaurs rushing hither and thither to escape the terrible onslaught from the demented god.

The shock of seeing people delayed Evans' reaction for a vital second as the last rocket found its target. It punched through the centre window and exploded in Prescott's office as though the wattage of the lights inside had suddenly increased a thousandfold.

Zeus was running out of lightning bolts and time as the sun struggled to regain its supremacy. It drove back the black clouds of Zeus's workshop, shrinking them with its returning warmth.

Government House was suddenly a formidable cliff racing at Evans with awesome certainty. He opened the throttle wide and hauled frantically on the yoke. The engine screamed, the biplane hung on to its propeller as it climbed steeply.

Another twenty to thirty horsepower and another 1000 revs and the tiny aircraft would've made it.

Its main gear hit the roof parapet. The biplane seemed to hang poised in mid-air like a children's mobile for some seconds before crashing down on the roof. The propeller chewed into hundred-year-old frost-weakened roof tiles. A flying hip bonnet, the biggest of the roof tiles, killed Harvey Evans instantly. The microlight somersaulted, the engine broke away, flailing petrol as it crashed through the roof's tile battens and ploughed into the mountains of dust-dry bat guano. They were a century's accumulation of beetle husks – more than just a fire waiting to happen, but a fireball.

Zeus was finished. He yawned and drew around him the blankets of his black storm-cloud bed.

310

Within seconds the entire roof space of Government House was ablaze, engulfing the wreckage of the Durand. Its tailplane broke away. It slithered down the roof and tipped over the parapet, fluttering lazily to ground, passing the windows of the blazing office.

Zeus found a tiny lightning bolt in his bed and tossed it out with casual disdain.

It fell to the ground just as Radio Pentworth went off the air.

Eighty-Nine

V ikki was within 200 metres of Pentworth Lake when she heard the microlight passing overhead. She paused to stare up at the black sky. There was nothing to see. Only the angry buzz of the little air-cooled engine to mark the aircraft's passage. She wondered why Mr Evans was flying at night again. The sound seemed to be heading towards the faint lights of Pentworth. She felt a sense of foreboding and shivered.

Vikki!

Yes – I'm coming.

She resumed her journey but her pace lost its certainty. Why was she here? What could she do? Her footsteps faltered when the grass gave way to sand. She could hear the gentle lapping of the breeze-stirred lake.

She concentrated on the words: I'm here.

No answer.

I'm here! Was it possible to *think* louder?

The sharp yap of a vixen answered as though it had read her thoughts. She flashed the feeble beam of her torch along the black line of the water's edge. Doubts assailed her. Perhaps she had dreamed that she had been summonsed to the lake? She would have to return to the cave and face Ellen and Claire in the knowledge that she had compromised their safety by venturing out. The darkness was almost total and she suddenly felt very alone and afraid. Her torch suddenly dimmed. Shaking it caused it to brighten for a few seconds, and then it went out for good.

This time her mounting sensation of dread caused her to call out, "Hallo! I'm here!"

"Who's that?"

Vikki gave a gasp of fear. The voice that had answered was very close, male, deep with a strange, resonant quality. She wanted to turn and run, but without the torch she would be certain to fall and injure herself. She preferred not to think about the terrible consequences of being caught in daylight with a twisted ankle or a broken leg.

The radio station had reported that Pentworth House was offering a huge reward for her capture.

Suddenly a faint glow suffused the lake. She wheeled around and watched the rocket climbing into the sky above Pentworth. It burst into a brilliant white light that seemed to hang motionless in the night haze. At this distance the light it created was the equivalent of a full moon.

"You must be Vikki." Trinder had no idea why he said that – the words swam into his head.

Vikki's head snapped around and her eyes went wide with shock when she saw the figure of the man standing not ten metres away. His jeans, sweat shirt and anorak looked uncomfortably tight, as though they had been made for a smaller man.

Recognition was instantaneous. He was the tall, regal figure of a hundred daydreams. "Dario!" she exclaimed.

She will probably call you Dario, they had told Trinder.

"Is that my name?"

It is now, they answered. *Her name is Victoria. You must call her Vikki.*

Trinder was confused. One part of him was saying that the girl was a stranger, another was saying that he knew her.

"Hallo, Vikki." He smiled and held out his hands.

Vikki rushed at him and threw her arms around him. His body felt hard and unyielding as she remembered it. "Oh, Dario . . . Dario . . . I knew you would come. I just knew."

"Look." He pointed.

She turned and gazed at the sudden orange-yellow glow that permeated the haze over Pentworth. It grew brighter by the second. They could see flames leaping into the sky, silhouetting intervening rooftops.

Vikki reached up and kissed the man she knew as Dario, tracing his finely sculptured aristocratic features with her left hand as she had done on another occasion. When she touched his lips, his incredibly white teeth parted to gently grip her fingers, drawing them in, sucking slowly while pushing the tip of his tongue between her fingertips, melting away her reason.

All Vikki would ever be able to recall of the next ten minutes was the divine moment when she threw back her head and uttered a primeval cry that was neither ecstasy nor pain, but triumph.

As they dressed in silence, Vikki became aware of a mounting sensation of joy. It was almost the same feeling of euphoria she remembered when her new hand was growing. But this time there was a difference; this time pictures formed in her mind with a vivid, almost frightening clarity of what was happening to her body. She saw a huge globe surrounded by millions of wriggling, tadpole-like creatures, their tails lashing furiously. One broke through and the cell divided instantly into two cells. They, in turn, became four cells, swelling rapidly to maintain their size.

And 4 were 8 . . . Then 16 . . . 32 . . .

They heard the harsh crackle of distant gunfire.

64 . . . 128 . . .

"There is much to be done," said Dario softly.

256 . . . 512 . . .

The hundreds of dividing cells in her body would become thousands . . . The thousands, millions . . .

Together the couple walked hand in hand towards the orange glow that was lighting up the sky.